P9-BZT-316

A CRIMSON PASSION

Pleasure rocketed through Mika. But instead of giving her more, McCabe jerked away. He shook his head as if coming out of a daze, and released his hold. "I'm sorry. I didn't mean to…" He trailed off and started to roll to the side.

Mika stopped him. She raised her knees, cradling him between her legs, and brought her hands up to hold his shoulders. "Don't apologize—I loved it. I'm only sorry you stopped." Then it occurred to her what was going on. Damn, she should have realized at once. "I'm just the same as you. I can take you just as you want—hard and fast. Just like who you are. You don't have to hold back. You don't have to be careful like you have been. You can't scare me, and you won't hurt me. Give us what we both want."

Through a Crimson Veil

Patti O'Shea

LOVE SPELL

NEW YORK CITY

For Mom and Dad.
Thank you for everything you've done.
I love you.

LOVE SPELL®

October 2005

Published by

Dorchester Publishing Co., Inc.
200 Madison Avenue
New York, NY 10016

ISBN 0-505-52647-6

The name "Love Spell" and its logo are trademarks of Dorchester Publishing Co., Inc.

Printed in the United States of America.

Visit us on the web at www.dorchesterpub.com.

Thanks to:

Theresa Monsey and Melissa Lynn Copeland for always coming through for me.

My friends at NWA, TDD, PTN, RBL, and the Lunatic Café for their support.

Liz Maverick for the cool world.

And Chris Keeslar for allowing me to color outside the lines, and for always seeing the heart of my characters and their stories.

THROUGH A
CRIMSON VEIL

Prologue

Allison Walters lightly touched the comm device at her waist as she turned down the hall. Being included in this after hours experiment was an honor she deserved. Of all the trainees, *she* was the best and brightest. Everyone knew that. Or they soon would—and that included her father. She'd make certain of that. Once she climbed high enough, he'd have no choice except to acknowledge her achievements.

With a determined nod, she walked through the double doors of the Los Angeles Department of Paranormal Research & Development and paused. The area seemed strangely deserted considering how important she'd been told this experiment was. Hesitating, she tucked her short, dark hair behind her ears. Maybe this was a joke: Her fellow trainees were envious of her brilliance, and she wouldn't put it past them to pull something. Allison knew they called her an arrogant bitch behind her back, and embarrassing her would be good for a laugh.

Firming her jaw, she strode purposefully down the hall. If this was some prank, she'd make them pay. She was so intent on her plans for retribution that a banging noise to her left made her jump. Allison stopped and eyed the door warily. The research subjects were housed in that wing, and one of them could have gotten loose. It had happened before.

"Grab the dog!" The muffled voice held urgency, adrenaline.

Dog. It was a werewolf then.

She heard a growl and involuntarily stepped back before catching herself. A body hit the door, the thud hard enough to make her wince, and then men were yelling. It was impossible to distinguish words, not with so many voices shouting at once, but Allison relaxed. The guards outnumbered the research subjects at least six to one here; they'd have the werewolf back in its pen shortly. As dangerous as this situation was, it was worse when one of the vampires escaped. They were creepy and their physical abilities were—

An expletive came through the metal door, then, "Tranq him! C'mon!"

The sounds of scuffling ended abruptly and Allison knew someone had knocked out the escapee. It grew quiet, but she didn't move. Without weapons, humans were no match for dogs or vamps. Did she want to work with these creatures? Put herself in jeopardy if something went wrong?

She tensed at the sound of footsteps, but it was Jeff Riker who came around the hallway corner. Although he was one of the younger members of the development team, he was slated to be part of the test tonight.

"There you are," he said brusquely. "They sent me to look for you. Come on, then. We don't have all night."

He headed back the way he'd come, expecting her to follow. Allison did, but only because he worked with Doctor Stowe, the head of tonight's team. She didn't like Riker, and the feeling was mutual. He was jealous of her like the others, since he knew his label of up-and-coming young genius was soon to be eclipsed—by her. Asshole, she thought with a smirk.

They reached a black door marked Cleaning Supplies. Allison stopped as Riker opened it and strode inside. This was a gag; it had to be.

"Come on," he ordered.

"If you think I'm walking in there with you, Riker, you can think again."

He snorted. "Don't flatter yourself. You're not sexy enough to overcome your attitude problem."

Allison puffed up. "You're envious because I landed the *top* researcher position, because I'm—"

"Yeah, yeah, yeah," Riker interrupted. "I've heard it before. Everyone in the department has. You're brilliant, you soar above the mediocrity of us poor, average human beings. But obviously you're not brilliant enough to discern why no one likes you."

She stiffened. "The inadequate always project their deficiencies on others."

Riker shook his head. "Keep telling yourself that while you eat lunch alone. Now, follow me or I'll leave you behind."

Allison scowled. Riker ignored her until reluctantly she walked into the closet. As soon as the door closed, he did something that created an exit in the back wall, and Allison found herself standing in a small lab—one she'd never known to exist. Curious, she looked around. There was a library filled with books—some lying open—but she couldn't see the titles.

The equipment present was impressive. There were monitors, digital equipment, a row of Bunsen burners and tools she couldn't identify. Walking deeper inside, she continued examining the room. There were desks as well as high-countered lab stations, and she couldn't help but wonder who worked here.

And what they did.

Doctor Stowe caught sight of her then. "Walters," he said when he reached her, "welcome to the Demon Research Group. You've displayed an interest in demonology, and we'd like you to see what we do." He smiled. "We'll be starting in a moment."

"Doctor, what's happening tonight?" she asked.

Stowe's angular face sobered as he measured her. "We're calling through demons, of course. Only a few," he assured her quickly. "We've located a new summoning ritual."

Allison was never speechless, but she didn't find her voice until after the doctor rejoined his colleagues. She was the only woman present, the only trainee. Not that the lab was filled with people. There was Doctor Stowe, Riker and two other men—that was it. She straightened, pulling her shoulders back. She was the best *and* brightest. They were grooming her for great things, asking her to pick their group for assignment when her training finished. Too bad this was a secret and she wouldn't be able to inform the others of her latest distinction.

Riker returned. "Doctor Stowe asked me to fill you in," he said. He sounded about as thrilled as a man headed to the dentist. "The summoning ritual they'll be trying tonight is open-ended. That means the demons—if this works— will remain in our world until we choose to send them back."

"I know the definition of open-ended," Allison informed him, lifting her chin. "A closed summoning means the demon is only allowed to remain until he completes the task he's been called for. But I thought there were no open-ended rites."

She shouldn't have said that. "Guess you don't know everything after all," Riker replied smugly.

"I understand more than you believe. For instance, the term 'demon' is used to refer to creatures native to Orcus and has no relationship to any theology. They appear humanoid, but have powers greater than vampires or werewolves." Unobtrusively, Allison took a deep breath and tried to recall specific abilities. She wouldn't permit this jackass to outshine her. "They can shapeshift, and control the elements—"

"*Some* can shapeshift," Riker corrected in a tone that put her back up. "Not all demons have the same talents."

"Of course not. I was speaking generally," she lied easily, then quickly moved on to another aspect. "Demons have incredible strength and stamina, and if injured, their wounds heal at an astonishing rate." Allison smirked at her adversary. "Should I continue educating you?"

Riker's face went red. "Right," he drawled sarcastically, "you're teaching me. Why don't you explain the hierarchy of Orcus, beginning with how they govern themselves? Include a breakdown of the different branches, their standing within that society, and the powers generally associated with each breed."

Curling her hands into fists, Allison struggled to hide her temper. She couldn't display weakness or it would be used against her. "Didn't Doctor Stowe request that you fill me in?" she asked with mock sweetness. "*I* haven't been part of the Demon Research Group for two years. That's how long it's been since you finished training, correct?"

"Fine," the boy genius snapped. "They govern themselves via a council believed to be comprised of four members. Pinning down how many types of demons there are is more difficult, but there are a lot of them. Those with weaker magic are viewed with scorn by the more powerful. The stronger of the branches such as Grolird, Setonian, Kiverian and such have the ability to use fire as a weapon. We've seen them shoot balls of flame as well as streaks of it. Most have some telekinetic capability, but again, the degree differs from demon to demon."

Despite herself, Allison was interested, and she worked hard to keep her voice nonchalant as she asked, "What about the talents of one of the weaker breeds? What can they do?"

Riker studied her, then shrugged. "Some of the lesser

branches also have control of the elements, although not to the same degree. There's one kind"—his eyes became slightly less remote as he became involved in the subject—"that manipulates air and wind. We're not sure what they're called since we've heard three different names, but they are definitely viewed as inferior by those of greater power."

"Demons." Allison shook her head. "As if vampires and werewolves in this city weren't enough."

Riker gave her a mild look, then went on. "What's particularly interesting, is how the weaker demons compensate for their shortcomings. They might lack punch in their magic, but they make up for it in other ways—like cleverness. Those perceived as strong in Orcus rarely are anywhere near as crafty."

Allison nodded. It made sense. The weak had to compensate in some manner. Hadn't her father tried to do the same with his sarcasm and derision? He'd been jealous of her intelligence from the time she was a child. "The myths I've heard—"

"I'm getting there," Riker said, sounding impatient. "As I was saying, all these types of demon are different. The ones that use air and wind? They're playful. Like Loki from Norse mythology—"

"Or Coyote from Navajo stories," she interrupted, refusing to let him lecture her as if she were a high school student.

"Exactly!" The boy wonder actually sounded pleased by her interjection. "What if those two really did exist? After all, these demons weren't always imprisoned in Orcus."

"The veil," Allison murmured. Her confusion over Riker's response had her asking him a question instead of researching it herself later. "How were the demons trapped?"

He shook his head. "If you're asking what the veil is and how it confines them, we have no conclusive answer. The stories we've found, though, seem to suggest that the barrier was created when a particular group of demons did some especially horrible deeds."

"And we're calling them forward?" Allison wasn't sure that sounded too bright.

"Most aren't too bad, and demons are stronger than either fangs or dogs. That's what the DRG's purpose is: to learn about the inhabitants of Orcus in the hope we'll be able to use them."

For a moment, Allison was disconcerted by the implications, but she pushed them aside. "If their abilities are beyond those of the vamps and dogs already here, that means they'll be very dangerous to us. We're already at a disadvantage."

"True, and we've thought of that." Riker gestured toward a table near the older men; it held nothing except an oversized pistol. "That weapon is still experimental, but it's killed every demon we've tested it on. Besides we humans can control them. Once they've given their word, they're bound to it. If they break a spoken promise, they lose their powers forever, and in their world, to be without magic is the same as being a serf."

The idea of commanding demons, creatures more powerful than anything in Crimson City, enticed Allison. Once she ruled them . . . "How do you get them to agree—"

"Quiet," Stowe called. "We're about to begin."

The team except for Riker chanted in a language Allison couldn't identify. The three men must have spent hours memorizing the words, since there were no papers or books in their hands. Allison tucked her fingers in the pockets of her trousers and watched in fascination.

As the final word faded, there was a strange wavering to the air in front of the doctors. Allison closed her eyes to clear her vision, and when she opened them again, two tall new masculine figures stood in the room. One had dark hair and the other was blond. Both wore it down to their waists and had thin braids at either temple used to pull their long tresses back into ponytails. Neither wore a shirt, but with their impressive chests, why would they want to?

Doctor Stowe approached the—demons? He spoke to them quietly enough that Allison couldn't hear the words. She pulled her hands free and smiled. Another honor for her: *She* was meeting the first demons allowed into Crimson City in years, would be part of the group directing their actions. Truly she did—how had Riker put it?—soar above the mediocrity of other humans.

One day she'd be in charge of the entire Department of Paranormal Research & Development; it was simply a matter of time. Why shouldn't she command demons now? The figure with dark hair turned his head and looked directly at her. His strange, light-colored eyes were unreadable, but there was a cruelty to his lips that sent a shiver down her spine. Allison shook it off. He hadn't acknowledged Riker or anyone else in the room—only her.

The air shimmered again and a third demon appeared. Allison stared at him. He was different than the first two. This one had shoulder-length, light brown hair, and while as muscular as the others, he wore a shirt.

Riker approached the newcomer. The demon ignored him, and Allison smirked. Even the creatures of Orcus saw how special she was, understood that she was the one they should obey.

A shout jerked her attention back to the first two demons. The dark-haired one had lifted Doctor Stowe off the floor by his throat. There was more yelling, and Riker rushed over. Lights popped, dimming the room. Involuntarily, Allison backed up a step.

The demon threw Stowe to the ground. He was dead, his neck at an odd angle. Two of the three remaining members of the team drew syringes and headed for his killer. Riker went for the weapon he'd pointed out to her, but it suddenly sailed across the room as if thrown.

The last demon to arrive began walking toward the door.

"You are not going to assist us?" the golden-haired demon asked. Despite the fact that the first two demons were focused on the third, Allison saw the research team was unable to close the distance and sedate them.

"I'm a healer," said the third demon.

"You will wait for us outside the chamber," the dark-haired one ordered, and the healer nodded.

As soon as he left the room, all hell broke loose. Allison tried to run, but her feet wouldn't move. The dark-haired demon looked at her and nodded, letting her know that he was responsible for her paralysis. The blond demon shapeshifted, probably into his true form—burning red eyes, black-scaled body, claws, fangs. Fear rose in Allison's throat, nearly choking her.

She turned her head away, unable to watch what the demons were doing, but the screams of Riker and the others seemed to echo through the lab. The ensuing silence was much worse.

"Think you to be special?"

Allison refused to look over, but a rough hand forced her face around to meet the dark-haired demon's eyes.

"Think *you* to command the Bak-Faru?"

Her lips trembled, but she couldn't speak, couldn't think of anything to say with those icy purple eyes staring at her.

"We saved you for the finale," the demon continued. His smile made her gulp. "You will pay for your hubris. Your thoughts, your arrogance reached us even in Orcus. You, human—you are *nothing*." The demon increased its pressure on her chin, forcing her head back.

He and his companion looked at each other, then they changed back into their humanoid forms. Up close, they were movie-star handsome, but Allison couldn't see beyond the earlier scales and claws.

"*You* will command *us?*" the dark one repeated. "I think not. Demons ruled the earth before our imprisonment, and we will rule it again. You are no better than the dirt beneath our feet, and we are your masters."

He pushed her, and Allison fell. For a moment, she simply stared at him; then she realized she could move. She scuttled backward on her butt, using her hands and feet to propel herself across the floor. That lasted only a moment before the demon's foot came down on her hand.

Allison tried to swallow her shriek, but as he ground his boot down, her bones snapped—he was pulverizing them, turning them into dust. By the time he stopped, she was crying and sweat beaded on her brow. She wouldn't beg. That was beneath her.

"Oh, but you *will* beg, human. You will beg me to kill you and you will acknowledge our superiority."

He tore the fingernails from her crushed hand, then did the same to the other. Every time she passed out, he forced her back to awareness. Every time Allison's brain distanced itself, he ended that numbness. The demon refused to allow her any respite from agony. She screamed until she was hoarse, pleaded for mercy, but there came none. He used her body as a weapon against her mind, used it by inflicting excruciating pain without killing her.

"Still believe you that the Bak-Faru are yours to command?" he asked.

"No." Allison hardly recognized her voice; her screams had destroyed it.

"Who is the master?"

"You." At his frown, she quickly added, "Demons are master."

"Now beg for your death."

She didn't hesitate; death would be welcome. "Please. *Please* kill me."

His hand morphed, and long talons appeared. He slid one sharp nail along her throat. The cut wasn't deep enough to kill, but warm blood ran down her neck. Please, she thought, unable to speak. Please, end it.

She never felt the bite of the claw that severed her head from her body.

. . . and in the time of darkness, will come knowledge of one not of Orcus. Some shall ascribe to him the role of deliverer, others shall fear him with just cause—he is a slayer, a powerful mage—and he alone possesses the magic to lower the wall. Through the crimson veil shall he peer, and if it be ill, he shall tear it asunder. Thus shall the freedom of Orcus be known—and its enslavement . . .

—from a sacred parchment,
Predictions of An-Tul, Setonian Prophet

Chapter One

McCabe was hunting; Mika knew it.

And she was hunting the hunter.

The thought amused her, and she struggled to rein in her merriment. This was serious business, not a game. Her ability to find humor at any given moment had been one of the arguments of the Council against using her on this assignment, but when it came right down to it, there was no one else. Of all those she knew who lived in Orcus, only she had a human parent. This time, that was an advantage.

For one thing, only she could cross the veil at will; she'd been doing it for years. For another, it was unlikely any full-blooded demon would survive McCabe long enough to find out what they needed to know. Of course, there were no guarantees that she'd live either, but the Council believed McCabe would be slower to attack her since he'd recognize her mixed parentage.

Mika shrugged. She wasn't going to worry about it. Tipping her face up to the night sky, she let her senses stretch. McCabe continued to move like a predator nearby—not too quickly, to avoid missing something, but not slowly either. Mika stayed just within her range, no closer, and didn't think he was aware of her yet. When the time felt right, she'd change that.

Anticipation zinged through her. She hadn't wanted this mission. Not really. Yeah, she'd been tempted for a few seconds when it was presented—until she'd realized how risky it would be. She was aware that it would be difficult to say no—the Council ruled everyone except Orcus's darkest residents—but she wasn't willing to put her life on the line.

Then they'd handed her a sheaf of papers and, as she fanned through them, she'd caught a glimpse of the man. For a moment, her heart had stopped beating. And when Mika could breathe again, she knew Conor McCabe was her vishtau mate.

Her logical side—and contrary to popular belief, she did have one—said it was unlikely, that she couldn't know from a mere picture. But she could meet him and find out for certain. She'd planned to turn down the assignment and seek him out on her own when it dawned on her that McCabe had been marked for death.

And so she'd bargained—his life in exchange for her participation in the mission. The Council had commented on her softness, that she was too weak to be even half demon, but she'd secured their promise to spare Conor and given her own oath in return. They'd nailed her down on this assignment, forcing her agree to more than she'd meant, but demons protected their vishtau mates no matter the cost. If she were mistaken, then no great harm was done, but if he were her mate . . . Mika's heart rate accelerated. Soon she'd meet him; soon she'd know.

For now, she kept her distance from McCabe, strolling through the night with assurance. She'd cloaked herself. Though she wasn't putting much energy into it, she was invisible to humans. To average humans, she corrected. A *sensitive* might be able to feel her, but it was unlikely there would be one around in this neighborhood: Not many existed, and this was a bad part of town with few inhabitants.

How did people live like this? The buildings were mostly boarded over, and many had yellow *Condemned* notices stapled to the plywood. Graffiti covered almost every inch of available space, and grime coated everything heavily enough to make the structures look as if they'd been fire-bombed. Only her ability to control her body's sensitivity kept her from overloading on the stench, noise and ugliness of the place.

If humans, vampires and werewolves acted together, maybe they could clean up areas like this. Of course, it would mean putting aside their differences to work with each other, and Mika guessed she'd be respected by the strong demons in Orcus before that ever happened. She shook off her cynicism. Los Angeles hadn't earned the nickname Crimson City because the different species lived in harmony. There had been tension and distrust here for her entire life.

She rounded a corner and stopped short, face-to-face with a woman. It was a vampire, Mika knew; demons like herself could read energy. There was a moment of surprise for both of them, then the female stared at her in challenge. Mika met that challenge head-on—she might be Mahsei, one of the weaker branches of demon, but she was more than strong enough to take on a vampire.

Shifting to balance her weight more evenly, Mika waited to see what happened. She'd read the newspaper articles about and seen evidence of the bloodshed in Crimson City right now. Humans and vampires and werewolves were all plotting and killing each other, and becoming bolder about it, their truce all but forgotten. She was prepared to fight, but she wouldn't be the one to start something; that wasn't part of her mission.

Patience turned out to be the right course of action. The vampire broke off the confrontation, inclining her head and stepping around Mika to continue on her way. Mika watched her disappear down the block, then tried again to pick up McCabe's trail. She had to locate his energy pattern, and quick.

A breeze whirled past, blowing her dark hair into her face. Pushing it out of the way, Mika sensed something and looked up. She knew just enough about birds to guess it was a great-horned owl. Another hunter. Busy night, she thought. Her lips curved again with amusement.

She'd carefully planned her first meeting with McCabe. Though he might be surprised to know it, seeing as they existed in another world, the Council had a very detailed dossier on his life. He was a demon hunter, one who'd killed many of her kind, and the leadership subscribed to the theory of *know thine enemy*. They'd allowed Mika to study McCabe's file before she left Orcus, and among other things, she'd discovered he was a man who protected those he perceived as weaker than himself.

To capitalize on that, her approach would be hesitant, almost timid. She would also use her appearance. She looked younger than she was and there was a naivete to her face. But along with that seeming ingenuousness was a sensuality that attracted males—each wanted to be the one to introduce her to passion. At least, until she showed them her demon side.

She laughed quietly. Once they realized her innocent face hid a darker nature, they couldn't get away from her fast enough. But if McCabe reacted to her the way human men did initially, she'd have time to spin her tale even if he did know what she was.

Her amusement drained away as she spotted hopscotch squares chalked on the sidewalk. Mika stopped in front of the game, stared at it for a moment, then jumped in with two feet. Next she used just her right foot, then both again. Then she went still. Surely there was more to it than this, but she couldn't recall what she'd seen girls do as they played. She quit hopping and strode away. Her difficulty was illustrative of all her life's problems: She'd divided her time between her parents, never fitting in to either this world or Orcus—but it had been worse when she'd lived here with her dad.

Not that things were a picnic in Orcus. Because of her mixed genetics, demons viewed her as an aberration, a freak, and most kept their distance. But at least in the Other World, she could be herself. She didn't need to be concerned about her eyes glowing red or worry that she might inadvertently hurt someone with her physical strength. With humans, she had to remain watchful and make sure she camouflaged her true nature.

Scowling, Mika forced such thoughts aside. She should be concentrating. Even if he were her vishtau mate, Mc-Cabe might kill her before he realized they shared a bond. Although, according to the intel the Council had gathered, he hadn't slain any weak demons; the deaths attributed to him were all from the strongest, most aggressive branches, and there weren't *that* many. Of course, there weren't that many demons loose in Los Angeles either, but it reassured her that he spent most of his time working for the government, hunting down outlaw vampires and werewolves.

Several blocks ahead, under the first unbroken street-light she'd seen in the area, she spied a heap lying on the sidewalk. Mika scanned its energy and recognized the bundle was a human male, and thus no threat, as he'd never know she was there. But as she skirted around him, she nearly squeaked with surprise when his hand closed over her ankle.

He wasn't that old, but with the whiskers and filth on his face, he looked far more ancient than his years. His blood-shot eyes clearly showed something was altering his perception of reality—probably drugs, which were also the reason he could see her. Mika tried to pull her leg free, but she was reluctant to injure him unnecessarily. "Let go," she ordered.

"It's not safe away from the light," he said, his voice slurred. "There are monsters out there, you know."

"There's a monster right here too." Mika made her eyes

glow red, but he was too far gone to have something so subtle scare him.

Time to go for the drama, she decided. After a moment's thought, she created the illusion that she had three heads—one belonging to a bull, another to a dragon and the third to an ogre. When the old man only stared, mouth agape, she added fanged snakes shooting from her belly. That did it. Shrieking, he scrambled backward, only trying to stand once he was some distance from her. He kept screaming as he stumbled away.

Ending the illusion, Mika tried to home back in on McCabe, but she couldn't find him. Damn it, he was probably out of her range by now. How long had that doper kept her busy, anyway?

Yet it wasn't all his fault. She hadn't been paying attention for a while now. Perhaps those opposed to her participation in this mission had been right: She couldn't be trusted with something so vital.

Mika pushed her hand impatiently through her hair and looked around as she scanned again. Still nothing. But maybe she could catch up with him. McCabe hadn't been moving that quickly; if she hurried, perhaps she could get within sensing distance again.

Deciding it was worth taking a chance, she rushed off in the direction in which he'd last been headed. She didn't have to find him tonight, she knew—she'd been given no definite time restriction. But if the Council's human minion showed up for a progress report, she didn't want to say, *I screwed up and lost him.*

The far-off wail of a siren echoed through the night, car doors slammed maybe a street over, and a domestic dispute reached her ears; yet Mika didn't let herself become distracted. She wouldn't fail, wouldn't give her detractors the satisfaction.

As she walked, she continued to scan, but there was no sign of McCabe. A few blocks later, she spotted a second illuminated street lamp, and not far past its pool of light was the dark maw of an alley. Mika slowed, tried to sense if anyone else was present, but the area was clear. She picked up her pace again.

He came at her from the alley. Before she could react, before she could blink, she found herself pinned against a building, a hand at her throat. Chipped brick cut into her back, but she ignored the minor discomfort and reached for her powers. There was a bottle in the gutter. Mika tried to use telekinesis to lift and hurl it at his back, but it didn't work. Next she called on wind, her strongest ally. Again, nothing happened. She couldn't bring up even a gentle breeze.

Since levitation would be of no help here, not with his hand around her neck, Mika tried to use the wind a second time, but still came up empty. Taking a deep breath, she investigated why and discovered her powers were frozen. That meant she had to take him on physically. Although his size was daunting, she knew how to fight down and dirty. She tried to raise her arm to knock her assailant away, but she couldn't move her body.

Belatedly, she realized he'd done something to paralyze her, and for the first time, Mika felt a frisson of fear trickle down her spine. She raised her gaze.

Conor McCabe.

In a split second she read the hatred on his face, realized she was in a bad situation, and recalled her plan. But surprisingly, bizarrely, impossibly—instead of acting fearful and meek, as she'd intended, she curled her lips up into a smile; she couldn't control it. From what she saw reflected in his sunglasses, it wasn't her usual impish grin, either, but a sultry, sexy smile. Pure seduction. Pure invitation.

"Sunglasses at night, McCabe? That's not very original." Her voice emerged as a husky murmur. It wasn't intentional, and for a moment she wondered if it were the vishtau that had her acting this way. She wouldn't know until their eyes met without those dark lenses blocking her view.

He didn't reply, just stared at her and Mika stared back.

She was tall, but he was taller—at least half a foot, maybe more. And muscular. She eyed his biceps beneath the sleeve of his forest green T-shirt and doubted she could span his arm with both hands. There was enough illumination to glint on the gold highlights in his close-cropped, dark brown hair. That made him look boyish —until she took in the uncompromising set of his mouth.

As she continued to stare, Mika picked up something else from him: an overwhelming sense of aloneness. Not just loneliness; this went far beyond that. It was a soul-deep sense of isolation, and it struck her hard enough to make her heart ache. She wanted to gather him close, to hold him until his hurt went away. And this urge was so atypical that it made her almost certain they were bonded.

The vishtau. It encompassed every level of being—heart, mind, body and soul. Humans had soul mates, but this went far beyond that. It was a connection that grew more powerful the longer the pair were together, and demons held it in reverence. Probably because it was only within the vishtau that they could conceive children. Mika had given up hope that she shared this rare and special bond with any male—until she'd seen McCabe's image. She studied him more closely. Was he her mate?

Before she realized what she was doing, she licked her lips. *I'm not completely paralyzed,* she noted, but she didn't test what else she could move.

Her kind—most demons actually—were highly sexual creatures, and so she instantly discerned the change in him. He wanted her. That was another piece of evidence that they shared the vishtau. Her smile deepened. She could almost hear his thoughts.

"Yes, it would be good," she said, again overcome by elemental attraction. She ran her gaze over him. "*Very* good." She looked back up at his face. Even through the dark lenses of his glasses, she knew his eyes burned. For a moment, she thought he was going to press his body against hers—his desire was pulsing that hotly—but he curbed himself.

"I don't want you," he said.

"Liar." She laughed, trying to ignore the shiver of awareness that shot through her. He should know better than to try to deceive her about this. Sexual attraction had its own energy signature, which Mika identified easily; she'd had it directed at her before. But this time she reciprocated, and it was an incredible rush to feel it building between them.

"Don't push me," McCabe said. His hand tightened around her throat.

"You might not *want* to want me, but you do. You're already picturing this, aren't you? What's your fantasy? Pulling me into the alley, tugging my pants out of the way, unzipping your jeans and thrusting inside me?" She asked because, incredibly, that was what was going through her own mind, and she couldn't deny it. "Our first time would be hard and fast, but the second—maybe that would be slower. Or maybe not. Not the way the fever's raging between us."

"I told you not to push." He gritted the words out.

"Why? Am I making you hot?"

Mika didn't know why she couldn't stop herself. Unlike the way she was acting, she knew how dangerous this man was, and that he could easily kill her. Every time she opened her mouth, she surprised herself. Perhaps it was a good thing she couldn't move, because who knew what she'd be doing if she were able to touch him. Her eyes dropped to the front of his jeans and the fantasies in her mind intensified.

"You're practically vibrating with desire," she found herself saying.

"Lust," he corrected. "And yes, you're causing it."

Her smile became a self-satisfied smirk. "Yes, I am."

His face became even more forbidding. "You're using some dark power to cause it," he elaborated.

She laughed again, before she could stop herself. Her, using powers on him? That was impossible, because she was just as affected. "You wish that's what it was. Then you could tell yourself I'm manipulating you. That's excusable, understandable even—but it's not the truth. Face it, McCabe, you just want me. There's nothing supernatural about it."

They stared at each other: she, with surprised delight, and he, with barely suppressed fury. She knew when she won, when he stopped lying to himself about their attraction, but she also knew it wouldn't make anything easier.

"Why are you following me?" he asked. His hand left her throat and he took hold of her shoulders.

"Ooh, changing the subject. Good way to avoid—"

He cut her off with a surprisingly gentle shake. "Why are you following me?" he repeated.

It was time to stop messing around. She wasn't normally flighty like this, captive to her body's demands, but no one witnessing her behavior tonight would ever guess. Mika forced herself to become serious, to stop being ruled by desire.

"I want to hire you." There. See? She could do it. This was the plan.

His voice was cold. "I kill things like you," he said.

But his face showed so much desire that Mika nearly laughed once more. She restrained herself to a mere twitch of her lips. "I know you do. That's why I'm here."

His expression changed as he regained control. "Start talking," he said.

"You know what I am, right? What species? You know how . . . dangerous my kind is, how malicious, compared to others?" She waited. A long time.

"Not very," he admitted grudgingly.

She'd been pretty certain he was aware of the differences between types of demon. Even if he'd never studied anything or had exposure outside of his life, here in Crimson

City, he still should be able to recognize such things; she'd simply wanted to make sure. But it probably hurt him to admit that not every demon from Orcus was pure evil.

"Then you'll understand why I need you," she went on. She took a breath. She had to get this right, had to get him to buy her next lie or she was sunk. "I have a Kiverian after me."

Kiverians weren't the darkest of demons, the most powerful or bloodthirsty, but they could be close, and one of her kind wouldn't stand much of a chance against one of them. He'd know that. But that wasn't why she'd chosen that specific type.

"Why? You demons rarely hurt each other without cause," he said.

"Rarely isn't never, and this particular Kiverian believes he has a reason. He hates mortals and thinks my human parent makes me an abomination. He wants me dead."

McCabe stared at her. Hard. Finally, when she'd about given up hope, he released her from whatever magic kept her frozen. He didn't let go of her arms, but Mika suspected that had less to do with protecting himself than with his desire to touch her. And she was aware he'd never confess that, not even on pain of death. She almost pointed it out, merely to see his reaction, then thought better of it. If she couldn't keep a tighter rein on her impulsiveness, she was going to mess up this assignment before it really began.

"You expect me to believe that he took one look at you and decided you had to die?"

Well, she'd hoped, but . . . "I might have said a few things that irked him. Unintentionally, of course."

"You taunted a Kiverian until he became fixated on you." McCabe shook his head, but he didn't look surprised.

"He was insulting my mother. I couldn't ignore that."

Something Mika labeled as understanding flitted across McCabe's face. "How did you cross paths with one of those monsters, anyway?"

Interesting that he chose that word: monsters. "Bad luck and bad timing," she replied.

"You're lying." He stepped back from her, his face as flat and emotionless as his voice had been.

Mika hated those damn sunglasses; she needed to see his eyes. "Why would I lie? And why would I seek you out if I didn't need help? I'm not stupid. I understood it would be a risk to approach you, that you might shoot first and ask questions later, so to speak—and that's almost exactly what you did."

He grunted and crossed his arms. "I'm supposed to believe a Kiverian is after you because of your smart mouth? That's too convenient," he said.

"There's nothing convenient about this situation," she snapped. Though he'd released her, she didn't move. She didn't want to do anything he might construe as preceding an act of aggression. "It's disrupted my life for far too long, and I can't go home to Orcus until he's taken care of."

"And you just happened to come to me. That's the part that's too pat."

"Perhaps I opted to come to you *because* of the type of demon after me. Have you considered that? You're not the only slayer out there, you know, and it would have been less risky for me to go to one of the others."

"Maybe, but I'm the best," he said. There was no arrogance in his voice; he merely stated a fact.

She wasn't able to smother her smile. "I know you are," she agreed.

"That's why this could be a setup. I'm too good."

"Oh, please," she scoffed. "If this were some setup to kill you, you'd already be dead. You haven't paid attention to anything but me since you leaped out of that alley."

And she hadn't been aware of anything except him either. Idiotic, considering that she already knew there were other dangerous things out tonight. There always were in Crimson City. And there were any number of beings who wouldn't mind both her and McCabe permanently out of the picture.

McCabe scowled, the first strong reaction she'd had from him since he'd locked down his desire. "Why were you following me?" he asked again.

"Instead of showing up on your doorstep? I did, but you were leaving as I arrived, so I followed. When it became clear what you were up to, I decided to see if you're as skilled as your reputation. An audition, if you will."

His frown became fiercer; he hadn't liked that. Amusement welled up in her again and Mika struggled to keep it under control. There was nothing quite like the male ego, no matter in which species of animal. When her laugh escaped despite her efforts, she received a heated glare. Then McCabe shook his head and reluctantly smiled. It transformed his face, made him look younger and much more approachable.

"You're a pain in the ass," he said. "And I'd be insane to help you out if I'd have to put up with this shit."

"Maybe," she conceded soberly, "but could you live with yourself if you turned me down and I ended up dead? I'm half human and my demon blood comes from a weak branch. You know as well as I do how powerful Kiverians are. Even if I hired another slayer, he could die with me. You're my best hope of survival."

He sighed, looked away for a moment, then drilled her again with his gaze. Or at least she suspected he did. She was becoming damned sick of those sunglasses, and if she succeeded in nothing else tonight, she was getting them off his face.

Mika crossed her arms over her chest, mimicking his stance, and waited. It was make-or-break time for her mission.

"So . . . you want me to kill this demon for you," he asked.

She shook her head. "I want a bit more than that. I'll need around-the-clock protection too." Before she could explain, something strummed at her senses. She lost her relaxed pose and turned her head, trying to discern what it was that had intruded.

McCabe stiffened too, and in an action that she found very telling, he moved in front of her. The position was purely protective; it was instinct, not thought, guiding him.

"What did you pick up?" he asked, his voice lower than a whisper.

"I'm not sure." She was just as quiet. "I only caught a wisp, but whatever or whoever it is, he doesn't like us."

"Your would-be killer?"

"I don't think so."

McCabe looked over his shoulder at her, and she read deep skepticism on his face. He thought this whole thing was a ruse, that she was putting on an act to convince him she was in danger. Then she felt it again. So did McCabe. He focused his attention in the same direction as she'd sensed the presence. Mika moved from behind his back to his side. She hadn't picked up any intent to harm them, only curiosity and dislike. But not of the intensity that led to violence.

"He's cloaking—has to be a demon," McCabe said. He didn't look at her.

"Only if he's very young, a demon who doesn't have practice holding the mask in place. It's wavering. You know, others with psychic abilities can pull the invisible act, too," she reminded McCabe.

"But it's not as natural for them."

"Which could be why he's unable to hold it steady," she argued. It required great skill and a lot of energy to hide from a demon—much more than it took to cloak from a human, vampire or werewolf. Few who weren't demons themselves had the ability to do it.

"We need to get out of the light," McCabe grunted, and Mika figured the change in subject meant he had no good argument.

She said, "I don't think we're in danger—at least, not right now."

"And what are you basing that theory on?"

"I don't sense any hostility, just distaste."

Conor muttered under his breath, but Mika ignored it. When he spoke again, she could tell it took a great deal of self-control for him to keep his tone even. "Threat or no threat, we are getting out of this pool of light. Understand me?"

"Yes, I understand, but where are we going? That alley's dark, but it's a dead end. That's a disadvantage."

"It's a bigger disadvantage to stand here, making ideal targets." He looked around. "Okay . . . to our right, there's a Dumpster about a block away. We can get behind it."

Mika glanced down the street. "That's a long block. Easy to take us out before we reach it," she said. She waited for his reaction.

"I thought you said there wasn't any risk. So, which is it—are we safe, or are we going to be picked off?"

She grinned. "Just because I said I didn't sense anything ready to attack us, that doesn't mean we can expect to be safe."

"Which is why I said we need to get out of the light."

"But—"

He cut her off. "Do you have to argue with me about everything?"

"I'm pointing out things that need to be considered," she explained happily. She still didn't have any sense that their watcher was going to attack.

Conor shifted, putting his shoulder in front of her. He was trying to shield her again. "Is this how you'd be if I took on the job of protecting you? Shit, we'd both be dead before we finished our first fight."

"You want unthinking obedience?" she asked.

"Damn straight. Now when I say go, you run to the right—are we clear?" he growled.

"I say we prepare to attack," she argued. She threw that out there deliberately. Not to jab Conor but to test their watcher, who had just moved closer. Her plan worked: The words barely cleared her mouth when whoever it was started making tracks away from their position. He was still cloaking himself, enough so she was unable to identify who or what he was, but Mika knew the instant he was gone.

Almost as soon as she relaxed, McCabe turned and herded her against the side of the building. He was furious and trying to use his size to intimidate her, but unfortunately for him, not only wasn't she cowed, but she liked his nearness. His hard body pressed her shoulders into the ragged brick, but his hands cupped her butt and pulled her flush against him. "You don't have to worry about the Kiverian that's after you. I'm going to fucking kill you myself," he snarled.

Mika wrapped her arms around his waist and gave him a seductive smile before she realized what she was doing. "Yeah? I hate to tell you this, but if you're trying to wring my neck, it's farther north."

His hands immediately stopped kneading her rear, and Mika pulled free. She ignored his cursing and walked a few steps away. McCabe grabbed her, tugged her back, and put her in a bear hug. It was supposed to be a method of restraint, but the feel of him against her bottom made Mika wriggle. His hold tightened, forcing her to still, but not before she felt his body begin to react to hers. She turned and ran her hands up his chest.

"Are you trying to convince me to protect you by offering me your body?" he asked.

It was meant to be an insult, there was no doubt about that, but she wasn't prostituting herself and Conor knew it. He'd said that to make her mad; he wanted her to storm off in a snit, then he wouldn't have to deal with her. Too bad for him that she knew what he was up to, and Mika refused to let him push her buttons.

"No, but I might offer you my body for other reasons," she answered easily.

Turning her head, she snuggled into his shoulder and nipped at the pulse point in his throat, then ran her tongue over it. She couldn't have chosen a worse action if she'd planned it—not if her goal was to stay close to Conor McCabe. He released her so fast, Mika staggered to catch her balance.

Damn it, why did she have this need to always push? She knew he didn't want to want her, that if she had any hope of him agreeing to her scheme, she had to do everything she could to play down the overwhelming physical attraction flaring between them. But was that what she'd done? Hell, no. She'd *maximized* his awareness of her. How stupid.

"I'm sorry," she said, and tried to sound contrite. "Let's start over, shall we?" He pivoted to face her, and she could sense his reluctance. *Be businesslike,* she told herself. "Conor McCabe, I'm Mika Noguchi." She took a few steps toward him, arm outstretched. For a moment, she didn't think he was going to take her hand, but he surprised her. The shake, however, was perfunctory. "I'd like to hire you to protect me, and to slay the demon that's trying to kill me," she said.

He tucked his hands in the back pockets of his jeans. "I don't work cheap," he warned her.

She knew she had him then. McCabe might not realize it yet, but they were now negotiating price. Mika managed to keep her satisfaction in check. "That's okay. I don't value my life cheaply." With a shrug she added, "And I can afford you."

"Can you afford *this?*" He named a price that made her eyes bug out. "That's per day," Conor added.

"That's outrageous!"

"So? Usually I only kill demons. You're going to have to pay for my time if you want around-the-clock baby-sitting."

Mika reined in her temper. She made a counter-proposal, offering a fraction of what he'd suggested.

"Is that a joke?" He shook his head. "Never mind. I don't know why we're discussing money anyway. I don't want the work." He started to walk away.

"You thought if you threw out that ridiculous figure that

I'd tell you to forget it? Well, think again, McCabe." She closed the distance until she was toe-to-toe with him. "I want you." When he tensed, she realized her wording. "I mean, I want your skills as a hunter," she amended.

He didn't respond.

"Would you really trust my life to someone else?" she asked.

"What do I care about your life? You're a demon."

"Half demon," she corrected. "And half human." The flash of anger she felt seeped away and humor returned as she realized he was grumbling more for appearances sake than for any other reason. She upped her offer.

He countered, tacitly admitting he was taking the job. They went back and forth until they agreed to a figure that was about midway between their opening proposals. It wasn't that the cost was important—her dad had plenty of money and was extravagantly generous—but if she didn't dicker over such an exorbitant amount, he'd become even more suspicious.

Their next argument was over what, precisely, his job would entail. She couldn't give in on this; he had to put her up in his home. Mika needed access to his things in order to find and retrieve the incantation the Council believed he had. That was the plan.

Reaching an accord was easier than she expected, once she agreed to obey his orders without discussion. Unless what she had to say was critical; she tacked that on.

"Deal." McCabe held out a hand.

"Take off your glasses," she ordered.

"Why?"

"Two rules. First, when I make an agreement, I always know *exactly* what I'm giving and what I'm getting in exchange. We took care of that. Second, I never seal a bargain if I can't see the eyes. My mother told me if I followed both these principles, I'd never be rooked when dealing with a demon. And, Conor? You have as much demon blood as I do. I'll see your eyes before I shake."

Reluctantly, he pulled the sunglasses off his face. His irises were the color of celery, a pale green shade that wasn't human.

Demon eyes.

Chapter Two

McCabe's palm was warm and calloused, his grip firm but not overpowering. The handshake lingered, giving them both a chance to measure the sincerity of the other. In Mika's experience, those with demon blood would die before going back on their word, but not only would they use any shade of gray to their advantage, they'd also try to fool any other party into thinking they were making a promise when they really weren't. That was why eye contact with McCabe was so important. What she saw reassured her, and she felt confident the bargain was sealed.

It was only then that Mika dared to peer deeper. Her knees buckled, but she quickly locked them. He *was* her vishtau mate. She actually had a mate. Part of her was scared; it was a momentous discovery, a life-altering event. But another part of her wanted to throw her head back and laugh in sheer joy over their connection. It was one thing to suspect, to hope, but something else entirely to be certain.

When he tried to pull his hand free, she tightened her grip before reluctantly releasing him. For a few seconds after they broke the connection, they continued to stare at each other, then McCabe tucked his sunglasses into the pocket on his T-shirt and said, "Let's get out of here."

"You're not putting those back on?" she asked.

"And sacrifice my superior night vision while protecting you from a Kiverian? Not a chance." He took her elbow and steered her down the sidewalk.

"Wait!"

"Oh, hell. What now?"

Mika rested her hands on her hips, unsure whether she was irritated by his tone or amused by it. "We should check where our watcher was standing, see if he left any clues."

McCabe's sigh was loud and long. "Listen," he said, his voice tight. "You wanted protection. The most important thing is to get you off the street. You'll be safe in my home. Besides, we don't know precisely where the hell he was, and we're not going to take time to canvass the area."

His first point was valid and hard to argue with if she really were being hunted by another demon, so she addressed his second point. "I have a fairly accurate idea where he was. We could just stroll by and see if we notice anything."

"This is how you're going to follow my orders?" The soft glow of McCabe's eyes showed he was angry.

"I promised I wouldn't argue unless it was critical." Mika moved closer, tilting her face up to give him the full effect of her glare. "Finding out who was observing us might be that important." *Duh,* she wanted to add.

"Fine." His voice was clipped. "If that's what it takes to get you out of this damn light, then we'll detour in that direction." McCabe leaned forward till his nose nearly bumped hers. "But if you think you're going to continually use that loophole to wriggle out of your promise, you better think again."

"I won't *continually* use it." Mika gave him her nicest smile. "I swear."

The glow in his eyes brightened, but McCabe took deep breaths until they dimmed. "That assurance has a hole big enough to fly a 747 through, but I'm not going to fight you out here. Come on."

Silence and cooperation were her best options right now, Mika decided, moving when he did. And maybe by the time they were somewhere he considered safer, McCabe would have forgotten about her dodge. She cast a sidelong glance at him and noted the tension in his jaw. Or maybe not.

As they neared the place where the watcher had been, Conor hung back and let her lead. It was logical, as she knew where they were headed and he didn't, but still it gave her a moment of surprise. Everything till now had indicated he had trouble giving up control.

They were across the street and maybe fifty feet away, when she gestured toward a wide gap between two buildings and said, "That's the spot."

Despite how large the area was, despite the light coming from the moon, and despite her excellent eyesight, the shadows there remained impenetrable—far darker than they should be. Eerie. A shiver slid down her spine. Mika hesitated, stopped. Her stomach roiled at the very idea of going any closer, and McCabe wasn't moving either.

Something was wrong, but she couldn't name what. Clenching her hands, she pushed forward, but as she took a step, Conor grabbed her arm and drew her back. "Don't," he said.

Mentally, she reached out and probed the area. It felt as if a billion spiders were crawling inside her skull. She quickly pulled back. Nausea welled up inside her, and Mika swallowed hard. She wouldn't attempt that again. "Do you know what it is?" she asked.

He didn't answer. As she started to edge away from him, he tugged her to his side. "Yeah, I know," he said. His face was grim. "It's a trap—one created by a demon. We need to get out of here, and don't argue with me about it."

Without giving her a chance to disagree, he hauled her down the street. He needn't have worried; as dark and repugnant as that area had been, she wasn't about to voice any objections.

Conor was alert, intense, and Mika kept close watch on their surroundings as well. If that had truly been a trap, whoever set it was probably nearby, waiting. There was no doubt in her mind that it had been meant for them, and from the expression on McCabe's face, he thought so too.

But had it been meant for both of them? Or just one?

Mika considered, as they sped along the deserted streets. Orcus didn't have a cohesive, democratic government. Power was maintained through fear, intimidation, bribery and favors—and there was always some faction that opposed a decision the Council made. No doubt this particular mission had incited more than the usual controversy among those who knew of it.

But then, the legend itself was a bone of contention.

She glanced over at McCabe. "You're lucky I'm half Mahsei," she remarked, smothering a smile. "No human could keep up with you—not at the speed you're going."

He immediately slowed. "Sorry. I wanted us out of the area as quickly as possible."

The apology startled her. It was the last thing she'd expected, she'd just wanted to remind him of his heritage. "I wasn't complaining. If you think we need to move fast, we'll move fast. I *can* keep up with you."

He shook his head. "No, we've traveled far enough that we're okay." He turned and looked at her. "You realize the trap ups the stakes considerably," he added.

"You're not going to ask for more money, are you?" She tried to sound worried, but she couldn't keep a teasing note from her voice.

He drew to a halt and took her shoulders. "Be serious. That snare was set by a very ugly demon—you know that, right?"

She didn't. "I know the energy was repulsive, but I've

never encountered anything like it before. What do you think—"

He gave her a soft squeeze, looking uncomfortable. "Come on, let's move. I don't want to stand here analyzing."

McCabe didn't take her elbow this time, so with a small tilt to her lips, she threaded her arm through his. When he stiffened, she put a questioning look on her face. He simply shook his head and kept going, and her smile became full-fledged. Her vishtau mate would get used to her yet.

As they traveled, Mika looked around. Conor hadn't cloaked, so she hadn't bothered to either, but it didn't really matter. While this neighborhood was slightly better than the other—there were bars on the windows instead of plywood—the streets remained empty.

As they zigged around an open trash bag lying on the sidewalk, a thought occurred to Mika. "When you set a trap, you bait it and try to lure in your prey, but neither of us wanted to go forward. Since they were hoping to catch at least one of us, why wasn't it appealing?"

"The trap was baited," McCabe disagreed. "I think you didn't sense it because whatever repelled you was stronger than the lure they created, but it was geared for one of us."

There was a figure huddled in a doorway, the first person Mika had seen in a while, but he was out cold and didn't stir as they passed. Just in case, she waited till she and Conor were farther away before continuing.

"How could anyone be sure where we were going to be tonight?" she asked. "I didn't know where I was going; I was merely following you. You didn't seem headed for a particular destination either."

Three young male figures—their energy patterns told Mika they were werewolves—separated from the shadows of a rundown building, but one hard look from McCabe, red fire burning in his eyes, and they slunk away. Mika laughed quietly. There were definitely perks to having demon blood.

"You're assuming it takes a long time to erect one of

those things," he said when it was clear again. "You're be-lieving that . . ." He drifted off into silence.

"What are you thinking?" Mika asked.

He didn't answer.

"Well?" she prompted.

"How close are you to your family?"

"What? Why are you asking that?" He shot her a look, and Mika rolled her eyes before she answered. "Very close. Now, tell me why you want to know that."

"Mika," Conor said, his voice serious, "that trap was meant for you. There was an energy signature inside, and my guess is that it matches someone in your family. It fit yours very closely. Whoever's after you was counting on you charging to the rescue. Is that something you would do?"

She frowned at him and gripped his arm. Hard. "It was faked, right? No one was really there, were they?"

"No, no one was inside, I promise."

Mika relaxed. If Conor gave his word, then no one in her family was in trouble.

"So, you couldn't read the snare's energy." He sounded grim.

She shook her head.

"I've never felt anything that evil before," he told her. "Ever. You've got something a hell of a lot more dangerous than a Kiverian after you."

Mika felt a chill. This explained the soberness of his voice. As she'd sensed, McCabe was half Kiverian himself—so he'd know that energy and wouldn't misread it. There were only three breeds of demon that were darker, more prone to violence and gifted with power, and at the top of that list was a group to inspire nightmares. And not just among humans. This wasn't good. Not if that trap really had been for her.

"What happened to the demons you saw caught in the snare?" she asked. She wasn't certain she wanted to hear, but she'd better know. Just in case.

"I'm not sure. There was never anything left." He cast

her a sideways glance. "Whatever happened, though, caused a hell of a lot of screaming—and it lasted for a long, long time."

He never should have taken this job. From the minute he'd felt this demoness half-breed trailing him, Conor had known she was trouble. He'd been right. Her energy now seemed to burst through his small house, filling every inch of the place with her essence.

She was unpacking in his bedroom, stowing her things in the drawer he'd cleared out for her. Judging by the weight of the suitcase he'd pulled from the trunk of her car, she'd be at it for a while. His position in the great room gave him the perfect angle and he could see her every time she went past the door. He found himself waiting for those moments, anticipating them. Hell. With a scowl, he swung his chair back to the computer console and typed *Mahsei* into the search engine.

No results. None related to demons anyway. Of course, humans didn't always use the same terminology as the inhabitants of Orcus, and while he hadn't heard of this group before, he knew where Mika's type ranked as far as strength went; her energy sig gave it away. He put the Mahsei in the bottom twenty-five percent, but probably on the upper end of that spread since he'd felt her try to control the wind. Power and malevolence seemed to go hand-in-hand with demons, so he doubted she was a danger to him —not magically at least.

After casting a glance toward the bedroom, he typed in *Mika Noguchi*. It was another dead end, unless his houseguest was an Asian women's wrestling champ—though the idea of her pinning him down had Conor shifting in his chair. He'd always been able to master his sexual urges, but with Mika, he was hanging on by his fingertips. Every instinct he had was clamoring to throw her on the bed and claim her. She'd be willing, he knew.

He shook his head, denying his thoughts. She was a

demon—he couldn't want her. But he did, and it wasn't simply lust she inspired. Since he'd met her, he'd felt frustrated and protective. He couldn't afford either. The only way he could maintain control of his Kiverian side was to not allow himself any strong emotion; he'd learned that long ago. He had to stop reacting to her, had to rein himself in. If he lost too much self-command, he wasn't sure he'd ever be able to cage his demon half again.

The task wasn't going to be easy. Mika enjoyed forcing a response from him—she pushed until she got one—and she wasn't particular about what emotion she triggered. It seemed anger satisfied her as much as anything else.

The memory of their previous interaction was seductive. His fury hadn't frightened her, not even a bit. She'd wrapped her arms around him and smiled. Conor scrubbed both hands down his face. He'd liked that. A lot. Never before had anyone seen his rage and not been scared. Even his mother—

He cut that thought off.

The volume on the radio in his bedroom became louder, and he heard Mika start singing along. Her voice was good, clear and on-key. His body responded as if she were caressing it.

Conor swallowed a curse and pushed out of his chair. A sometimes freelance agent for Los Angeles Battlefield Ops, an intelligence agency founded to keep tabs on the city's paranormal populations and to keep them in line, he worked out of his home—at least as much as possible. To make things easy, he had set up a makeshift office in a corner of his great room, and the bookcase was maybe three steps from his desk.

About half of his reference materials covered vampires and werewolves—his jobs were often to hunt down badass outlaws of those two species—but the other half was about demons. That was his personal interest. Scanning titles, he searched for a volume that would include the widest number of breeds from Orcus, pulled it off the shelf and returned to his desk chair.

Mika danced past the doorway, hips swaying as she slipped something onto a hanger, and his hands clenched around his book. His body howled with need. Her black pants fit her like a second skin, and the sleeveless black top wasn't much looser—the view was riveting. He didn't look away until she moved out of sight.

Hanger? Shit, she was taking over his closet too. Resigned, he shook his head. That was the least of his worries.

Determined to ignore his desire, Conor opened the text and started skimming. He just wished the damn thing had an index. Doggedly, he flipped pages and kept going, but he didn't find any mention of the Mahsei.

Heat filled him and he lost focus. Conor glanced up. Sure enough, Mika stood in the doorway watching him. Her pose made him stir again; her left hand was above her head, resting against the side of the jamb, and her right hand was on her hip, just below the low-slung, silver concho belt. Her lips were quirked up at the corners, giving her a mischievous look.

Her smile changed as she sauntered toward him, became that provocative, come-and-get-me expression that had derailed his common sense earlier. He gripped his book tightly, fighting what she was doing to him.

Control. He had to keep control.

When she reached him, she leaned over his shoulder and looked at his console, her breasts brushing his back. His senses flooded with her. The soft sounds of her breathing, the sexy scent of her skin—even her laugh was intoxicating.

"Conor, you pervert! Women's wrestling?"

Unbelievably, he felt himself blush. Hell. "I was researching you," he grumbled.

That earned him another laugh, and she moved closer, resting her chin on top of his head. He should have told her to back off, but he liked the feel of her pressing against him too much. Yeah, she was trouble, and that was with a capital T.

"Well, how about that? I brought home a gold medal for Japan." Mika wrapped her arms around him, her mouth moving next to his ear. "Do you want to practice some moves?"

His entire body went rigid. "Knock it off," he said. He managed to sound mostly nonchalant.

She lightly nipped his earlobe before moving back, giving him some space. Conor closed his eyes and struggled for command. He wouldn't lose it. He couldn't.

Mika settled on the couch a few feet away from where he sat and brought her left knee up to her chest. She wrapped her arm around her leg and stared at him. Great. Just what he needed: her assessing the damage she'd done to his self-control. But he shoved his demon nature into the background and met her gaze coolly. At some point, he noted, she'd taken off her boots, and damn it, her bare feet made her look innocent. He knew that was a huge lie; she was a demon.

Half demon, a small voice whispered. Just like you.

She had the eyes. They were the color of champagne, and he doubted she wore tinted contacts to hide them like he usually did. His gaze drifted, taking in the rest of her. Her hair was dark brown and fell to the tops of her breasts. It had felt soft pressed against his cheek. Her body— He caught her smile and realized where he was staring.

"Like what you see?" she asked.

He ignored it. "There's nothing in here"—he raised the book—"about the Mahsei."

With a shrug, she said, "I doubt any human has written about us."

"Why?"

"Most have a skewed idea of what demons are. We're all supposed to be evil and make small girls hurl split pea soup." Her grin returned. "But we Mahsei aren't particularly dark. One of my kind might sneak into a house and short-sheet the bed, but we don't indwell—that means possess someone."

"I know what indwelling is," he growled. Maybe he hadn't gone to college, but he was practically a Ph.D. on demons.

"Sorry. Most people don't use that term." She seemed more amused than apologetic. "In any case, our existence has largely been ignored, as we're not dark enough to attract much notice."

"All demons have darkness in them," he said. He knew what he lived with, knew what he fought almost every day.

"So do all humans."

"That's . . . different." It was a lame reply and he wasn't surprised when she laughed.

Mika stretched her legs out from the couch and swiveled to put her feet on the battered coffee table. "You have a nice house," she said. "It looks like you've done some remodeling."

"Subject closed?" Conor asked. He shut his book and tossed it on the desk. He'd do more research later. Demons lied. He had no reason to believe Mika was being honest about her race being left out of the books—or about anything else she'd told him. It was infuriating.

"Did you really want to debate this when your best argument is 'that's different'?" She waited a beat, then asked, "Now . . . I'm tired. Are we sleeping together tonight? Not that I mind," she clarified, "but you're kind of prudish."

She was doing it again, trying to wind him up to get a reaction. He wouldn't fall for it this time, "No," he answered.

Mika looked amused. "The second bedroom is filled with a weight bench and its accoutrements. There's nowhere else to sleep."

She stretched, a deliberate action to call attention to her breasts. To Conor's disgust, it worked. He fisted his hands, his palms itching with need. When he was able to tear his gaze away and look into her eyes, she was smiling again.

"I don't want to play this game," he said. He knew his irises were glowing, damn it, and it wasn't from anger.

For a minute he thought she was going to persist, then she gave up and said, "My question was serious. Where are you sleeping?" She looked unperturbed.

Whether or not she was disappointed by his refusal was anyone's guess, and he couldn't keep ascribing other motives to everything she said or he'd drive himself nuts. "I'll sack out on the couch," he decided.

She looked from one side of the sofa to the other. "You're kidding, right? You're too tall to be comfortable. It's so short that I don't think *I*'d be able to sleep on it."

"It'll be fine." She was right, he was going to be miserable, but he'd get more rest out here than he would lying beside her. And if things became too unbearable, he could always use the floor. He'd slept in worse places. A lot worse.

"Whatever," she said.

Her amusement came through loud and clear—as did a certain smugness. His temper started to simmer again and he struggled to tamp it down.

"Do we need to discuss strategy about how we're going to hunt the demon that's after me?" she asked.

"We? What the hell do you mean, *we?* You're staying here."

She pursed her lips, crossed one ankle over the other, then asked, "Why do you get to have fun while I sit home?"

Conor realized then that she was teasing him again—no way was she serious about hunting demons—but just in case, he said, "You hired me, so you should stay out of the way and let me do my job."

"Sweet talker," she murmured, giving him a flirtatious look from under lowered lashes. "You just don't want me along because I distract you. Say otherwise all you want, but I know you were this close"—she held up her hand, her thumb and forefinger maybe a quarter of an inch apart—"to taking me against that alley wall, and you didn't even know my name."

Conor took a deep breath, then another. How much of this woman's forwardness was a ploy? She was looking for a response, and he wasn't going to give one to her, no matter how tempting. He wanted to tell her she was wrong—it wasn't the alley he'd had in mind; he'd been thinking of taking her right there on the street. But that would be playing into her hands. And it might not shock her the way he wanted. She seemed unshockable.

Control, he reminded himself. Ignore the provocation.

"Besides"—he actually managed to sound halfway normal—"you'll be safe here. I've got protection around the property. No one—demon, human, or anything else—can enter."

His home was a damn fortress. He wasn't sure how it worked, but from the day a human woman, a psychic, had buried four stones at the corners of his land and performed some odd ritual, no one had been able to cross the boundary. If he wanted to make an exception, he needed to chant a spell using the person's full name. To get Mika inside, he'd intoned the words, his voice not even a whisper, while he'd been retrieving her suitcase.

"I walked right through," Mika continued blithely, "without feeling any barrier. Are you sure no demon can enter?" she asked.

"You're not supposed to feel it, but it's there. And I gave you permission to come in," he growled. Was she intentionally questioning his competence?

"How many others have you given permission?" she asked. Her tone of voice was making it difficult for him to hang on to his cool.

"No one you need to worry about."

She continued pushing him: "Kiverians have been known to indwell. I'd hate to have to fight a stream of possessed ex-lovers."

He was standing in front of her before he realized he'd moved, and his hands were on the back of the couch, on either side of her head. Conor never allowed himself to use his demon powers when he wasn't out slaying, yet he'd just broken his own rule. Mika blinked, but that was the only sign his unnatural speed had unnerved her. He leaned in closer, eyes no doubt blazing like two bonfires, and growled an answer. "One other person. One. My former mentor. You don't have to worry about him. Not only does Ben now live hundreds of miles away, he's too old and frail for any demon to possess." Everyone knew if a human died before indwelling was complete, the demon died too.

With a satisfied smile, Mika sat forward and rubbed her nose against his. Conor jerked away as if she'd jolted him with a million volts of electricity.

"Why do you keep doing this?" he asked quietly. He expected some flippant answer along the lines of *Because I can*, but that wasn't what he got. She sat back on the couch.

"You're too tight. You need to let loose and live."

"I can't 'let loose.' I'm half Kiverian—you know that. I have to keep the evil leashed."

She shook her head. "Kiverians aren't evil. They're . . . dark. There's a difference." She looked at him intently.

He didn't agree, but he wasn't going to argue with her.

Mika's mouth twitched into a frown and she said, "There's a Japanese proverb: 'The bamboo that bends is stronger than the oak that resists.' You're resisting what you are, and some day you'll snap. It's inevitable. But if you accept your demon self, integrate it into who you are, you'll be the stronger for it." She continued to stare at him.

Conor shifted uncomfortably. Did she expect him to believe she was offering this advice because she cared for him? More likely she wanted his demon side out for some reason of her own. He changed the subject.

"Your mother is Japanese?" At first, he didn't think

she'd go along, but he could almost see her give a mental shrug.

"My dad. But he prefers to be called American. He's the fifth generation of his family to be born in this country."

"Your *mother* is the demon?" Conor asked. When Mika nodded, he felt shock course through him. This put a whole different spin on things. He'd assumed her mother had been raped the way his own had. "Did she trick him or force him in some manner in order to conceive you?"

Mika looked confused. "How would I know? But I doubt it. I don't remember any tension between them." She suddenly scowled. "Why would you even ask that kind of question?"

He kept his face blank, but it didn't make any difference; he saw the truth dawn on her. Though he thought he'd been oblique enough, somehow he'd tipped her off and given her another weapon to use against him. Conor braced, waiting for her to wield it. She surprised him.

"I'm sorry," she said quietly. Then, after a short pause, she started a monologue about the wood floors in his house. Their eyes met and her lips twisted—not in humor, but in understanding. For the first time, Conor realized he could really like Mika.

And that made her far more dangerous than he'd first believed.

Chapter Three

The sound of a door closing jerked him from a light doze, and Conor's whole body tensed. Then he remembered Mika. He didn't relax until he heard the water come on in the bathroom. With a soft curse, he pushed into a sitting position and leaned back against the couch. It was daytime. He didn't remember the floor being this hard, but his body ached from sleeping on it. Or from trying to sleep.

It wasn't only the discomfort that had kept him awake, either. Mika had insisted on leaving the door to his bedroom open—said it would make her feel safer. Talk about bullshit. It had been another invitation, pure and simple.

Conor brought his knees up and rested his forearms on them. Every time she'd shifted in bed last night, he'd heard. And as the hours passed, resisting the pull he felt to Mika had become tougher and tougher. He rubbed a hand over his eyes. The time spent lying awake had allowed him to think, and he'd come to a realization: Despite her behavior, despite her willingness, Mika wasn't as experienced as she wanted him to believe. There was something in her eyes, a watchfulness maybe, that made him think she was studying his reactions and learning from them.

And damn, if that wasn't an even bigger lure.

She liked to play games; he was aware of that. And demons lied. He knew that too. But her lust for him was real and unconnected to the reason she'd sought him out—it was a truth he could sense. Of course, that didn't mean she wouldn't use it to her advantage.

When the water went off, he stood and stifled a groan as his body protested the movement. Conor eyed his shirt and decided to leave it; Mika wouldn't be offended by a bare chest and he didn't feel like pulling it on.

He stopped short when he saw his home comm was blinking, indicating he had messages. Swallowing a curse, he sprawled in his desk chair and brought the unit online. When some slick salesman went into a spiel about home siding, Conor minimized the window and pulled up the day's headlines. Demons tended to do things that got them noticed, and part of his plan to hunt down the Kiverian after Mika was to scan the news.

Maddox Clan Denies War Prep Rumors. Conor snorted. Like the dogs were going to tell reporters anything different.

Donner: "Business As Usual." Donner might head B-Ops, but he was a politician, not an agent. He had no clue what *usual* was. At least he knew enough to keep his nose out of operations. Conor grimaced, scrolled down the page.

Strange Events West of City. He skimmed the article. It didn't say much, but it sounded like someone was shapeshifting or maybe creating illusions. Definitely worth checking out.

Finally, the siding salesman ended his pitch and the comm unit beeped. When McCabe heard the next voice, he brought the image back to full-screen. Ben looked older than the last time Conor saw him. His mentor's hair was more gray than brown now, the skin wrinkled and sagging around his face. It gave Conor a pang to see how his friend had aged in only a few months, but he reluctantly smiled as Ben muttered about "all the damn technology."

Ben ground to a halt, shook his head, and said, "I was hoping to talk with you, but I should have realized you'd have your comm turned off. Kid, you can't stay so isolated. It's not good for you." There was affection laced with the exasperation in his voice. "Never mind," he said, "I'll lecture you in person when you call me back. You know my code."

There was a close-up of his mentor's nose and more complaints about "gizmos" before Ben managed to disconnect. The double beep signaled the end of messages, and Conor leaned forward to return the call. The last thing he wanted was a reprimand about being such a loner, but he owed too much to his friend to blow him off; he'd endure the speech, even if he'd heard it so many times that he had it memorized.

No answer. A glance at the time told him Ben was probably at his usual afternoon poker game. Conor left a message and pushed to his feet.

He entered the kitchen grimacing, and not just from the late afternoon sun pouring in through the uncovered windows. His next—and final—project for this house was remodeling this room. Conor hated the yellowed linoleum, and the way it had started to curl near the walls, but time had been hard to come by lately. He couldn't remember when more vampires and werewolves were listed as wanted by the government, and freelance work from B-Ops had kept him busy.

Tensions were high and had been for a while. The Preemptive Defense Initiative against vampires had ended, but the armed truce Crimson City's inhabitants lived in was tentative. It wouldn't take much to set off a damn interspecies war.

As if that weren't bad enough, word on the street was that the werewolves and vampires had formed an alliance. Conor had no problem believing that. Fangs were snobbish as hell, but they were opportunistic and would realize it was to their benefit to team up with the dogs. It probably hadn't been easy to convince the werewolves—not at first—but the packs had no doubt realized if PDI were successful, humans would eliminate their species next.

Frowning, he reached into one of the kitchen cabinets, pulled out a plastic glass and put it on the table. For a few days, he didn't have to worry about B-Ops or alliances—he'd just be protecting Mika. A nice, straightforward job.

He snorted at that thought. It had been maybe fourteen hours since he'd met her, and she'd already turned his life upside down.

Taking out a carton of orange juice, he filled his cup to the top, then returned it to the fridge before settling in the wooden chair facing the hallway. Something made him freeze—a shift in energy maybe—but as he tried to focus, he heard the bathroom door open and he lost the sense. Had it even been there? He shrugged and raised his glass as Mika made her entrance.

His hand jerked, causing a wave of juice to slop over his fingers and pool on the wooden surface of the table. Quickly, he put down the cup in order to stare. Mika's legs looked impossibly long, and he let his eyes trail over every inch of them. By the time his gaze reached the edge of her red, high-cut panties, his jeans had become restrictive. He shifted in his chair seeking relief.

Her midriff was bare, her skin golden. She was wearing a red tank top that ended above her navel. It clung to her, especially her breasts, and outlined her erect nipples. More blood surged away from Conor's brain. He wanted his mouth on her, wanted it bad.

Her dark hair was mussed, her eyes heavy-lidded—probably from sleep, but it made her appear even more sultry. Conor swallowed hard as she started walking toward him. For a moment, he was mesmerized by the sway of her hips. Then he snapped himself out of it.

"What the hell are you wearing?" His voice was a combination rasp and growl, but he was relieved he could form a coherent sentence. He slid his chair back from the table far enough to reach the dish towel looped through the oven handle, and wiped the orange juice off his hand.

"What's wrong with my pajamas?" she asked. She stopped in front of him and rested her hip lightly against the table. She looked confused, which was bullshit.

"Pajamas? You're in underwear. Go put some clothes on."

"Everything's covered," she agreed. "Besides, women wear less than this at the beach every day."

"We're not at the beach," he forced himself to say.

She smiled, and Conor tensed, but although he realized she was up to something, he wasn't prepared for it. Before he could react, Mika straddled him. It was a bold action except for one thing—she leaned backward, away from him.

He dropped the towel he held and took her waist, but instead of lifting her off his lap, he drew her tightly against his body until her breasts pressed against his chest. Nothing before in his life had ever felt so good. He managed to stop his groan, but not the shudder. She smiled at his reaction and nipped his chin. He hated that he wasn't indifferent to it, hated that Mika's teeth on his skin made him so much hotter, but Conor arched forward anyway.

Why her? He'd been immune to the few other female demons he'd met, but from the instant he'd sensed Mika, he'd skated on the edge of control. "Stop that," he said, but she ignored him. Even he could hear the lack of conviction in his tone.

Her mouth moved up his jaw, kissing, licking and nipping. Conor had his hands on her waist again, and he stroked the bare skin over her spine, tracing each of Mika's vertebrae. He was losing himself in lust when he felt the disturbance again. It had something to do with the protective barrier around his house, but he couldn't figure out what. His residence was tamper-proof. Or as close to it as possible.

He attempted to zero in on what he sensed, but Mika reached his ear and traced its outside edge with her tongue. He shuddered more strongly and his hands went to her hips, pulling her against his erection. She eased back, letting him see her smile, then rocked her body into his.

Conor wouldn't have guessed he could get any harder, but she showed him differently. His world narrowed to Mika: the feel of her curves against him, the sight of her eyes glowing red, the scent of her arousal. She took his mouth in a kiss as wild and unrestrained as he felt. At first he tried to hold back, tried to keep from scaring her, then he realized he didn't have to do that—his relentless hunger wouldn't frighten her. The part of him that was Kiverian strained at its tether.

Which was enough to knock him out of his sensual daze. Breaking the kiss, he said, "That's enough."

It wasn't, not even close, but he couldn't risk it, couldn't let his demon nature loose. Mika was bad for him. Very bad. And she still leaned into him, tempting him to throw control aside and take what he wanted with every cell of his being.

His grip tightened and he shifted her back so she wasn't molded to his torso. He nearly groaned in protest at the separation, but closed his eyes and fought the need.

Mika didn't help. Although he kept her from sliding forward again, her hands were roaming his chest and belly, even dipping beneath the waistband of his jeans. He pinned her with a hard stare. His resolve faltered for a moment as he saw the thick glaze of arousal in her eyes, but he said, "Stay still."

She froze. Her obedience shocked the hell out of him before he realized she was probably trying to keep him off-balance. It worked. He didn't know which end was up. "You're trouble," he said stupidly, his voice still thick with need.

She grinned. "Why? Because when you're with me, you actually start to feel things? That means you're alive."

"No." He shook his head, denying what she'd said.

"*Yes.* Look at you, Conor. Your eyes are burning, your skin is flushed and—"

He sensed something. Immediately, Mika tensed and stopped talking, trying to figure out what had made his body go rigid. Conor forced his awareness of her out of his mind; he couldn't afford the distraction. His protective shield: someone definitely was testing it. If he had to make a guess, he'd say they were probing, trying to find out if there was a weakness and where. He needed to figure out who or what was out there.

As hard as he focused, though, he couldn't get a good read. Whoever it was had shielded himself, and had done a damn good job. That tipped the odds in favor of this uninvited guest being a demon. If he weren't in tune with his security, he might not have picked up on it at all.

"What is it?" Mika whispered.

Conor shook his head, silently telling her to stay quiet.

The fact that she didn't sense anything wrong reinforced his belief that it was his familiarity with his defenses that had allowed him to pick up the problem. He should go outside and check, but he hesitated. If he left her alone, and if somehow whoever it was made it through the barrier, Mika would be virtually helpless.

Okay, as helpless as a demon could be.

He was under no illusions about Mika's nature. She might be on the lighter end of the demon-breed spectrum, but she was dangerous. She could kill. Maybe not in cold blood, but in self-defense? Hell, yeah.

Still, if this was the same demon that had set that snare last night, she wouldn't stand a chance. It wouldn't matter what kind of powers she had or how skilled she was, he'd have her in seconds. Conor wasn't positive even *he* could battle something so dark and survive; but his odds were a damn sight better than Mika's.

No, he decided, he'd stick with her until he was positive his protection wouldn't be breached; then, after the intruder was gone, he would look around and see if there was any remaining evidence.

He breathed a silent sigh of relief when the would-be trespasser gave up: His shield had held. As soon as he relaxed, Mika did as well. Her arms went around his neck and she rested her forehead against his. She was plastered against him, and Conor cursed silently. He'd done it again, drawn her close.

"What was it?" she asked.

"Someone was trying to bypass my security. Probably to get to you." He ran his palm unthinkingly down the length of her hair a couple of times, letting the soft strands slide between his fingers.

"Me?" She straightened, and he let his hand fall to her waist as she studied him. "Are you sure about that? Maybe they were after you. I mean, I only hired you last night," she added quickly. "That would be fast to find me here."

"Maybe." He shrugged. "But the timing is coincidental after running into that trap last night. I think it's likely you're the target. I have to watch out for you, remember."

"True," she agreed. She smiled mischievously, moved her hand to his nape and toyed with his hair. "So what's the plan for tonight? There's only a few hours until the sun goes down."

"You're staying in the house until this whole situation is resolved. Think of it as protective custody," he added at her frown. "I'm going out to see what I can scare up about any Kiverians that have arrived in Crimson City recently. I'm guessing your stalker came from Orcus." Damn, he should have asked these questions last night. Conor frowned. She'd messed up his head till he could barely think.

As he expected, Mika nodded. If there had been a Kiverian in the Overworld, he would have hunted it down already.

"What did it look like?" he asked.

"I don't know."

"How can you not know?" he snapped. When her eyes started dancing with amusement, he realized she'd picked up on his frustration. Was she withholding information on purpose? What was her game?

"Some demons can shapeshift," she said.

"Yeah, but you should be able to see through that." It was damn hard for one demon to fool another. Illusions didn't work very well, as they took a hell of a lot of energy—not to mention, concentration—to maintain when another demon tried to see through them. That was why demons rarely fought each other while cloaked. Shapeshifting would drain even more power.

"I couldn't," she disagreed. She trailed a fingernail across his nape and a shiver went through him. "I was too busy fighting to stay alive and looking for a chance to escape."

Shit, he hadn't considered that. Mika would have had more on her mind than seeing through an illusion. But that raised more questions than it answered. "What about while you were mouthing off to him? Was he cloaked then? And why did he disguise himself to attack you?"

"I don't know."

She shrugged, her breasts moving against his bare chest. The flimsy tank top she wore teased him, and he took hold of the hem, ready to tug it over her head, before he realized what he was doing. Conor released the cloth and took his hands off her.

"Give me a break. Just because I didn't question you last night doesn't mean you're off the hook. You want me on the job, then give me the information I need to take care of things."

"I don't like to talk about it," she said.

She looked uneasy, but how much of that was real, and how much was some act? "Let's start with the basics. Where were you when you first saw this Kiverian?"

"Biirkma." A rumbling noise escaped him, and she quickly added, "It's a major city in Orcus. Unless you're familiar with it, what good does it do to be more specific? If

I tell you I was in a square near the palace, does that mean anything to you?"

"You have a point. So he insulted your mother and you made a few smart-ass remarks, right?" Mika nodded and squirmed a little on his lap. "Okay, he wasn't shapeshifting during this time, right?"

"No, but I'm not sure I can describe him. I wasn't paying attention until he confronted me, and as soon as I realized he was looking for trouble, I started trying to get away from him. I'm a weak demon," Mika said, sounding apologetic.

"Of course, you didn't realize he was *looking for trouble* until after you lipped off."

Her contrition increased. "I'm Mahsei. We're impulsive."

Conor took a deep breath and realized he was getting sidetracked again. That happened a lot around Mika. "Describe him. Give me his height, weight, hair and eye colors."

"He was maybe your height, but not as big as you are. His hair was dark, and he wore it long." Mika shrugged. "I can't say what color his eyes were. It was night."

"You've just described about half the male demons," he commented, voice neutral. "It seems to me that since you were targeted, you would have paid more attention to detail."

She shrugged. "There was a lot going on."

Conor bit back a curse. "Let's try this instead. How did you and the Kiverian get across the veil?"

"My dad can do summonings. How do you think he met my mom? As for the Kiverian, he must have a human minion."

Looking past Mika's shoulder, Conor considered her answer. It wasn't quite as easy as she made it sound. First off, *minion* wasn't all that accurate a term. Though they probably wished otherwise, the residents of Orcus couldn't control humans. Secondly, not just anyone could successfully call out demons—only those who had an innate magical ability. Few humans fell into that category, and most of those were too well-trained to be used. Even the handful who were open to trading a summoning for a favor knew enough to put tight boundaries on the demon.

"So you're saying your fath—"

Mika rocked her pelvis against his. Conor swallowed a curse. That response made her smile; then she trailed her mouth over his left shoulder and upper arm, down to his biceps. She bit the muscle, and Conor lost his train of thought. All he could think about was how her position gave him access to a wide expanse of her bare skin. He lightly bit the curve where her neck met her shoulder, then pulled away, appalled. Even though he was half Kiverian, he didn't bite women in passion. Ever. Until today.

"Stop," he ordered.

She didn't. Instead, she used her teeth another time. He felt the beast inside him struggling for freedom, and its strength scared him. He would be swamped, taken over—he didn't doubt that.

"Mika," he said.

She ran her tongue over his collarbone, and he knew she planned to ignore him. It was time for drastic measures. He took hold of her waist, picked her up and sat her on the table. Her eyes widened and she gasped. That's when he remembered the spilled orange juice.

He didn't apologize. "Maybe that will cool you off," he said instead, taking another step back. Three feet didn't seem a safe enough distance, not with how he reacted to her.

"Conor," she purred with a smile that made him twitch, "there are more pleasurable ways to get my panties wet."

He opened his mouth, then shut it again without speaking. Taking in her tousled hair, her softly glowing eyes, that tempting grin and her incredible body, he knew there was only one thing for a smart man to do: Retreat.

Her laughter followed him as he fled.

Mika sat cross-legged on the couch and frowned. Conor McCabe clearly came from the minimalist school of home decor. The walls of the great room were a soft ivory, without so much as a cheap print to break the monotony, and the furnishings were simple—one sofa, apparently picked for durability rather than comfort or style; one coffee table that looked as if he'd rescued it from a trash heap; and his oversized desk.

The office area held most of her interest. Not only was the desk huge, the bookcase was as well, and it was crammed with texts. The desktop was empty except for a computer screen, a keyboard, and a stack of papers with a geode paperweight on top of them.

Mika rubbed her forehead. It felt so lonely here, so barren of life and joy. Looking at the room—at the whole home—made her hurt for Conor. Not that McCabe would appreciate that. He'd get prickly if she said anything, but if she were living here, she'd make the place burst with color and vibrancy. It was just what he needed.

She blew out a sharp breath. Conor had disappeared for good, and she guessed he was out investigating or doing whatever the first step was in his plan of action. The house seemed emptier without him.

Her intention when she'd walked into the kitchen earlier had been to test how strong the bond between them was. Already she was comfortable with Conor, as if she'd known him forever, but he'd lived his entire life in the human world. How much did he feel? Before she'd been able to get any answer, he'd begun questioning her. Mika's scowl deepened. There had been no choice except to divert him, and she'd used their attraction to do it. She certainly couldn't tell the truth.

Not with the way her promise to the Council was worded.

The Council. Mika stretched out her legs, resting her heels atop the coffee table. She'd finally figured it out. The reason why they needed her, the reason why they hadn't had Conor killed and then ransacked his home at their leisure, was the protective field surrounding his property.

They must have tested it, and once they'd discovered it couldn't be breached, they must have decided they needed someone he would allow inside.

They'd laid out a plan for her to enlist his aid and she'd never asked the one question that would have occurred to any idiot. Why didn't she just break into his home and find the spell? If she'd raised that issue, odds were good she would have gotten a better bargain than the one she'd agreed to.

Slouching in her seat, she gazed at her bare toes. At least she'd protected Conor. He might hate her when the spell disappeared, but her vishtau mate would be safe.

The vishtau. Mika sighed. The timing and the man couldn't be worse. Yet she couldn't imagine wanting any other now that she'd spent time with him.

Sex was casual among the inhabitants of Orcus. She'd never embraced that lifestyle, maybe because she'd lived too long in the Overworld, or maybe because her grandma Noguchi had such a huge influence on her, but Mika didn't condemn others for taking their pleasure. And in all honesty, there had been several demon males she would have gone to bed with—if they hadn't scorned her because of her damn human blood. Since she wasn't willing to settle for some weak creature, and certainly not for a human, she didn't have much in the way of firsthand experience.

Still, she'd grown up with the openness—she'd witnessed plenty—so she wasn't ignorant. Nor was she shy. Conor was her mate and she wanted him, why shouldn't she touch him?

It wasn't as if he were fighting her off. She hadn't been bold enough to straddle him torso to torso, not with the memories of her previous rejections, but he hadn't hesitated for more than a second before pulling her the rest of the way forward. He'd told her to stop kissing him, yet at that very moment, Conor's hands had been underneath her tank top, exploring the bare skin of her back. He didn't want to want her, she was aware of that, but his desire was as strong as hers.

Nothing would be casual between them, not with this bond. The thought made her shiver. And while it was a connection that they could fight for a short time, the longer they spent together, the more difficult it would be to resist. Which made it a foregone conclusion where they'd end up.

And once they became lovers, their link would only solidify. They would want each other more, and the need to protect the other would grow. She felt it already, suspected Conor did too, and that it played a part in his agreeing to watch over her.

Mika sighed. She needed to get off the sofa and begin searching. It was already full dark and she had no idea how long McCabe would be away, but she didn't move. She was in no big hurry to find the spell. It might be a longshot, but if Conor had more time with her, grew to like her, maybe he wouldn't be unforgiving when the truth came out about her duplicity.

Did he know of the vishtau? Probably not, and that was to her advantage. He couldn't battle it as easily if he didn't understand what it was. Since the bond was viewed with reverence in Orcus, it was unlikely any demon had spoken of it to a human, and it wouldn't be in one of his books.

At some point, she'd have to explain it to him. The thought was daunting. He wouldn't want that kind of tie with her—especially after she completed her mission.

She tugged at her shirt, pulling the hem down to the waistband of her shorts, and laughed as her sense of humor surged back. Poor Conor. Part of the vishtau was overwhelming sexual desire. More than desire, it was need, craving, yearning . . . There wasn't a word in any human language strong enough to describe the urge to mate. And the longer they were together, the more powerful it would grow. It was part of being a demon even he wouldn't be able to deny. Not for long.

With another laugh, Mika pushed herself to her feet. She

could think while she searched, and she needed to start looking. The Council was positive McCabe had the incantation of legend, and that he was only one capable of using it. After spending time with him, she had some doubts. Not that he had it—*that* wouldn't surprise her—but that he might perform it.

According to the legend, the spell not only enslaved all demon will to the one who wielded it, but would lower the veil that kept her people imprisoned in Orcus. Given his feelings, Mika was sure the last thing Conor McCabe would want was demons loose again in the human world. It didn't matter if he had control; simply seeing them would remind Conor of what he was—and of what he hated.

Though she doubted McCabe would ever use it, Mika knew she couldn't take any chances. As long as that incantation existed, so did the possibility that it would be enacted, and she wouldn't allow her family to become thralls to anyone.

She looked around, trying to choose a starting point for her search. It was difficult. If the spell wasn't part of a grimoire, it could be anywhere: tucked in one of his books, in a pocket of a jacket, on his computer. And while Conor was neat, he also seemed to have accumulated a hell of a lot of paper.

Mika huffed out a long breath and, with one hand, pushed the hair off her forehead. She'd begin with his desk and work her way through his office area first. That was the most likely place. If that failed, she'd keep looking. She had no choice.

When she sat in his chair, she felt his essence strongly. Obviously Conor spent a lot of time here. For a moment she stopped and indulged herself in the sense of him, at least until she felt the ache of the vishtau return between her thighs. Mika squirmed, trying to make it ease, and reached for the deep purple geode paperweight. It was heavy and big enough that she needed two hands to hold.

The geode held Conor's vibration too, and as she cradled it against her chest, she found it somehow calming.

Reluctantly, she returned the stone to the desktop and, with a sigh, forced herself to get to work—the Council wasn't going to accept any excuses. She opened the top left desk drawer. Pulling out a stack of papers, she began sorting through them. Receipts. Half a bazillion of them. She groaned. McCabe needed to get better organized. Unless she was mistaken, these were income tax documents. Some of the papers were crumpled up. The damn man better hope he never got audited.

Mika began to itch with the desire to set up a color-coded system. It wouldn't take long, and if he remembered to follow her instructions, it would make McCabe's life much easier.

She laughed. Her human family teased her about her need for order, but her family in Orcus understood. All demons had an obsessive streak, and it generally manifested itself with one quirk. For her gran it was perfect fingernails, and her mom had a shoe collection that filled the house, though she preferred to be barefoot. Mika's happened to be a compulsive desire for organization. It was honestly funny given her general disposition, but idiosyncrasies seemed to work that way.

When she realized she was checking his bottom drawer for tabbed folders, she stopped short. Setting up this office wasn't her job—finding that incantation was, and although she didn't want to locate it immediately, she'd given her word.

She returned to sorting, thinking about her task. The plan was, she'd give the spell to the Council so they could destroy it. She wasn't naive; she knew that if they could use it to gain more power, the Council members would. But no full-blooded demon could wield it—that was part of the legend. And since they couldn't cast it themselves, the Council wanted the incantation eliminated.

She finished with the pile, then slid the drawer all the way out and turned it upside down. There was nothing attached to the bottom, and tapping revealed no hidden compartments. She put it back and arranged the papers inside as she'd found them.

Nothing turned up in any of the other desk drawers either. Pushing the chair back, she crawled on the floor and examined the desk's underside—she even felt along the back. Not a damn thing.

She emerged from beneath the desk and eyed the shelving unit. There had to be a thousand books jammed in there, and she'd have to glance through each and every one. She was bored, sweaty, and the last thing she wanted was to go through every one of those tomes. Mika perused the titles. Some had nothing written on the spine, but of the ones that did, about half dealt with demonology.

She'd already spent four and a half hours digging through Conor's things, and had discovered nothing. Well, nothing except the fact that the man didn't throw papers away and didn't have a filing system. Mika shook her head and laughed. She'd bet McCabe would be shocked to his core to discover a demon who wanted to rearrange his file cabinets. That was the ultimate in evil, she knew.

Deciding she'd feel more like tackling the bookcase after a short break, she padded barefoot into the kitchen and turned on the light. It made her feel vaguely uncomfortable to stand there, fully illuminated. The windows didn't have any kind of curtain or blind, and anyone lurking outside would see her clearly. It was silly, paranoid—who would be watching her? Did she believe his earlier suggestion that she was the one being targeted? No. But her laugh was uneasy, unamused.

She opened the refrigerator and pulled out the orange juice. Lifting the container, she knew it was nearly empty and decided not to bother with a glass. Her head was back and the carton almost vertical when she felt it: Someone *was* out there. Mika started and juice soaked the front of her shirt. Ignoring it, she dropped to the floor—right into a puddle of juice. She didn't bother to swear, but reached out magically and turned off the lights.

She tried to focus outside, but her night vision was impaired from the earlier light. Damn it, she hadn't needed the overhead on, she could see as well in the dark as with the lights on, but flipping the switch was a human habit she'd never broken.

Extending her senses, Mika tried to read the watcher's energy. He was cloaked in invisibility, but that cloak wavered—the same as she'd felt last night when she and McCabe were under observation. What were the odds that there were two different people who couldn't hold a shield while watching her? Slim—she'd bet on it.

There hadn't been any heated animosity earlier, and she needed to know if that had changed. She reached out again, but it was distaste she sensed, not hatred. Of course, she was making a huge leap and maybe a foolish one. There didn't have to be rage for this watcher to kill; that had been a hole in her logic yesterday. If Conor hadn't been so furious with her, he probably would have pointed it out right then and there.

At least the protection around his home was holding. It was barely discernible, but she thought she had its signature now. Mika turned her attention back to the watcher.

"Who are you?" she asked and held her breath. If he heard, he chose not to answer.

She needed to figure out as much as she could. This wasn't a demon, she was sure. As she'd told Conor, only one very young would be unable to hold his cloak, and this wasn't a child.

So vampire, werewolf or sensitive—which was it?

When her eyes adjusted, she shifted into a crouch and carefully crept to the window. Scanning the scrub-filled land behind Conor's house, she didn't see anyone. Of course, her field of view was restricted, not only by the overgrown bushes at the back of the property line, but by her position in the house. She debated moving to check from some other vantage points, but decided not to. Maybe the peeping tom would grow impatient and give himself away; she simply had to wait.

For more than half an hour she knelt on the floor and watched, but while she felt the presence from time to time and knew he was directly across from the window, she never saw him. Restlessness gnawed at her, and it became more difficult to remain still. The thought of going outside for a confrontation was tempting, but she decided that would be precipitous.

She continued to bide her time until she felt McCabe approach. Then the observer changed position. Mika's heart froze, resumed beating in double-time. It was difficult to be sure with the energy fading in and out, but she thought the spy was moving to intercept Conor. She had to do something.

Mika raced to the front of the house, and for a split second she hesitated. McCabe would have a fit if she went outside, but she had to warn him. To hell with it.

She threw open the door as Conor turned into the yard. His scowl was immediate. "Get back in the house," he said. Despite his quiet voice, she heard his anger.

Realizing the brightness from within the house silhouetted her, she telekinetically turned off all the lights, but she didn't go inside. Conor's expression became fiercer, and she knew there would be hell to pay later. Ignoring that, she reached out to find the watcher. She couldn't locate him, but something pulled at her senses.

Mika tensed, caught the vaguest sense of motion.

She went from zero to warp speed in a nanosecond and tackled Conor to the ground. He rolled, covering her body, and they both watched a glowing streak flash through the night, slicing directly through the space where he'd been standing.

She'd been wrong. The stalker was a demon.

But things were even worse than that. Even among the

darkest of demons, only a few were able to wield auric killing energy. And those few performed one job and only one job: Assassin.

Which meant someone wanted Conor dead.

She had to get him inside. "We need to move."

"I know. Stay behind me," he replied.

He was the one in danger, but she remained quiet; Mc-Cabe wouldn't let her shield him, and arguing about it would only keep them outside longer.

When he shifted into a crouch, she did exactly as he'd ordered. The sight of a gun in his hand startled her. Conor should know that demons weren't affected by bullets. His other arm went around her waist and he hauled her to her feet.

He didn't let go of her. Keeping his body between her and the assassin, he propelled her toward the house. She didn't resist, not wanting to give him any reason to slow down. Mika wanted him out of the line of fire. When her heel hit the bottom stair and she started to fall, Conor tightened his hold and nearly dragged her into the house.

The door closed behind him, and he holstered his weapon. "What the hell were—You're hurt. How bad?"

She followed his gaze. It was only then that Mika realized she was bleeding.

Chapter Four

"Ow!"

"Sorry," he apologized, "I know it stings."

Mika frowned, but Conor bent his head to dab at her leg. She sat on the coffee table—too sticky and dirty to sit on the sofa—and McCabe knelt in front of her, administering first aid. "It's barely more than a few scrapes from the concrete. They'll heal within a few hours. There's no need to do thissss." Her last word came out a hiss as he found a deeper laceration.

"Who would have guessed that a demon would be such a baby about antiseptic?" he jibed. She snarled, but McCabe ignored her and kept cleaning the wounds.

"This is a waste of time," she said.

"No, it's not. You've got dirt in there. You'll heal better if I get it out."

Since he sounded determined, Mika vowed to be tough. She wouldn't let him think her weak, not over this. But as he scrubbed another of the deeper cuts, she inhaled sharply, her fingers curling around the edges of the coffee table.

Somehow, she needed to keep her mind off what Conor

was doing. She closed her eyes and replayed the ambush. Yeah, that would keep her thoughts occupied.

The attack had to be orchestrated by the Council. Bastards. They'd promised her they wouldn't kill Conor, but if an auric assassin was involved, odds were good they'd sent it. Mika tried to remember the precise phrasing of the oath they'd given her. She was sure she'd covered every contingency.

But was it the Council? For one thing, she'd only been here a little over twenty-four hours. Even a strong demon couldn't be expected to find the spell so quickly. And for another thing, they would never risk their magic by breaking a vow. There were other factions who might want Conor dead. She'd been assured that no one except a few high-level advisors were aware McCabe was thought to have the spell, but word might have spread. Information was power in Orcus and all loyalties were for sale.

She sighed silently. The rats' nests of alliances among demons were always troublesome. Weaker branches regularly gave their oaths to stronger ones for protection. All it took was one word in the wrong place and a secret was compromised.

Mika reached out and ran her hand through Conor's hair. With his close call so fresh, she needed to touch him. He froze and shot her a questioning look. Smiling faintly, she rested her hand on his shoulder. After a moment, he glanced away and resumed his ministrations.

She had to think. What did she know about auric assassins? The answer wasn't much—demon breeds never shared info about their talents. But she had a few facts. Only a handful of males from the five darkest groups were capable of wielding such energy.

And how many did she think there would be, all told? Mika rubbed her forehead with her free hand and tried to make an educated guess. Probably fewer than twenty, she speculated.

Conor interrupted her thoughts. "There, that should do it. Why don't you go clean up?"

His voice made Mika slowly turn her head and meet his eyes. "He was after you, not me," she said, ignoring his suggestion. She did want a shower, but there were more important things to take care of first. McCabe needed to understand the danger he was in, and she wasn't sure he did. He was much too calm for a man who'd avoided death by a matter of seconds.

"We don't know that," he said.

"The hell we don't!" Mika glared at him. "He was aiming for you."

Conor took her shoulders and looked deep into her eyes. "What do you think would happen to you if I were killed? If he takes me out of the picture, the path to you is wide open. That's the way assassins think. They prefer easier kills."

For a moment, she merely stared at him. "How do you know it's an assassin?"

"Come on, Mika." Conor began to pull away, but she caught him and dug her fingers into his shoulders to keep him close. "Give me some credit. I've been around for a long time."

Bullshit. He lived in the human world, he shouldn't have a clue that the demon who'd shot at him was an assassin. But Mika opted not to question him about his knowledge; she might discover more by pretending to believe him. Not that he was lying, strictly speaking. She was sure every word he said was a hundred percent true. McCabe was such a boy scout, it was unlikely he'd tell an outright fib.

"You're right," she said. He looked smug until she continued, "I do need a shower." Mika stood and stepped around him. The laugh she let escape while sauntering toward the bedroom was deliberate. Let him stew over that for a while.

Grabbing some clean clothes, she went down the hall to

the bathroom. She left the door open about six inches. It wasn't precisely an invitation, but if he wanted to join her, she wouldn't say no. Still, Mika doubted Conor would come in. He wasn't at the breaking point. Yet. Her lips curved. She might have to give him a few more nudges.

His bathroom had an art deco look. The ceramic tiles were a warm coppery-brown color, and the vanity was a few shades darker. Rising up from the tub was a decorative curved wall with a stripe down the center that made her think of water. The shower was separate, the floor inlaid with small tiles in a pattern that complemented the retro feel.

Mika's eyes narrowed. There was definitely a woman's influence in the decor. No way did any guy, especially one like Conor, buy a mirror with a design etched into the corner, or a window with a frosted ocean wave on one side. Jealousy burned in her, and Mika tried to push it aside. This possessiveness was associated with the vishtau. She knew that, but it didn't help.

She started the shower. Whoever the woman was who'd helped McCabe pick out the tile and fixtures, she was long gone. That was obvious, since her presence was notably absent in the other rooms. Besides, she didn't matter; Mika was around now.

With a shimmy, Mika let her shorts drop to the floor and kicked them into the corner. Placing her clean clothes atop the hamper, she leaned forward to study her face in the mirror. There was a small cut on her left cheek that McCabe had missed swabbing with antiseptic. For a moment, Mika toyed with the idea of calling him and asking him to clean it, but decided that was too much—it would be gone in a few hours, anyway. But the laceration was a reminder of how dangerous the situation was.

When she'd taken this assignment, Mika had never dreamed she'd end up playing bodyguard to a man who was half Kiverian. Despite the oddity of someone as weak as herself protecting a much darker demon, she'd do it. No one would hurt McCabe, not if she could prevent it. Not the damn Council, not any other faction, and most definitely not the shooter.

Mika snorted. Yeah, right, *she* was going to defend *him* from an auric assassin? Demons a lot less powerful than that could kick her ass. She shook her head. There were ways other than confrontation to keep Conor safe, and she'd have to rely on those.

Steam billowed out of the shower and she stepped back from the vanity. Tugging her shirt over her head, she tossed it near her shorts and shed the rest of her clothes. When she got in, the hot water felt good and she let it sluice down her body and relieve her tension. She only allowed herself a few minutes before reaching for the shampoo.

As she scrubbed her hair, Mika noticed how her things were intermingled with Conor's. Her shampoo and conditioner sat on the ledge next to his. Her soaps rested against his bar in the shower caddy. There was an intimacy to the way their personal items had become tossed together and, no doubt, that familiarity would drive McCabe nuts. She laughed quietly.

After rinsing out the suds and conditioning her hair, Mika worked on getting the rest of the dirt off her body. With a sigh, she straightened, then froze. She heard something. Cocking her head, she listened intently. Then she made a guess as to what was going on. That son of a bitch. And after she'd saved his life, too!

As quietly as she could, Mika stepped out of the shower. She left the water running. Quickly, she dried off, then wrapped the towel around her. It barely covered the essentials, but that didn't bother her. Conor, however, would be affected.

Since the bathroom door was already ajar, she didn't have to do more then ease it slowly open. She knew how to move without making a sound, and she used that skill as she walked down the hall to the bedroom. Yep, she'd read the noise exactly right.

Mika stood in the doorway and watched Conor search her things. He was fast, he was silent and he was careful—just not fast, silent or careful enough.

It was impossible to be offended by his lack of trust. She had searched his desk earlier, and she herself was lying to him. He was smart not to put his faith in her. But that didn't mean she was going to let this go. As he opened the second dresser drawer—the one she'd appropriated without permission—she knew the perfect opportunity was fast approaching. She bit her lip to prevent a laugh from escaping.

He went through the half that held her socks first, and Mika rolled her eyes. If he planned to do a thorough search, he was merely delaying the inevitable. But that was no big surprise. He was resisting the need to mate with her.

Finally, Conor moved to the other side of the drawer. He gingerly removed each piece of lingerie and set it down on top of the dresser. She waited until he was holding a tiny pair of lime green, lacy panties before she called out, "First women's wrestling, now a panty fetish? McCabe, you *are* a pervert!"

His expression was priceless, but it didn't last long. A neutral mask settled over his face. With a smirk, Mika sashayed into the room, not stopping until she had invaded his personal space.

"What were you planning to do with those?" She trailed her fingers over the hand clutching her underwear. "Were you going to use them while you indulged in self-pleasure, or were you thinking about wearing them?"

"Mika," he growled in warning, but she was close enough to see the flush beneath his tan.

"Don't you think I have the right to ask what you're doing with my panties?" she asked. She slid her fingers through his till their hands meshed in her silky lingerie.

He bent forward so he could scowl in her face, but Mika wasn't intimidated.

"Maybe you'd rather I lose the towel and put them on myself," she said. "Then you could tug this out of the way"—she hooked her finger in the gusset of the panties, pulling the fabric to one side—"and slide inside me." Mika let her lashes drop and ran her tongue over her upper lip. "Mmm, I think I'd like that too."

"Will you stop that?" he said. He tried to take a step back, but the dresser was in the corner and there was nowhere for him to go. Mika edged forward, pressing her breasts against his forearm.

"I suppose a thing for panties isn't that kinky, and if this is what it does to you"—she put her palm on the front of his jeans and stroked his erection—"then I can live with it."

His hand covered hers, stopping her from continuing her motion, but he didn't pull her free. She squeezed him and saw the color burn brighter in his irises. Mika squeezed it again, heard the change in his breathing, and when his hold loosened, she resumed caressing him.

"How do you want me?" She wasn't calm herself, and the more she touched him, the more she wanted him. He'd feel so good moving inside her—she just knew it. "Against the wall? Or would you rather have me leaning over the dresser?"

Conor blinked, and she saw him rein himself in. She nearly groaned aloud. It didn't surprise her when his hand captured hers again and removed it from his pants.

"You left the water running," he rasped.

"What?"

"You're wasting water. Turn the shower off."

Mika didn't have to go anywhere to do that. She reached out mentally and stopped the flow. "I'd ask if you were happy now, but we both know you're not. Nothing except your body shuddering inside mine is going to satisfy you. Trust me."

He pivoted, caging her in the corner, and growled. It

was purely the sound of a frustrated demon male, but she didn't tell him that. The situation was much too volatile at this moment for her to goad him. He might not realize how dangerous he was right now, but she did. Conor wouldn't hurt her, she trusted that, but nothing good would come from too much pressure.

Though she didn't do it often, Mika backed down and dropped her eyes. It was a submissive gesture, one his Kiverian instincts would read and accept even if his human side was unaware.

"No," he said, and his finger went under her chin, carefully tipping her face up until their gazes met. "I'm not happy."

Before she could say anything, his mouth brushed over hers in a surprisingly gentle kiss. For an endless moment, they stared at each other, then Conor took a step away and strode out of the bedroom.

Mika raised her fingers and touched her tingling lips. Something had just happened. She wasn't sure exactly what, but his actions had left her feeling off-balance and confused. McCabe had turned the tables, and Mika didn't like it.

It was ten A.M., and though she'd been in bed for a couple of hours, Mika couldn't sleep. Whenever she closed her eyes, she saw that streak of energy headed toward Conor. It easily could have killed him. What if she hadn't sensed it? What if she hadn't been fast enough? What if the assassin had fired again? Rumor had it that some of them could shoot that killing bolt twice.

Conor was as restless as she. Mika heard him moving in the other room, trying to get comfortable. Demons could go indefinitely without rest, but their powers declined as fatigue increased. And with their human genes, she and Conor would be affected more quickly. They both needed to sleep.

Mika sighed and rolled onto her side. She was too aware

of him. Despite the room-darkening blinds, she could see him clearly whenever she looked through the open door. The mid-morning noise outside the house seemed remote, but she could hear every breath he took. In one day Conor McCabe had become important to her, and she felt as if she'd known him forever. It was tied to the vishtau, but there was more than that. There was a lot about this man that she liked. That she'd liked since reading his file. He was honorable and intelligent, kindhearted—but with an edge that made him sexy as hell.

What was she going to do? Tonight Conor would want to go off on his own again, to look for the demon that was supposed to be after her, and that might cost him his life. She couldn't expect him to stay in his house indefinitely. It wasn't in his nature to hide. He was a warrior, a man who would always confront a threat, not cower from it.

Mika reached out a hand, resting her palm on the empty mattress beside her. She needed Conor close, needed to touch him, and it had nothing to do with sex. This came from her soul.

She heard him shift again, mutter some obscenities about the sofa and make a low growling sound. His bed was king-sized and there was plenty of room, but he wouldn't join her. Not today. She struggled against the pull, against the overwhelming loneliness, but Mika conceded the battle after a few more minutes.

Tossing back the covers, she slipped out of bed and went to him. As soon as she entered the darkened great room, his gaze locked on her. She stopped when she reached the couch and looked down. Conor lay on his right side, his knees bent as he tried to fit in the too-small space. All he wore was a pair of shorts, and she took a minute to admire his muscled chest and ripped abs. The man clearly made use of his weight-lifting equipment on a regular basis. His eyes were glowing when she glanced up again.

"Did you have to come out here in that?" he asked.

Mika looked down, and her cheeks heated. She'd forgotten she was wearing the green panties he'd had in his hands earlier, and along with them, she'd put on a matching camisole that dipped low between her breasts. There were a variety of responses she could make to his question, but none of them felt right. She wasn't desiring to spar with or to tease him. "Move over," she said softly, and was surprised when he did.

She settled beside Conor, her back to his front, and the tautness inside her eased. And when his left arm went around her waist, anchoring her snugly against him, Mika experienced something oddly close to contentment. This seemed . . . *right*.

They were very different people. Conor was serious, she often wasn't—many had called her flighty, although Mika didn't agree. Conor came from one of the darkest groups of demons, she from among the most carefree. But the biggest obstacle to their vishtau bond would be his black and white view of the world, and the lies she'd told.

She was brooding about that, her hand lightly resting atop his, when Conor asked, "You were born in Orcus, weren't you?"

"Yes, born and half raised."

"Half?"

Mika felt the heat of his breath against her neck and she took a second to enjoy it before she answered. "I spent equal time with my dad. An informal joint-custody thing."

"Why didn't you tell your mother that you'd rather stay in the human world?"

For a moment she hesitated, but Mika decided to answer honestly. "Because I didn't want to stay here. If I didn't love my dad, my grandma Noguchi and my other relatives, I would have happily remained in Orcus. And although I still spend time here, it's the Other World where I feel most comfortable."

He stiffened. "I find that hard to believe."

"It's my home." She didn't want to get too deeply into it, but despite the fact that she didn't fit in anywhere, she could be herself in the Other World. Though she was largely shunned there, she at least understood why. She was from a weaker branch of demon and had been made less by the genes she'd gotten from her father. The cruelty of the human children had been far more difficult to comprehend. Her only sin seemed to be that she was different, and in their eyes, all differences were bad.

"I guess a person can get used to anything if they grow up with it," Conor said. He shifted, but the short couch gave him almost no way to relieve his cramped muscles, and her presence didn't help.

"There are good and bad things about every place," she said with equanimity. "Do you think Crimson City is a paradise? If it was, you'd be out of a job."

His only response was a grunt. Mika swallowed a laugh. McCabe was damn stubborn. She ran her hand up and down his forearm. "Come on, admit it," she coaxed softly.

His arm tensed under her fingers and he said, "You're going back to Orcus then, after this is finished?"

Mika nearly told him that of course she was returning home, but closed her mouth without speaking. What if Conor didn't despise her at the end of this? He was her vishtau mate, half Kiverian, and he could never live in the Other World. He'd slain demons merely for roaming the streets here, and that wouldn't be well-received. Even if that remained secret, his hatred of demons was so ingrained, it would take years to overcome.

"I'm not sure," she hedged. "I can be happy here too, but it would depend on a few things." Since she didn't want him to ask what those things were, Mika kept talking. "I'll always have ties to Orcus, though. My mom, and gran, and brother are there."

"You have a brother?" He sounded shocked.

"Half brother," she corrected easily. "Our mom was mated to his father before she met mine. We're pretty close, considering he was nearly twenty when I came along and we didn't grow up together. His dad was Grolird—that's the second darkest of the demon branches—and Nic's always been protective of me." She couldn't contain a laugh at the thought. "Other demons have no clue how to respond to him. He has the bite of his father and the sense of fun of the Mahsei. It confuses almost everyone."

"Why isn't he protecting you from the Kiverian then?" Conor asked.

It took all of Mika's will to keep her body from becoming rigid. Damn, for a second, she'd forgotten about her story. Conor was her mate; she didn't want to add more untruths to their relationship, but what the hell could she say?

"Nic doesn't know about this," she said, *this* being her mission for the Council—"and I'd like to keep it that way." Oh, yeah, would she ever. Nic would chew her out for even agreeing to undertake the job, but she'd had to protect the man she'd thought her vishtau mate no matter what.

"Why?" There was a note of suspicion in Conor's voice.

Mika had to be careful. "For much of my life, I've run to my brother to fight my battles when they became too tough for me. I'm tired of that, McCabe. Maybe you think it's stupid—what difference does it make if you fight for me or Nic does—but I hired you. And I'm giving you something in return."

He exhaled long and hard, his breath tickling her ear. "I think I understand. You feel like a burden."

She nodded, if hesitantly. "Sometimes. I don't go to Nic often, and haven't since I reached my teens. I'd rather take care of things on my own."

She wanted him off this line of questioning. When he'd quizzed her yesterday about the Kiverian that was supposedly after her, she'd used her body to derail him, but if she pulled that again, he might suspect. She needed an alternate plan.

Stoke his temper. Mika smiled. That would work, and

when it came to infuriating Conor, she was the world champion.

"Of course," she said with exaggerated patience, "you'd never understand how I feel."

"Why the hell wouldn't I?"

No doubt he thought she'd blame it on his being male, but that wasn't a hot button for him. "Because you're Kiverian," she said instead.

She felt the rumble in his chest, but she couldn't hear it. He wasn't quite mad enough. She needed to torque him up another notch or two. "After all," she continued blithely, "you're from such a dark branch of demon, you must be the biggest badass in Crimson City. You can take down vampires and werewolves without difficulty, no human would dare challenge you, and even other demons are going to be careful. How could you know what it's like to be powerless?"

"I am not a demon," he snarled. His voice was hard, dangerous.

And she had ignition. Mika guessed she couldn't take full credit for getting McCabe angry so fast, not with the frustrated sexual tension brewing between them. But the whys didn't matter. The important thing was that Conor had stopped questioning her.

"Demon traits are dominant. The scientific claim could be made that you're more Kiverian than human."

His growl only proved her argument. Only a demon male could manage to produce that noise. Mika, however, wasn't about to point that out. "Sorry," she apologized, "I'm touchy about being weak, because some alliances in Orcus leave the lesser demon little more than a serf."

He firmed his hold on her. "You don't have to worry about that, honey. I'll make sure that doesn't happen to you."

Mika froze at the endearment and her heart stuttered. Then guilt overwhelmed her. She'd been lying, searching his house, was prepared to steal the incantation when she found it, and here he was telling her he'd keep her safe—not merely from the fictitious demon for which she'd hired him, but from others as well. And after she'd deliberately enraged him. She couldn't speak around the lump in her throat. Taking his hand from her stomach, she brought it to her lips and pressed a kiss in his palm. It was the best she could do to convey how much his offer meant to her.

When she released him, he rested his hand below her collarbone, his fingers spread above the swell of her breasts. Conor's heat warmed her heart and her eyes drifted closed as she immersed herself in him, in the essence of his being.

It wouldn't last, but she decided not to worry about that. Not today. Conor had his arms around her, his body at her back, and she felt as if she'd finally found somewhere that she belonged. It was more than she'd expected.

And for right now, Mika decided it was enough.

Chapter Five

It was the muttered curse that woke her. Mika blinked and took a minute to orient herself. "Conor? What's wrong?"

"Nothing, go back to sleep."

His gruffness told her it wasn't nothing, and she forced some of her drowsiness aside. Somehow, while she'd been sleeping, she'd ended up sprawled atop him. She suspected he was responsible for that. As narrow as the couch was, Mika didn't think she could have moved on her own without falling to the floor. His heart raced beneath her cheek, and for a moment, she let herself be lulled by its rhythm.

It wasn't until she shifted that she realized he was aroused and that her body was perfectly aligned to feel every inch of him. Since she herself felt all tingly, she figured they must have been in this position for a while. Involuntarily the muscles in her legs tightened, sliding her pelvis against him. Conor made a choking noise, and Mika gasped as his erection found a strategic groove.

Surrendering to desire, she turned her face and bit his chest. His reaction was immediate. His hands went to her bottom, and he rocked her against him. Her panties were damp and so were his shorts; she could feel it as he pushed against her cleft. She wanted exactly what she'd taunted last night: for him to pull the lacy cloth aside and drive himself inside her.

When he stopped the movement, she groaned in protest, but she quieted as his fingers slipped beneath her underwear and grasped her bare bottom. Mika propped herself up on his chest and gazed into Conor's face. His green eyes burned, and he was so tense that a muscle jumped in the corner of his jaw.

She'd done this to him. Her, the weakling half-breed no real demon wanted. But Conor wanted her.

With a smile, she leaned forward and lightly nipped his lower lip. One of his hands left her rear end and his fingers splayed through her hair, holding her in place so he could kiss her. His mouth was hot, hungry, and his tongue stabbed against hers, demanding absolute surrender.

Conor didn't have to worry. Anything he wanted, any way he wanted it, she would give it to him. Mika rocked again, needing to feel that friction between her legs. Conor broke the kiss and she started to complain, until she felt him grip the hem of her camisole. She lifted as he drew it up, helping him remove it, and he tossed the scrap of lingerie aside.

As she started to lower herself again, he stopped her. "Wanna look at you," he growled.

His eyes were glued to her breasts and her nipples grew harder under his stare. When his sex pulsed between her thighs, Mika smiled. "Yeah, I feel it too. It's going to be so hot with us," she said.

McCabe's reply was unintelligible, but the guttural noise was worth a hundred words. Lazily, Mika dragged her fingers over his abs, tracing the ridge of each hard muscle. She lightly circled his navel, then trailed the tip of her index finger down the line of hair that started just below his belly button until she reached the waistband of his shorts.

He arched back, but his arms remained locked at his sides—which wasn't good enough. Mika wanted him out of control. Completely, totally, utterly lost in her. The position of her body prevented her from exploring beneath the elastic, but with agonizing slowness she slid her palms up his skin until she could tease his nipples.

Conor bucked. He grabbed her hips, holding her in place for an instant, then ran his hands up her back. As he pulled her down to him, Mika braced her palms on either side of his head. The nubby fabric of the sofa abraded her skin, but she was only aware of that for the briefest moment before his lips were on her breasts. He kissed, licked, took her nipples into his mouth and used his tongue to pleasure her.

"More, please," she gasped. When he gave her more, it wasn't what she wanted. If the man couldn't take a hint, she'd have to spell it out for him. "Damn it, *bite* me," she ordered.

He did, light little nibbles that made her whimper and grind against him. She was close to orgasm, but she wanted Conor inside her when she came, and she told him that.

Wrapping his arms around her, he held her close and began to shift his body. It didn't surprise her that a Kiverian male wanted the dominant position during sex. The realization made her inner muscles clench, and Mika pressed her teeth gently into his shoulder. His groan was silent, but she felt it vibrate through him.

Conor shifted faster. The solid support of the couch gave way to empty air, and Mika only had enough time to widen her eyes before they landed on the floor. McCabe took the brunt of the impact, his body cushioning hers. For an instant, Mika was dazed, then she realized Conor wasn't moving.

The coffee table—it was so close to the sofa that he must have hit his head. She scrambled off him, but was careful not to hurt him further. "Conor!" She knelt beside him.

His eyes opened, the glow banked. "I'm okay," he said.

She leaned closer, but there wasn't much space. Impatiently, she gave the couch a shove, sending it halfway across the room, then pushed the table the other direction. "Are you sure?" Without waiting for answers, Mika started feeling the back of his head for bumps.

Conor grabbed her hand and sat up. "I'm fine," he said.

The thread of impatience in his voice froze her. Then she smiled. His annoyance was understandable; they had been on the verge of mating. "Well, since you're fine . . ."

She pressed herself against him, and freeing her hand, turned his face toward hers to kiss him. He didn't respond. Confused, Mika eased back. "What's wrong?" she asked.

"Nothing." He pulled away from her and stood. "Get dressed." His voice was flat, almost cold. He put a few steps' distance between them.

For a split second, she felt strangely uncomfortable kneeling in front of him in nothing but her panties—embarrassed, ashamed—until she saw the way his sex strained against his shorts. Mika sat back on her heels, arching to accentuate her breasts, and looked at him from beneath lowered lashes. A rumble came from low in his throat, but she didn't need it to know the effect she had on him. She could see it.

"Are you sure you wouldn't rather have me finish *un*-dressing, McCabe?" she asked.

He didn't reply, so Mika lifted her gaze. His eyes were glowing red. Oh, yeah, he definitely liked looking at her. She rose to her feet, going to him and winding her arms around his waist. His muscles became more rigid. Another rejection. The pain was so sharp, she couldn't move; then she remembered that he'd been the one to start this.

For a moment, she stared at him, trying to figure out why he pulled back. What was he afraid of? The bond. Some demons ran from it, and since he was unaware of why he reacted so strongly to her, it probably frightened him more than most. Mika made a decision to show him a sliver of her own vulnerability. "I've never chased anyone before, never begged a male for sex, but with you it's different. I need you, Conor. I need you on top of me, I need you"—she slid her hand between them so she could stroke his erection—"inside me."

"I don't want this," he said, his voice low and tight. But he didn't prevent her hand from moving.

"Liar. There's nothing you want more. I can feel it." Mika slipped her fingers past the waistband of his shorts and ran her thumb across the moist head of his sex.

Conor jerked at her intimate caress, but he remained rigid, not returning the touch. Mika took her eyes off his bulge and looked up. His face was set in severe lines, and from the tension in his jaw, she knew his teeth were clenched. "You *want* me," she repeated.

"My body wants yours, but *I* don't want this."

Mika studied him more closely. He was still in control and fighting what she made him feel, but she could break through his resistance. She was certain of that. And it wouldn't take much.

Her hand stopped moving on his shorts, but she didn't withdraw it. If she pushed, she'd have what she wanted—him. It seemed as if she'd been waiting her whole life to join with Conor. But if they had sex like this, with him compelled by her and the vishtau bond, he'd regret it afterward. And he'd be pissed off at her. Big time.

When it came right down to it, she'd more or less be forcing him to do something he didn't want to do. That wouldn't be as satisfying as being taken by someone who truly wanted her.

And he might even hate her the way he hated his father. The dossier the Council had about Conor's life had clearly cited his feelings about the demon who had sired him, but Mika might have guessed it on her own. She clenched her free hand where it rested behind Conor's back. Her need to have him warred with her awareness that he wasn't ready. If she goaded him, broke his control and spent the night in bed with him, that would be all she'd ever have with Conor. There wasn't a doubt in her mind about that.

Of course, once he discovered that she'd lied to him from the moment they met, she'd lose him anyway.

She struggled some more, but finally decided there was only one thing she could do. Regretfully, she stepped back and stopped touching him. She hesitated a moment longer, then stooped to pick up her camisole. It was inside-out, but she didn't bother righting it before pulling it over her head.

Conor's facial expression didn't alter, but she sensed a change in him. Something seemed to ease in his features, and Mika knew a moment of bittersweet satisfaction. She'd done the right thing, there wasn't any doubt about that—but had she given up her only opportunity with Mc-Cabe? Her only opportunity to mate with a strong demon? If she found the spell today, and was able to learn the other information the Council wanted, she'd have to go. And she wouldn't be able to return.

Yes, he'd know she was the one responsible for the theft, and he'd never forgive her for the betrayal. Mika's lips curved, but not with humor. So be it, she thought fatalistically. Despite his fury, Conor would know she'd backed off for him tonight. Maybe that would balance things out.

Even though she'd made the correct decision, she decided to torment him. It was only fair, since his withdrawal had left her throbbing.

Mika tossed her head, throwing her hair behind her shoulders with the motion, and strolled away, making sure there was just enough sway in her walk to hold him mesmerized. When she was halfway across the room, she paused, gave him a flirtatious look over her shoulder and said, "I'm going to be in the shower for a while. Try to ignore the moans—it'll just be the massager doing what *you* should have."

She waited until she saw that he understood. Then, with a soft laugh, she continued to the bathroom. This time, she closed the door.

* * *

Dried off and dressed, Mika followed the sound of grunting to Conor in his weight room. He was bench-pressing an impressive amount, and she was fascinated by his flexing muscles as he lifted the barbell. Since he only wore a pair of shorts, she was able to see quite a bit of his body. She stood in the doorway, fingers tucked into the front pockets of her faded jeans, and enjoyed the view. A light sheen of sweat covered him, and she guessed he'd been at it for a while. Mika smothered a smile. Since she'd hogged the shower, he'd turned to physical exertion for comfort.

As if sensing her presence, Conor put the barbell back in its cradle and lifted his head. Their eyes locked, and she quirked her lips. He muttered that she was trouble, and her smile widened—McCabe needed someone like her to shake him up.

Pushing away from the doorjamb, she sauntered toward the weight bench. As she neared, Conor sat up and grabbed the nearby towel. Probably he felt too vulnerable on his back around her, and the thought made her laugh quietly. When she reached him, Mika looked at the moisture on the black vinyl and then at Conor. With a loud sigh—one she was certain was for effect rather than any real sense of being put-upon—he ran the towel over the bench and then his chest and face.

Mika sat next to him, her body not quite touching his. The seat was high enough that her feet didn't reach the floor, and she swung her legs as he toweled off. She'd sought him out with a plan—to set up a story so she could leave the house when it was necessary to rendezvous with her contact from the Council—but she was reluctant to lie to him again.

Instead of starting her tale, she asked, "Are we okay?"

"Sure. Why wouldn't we be?"

She turned her head to look at him. "Because of what happened earlier."

"Don't worry about it," he said.

She reached for his arm to stop him from bringing the towel to his face. "You didn't want to have sex, and I nearly forced you. Given your background, I believe I have reason to worry."

His expression hardened and a spark came into his eyes. Mika couldn't put a name to it, but it made her heart pound. Maybe she shouldn't have said anything.

"You couldn't have forced me," he growled.

Tightening her grasp on his arm, she studied him. "I could have. You said no, but I saw you teetering and knew it would only take a small push. I almost did it, and I think we both would have regretted that."

McCabe's face held curiosity, and she wondered over it until she realized how serious their conversation was. He'd only seen flashes of this side of her before now. The thought nearly made her smile, but Mika suppressed it. This exchange needed to be earnest. While she wasn't sorry for her actions, she did feel he deserved an explanation.

After a sigh, she said quietly, "You know I was raised in Orcus—for the most part, anyway—and if two demons want each other, they have sex. It's that easy. I thought . . . I thought it could be that simple for us as well."

He tugged his arm free. "I'm not a demon," he growled.

The temptation to laugh was strong, but somehow she managed to resist. "You're half demon, Conor, just as I am. As much as you pretend you're human, nothing is going to change that. The drive and instincts of a Kiverian are deep inside you, whether you like it or not."

Some of the rigidity left his body. "I've got them caged."

"It's not easy to cage something like that."

Conor didn't reply.

She debated, then decided there was no point in continuing on this path. "So, back to what I asked originally," she said into the quiet. "Are we okay? It's important to me that you don't hate me like you do your father."

He hooked his towel around his neck, and hanging on to the ends with his hands, he considered her. "Your actions were nothing like what that bastard did." His voice was even, unemotional, but he couldn't quite contain the glow of his eyes. "Even if you kept pushing until I didn't care about anything but jumping you, it wouldn't be the same thing. You were teasing me, trying to make *me* take action." Conor looked away. "He restrained her, used force to take what he wanted."

Mika traced designs on her thigh with her index finger. She knew this was a volatile subject, one she should probably leave alone, but she had questions. "Who called him out of Orcus?"

"What?" The word was a warning. Too bad she'd never been good about heeding them.

"The veil keeps demons inside unless someone calls them forth. Who summoned your father?"

Conor didn't reply, but the tense silence told a story.

Leave it alone, Mika thought. But she didn't pay attention to her own suggestion. "Why did your mother invoke his presence?"

Conor's expression became more forbidding, and his body was so tense that he nearly vibrated. Mika didn't say anything, although she had a comment or two she was dying to make about the fact that his mother had shared any of this with him. Maybe she was wrong, but she didn't think it served any purpose to tell a child he was conceived through rape. It had colored McCabe's view of what he was, had made him hate the part of himself that was Kiverian.

When he spoke, his tone was as tight as the rest of him. "She was a college kid dabbling in rauthima."

Mika was shocked into momentary silence. Was he aware of what his answer revealed? "Women who practice rauthima only call demons forward for one reason."

"I know that," he snarled. "She changed her mind."

Okay, Mika decided, it was definitely time to shut up. She was ignorant of what had happened and it was unlikely that Conor knew the full story either. But his existence proved the vishtau had been in play between his mother and father—he wouldn't have been conceived if it hadn't—and that would have complicated an already charged situation.

Rauthima was practiced by a very small group of women who had some magical ability. They believed their powers increased if they had sex with a demon, and while not every member of the cult had the ability to perform a summoning, a majority did. This sect had never been well-known in the Overworld, but they were notorious in Orcus—and reviled. There was nothing a demon hated more than having their freedom stolen from them, and the ritual these women used to call them forth did exactly that.

Mika grimaced. The rauthima summoning was a random call, but it ensured that the male who appeared wasn't just ready for sex, but was aroused to a frenzy. Then, as soon as he finished his orgasm, he was returned to the Other World without even a minute to clear his thoughts or speak to his summoner.

Conor's mother, however, hadn't pulled just any demon. Against all odds, she'd somehow managed to call forward a male with whom she shared the vishtau, and that bond would mean *overwhelming* sexual desire. A human woman, especially a young one, could easily be frightened enough not to feel that need, but a Kiverian male who was already whipped up to the point of mindless coupling would immediately be aware of it.

Ugly was probably too mild a word for what had happened.

Conor should never have paid the price for the circumstances of his birth. But he had. That was obvious.

Mika leaned over and kissed his shoulder, before resting her cheek there. "You're not to blame for anything that happened before you were born," she said quietly. He stiffened and she kissed him again. "Nothing is your fault," she added.

"Leave it alone, Mika," he replied. His voice held a thread of weariness.

With a sigh, she did leave it alone, but Conor was *her* vishtau mate and she wanted to heal the damage that had been inflicted so many years ago. She shifted until her body rested against his, and enveloped him in a loose embrace. If anyone needed physical comfort, it was Conor McCabe. When he relaxed into her, wrapped his big arms around her, Mika knew she'd been right.

Somehow during this conversation, there'd been another shift in their relationship. He'd reached something inside her, and now his needs were as important as her own. This was *so* not good. In the end, she'd hurt him; there was no doubt about it. As much as she might wish otherwise, she couldn't abandon her mission. The Council had insisted she give them her promise to retrieve the spell from McCabe no matter what. And *a demon would die before going back on her word.*

She couldn't break her oath and lose her powers; they were too much a part of her. But it was more than that. The idea of going back on her word was repellent. The only loophole she had was if Conor didn't have the incantation. But her instincts said he did.

Mika kissed his shoulder again, a silent apology for her imminent betrayal. "Did I tell you that I have a cousin who lives near Crimson City?"

She was almost being honest; three hundred and fifty miles was fairly close. But she felt sick over the falsehood anyway. Why did things always have to become so complicated?

"Actually, she's more like a little sister to me," she continued. "After her mother became ill, she lived with my dad and me for a while." This part was true. "When I'm safe from the demon that's after me, I'm going to see her. That's number one on my list."

"You'll see her soon, Mika," Conor said. His arm tightened around her shoulders. "I promise you that."

"Thanks. I'm sure I will." Mika added a silent thank-you that he hadn't asked why she was bringing her cousin up out of the blue. She'd blurted the information instead of transitioning smoothly, but maybe he thought talking about his mother had made her think of her family.

This was enough of seriousness, she decided, enough of regret and angst; it was time to shake, rattle and roll his world. She turned so that she could put her mouth against his ear. "McCabe," she said in a voice just above a whisper, "I came three times in the shower and I still ache for you. Just so you know."

Then she hopped off the weight bench, shot him a grin and escaped before he could recover.

Conor wanted to take someone's head off. Thanks to Mika, he'd never be able to walk into his bathroom again without thinking of her. Of her body, long and lean, pressed against the shower wall. Of her soft mouth open, her chest heaving as she gulped at the air, feeling the water play over her—

"Damn it," he said, stopping his thoughts.

A breeze tugged at his open jean jacket, which he pulled back into place. It wasn't cool outside, but the garment hid the weapons he carried. Not that he needed them. He could take out most anything without the aid of a gun or blade. A vampire moved close and Conor eyed him with anticipation, but the creature obviously meant to try nothing.

"Chickenshit," Conor muttered. Who cared that his eyes were probably glowing red enough to show through his contact lenses? He was spoiling for a fight. The streets were full, but everyone was giving him a wide berth. Did they all have to show common sense tonight?

It didn't help that he was picturing Mika wet and naked

beneath him. Shit, how he wanted her. And the damn thing was, he'd had his chance. Mika wouldn't have said no. He snarled at a hooker who minced toward him, and the woman immediately pivoted and returned to her spot against the side of the building.

It was late, but this part of Crimson City still buzzed. Tourists mixed with vampires and werewolves, and he bet more than half the humans were unaware of with whom— or what—they were mingling. Stores were open, selling anything and everything at exorbitant rates. Their big, brightly lit signs competed with the skywriters beaming advertising to the masses. Cars cruised slowly up and down the boulevard; some of whose occupants were looking for a parking spot, others for a quick blowjob.

This was a bad area, a seedy area, but no one seemed to care, or to worry about their safety. The tourists were too busy oohing and ahhing over the stars embedded in the sidewalk, and that made them ripe targets. But tonight, they weren't Conor's problem.

He'd parked more than a mile away from the bar, hoping he could walk off some of his excess energy, but it hadn't helped. Conor knew he had to get his head on straight before he reached Hole in the Wall to meet his contact. The way he felt right now, all it would take was someone bumping into him to set him off, and that could cause repercussions he wouldn't want to face—even in his present mood.

Mika Noguchi. A week ago—hell, three days ago—he hadn't known she existed; now he couldn't think of anything but her. If he'd ever been this obsessed with a woman, he couldn't remember it. Everything about her appealed to him, and he didn't even care that she was half demon. What the hell; so was he. She'd teased him, taunted him, pushed him, talked with him—she'd even risked her life believing that she protected him.

And she'd stood down for him.

That's what hit him the hardest. Mika had apparently cared enough to stop goading him this afternoon. His control had been hanging by a thread and she'd known it. One more touch and he'd have had her on her back. He would have been on top of her, inside of her, before she could blink. The monster that lived within him had been screaming for her flesh, straining to join with her.

She hadn't been frightened, but he had.

Conor wasn't sure if anything could scare Mika. The closest he'd seen was when she'd caught him holding her panties. As he'd pressed her into the wall, there'd been a flash of wariness—not fear, not even then—but she'd dropped her gaze, stopped challenging him. And that had shaken him enough to drive the Kiverian back inside its cage. He didn't want her to ever be submissive with him. No, he liked her daring him, glaring into his eyes, invading his space, and yeah, even laughing at him, tempting him, provoking him. . . .

He swerved around three women who'd stopped short and began shrieking over the name on one of the stars. Mika would have gotten a kick out of this. Too bad he'd had to leave her home, but until he figured out just who the hell was after her and neutralized the threat, it wasn't safe for her to leave his protection.

Yet *she* was worried about *him*.

The knowledge gave him a strange warmth. No one had ever been concerned over his well-being, not even as a child. But Mika cared; she'd fussed over him as he'd gotten ready to leave. Conor wiped a hand across his mouth, trying to get rid of his smile. Either she was the best thing that had ever happened to him or the worst. He wasn't sure which.

Demons lied, he reminded himself. She might only be pretending to be troubled by the attack on him. Ben, his former mentor, had told him repeatedly to never trust anyone until they'd demonstrated their integrity beyond a shadow of a doubt—and even then, he'd said to beware. Mika hadn't proven a damn thing yet. Even if she had dived forward to save his life.

It could have been a selfish act, since he was her defender. Maybe she'd thought that by protecting him, she was protecting herself. That could be why she was worried about him leaving the house.

He'd nearly slipped. The urge to reassure Mika had been so strong, he'd started to tell her that he could defend himself against such a threat. Luckily, he'd stopped himself in time. She'd become suspicious when he used the word *assassin;* his explanation would have made her even more so.

Conor sighed silently. He wanted to question her, since she obviously knew things about the demon who'd tried to take him out, but he wasn't sure how to ask without tipping her off. Somehow, he had to find a way. Mika lived in Orcus; he might never have access to such valuable first-hand information again.

As he left the tourists behind, the crowds on the sidewalk thinned and part of Conor relaxed. Too many people left him tense, edgy. He'd always wondered if that was a demonic trait or a personal one, but there'd never been anyone to get answers from. Until now.

The lighting grew more sporadic, the lamps fewer and farther between, and he became more at ease. He'd always felt at home in the darkness, and that *was* a demon thing.

Conor paused and took a deep breath. He had a better handle on his frustration now. It continued to simmer in the background, but it wasn't clawing at him, not at this moment. Of course, it helped that Mika was miles away.

Taking another deep breath, he studied the area. He was a couple of blocks from the bar, but he had plenty of time before he'd arranged to meet his contact. Ben had told him years ago that nothing happened in Crimson City that Nat didn't know about, and Conor had always found that to be true. If Nat couldn't provide a hint of what was after Mika, no one could.

Mika. Conor found himself reaching beneath his jacket for his comm unit and stopped. Damn, he had it bad. Calling just because he hadn't heard her voice for an hour? Shaking his head, he let the denim settle back into place.

Conor took a few steps, then stiffened. He zeroed in on the energy sig, identified it. Rogue vampire. Something about the way it approached suggested an assault. At last, someone stupid enough to take him on. He suspected his grin was feral.

Come on, you son of a bitch, let's go, he thought.

He didn't bother drawing a gun, and he had no plans to use energy blasts or fire; he was putting this one down bare-handed.

Chapter Six

Mika yawned, bored already, and slipped the book back into place. She eyed the shelves and took a deep breath. Did McCabe really need so many damn references? After more than an hour of searching, she'd only made it a third of the way through the bottom shelf. It was a tedious task, since she had to check each volume carefully to make sure nothing was tucked inside.

If only she knew what format the spell was in, everything would be so much easier. Was it part of a grimoire? Was it written on a napkin and stuffed in some drawer? Even if the incantation had originally been part of a book, that didn't mean it still was. All Conor needed was the words. It could even be on a memory stick slipped in his computer, but Mika didn't think so. She knew her vishtau mate well enough to guess that he'd have it on paper. Somewhere.

She reached for the next dusty book and crossed her legs, cradling the ancient text in her lap. Her eyes drifted to the computer and she thought about checking her messages. Instead, she forced her eyes back to the tome in front of her. The members of the Council weren't the most patient of demons, and she'd be wise to accomplish as much as she could before they instructed their minion to meet her for a report.

With a loud sigh, she flipped open the book and started leafing through it. Some of her boredom vanished as she realized the text wasn't English, but in something archaic. It was demonic, too. Where the hell had he found this?

Some instinct told her McCabe could read this book, and that intrigued her. How had he learned when he hadn't grown up in Orcus? Even she had to concentrate to make sense of what she was looking at, and she'd received some education in the tongue.

Now that she had an idea of what she was perusing, it was easier to decipher the weird spellings and odd handwriting. Her training in the old language was incomplete, but she knew enough and could guess at the rest. Unless she was misinterpreting badly, this was a magic primer. But what she read reassured her—everything here was earthbased. She continued scanning anyway, just in case.

Mika was nearly at the end of the volume when she turned the page and found a sheet of paper. It was folded in half and she put the text on the floor to open it.

McCabe's writing was easily recognizable after having gone through his desk last night. His boldness and assurance came through in each slash of the pen, but there was an immaturity in the way the letters were formed that made Mika think he'd written this when he was much younger.

The sight of instructions on how to kill a Kiverian dismayed but didn't surprise Mika. Conor carried a lot of hate for his father. She found it easy to imagine a teenage boy intending to avenge his mother by killing the demon who'd sired him. McCabe hadn't grown out of this desire, though—he still wanted his father dead.

With care, she refolded the paper and slipped it back into place. Conor talked about keeping his evil side caged, but Kiverians weren't inherently monsters; they were simply dark. It was easier for them to justify malevolent actions than it was for many other demons, but their course wasn't preordained or anything.

Strangely, he'd put himself on the path he loathed. She'd told Conor she was worried about him, that he needed to learn to integrate his demon nature with his humanity. This proved she had cause for concern. If Conor murdered his father with the coldness and calculation his notes indicated, it would be his breaking point. She felt sure of that. He would become what he most hated, and there would be no way for him to contain it. By denying that part of himself, he'd guaranteed there was nothing to keep it in check should the worst happen. And with each action he took afterward, it would become easier and easier to ignore his conscience.

McCabe wouldn't believe her if she told him this, though. He was so certain his self-control would hold no matter what.

Mika brought a hand up and rubbed her forehead. Somehow, before she left this world, she was going to have to help Conor learn to accept his nature and forgive his father. She dropped her arm and sighed. While she was at it, maybe she'd negotiate world peace too. That couldn't be any harder.

He was ready when the attack came. The rogue's first blow would have killed him—if Conor had been completely human. His grin widened. This might be an interesting fight after all.

He used his speed to avoid the second strike, sending his opponent flailing into space. A boot to the vampire's ass sent the creature to the ground, but he rolled to his feet almost instantly. "You're not human," he said. "Not going to be so easy a lunch."

"No shit," Conor replied. "You gonna run like the coward you are, fang boy?"

It was the *coward* part that was the right button. Conor could see it in the vamp's eyes, but the vampire didn't move and Conor didn't either.

"What are you?" the vampire asked.

Conor didn't answer verbally. Instead, he sent an illusion into the vampire's mind—one he knew would cause fear. Some demons could project imagery over their real bodies, but he'd never been able to do that. The best he could manage was to make one person think they were seeing something they weren't.

In the deception, he shapeshifted into a being with large, leathery wings and black eyes that glowed red. He increased his size, making his body huge, and added fangs and claws. For the hell of it, Conor also covered his illusory form with dark, impenetrable scales. It was cliché demon, but going with the obvious worked best.

For a minute, he thought he'd laid it on too thick and that his opponent would run, but then the vampire gathered his courage. Conor watched him sail past. He sighed; the creature had tried to attack the illusion. He quit projecting—he wanted to work off some frustration, not watch an acrobatic act.

He got his wish.

The next attack came at full power. Conor used his forearm to block the strike and delivered a hard blow with the heel of his hand to the vampire's throat. The two combatants broke off, circled, came at each other again.

Conor found his own momentum used against him as he went sailing over his foe's shoulder. He rolled as he hit the ground and came immediately to his feet, but his attacker was there first, ready to land a punch. Conor grabbed the vampire by the arm, whirled him into the side of a building. The vamp's shoulder hit the corner, but while Conor was able to bang him against the brick once, he couldn't hold him there.

The creature hissed and dove at him. Conor went down,

the vampire atop him. With his hand at his enemy's neck, he turned, getting on top, but it only lasted an instant before he was on his back again. Conor grunted as they rolled and he took a punch to his kidney.

Enough of this shit, he decided. He used his Kiverian strength to push the vamp back. The creature stumbled but didn't fall. It didn't matter. Conor was on his feet, ready for the next attack.

He blocked three blows in rapid succession before he delivered a roundhouse kick to the vamp's chest. Conor moved closer, and used the ridge of his hand to strike his opponent. The vampire moved and Conor's blow went off target. Damn.

With a quick whirl, Conor avoided a fist to his face and let loose with a front kick, leaving his attacker staggering. Conor ducked, avoiding another swing at his head, then used his demon strength to leap in the air and elude the foot aimed at his knee. He came down behind the vampire, and hit the side of the creature's neck before grabbing an arm and twisting it. Conor drove the bastard's head into a brick wall several times before the vampire broke away.

Then came the moment of truth: As he launched his next attack, the vampire left himself wide open. Conor pulled his arm back, then drove his hand into the creature's chest and tore out the heart. Time seemed to hang suspended before his opponent fell to the ground.

It didn't take long before a dead vamp turned to dust, but Conor didn't feel like dealing with the remains for any amount of time. The same demon power he had that froze living things also worked in reverse—it speeded up physical processes. He directed that energy to the heart he held, turning it to powder. Then, crouching down, he touched the corpse and did the same thing.

At last Conor straightened, looked down at the pile of coarse particles on the sidewalk and tugged the sleeves of his jacket back to his wrists. That was the nice thing about killing vampires—once they turned to dust, there was nothing to worry about.

A quick glance verified that there were no witnesses to the fight. Conor rolled his shoulders, easing the kinks. There were a few sore places, but nothing that wouldn't heal in an hour or two, and the physical exertion had done a lot to work off his frustration. Taking a deep breath, Conor headed for the bar.

As he neared it, he slowed. Once, it might have been a neighborhood tavern, but those days were long past. The building's red brick facade looked bleak, without even a splash of graffiti to add color. But then, the local gangs would think twice about irritating the owners and regulars of this establishment. Conor opened the heavy, wooden door and stepped inside.

Hole in the Wall was mostly a werewolf hangout, and the shadowy, almost nonexistent lighting made them feel at home. He paused, his eyes scanning all occupants. The place was mostly filled with the dogs, but Conor picked up the energy of the occasional vampire and human too. Not the brightest move to come here. Why chance catching the attention of this group of killers?

Aside from the dimness, there was nothing out of the ordinary, nothing that gave the place away as a hot spot for monsters; it could be any booze joint in America. The wooden floor was battered and scarred, booths ringed three walls of the building, and tables filled the open floor. Along the fourth wall was a long, highly polished bar with stools.

Satisfied that everything was normal, Conor began searching for his contact. Nat—no last name—wasn't easy to spot, not even for a half-Kiverian hunter. It took two sweeps of the room, and even then Conor didn't think he would have succeeded if the man hadn't moved. Nat stepped out of a crowd waiting at the bar and, with a jerk of his head, signaled for Conor to follow.

The table the other man chose was in a corner at the back, somewhat secluded. Conor found it interesting how the best seat in the house remained open, but then Nat had that kind of luck. If the word *luck* applied.

The man was an enigma, someone Conor had never been able to pin down. For starters, he couldn't read Nat's energy signature and that was weird. Demons read *everyone's* sig, even other types of demons, but this man's pattern remained ambiguous. One moment Conor would pick up vampire energy, the next it would be werewolf or human or some type of demon. As many times as he'd met with Nat, Conor had never had a clear idea of what he was.

Even the man's appearance was changeable. Tonight, his hair seemed to have reddish highlights, but at other meetings it had been totally dark. If Nat were human, his age could be anywhere between thirty and forty-five. If he wasn't human, there was no way to guess. Conor knew one thing, though, his contact had the eyes of a predator; they were watchful, always taking in his surroundings. This was no innocent.

A waitress came over, and Conor ordered a beer then waited impatiently as Nat bantered with the woman. For someone so gregarious, it was strange the way he'd vanish. There were times when Conor searched high and low, times when he'd needed information badly but was unable to find a trace that Nat existed. On other occasions, the man practically flagged him down to pass on intel.

Everything about Nat raised questions, but his information was always one-hundred-percent accurate. Conor wasn't going to risk alienating his informant by probing too closely. Not yet.

Finally the waitress left, and Nat turned to him. "So," Nat said quietly. "What do you need, my friend?"

Conor quirked a brow. "Since when do you resort to bullshit, *my friend?*"

The corners of Nat's lips turned up, but the expression was so slight, very few would have caught it. "As charming as ever, McCabe. It's a wonder you haven't driven her off yet."

Although he was careful to display no reaction, everything in Conor went still. "Her?" he asked.

"Your houseguest."

Raising his other brow in question, Conor didn't speak. He wasn't sure what his informant was aware of, but he'd do nothing that might put Mika at greater risk. The fact that Nat knew about her strung Conor's nerves tight—and made his demon side rage within him.

"Play dumb all you want," Nat said, "but you didn't sneak her into your house. Lots of people are aware of her presence."

"People, or things?" Conor asked, tacitly admitting that Mika existed. His contact was right; he hadn't brought her into his home covertly. Hell, he'd seen Mrs. Howell, his elderly next-door neighbor, peeking out her window.

Nat nearly smiled. "Both."

The waitress returned, halting conversation. Conor stood, dug some bills out of the front pocket of his jeans and paid for the drinks. He added a generous tip, which earned him a smile of thanks, but the woman was enthralled by Nat. As Conor sat, waiting for the flirting to end, he opened his beer and took a swig. His source seemed to be in no hurry.

Mika was like a damn lightning rod. It shouldn't surprise him that others noticed her. Her life, her vitality, shone from her, and even he found himself fascinated: He wanted to watch her, to be part of her orbit. Maybe all Mahsei were like her, but Conor doubted it. Mika was special.

He raised the bottle to his lips. If it were only sexual attraction, it would be easy. But it wasn't. She had him engaged on so many different levels, he didn't know which way was up. And he was beginning not to care.

Mika was half demon, half Japanese and complete trouble. Damn, if he didn't want more of her brand of chaos.

A chuckle made him lower his beer back to the table and

focus on the man sitting across from him. "What has you so amused?" he snapped.

When Nat only shrugged, Conor scowled. He was willing to bet his preoccupation had been obvious, and Mika was a vulnerability he couldn't afford. He might have faith in his contact's info, but he didn't know or trust the man.

"What have you got for me?" he asked.

Nat gave another shrug and said, "Depends what you want to know. Might have nothing. Might have a lot."

Oh, hell, they were going to play games—just what he needed. Nine times out of ten, Nat would be upfront, but then there were the meetings where Conor had to ask precisely the right question. It irritated him in the best of circumstances, but with Mika in danger, he had no patience for this. His demon half roared inside him, pulled harder to get free. Conor had to pause and get control before giving Nat a warning look.

"Interesting," the man commented. He leaned back in his chair, and this time made no attempt to suppress his smile.

Conor ignored the comment and the smug expression. "Tell me what you know about the demons in the area," he said.

"Should I start with you or your girlfriend?"

This time Conor didn't bother to rein in the Kiverian—not immediately. He felt sure his contact could see the demon was at the end of its tether, but it didn't seem to rattle the man. Very deliberately, Conor let Nat watch him pull back and coldly take command. The biggest weakness demons had was their overly emotional natures, but by showing his human side dominating, he was demonstrating that he was stronger than the typical Kiverian.

Conor kept his voice even, though it took effort. "Do you really want to go there?" he asked.

Nat took a swig from his beer before he spoke. "There are a few demons around that weren't here a week ago, and they all seem to be focused on you and your houseguest."

"Why?"

After Nat gave another shrug, Conor leaned forward, eyes narrowed. Before he could issue a threat, his contact said, "I don't know, and that's the truth."

The man wasn't worried, but he should be. Conor wasn't going to let anything or anyone hurt Mika, no matter what he had to do. But despite making it clear he wanted answers, this game of twenty questions was apparently still on. "What kinds of demons?" he gritted out.

"You're assuming I'm familiar with the breeds."

"I *know* you are. What types?"

"Very dangerous," Nat said after a slight hesitation. "The nicest of the group is a Kiverian—that should tell you what a friendly batch of visitors has come to Crimson City."

Conor slowly rotated his beer bottle, thinking. The Kiverian wasn't a surprise; Mika had told him she was being hunted by one. But . . . "What are the others?"

"Two are Setonians—each much scarier than a Kiverian." Nat smirked as he said that, so Conor guessed he wasn't frightened at all. "Then there are the *nasty* ones."

"They have a name?"

Nat nodded. "Yep, Bak-Faru." He spelled it. "But you won't hear that term much; most only refer to them as the Dark Ones. Ask your houseguest about them. I'm sure she'll have more information than I do."

It was probably true—if Nat wasn't a demon. Conor tried again to read him, but the energy morphed so fast that he gave up trying to identify just what the hell his contact was. "How'd they get through the veil?" Conor finally asked.

"You're not going to believe me," Nat said, "but I don't know. There are rumors flying, though."

"Share them."

"They're unsubstantiated—I can't tell you if they're true." Nat seemed to watch him closely as he spoke. Conor nodded.

"I'll consider myself warned. What are the rumors?"

"Word going around is that a group of humans has been

playing with things better left alone. I've heard this enough to tend to believe it's true. It's after this that the stories diverge."

Nat stopped, and Conor had to swallow a growl. Was he going to have to drag it out of the man? "Keep talking," he ordered.

"One version," his contact continued, "is that humans conducted experiments that made a crack in the portal between Orcus and this world. Seems to me if this were true, we'd be overrun by demons by now, but you never know. The other story has a group of humans calling forth the Dark Ones with the hope of forging an alliance with the underworld."

"You believe version two?"

Nat shrugged. "With all the fear around about the vampires and werewolves, it wouldn't surprise me if the humans were looking to make a deal. They'd be stupid, though, to trust a demon." He paused before adding, "No offense."

"Demons lie," Conor agreed flatly.

"Whenever it's to their benefit," Nat agreed. "But you might want to find Hayes, and ask him about the current invasion."

Hayes? He was another freelancer for B-Ops, and while Conor didn't have much to do with anyone at the agency, he'd probably talked with him the most. "Marc Hayes? What the hell would he know?" Conor demanded.

With a smirk, Nat shrugged. "I don't know. But word is, Hayes is looking for intel on demons too. Might be nothing. Might be interesting." Nat raised his bottle, took a long draw, then said, "The other thing to keep in mind is that neither story might be true. Demons might have got to LA another way. Some in Orcus have human minions. They could have told their people to call these demons forward for reasons of their own."

Conor nodded grimly; but so few humans fell into this

category, he considered the odds negligible. "Why the focus on my houseguest?" He wasn't going to use Mika's name, not with this man.

"You asked that before."

"And you claimed not to know, but I don't believe you."

Nat's smirk returned. "I don't have the answer to that question, and I can't say for sure the focus is on her. What I do know is that our new friends seem to be interested in your house." The smile widened. "Maybe you're just parked over the gate to Orcus."

Without waiting for a response, Nat pushed his chair back from the table and stood. Conor got to his own feet. "We're not finished," he said.

Nat had other ideas: "You may not be, but I've told you what I know."

Conor figured that was unlikely. A war went on inside him, part of him wanting to keep Nat there, to make the man tell him more. The other part of him knew that being on friendly terms with his contact was smarter than antagonizing him, that honey would pay off bigger in the long run than vinegar. Common sense subdued him. "If you discover anything else, I'd appreciate you getting in touch," he said.

"Sure," Nat agreed. As he went past, Conor sat down again and reached for his beer bottle. "By the way," Nat added from behind him, "congratulations on the vishtau."

The laughter in the man's voice made Conor whip around, but there was no sign of his informant anywhere. He stood, scanned the bar again, but the man had disappeared. He felt a brief moment of concern.

What the hell was Nat? And what was a vishtau?

Mika couldn't concentrate. Conceding that she wasn't going to get any further tonight, she put the book back on the shelf and paced restlessly around the great room. Where the hell was McCabe? Damn it, the sun was already peeking over the horizon and he wasn't home yet.

He'd been so blithe about the danger from that auric assassin that she'd stopped worrying, but now the only thing she could think was that he'd been hurt, maybe killed. Who cared if demons didn't have any adverse reaction to sunlight like vampires, that he could stroll around Death Valley at high noon without any difficulty? She was still concerned.

She pivoted sharply and her dark hair fell into her face. Irritated, Mika dragged her fingers through it, pushing it out of her way. The least the man could do was call and let her know he was okay. Didn't he know that she'd be anxious?

No, she realized, it probably hadn't occurred to him that she'd worry. From the things he'd said—and things she'd read in his file—it didn't sound as if he'd ever had anyone who paid attention to his comings and goings. Mika ran her hand through her hair again. When McCabe showed up, she was going to set him straight; *she* cared and she expected him to let her know when he'd be late.

After a few more circuits of the room, she knew she had to do something or she'd start climbing the walls. Her eyes went to his desk. He'd go insane if she organized his workspace. She smiled. It served him right for stressing her out like this.

Mika started with his tax drawer, separating the papers into appropriate piles. She'd need to find some tabbed folders later, but at least everything would be ready to file. Digging in the shallow center drawer, she spotted a jumble of paperclips, and with a frown untangled them. Tucking one bare foot beneath her, she returned to sorting the documents.

"What the hell are you doing?"

Her head popped up. She hadn't been monitoring for Conor's arrival, and he'd managed to surprise her. Her eyes roamed over him, studying him from head to toe. There was no sign of injury. Mika looked out the window and saw it was full morning. She scowled at him. "Where the hell have you been, McCabe? Do you know what time it is?" She put the papers aside and stalked over so she was toe-to-toe with him. "You couldn't use your comm and let me know you were still breathing?"

"What?"

He stared at her as if she were speaking in some foreign language, and that calmed her temper. Winding her arms around his waist, she leaned into him and said quietly, "I was worried about you."

"Yeah?" She thought she detected a note of pleasure as well as surprise before he went all grumbly on her. "I can take care of myself, you know. There's no reason to get upset."

The gruff persona would be a lot easier to buy if he hadn't put his arms around her too and started rubbing her back. It told her clearer than words that he appreciated her concern.

"I know you can," she said. "But because I care about what happens to you, I'll worry from time to time. It's natural."

She'd managed to stun him, but it only lasted a second or two before he covered up with bluster. "Now, would you mind telling me what the hell you're doing over there?" Instead of freeing her, he nodded toward his desk.

"I'm organizing your paperwork."

"What?" He looked completely befuddled. "What are you? The world's first accounting demon?"

Mika stiffened. It was one thing for her cousins to tease her about her compulsive behavior, it was another thing for Conor to comment. "If you're going to be snide, at least be accurate," she told him, "That would be the world's first file clerk demon. I'm not doing your taxes, I'm sorting the papers."

"Why?"

"Because they're there," she snapped. "You should know demons get obsessive. My deal is organization, your fixation is staying in control. I don't mock you about that."

"I'm not mocking you," he said, rubbing circles on her back. "It's just . . . unexpected, that's all."

"I know." She sagged into him, and it was only then that she realized that a good deal of her pique had to do with her relief that Conor had returned safely. "By the way, you need a filing cabinet and tabbed folders. Get me the hanging things too. I'll set everything up, but it's your job to keep it going." She knew he wouldn't like her fussing over him, so Mika didn't say another word about his tardiness. Instead, she edged closer and nuzzled his throat. Feeling his steady pulse beneath her lips reassured her.

"I had a filing cabinet," he said, his breath warm against her ear. "I got rid of it when the IRS switched to the new, paperless system."

Mika shifted enough for him to see her laugh. "Haven't you learned? When you hear the words *paperless system*, you should buy a *second* filing cabinet. The documentation always doubles—and that's at the very least."

He made a growling noise, but didn't argue. She brought a hand up and turned his face to hers. For a moment, Mika gazed into his eyes. She wanted to kiss him—not a hot, take-me-and-do-me-on-the-kitchen-floor kiss, but one that showed her appreciation that he was here. Except, she found it impossible to close the distance between them when he always pulled away.

Not this time. McCabe brushed his lips over hers. He gave her exactly the kind of kiss she wanted—soft, tender, affectionate. And when he broke away, she leaned back in his arms and smiled gently. "I'm glad you're home," she said.

She started to turn out of his embrace, intending to explain the rudiments of her system, but Conor's hold tightened, keeping her close. "Tell me about the Bak-Faru," he ordered.

Mika gasped. Immediately she raised her hand to trace the glyph of protection, and she said, "Don't *ever* say that name aloud!"

Chapter Seven

Mika broke away from Conor and started pacing, trying to work off some of her agitation. He didn't know any better, hadn't seen what the Dark Ones could do, but to use their name like that . . . She twisted her fingers and paced faster.

It was superstition and instinct that had impelled her to make the pattern of protection in the air, but that didn't indicate weakness. Demons much stronger than the Mahsei would have done the same thing. Even those from the Grolird branch, the second most dangerous group, made the sign if someone was foolish enough to speak the name of the Dark Ones—she'd seen it with her own eyes. Nobody wanted to attract attention from a member of that group.

"Mika," Conor said.

She ignored him. How likely was it that they'd heard Conor? This wasn't Orcus, and no one of that breed should be here. But say there were a handful of the Dark Ones freed; what were the odds one of them would pick up such a quick utterance? She and McCabe were probably safe. She hoped.

"Mika."

But what if they weren't? What if one of the dark demons had heard their name? She wrung her hands harder.

There was no way she could hope to fight off such powerful beings. Hell, there was little chance *Conor* and her could fight them off. Maybe they'd be lucky and the Dark Ones would merely kill them. After all, they didn't always torture their victims.

"Mika!" Conor caught her by the shoulders and turned her to face him. "What's wrong? All I did was ask about the Ba—"

She put her hand over his mouth, cutting him off. "I told you not to say that! Don't even think it." Mika looked around, half expecting to see one standing there despite the security around Conor's home. The dark demons were capable of nearly anything.

Conor took her hand from his face, and held on to it. "You're scared," he said. There was surprise in his voice.

That made her stop and take a deep breath. "Only the foolish or ignorant aren't frightened of them."

"I guess you're not fearless after all." One side of his mouth quirked up.

He'd thought she was fearless? Mika studied him, but McCabe didn't appear to be joking. "Don't I wish," she laughed to herself.

Conor stooped and looked into her eyes. "Honey, even if these guys are total psychos, they're not omnipotent." His gentleness knocked her off balance, and Conor continued, "They'll never know we're talking about them. There's nothing to be scared of."

For a few seconds, Mika debated. It would probably be okay to say one small thing about them. "No, they're not omnipotent. But saying their name must change ambient energy or something, since they always seem to know when it happens. And they can listen from a distance then, or so it's believed. Conor"—she tightened her grip on him—"don't *ever* underestimate how deadly they are."

The expression on his face told her he was about to pat her on the head—figuratively speaking. With a low growl of frustration, she spun away and put space between them. He hadn't lived in Orcus, and odds were he'd never run across a dark demon, but he was ready to dismiss what she said because it didn't fit his view of the world. What could she say to convince him that she told the truth? The dark demons were the things of nightmares, and even if she were willing to talk about them, he wouldn't believe her stories. McCabe would think they were tales meant to frighten children, tales of imagined boogeymen.

She stopped pacing abruptly when she saw him at his computer. "What are you doing?" she demanded.

Conor didn't so much as glance at her, but she saw he had a search engine on the screen and made tracks. She stopped him before he could type the first three letters. Straddling him, she gripped his hands with hers. "Don't! Please don't, okay?"

"Your fear isn't rational." He shifted, adjusting her position so that they were both more comfortable.

"You've seen those old movies where the gunfighter comes to town looking to have a showdown," she said intently. "Remember how people would scurry off the street? Parents would grab their children and hustle them to safety? That's what it was like whenever the Dark Ones left their enclave. Everyone in Orcus—*every* other type of demon—hurried to get out of their way."

He looked skeptical, and Mika sighed. McCabe wouldn't understand what it was like. He was a demon living in a human world; there wasn't much here for him to be afraid of. "You have to trust me. They're malicious, ruthless—*evil*."

"Well, my contact tells me we already have a couple of these bastards out here. If they're the ones that set that trap for you, it's essential that I know as much as possible about them." He freed his hands from her grip and cupped her face, his thumbs running over her cheekbones. "Knowledge is power, and if I have to fight them to defend you, I'll need all the power I can get."

Mika felt the blood drain out of her face. "No," she said. It was the only word she managed to form. She rested her hands on his shoulders and leaned forward. "No," she repeated. Then, her voice thick, she choked out, "I don't want you facing them."

"There might not be any other option if they're the ones after you. I took the job to keep you safe, and—"

"From a Kiverian, not them!"

"That's not what I promised." His eyes were glowing behind his contact lenses. "I gave my word to protect you, period. I won't renege."

He was serious—there was no mistaking that. She ran through options. It wasn't possible to simply let him out of his promise; it didn't work that way when a demon made a bargain. The only thing that might break it was—

"I didn't pay you yet. That means I didn't uphold my end of the deal, and you're not bound by our agreement."

McCabe gave her cheeks another caress, then moved his hands to her hips, shifting her weight again. She wasn't sure if he was uncomfortable or if he simply wanted her body closer to his, but the change in position put them nose to nose. "That might work if you were human. But you're a demon, and you entered into this deal same as me. I know you'll keep your end."

With a soft sigh, Mika surrendered to the inevitable. At the beginning, this had seemed so easy. Tell a small lie, spend some time in his house, and complete her mission. Only, it had stopped being simple almost immediately.

She'd assumed that if Conor were her vishtau mate, things would work out. Generally speaking, demons tended to shrug off untruths from other demons. After all, the next day they might be the one lying. Only, McCabe didn't think that way, and his rigid code almost guaranteed that things wouldn't end well.

Even knowing that, she wouldn't change anything about him. She liked Conor. Liked his honor and intelligence, the way he gave his all once he committed himself. She liked his intensity, and yeah, she even liked how serious he was, maybe because it balanced out her tendency to be playful. Then there were those unexpected smiles. Just when she thought he was dour beyond hope, he'd flash that grin and make her melt.

"Promise me one thing," she said quietly.

"What's that?"

"Don't do anything stupid for me, McCabe, okay?"

He started shaking his head before she finished. "I know what you're saying, and I can't swear to that." His hands firmed on her hips. "I will give my word not to do anything . . . rash, but that's the best I can do."

Mika nodded. She knew why he wouldn't promise. The future was unknown. If he gave his word, he limited his possible responses.

What worried her, though, was their bond. The vishtau could override survival instincts. It wasn't something one could turn off; it simply was. Already she felt a need to defend Conor, and the feeling would be a thousand times stronger for a male demon. It was biological, genetic. A male would die to ensure his mate made it to safety. Mika figured it was a different kind of survival instinct, one that had to do with propagation of the species. Demon offspring were rare, and each child was considered precious—even a half human one.

It was terrifying. She and Conor hadn't slept together yet, but she already believed he'd die to keep her safe. In just a few days, the connection between them had become that solid, and it seemed to firm more every hour. Mika felt it happening.

"I wish you wouldn't wear your contact lenses," she said abruptly. "Your real eye color is beautiful."

Without a word, he reached up and took them out. Hanging on to her with one arm, he leaned forward and tossed them away. "Better?"

"Mm-hmm." Mika nibbled at his lower lip as a thank-you. She kept the kiss slow and languid, refusing to let her lust rule. Maybe he understood. Conor allowed her to set the pace, not taking more than she gave. When she felt her control start to slip, she left his lips and kissed her way up his jawline. She nipped his earlobe, then used her tongue to trace higher.

"Tell me about the Dark Ones," he whispered.

His sexy murmur blended into the moment. Then what he said registered and hit Mika like a slap. She stiffened, breaking away and standing. It hurt, the idea that he'd gone along with her kiss to lull her into compliance. It was manipulative, something a demon wouldn't hesitate to do, but she didn't expect it from Conor. "Nice, McCabe," she snarled. She moved away from him. "Do you always use seduction to get the answers you want?"

"That's unfair." He pushed himself out of the chair, and came to her. Mika held her ground, but was too hurt to look at him. He didn't allow that. With a finger, Conor tilted her face to his. "Did I pull you onto my lap? Did I start the kissing? *You* did that, so you can't say *I* was using seduction. Wasn't that *your* plan, to make me forget I asked you a question?"

"I never—," she started, voice hot, then realized what he was doing. "I'm not falling for that." Mika snapped her head to the left, freeing her chin from his touch; then she took a step forward, getting in his face. "I legitimately feel something for you. *I* was in the moment—which is more than I can say for you."

"It wasn't like that," he argued. "I didn't set out to persuade you or whatever the hell it is you think."

"You just saw your opportunity and you took it?" She hissed.

A soft glow came into his eyes, but she was sure her own were burning bright red.

"Yeah, I took it," he said. "You know why? Because I'm going to keep you safe, with or without your help. You don't want me to say the name of that branch of demons? Fine. I can do that. You don't want me to search info sites for them? I can do that too, but you've got to give me something to work with."

Mika felt herself start to slide into emotion and stopped. She needed to think, not to let anger and bruised feelings cloud her judgment. After a deep breath, she took a couple of steps back and turned away to consider what he'd said. Conor was willing to meet her part of the way. He was agreeing not to do anything that would call the attention of the dark demons, and that was what she'd wanted.

He came up behind her, but didn't touch her. "You experienced the energy in that trap the night we met. Take a second and remember how it made you feel." He paused. "Do you want me to face the demons that created it without knowing anything about them?"

She shook her head, grasping at straws. "No, but are you sure it was made by demons? I've lived in Orcus and I've never seen one of these things." She faced him again, wanting Conor to tell her he was mistaken, that it hadn't been a demon snare. Or maybe she just wanted reassurance that it wasn't the Dark Ones who'd built it. She didn't get either.

"It could be that you didn't sense them in the underworld because none of the traps were targeted on you. I told you, I've seen many demons walk right by them and never notice."

She thought for a moment. "Or maybe there's something in this world that allows for their creation, something that Orcus doesn't provide."

McCabe shrugged. "Does it matter?"

Mika shook her head. No. It didn't. She believed in him and trusted his instincts. What difference did it make why she hadn't identified one of those snares before? What did matter was: "Conor, I really don't want you to fight any of the Dark Ones."

He grimaced. "Neither do I. But withholding information isn't going to prevent a battle. All you're doing is ensuring I'm at a disadvantage. Is that what you want?"

She almost swore at him. He was a stubborn bastard, and if the dark demons were after her, McCabe would put himself in their path. There was no doubt. "No, I want you safe," she said.

"Then you'll give me some info."

She reluctantly agreed. Conor reached out, took her hand and tugged her to sit on the couch. With a sigh, Mika shifted so she could see him, brought her knees to her chest and wrapped her arms around them. Enough time must have passed since he'd spoken the dark demons' name. Enough time for the energy to settle and for no one to be eavesdropping. She hoped.

"I don't know much about them," she warned. "No one does. They make certain of that."

Conor seemed to accept that. "Then tell me what you can."

Mika lay in bed, her fingers linked at her waist, and thought. McCabe had said a couple of dark demons were here in Crimson City. He trusted his source, and she trusted Conor. If they were after her as he believed, it was surely because of her mission. For some reason, they didn't want the incantation destroyed. Did they think they could enslave other demons to their will? If the legend was correct, even the Dark Ones would be unable to pull that off.

She pursed her lips. Why were they trying to get to her now? Why not wait until she found the spell and left the safety of McCabe's property, since they could take it from her much more easily than Conor? Odds were, the spell was somewhere in his house and the protection he had was strong enough to keep them out. If it wasn't and they wanted her, they would have come inside already.

Unless, of course, McCabe was wrong. Maybe he thought the dark demons were after her simply because of her lie about needing protection. Maybe they were in town for something else completely. Maybe that trap hadn't been created by the Dark Ones, but by another kind of demon. Like the auric assassin that had been gunning for Conor. Were they separate? How many demons had managed to find their way through the veil?

The light seeping in through the top of the blinds made a pattern on the ceiling, and Mika stared at it as she contemplated the situation. It was unlikely there were many demons here. Mika could cross the barrier at will, but that was attributable to her human genes. Full-blooded demons were trapped unless summoned, and even then, their time in the Overworld was usually very short. That meant the chances were slim that one of those auric assassins had been living in Los Angeles. Someone with a grudge against McCabe had called him forth. Mika didn't want to believe the Council had rooked her.

She heard Conor shift out in the great room, and bit back a sigh. He'd questioned her intensely and for a long time. Mika had started out telling him things about the dark demons that she'd seen herself or knew were true beyond doubt, but he'd pushed even further. She'd begun sharing stuff that she'd heard, and as she'd predicted, he'd thought the information was exaggerated. He'd even suggested what *she'd* witnessed was distorted by fear.

Mika frowned at the memory. She never used the word *evil* when she talked about demonkind. It was a misnomer, a label humans had slapped on a society they didn't understand. But when it came to the Dark Ones, evil wasn't a strong enough word to convey their ruthlessness.

Yes, the Dark Ones were the monsters of human lore. They had no conscience, no compassion and seemed wholly irrational. Well, other demons at least found them irrational. Maybe their actions made sense to them. Sometimes Mika wondered if all demonkind had been painted with the same brush, banished to Orcus so long ago because of this one breed.

Not that it mattered. Still, it was late in the morning and she couldn't sleep. It had to be imagination, but suddenly Mika thought she felt Conor breathe. *The vishtau*. She hadn't experienced it before, and the effects were . . . different than she'd expected them to be.

She'd known of the sexual attraction, welcomed it even, although she hadn't known it would be this wild, this uncontrollable. And intellectually she'd understood there would be an emotional attachment. Mika tucked her arm behind her head and curled a hand around her hair. But the reality of the bond was overwhelming, and when she thought about it too long, it became frightening.

"Mika."

For an instant, she froze, then she smiled. He'd spoken so softly, she never would have heard him if she'd been asleep. Mika pushed her fear aside. To hell with it. She wouldn't be here long—she might as well enjoy him while she could.

"What?" she answered, just as quietly.

"Come here. Please."

"Why?"

Conor sighed, loudly, and Mika's smile deepened. His reluctance was obvious as he said, "I want to hold you, okay?"

It was more than okay. Mika pushed the blankets back and was on her knees before it dawned on her that they'd be lying on that narrow couch again. "Why don't you come here? We'll be more comfortable in bed."

There was a long pause. "Too comfortable," he finally said.

Damn, she loved that grumbly tone of his. She hesitated

only a moment longer before getting to her feet and going to him. She stopped before she came into his view. Today she was wearing turquoise. The panties were as skimpy as the green ones she'd had on yesterday, so high-cut, all she had was a strip of fabric over her hip bones. Her tank top was more revealing. The ribbed knit ended above her navel and clung to her breasts, outlining her peaked nipples. It would drive Conor insane.

With a smile, she stepped into the doorway.

The empty sofa puzzled her, then movement caught her eye and Mika zeroed in on him as he sat up. He'd made a pallet on the hardwood floor in front of the couch, and to create room, he'd shoved the coffee table against the wall. For a moment, he did nothing but stare at her, then he muttered a curse.

Mika walked toward him, an unhurried stroll. She came to a halt again about five feet away from him and posed— just a little. When she saw the glow in his eyes brighten, she did a slow revolution to give him a full view.

"I shouldn't have called you," he said, his voice choked.

"But you did." She knelt beside him, her breasts at his eye level. What difference did it make if she wasn't fighting fair? Mika wanted to experience everything with Conor. Didn't she deserve that?

"Stop playing games. I want to hold you—that's all," he said.

She laughed. "You want a hell of a lot more than that, but you won't let it happen." She ran a finger around her belly button, and Conor's gaze locked there.

"Don't tease."

He sounded dangerous, and since he was half-Kiverian, he probably was, but Mika knew McCabe would never harm her. She'd known it since meeting him. When she ignored his warning and started pushing up the hem of her tank, he grabbed her hands and held them.

"I'm not teasing, Conor. I want you," she said. "I've been

trying to tell you. I want to feel the weight of your naked body on top of mine. I want to arch my hips and feel you inside me. I want—"

McCabe had her on her back before she realized he'd moved, and Mika laughed with delight. He loomed over her, his hands pinning her wrists beside her head. Her top had ridden up, exposing the bottom of her breasts, and Conor's eyes were glued on her bare flesh. Her blood burned as she felt his sex grow harder against her thigh.

Lowering his mouth, he bit her left nipple through the knit of her shirt. She gasped, shuddering as pleasure rocketed through her. But instead of giving her more, McCabe jerked away. He shook his head as if coming out of a daze and released his hold. "I'm sorry. I didn't mean to . . ." He trailed off and started to roll to the side.

Mika stopped him. She raised her knees, cradling him between her legs and brought her hands up to hang on to his shoulders. "Don't apologize—I loved it. I'm only sorry you stopped." Then it occurred to her what was going on. Damn, she should have realized at once. "I'm as much demon as you are. I can take you just as you are—hard and fast. Just like you want. You don't have to hold back. You don't have to be careful like you would with a human woman. You can't scare me, and you won't hurt me. Give us what we both want."

His eyes flared hotter, and Mika saw she was on to something.

"Just think. For once you could have exactly what you've always wanted." She kept her voice as soft as she could, not wanting to scare him. She wouldn't push, but that didn't mean she couldn't offer a little encouragement—did it? "With me there's no need to restrain your strength or fight your arousal. No need to hide that glow in your eyes. You can bite me. In fact, I *want* you to bite me. I love it."

He stared down at her, one lock of blond-brown hair falling over his forehead, and desire made her muscles clench. She brought her legs up higher, positioning his flesh where she needed it most. McCabe pressed forward, sliding his length against her. She wanted their clothes out of the way, wanted to feel his bare shaft nudging her, filling her. Mika let go of him and grabbed the edges of her tank top. Conor didn't move, and because of that, it took some wriggling before she was able to tug the garment over her head and toss it aside. The sheen of sweat across his brow made her smile.

"Come down here and kiss me," she ordered, and with one of his slow, sexy grins, he obeyed.

There was no restraint, no gradual build-up. Their mouths met hungrily. For a moment, she couldn't focus on anything but his tongue against hers, then the pleasure the rest of her body was experiencing roared into her consciousness.

His hard-muscled chest felt so damn good that Mika arched and twisted, rubbing her breasts against him. She moaned in protest as he broke off the kiss, but it changed to approval as he nuzzled her throat. He didn't stay there long. Soon he moved downward, his hands and mouth driving her higher, making her gasp and groan. When he bit her, she dug her fingers into his hair and held him tightly. "More, Conor," she begged.

He gave her more, and she locked her ankles behind his back, pulling the lower half of his body closer as she rocked into him. He needed a shave, Mika realized, but the roughness of his whiskers against the tender skin of her breasts made her hotter. She wanted to touch him, wanted to yank his shorts down and wrap her hand around him, but because of their positions, she was unable to do more than stroke his back and shoulders. Mika thought about demanding equal time, but was worried that would make Conor remember why he didn't want to do this.

As if he'd read her mind, McCabe stopped. He couldn't leave her frustrated again. Could he?

When his hands grabbed her hips and held her still, she

decided that was exactly what he was planning. "Why?" she almost cried out.

Raising his head, he looked down at her for a long moment. "I don't want to come in my shorts," he said. His voice sounded rough, ragged. Sexy.

"I don't want that, either," she agreed. "I want you to come inside me."

His whole body jerked, and with a groan, he ground against her. Then he froze again. Breaking her hold, he moved to lie at her side, one arm dropping across his eyes. "You're a menace."

"Me?" Mika pushed her hair out of her face. "Well, whatever," she said more calmly. "At least *I'm* not the tease."

In her peripheral vision, she saw him uncover his eyes and turn to look at her. "What the hell does that mean?"

"What the hell do you think it means, McCabe? This is the second day in a row you've left me aching, and it looks like I'll be heading for the shower again. You realize that if our genders were reversed, there'd be a name for you."

The growling sound he made was pure Kiverian. It surprised Mika almost as much as the way Conor rolled to the side and pinned her to the floor with his arm. His eyes were hot, but not just with arousal; there was anger there as well. "No one and *nothing* is going to pleasure you except me. Got it?"

Mika glared at him. She knew he hadn't changed his mind about having sex; that was obvious from the look on his face. "You've got a lot of nerve," she said. It took effort to keep her temper. "You leave me hanging, then don't want me to take matters into my own hands? Well, to hell with you." She pushed on his shoulder, but he didn't move an inch. "If you're not going to satisfy me, I'll take care of myself. Again. I don't know what sort of strange human puritanism you—"

He interrupted her: "You want an orgasm? Fine, I'll give you one."

His arm left her waist, but surprise kept Mika from moving. Then his hand settled between her legs and her eyes went wide. What was he up to? He didn't keep her in suspense. His fingers lightly stroked her through her damp panties. She moaned.

After a moment, Conor tugged the fabric out of his way. Arousal had left her open, giving easy access to the center of her pleasure. McCabe never took his gaze off her face. She knew he was reading her, finding out what she liked the most, but instead of being irritated with his arrogance, Mika felt joy. She smiled at him and opened her legs wider.

She was undulating against his hand when he stopped. And when she threatened his life, the man actually had the nerve to grin.

"Why don't you see what you think of this before you kill me?" he asked, slipping two fingers inside her.

Mika's head fell back and her hips came off the floor. Oh, yeah, she liked this. A lot. Especially once his fingers started moving in and out of her.

"Damn, honey, you're so tight. You're squeezing me." He sounded surprised. He pressed his fingers deeper, and she gasped from the sensation.

When she regained her voice, Mika said breathlessly, "If you weren't so stubborn, we could do a lot more than this. Imagine how good I'd feel wrapped around you, Conor."

McCabe's groan told her he was thinking of it.

Something she could only label as resoluteness settled across his features, then his thumb came up to circle the area he'd been teasing earlier. His fingers continued to thrust. The combination was delicious, and with little pants and moans Mika let him know how much she enjoyed it.

As her climax approached, Mika fought to keep her eyes open and her gaze locked with Conor's. She wanted to share this with him. And maybe to torture him—just a bit—with what he was missing out on. Torture. That gave her an idea. Mika reached up and pinched her own nipples, rolling them between her fingers. Conor's hand moved faster inside her and she suspected he wanted her to find release before she shattered him. She could see the lust in his eyes.

But the odds were in his favor: she was close and he was determined. Then he started talking dirty to her, telling her how good she felt, how much he liked the scent of her arousal and what he wanted to do to her besides this. That was all it took to push her over the edge.

He didn't stop, not even after she climaxed a second time. Mika grabbed his wrist. "Enough," she begged. There was only so much pleasure a demon could handle.

"You said you came three times in the shower. Don't you want to come three times for me?"

Chapter Eight

Half an hour later, Mika could still feel fine tremors coursing through the muscles of her inner thighs. Though she wasn't about to share it with McCabe, she'd never come so hard before. The man was already too pleased with himself. No way in hell was she going to let him crow any more.

Not that he'd escaped scot-free. After she'd made a few pointed suggestions on how to continue if he wanted to give her a third orgasm, Conor's eyes had become inferno-bright. His internal battle must have been fierce, but he'd managed to hold out. Because of that, they were now both paying the price.

McCabe, though, was getting the worse of the deal. Mika, at least, was somewhat replete; but she still could feel his erection pushing rather firmly into the leg she rested over his. She couldn't prevent a smirk at the pained expression he wore.

"Do you want me to kiss it and make it all better?" she asked.

With a growl, he opened his eyes and glared at her. Desire and frustration warred for dominance on his features. "Knock it off."

"I just want to make you more comfortable. After all, you helped me out, right?" The innocent look she gave him earned her another snarl. She was beginning to like that sound.

Mika didn't plan to tease him too much more. Really. He was adequately torturing himself without her needing to do anything. Of course, since it *was* his own fault, and since he wasn't taking steps to alleviate his suffering, she suspected he enjoyed his predicament. He could have told her to get dressed like he had yesterday. Or he could have kept his distance from her. But McCabe had done neither of those things. Instead, he'd pulled her into his arms. He'd even cupped her bare breasts several times. Mika found it amusing that he tried to make the touches seem accidental. Did he think she'd tell him no?

"I don't understand why you keep resisting the inevitable," she said, shifting her head to get a clearer view of his face.

"It's not inevitable," he gritted out.

"You don't think so? Every time we're together, this goes further, becomes more intense. At the rate we've progressed, how much longer do you think you can hold out? A day? Two?"

"Mika—"

"I'm not teasing you." Regretfully, she removed her leg from atop his thigh and propped herself up a bit on one elbow. "I'm honestly curious. We want each other, we're both adults, neither one of us is tied to another. Why are you fighting so hard?"

When his jaw tightened, Mika knew she wasn't going to get an answer. With a sigh she trailed her palm across his collarbone. This wasn't a discussion she could force.

Conor caught her hand, pressing it flat against his chest. "Let me turn it around. Why are you fighting so hard for sex?"

She grinned. "Never had a woman all over you before, huh? Well, I find you irresistible."

"That's a load of bullshit," he growled. But he half-smiled as he said it.

"You're even sexier when you smile," she added. He sobered immediately and Mika regretted having said anything. Freeing herself, she ran her forefinger over his bottom lip. "You're too serious. Why don't you just let yourself have some fun?"

He recaptured her hand. His was much larger than hers, his palm and fingers calloused, but Conor was careful with his grip, making certain he didn't squeeze too hard. The silence lengthened and Mika sighed. He'd told her something the night they'd met, but now she suspected it pervaded his life even more deeply than she'd thought.

"Does everything go back to keeping your Kiverian half in check?" she asked.

His body tensed. She expected him to tell her to go back to bed and leave him alone, but he didn't. That encouraged her. "Do you believe you can't laugh and have fun, that you can't make love without becoming some ogre?"

Again, there was no answer, but his stubborn expression said a lot. Mika pulled her hand loose, rested her palm against his jaw and turned his face to her. "You're not a monster," she said gently. "Emotion isn't going to turn you into one."

"Strong emotion makes it harder to maintain control."

Amazement held her speechless. He *did* believe that he had to remain this stoic, careful man or he would become some fiend. Did sex truly scare him so much? "I was thinking of the night we met, recalling something you said," she said. She slid her fingers along his jaw. "And what I told you. Remember? 'The bamboo that bends—' "

There was an intractable note in his voice, when he snapped, "If you want to spout Japanese adages at me, pick a new one."

"I don't know any other Japanese proverbs. I'm afraid you're stuck with this one." Mika leaned forward, brushing her lips across his. It wasn't meant as seduction, but something else. She didn't waste time trying to put a name to it, instead she gathered up her courage. Here was her vishtau mate, and while they didn't know each other well yet, she was somehow certain she could trust him with things that she'd never shared with anyone else. "My father told me that when I was a teenager. He'd noticed how I tried to deny my humanness and knew it was an unhealthy way to live. I was doing the same thing you're doing, only in reverse."

He rolled so that he was face-to-face with her, and this time, he was the one who offered a gentle touch. Running his thumb across her cheek, he said, "You still deny your humanness."

She shrugged off the pity she saw in his eyes. "No, I've accepted it, integrated it into who I am. I don't like it, I'd much rather be full Mahsei, but I know I'm not, and unlike you, I quit pretending otherwise long ago."

McCabe jerked away and sat up. Slowly, Mika got to her knees. She wasn't uncomfortable with him even though she was only half-dressed, but she looked around for her tank top anyway. This conversation was serious, and Conor might have trouble focusing if she wasn't covered. Once she had herself fully clothed again, she moved behind him.

At first, Mika didn't speak, but leaned in to kiss his shoulder. It wasn't much in the way of an apology, but she wanted him to know that what she'd said—what she was about to say—wasn't something she took lightly.

"You're not human, Conor," she said gently. "You're never going to be human." She felt his muscles become more rigid with each word. "If you don't find a way to meld with your true nature, if you keep it locked up, one day something will happen." He shook his head. "It will," Mika insisted. "And when your darkness breaks free, it'll be your humanness that's lost. Only if you integrate both parts of who you are, will you not have to worry about it. One will temper the other and you'll bend, not break."

He didn't respond, and Mika ran her hand across his

back. She nestled her body closer to his, pressing into him, but left her arm around his shoulders. "It isn't easy to blend the two. It took a long time before it was natural for me. But every day it will become easier, and at some point, you won't have to think about it."

McCabe turned his head. Since she sat as close to him as she possibly could, the movement put them nose-to-nose. When she saw his eyes, Mika braced herself, but she didn't leave his side.

"It's real easy for you, isn't it? But you only have to deal with being half-Mahsei. It's not like you're much of a demon."

She was able to keep from reacting to his words because she'd expected him to lash out; but still, he'd hurt her. He knew where she was most vulnerable and had gone straight for the heart. Of course, he probably thought she had done the same.

"No, I'm not a powerful demon," she admitted, "but I was a child—maybe thirteen—when I started bringing my two natures together. If I could do it with my hormones running rampant, you should be able to do it too."

"The difference is"—Conor used his strength to pull her from his flank across his lap—"that you used your good, human side and tempered the demon. Kiverians are . . . we're evil."

Mika shifted, moving her legs to either side of his, and scooted forward. The conversation had accomplished one thing—he'd lost his arousal. She smoothed the hair off his forehead, gazed into his eyes and made a decision; she was going to push all the way to the root of the matter and risk his anger. "She never should have done this to you."

"Who?" The word was a warning.

"Your mother."

The words hung there and Mika felt as if she had a guillotine poised above her neck. McCabe vibrated with fury, but he didn't move her from his lap.

At first, she didn't understand the feelings coursing through her, but then she figured it out. The bond between them had strengthened to the point where she'd begun to feel his emotional pain. She deeply regretted causing it, but in the long run, he'd be happier once this ache was excised.

He wasn't looking at her, and she didn't force it. "You were a child, completely innocent," she said. "She never should have taught you to despise any part of who you are."

Conor's hands went to her waist, and she expected him to dump her to his side and leave; but while his hold tightened for a moment, he didn't follow through. "You don't think she had the right to hate demons?"

"Maybe one Kiverian, but you're her son. She never, ever should have hated you." His gaze snapped to hers and she easily read it. Before he could argue, she said, "And don't tell me she didn't. Maybe it wasn't all the time, maybe it was only when she thought you were acting like a Kiverian, but you must have learned as a small child to hide that part of yourself, to suppress it."

"It wasn't like that," he denied thickly.

"Then tell me what it was like," she said.

Mika started stroking his brow again, trying to soothe him. She thought that would be it, that he'd end their talk instantly, so she was more than surprised when he lay back down and positioned her at his side. His arms went around her and she curled into him, offering the only comfort she thought he'd accept.

For a long time, he did nothing but hold her. Occasionally, his clasp would firm, bringing her closer against him, but he'd ease off almost immediately, as if he were concerned he'd crush her. His grip wasn't too strong, but she stayed quiet.

She heard the air-conditioning kick in, and more distantly, the muted sounds of Los Angeles, but it was Conor she was focused on. One of his hands slipped under her top and circled the bare skin of her back. He probably would have been happier if she'd left her tank off, she decided, but carefully kept her expression neutral. Mika didn't want him to think she was laughing about something so crucial to his life.

"She said that looking at me made her remember him," Conor said quietly. "I used to wonder if that meant I resembled him or if my presence alone was enough to remind her of what he'd done."

Mika ran a hand down the back of Conor's upper arm, but remained silent. It shocked her that he was talking about this. He normally held everything tightly inside. She'd expected him to stonewall her. That he wasn't told her that he needed to discuss this with someone, needed to let it out. It must be the vishtau that had made him choose her to share it with, and the idea brought a lump to her throat. The amount of trust this required was staggering.

And that caused a huge wave of guilt.

She'd lied to Conor since the moment they met. No more, Mika vowed silently. She couldn't come clean about what she'd already told him, nor could she say anything that would divulge her mission, but with everything else, she was going to be as honest as possible from now on.

"She wouldn't look at me, wouldn't touch me unless there was no other choice," he continued after a lengthy pause. "I always thought that if I could be human enough . . . I never could."

Conor's voice was cold, but she knew he was hardly indifferent. The more emotional something was for him, the harder he clamped down. This had to be the most painful part of his childhood: a mother who wouldn't touch him.

"It wasn't only her. A lot of people don't look me in the eye for long." McCabe's smile held no humor. "They must sense what I am, although I hide it." For the first time since he'd started talking, Conor looked at her. "That's one of the things I like about you. I don't scare you or make you nervous. You meet my eye. You touch me." His grin became more genuine. "Hell, you even laugh at me. It may frustrate me to no end, but at least I feel like I'm real when we're together."

For Conor, that was one hell of a speech. Mika couldn't blow it now, couldn't make him feel uncomfortable for opening up to her. "I *do* understand," she said quietly. "You wondered if you were a shadow or something, right? That people knew you were there, but didn't quite acknowledge your existence."

"Yeah, a shadow. Or that I was invisible."

Mika shifted nearer, sliding her thigh between his legs. "I felt the same way much of the time, both in Orcus and in this world. The only people I spent time with who made me feel normal were members of my family. I don't know what I would have done without them, and I don't know how you survived."

His eyes closed and Conor moved onto his back, putting distance between them again. "I did have someone—Ben. I met him when I was eighteen and he taught me to hunt vampires and werewolves. He even talked the powers that be into letting me work as a freelancer for the city because he knew I didn't have the temperament to hire on officially. As for my mother . . . I think she tried," he said at last, sounding tired.

She hesitated. "Do you realize how you sound when you talk about her?"

McCabe didn't say anything. The air conditioner turned off, making the silence seem more absolute. When it became obvious that he was finished, Mika decided he'd come as far as he could today; but there was one more thing she wanted to say. "If she was unable to accept you, to love you, she should have given you to someone who could. She should have found a demon to bring you to Orcus and your family."

Conor's eyes opened and he rolled, pinning her under him. "What the hell do demons know about love?"

So, he believed that old stereotype, that demons were incapable of tender emotions. It wasn't true, although there were distinct cultural differences between the races.

"We know as much about love as any other species," she said gently. Maybe she wouldn't have been so sanguine if Conor hadn't revealed something of his past, but how could she chew him out after the last fifteen minutes?

"Why would the demon that fathered me—or his family for that matter—want me?" Conor asked. His eyes blazed.

Mika took a deep breath, needing to say this right. "All demon children I've ever seen are loved and wanted. Every baby is considered a gift and treated that way. If for some reason the child's family is incapable of caring for them, there are many others willing to raise and love them."

Conor didn't say anything. His arms held most of his weight, but that kept him too far away. Putting her hands on his shoulders, Mika tugged him close. "But they would want you because you're you."

"Right. And then I could have grown up feeling invisible in two worlds the way you did." The skepticism in his voice annoyed Mika, but she decided not to argue.

"I want to be on top, not underneath," she said instead. Since sex wasn't involved, he'd be able to tolerate it.

Bemusedly McCabe shook his head, probably wondering where the hell that had come from, then rolled. As he stopped moving, Mika settled herself on his chest. With a sigh, she said, "You wouldn't have had to deal with feeling like a shadow in Orcus." She watched his face, but his expression didn't change. "You're half Kiverian. That would have overcome your human heritage in the minds of most demons." She smiled. "Just think, we could have met years ago and been enjoying *this*." She rotated her pelvis against his, and his hands went to her hips to hold her still.

His eyes were wide, his voice hoarse. "Damn, Mika, does it always come down to sex with you?"

She sobered. Though it would leave her vulnerable again, she answered honestly. "Only with you."

Mika lowered her head to rest it on his chest, ignoring

his unspoken demand that she explain. Let him keep guessing. There was no way she was telling him about the vishtau yet, not when he'd feel it necessary to fight such a demonic thing even more strenuously than he was already.

Besides, they'd already covered a lot of ground, much more than she'd expected, and she needed to think. Needed to find some way to keep Conor from despising her for her betrayal. For he would hate her when he found out that she'd lied to him; she had no illusion about it.

No, he probably wouldn't discover it until after she left, but even then, she wanted him to remember her with affection, not hate. And the most important thing was that he believe that her touching him was never part of the lie. She knew him better now, and thinking she'd been *that* dishonest with him would shut McCabe down more than he was already.

She stroked his right biceps. No matter what she had to do, she couldn't let her promise to the Council hurt Conor.

Mika had finally fallen asleep. Conor knew he was a long way from that. It had to be close to noon, but it didn't matter; his head was too full of her. And everything she'd said—hell, everything he'd said.

What the hell had he been thinking? He never shared anything as personal as what he'd told her. Not with anyone. Not even with Ben. And if he tried to blame it on some demon spell, she would laugh at him. Conor scowled. It hadn't been a Mahsei power that had made him talk; he knew that. It was simply Mika.

He levered himself up on his elbow to look at her. The blanket he'd covered them with had slipped to her waist, and he carefully tugged it over her arms to keep her warm. He should carry her to bed. The floor was uncomfortable and she'd be stiff when she woke, but selfishly he wanted her next to him. Almost involuntarily, his hand reached out and smoothed a lock of hair from her cheek. Her skin was soft, warm, and he lingered for a moment, studying her.

Her lips were curved, as if she were amused by her dreams, but because her eyes were closed, he couldn't see the mischief that usually danced there. She was incredibly changeable—laughing one moment, serious the next, and always getting underneath his skin one way or the other.

He'd never met anyone like her.

For sure he'd never met anyone who affected him the way she did. Emotion: It was his enemy and Mika made him feel too damn much, too damn intensely. There were no low or medium settings with her. Whether anger, arousal, humor, frustration or anything else he could name, hers were full-out, super-charged emotions. The damn woman tied him in knots.

Only with you. Just the memory of her saying that was enough to kick up his heart rate. Since they'd met, her actions had been sexual; he hadn't considered the possibility that her behavior with him would be unique.

He was reading too much into it. His desire to be special was giving her words a nuance she hadn't intended. But telling himself that didn't help. Besides, what else could she have meant except that it was different between them?

He ran his fingers lightly over her cheek again. The need to touch her sometimes overwhelmed him, and he guessed she was right about the inevitability of them becoming lovers. But Conor intended to fight anyway. When things were intimate between them, his control became too tenuous. He couldn't afford to lose his self-command.

She'd said he wouldn't have to be careful with her. That he could be himself. It was another memory that sent him into overdrive. A memory that tempted him to drop his restraint.

He'd damn near lived like a monk for the past two years. Sex had become almost more work than it was worth, and he'd taken to waiting until the urge was undeniable. There was too much he had to be cautious about. He couldn't let his eyes glow or it would show through his contact lenses. He'd had to fight the need to bite, and had restrained his strength to ensure he didn't hurt the woman he was with.

Everything would be different with Mika. Her eyes glowed the same as his and she liked it when he bit her. Hell, she'd demanded that he bite her. Conor ran a hand over his mouth, trying to wipe away the unexpected smile, and shook his head.

Could he really have her as he wanted? She'd said yes, but Mika was finely built. It was difficult to imagine her withstanding his force. Such thoughts had his unruly body reacting and he had another damned hard-on. The state seemed to be perpetual since Mika had first smiled at him on that darkened street.

She turned toward him, her hand landing on his abs and her fingers flexing against his bare skin. "Go to sleep," she murmured. "Rest."

"How long have you been awake?" he asked.

Her eyes didn't open, but her smile grew. She put a leg across him and her thigh sandwiched his erection. "Not long." She yawned. "And I plan on going right back to sleep. Unless, of course, you give me a good reason not to." She squeezed.

Conor didn't say anything, and in a few moments, her breathing became even. It wouldn't take long until she was out again. "Mika," he said. He kept his voice low.

"Hmm?"

She was almost asleep. Good. He couldn't ask this while she was aware. It would be too embarrassing if she knew he was this needy, too dangerous to put this kind of weapon into her hands. He'd already trusted her with too much. But she was so drowsy, Conor doubted she'd recall anything he said now. "Am I really the only man you've reacted to like this? Sexually?"

"Mmm-hmm. Only you, Conor," she murmured.

Something inside him eased. It was odd for a paid killer,

a bodyguard, a hard man to admit, but all his life he'd wanted to be important to someone else. Maybe he finally was. Maybe.

Mika stretched and swallowed a groan. Honestly, she needed to get McCabe in bed with her ASAP. One more night on the floor or his narrow couch, and she was going to be hobbling.

She sat up, massaged the crick in her neck and tried to locate him. It wasn't a surprise to wake up alone; as contained as Conor was, he must be appalled at how much he'd revealed. Especially with that last question, the one Mika bet he wished she wouldn't remember. The one *she* wished she didn't remember.

Propping her elbows on her thighs, she dropped her head into her hands. All along she'd told herself this assignment wasn't a game, yet that was exactly how she'd treated it. The lure of playing covert agent had been irresistible. Her other reason for agreeing to do this was just as self-serving. Finding her vishtau mate. The idea of protecting her people, of protecting her family, only arose when she needed to justify her actions.

She hadn't considered for even a minute what she'd be doing to Conor. He was a big, tough Kiverian male. Maybe she'd thought he was indestructible—emotionally, at least.

Mika knew differently now. When he found out what she'd done, it would destroy something inside of him, something that barely managed to cling to life. His mother hadn't killed it but Mika just might. She rubbed her temples. How could she keep from devastating him?

Not completing her mission wasn't an option; she'd given her word. And even if she hadn't, there *was* her family and the other residents of Orcus to consider. Maybe she hadn't thought of them very much before this, but they definitely needed to be factored in. She couldn't let their wills become enslaved. What if McCabe decided to wield that incantation? To pit demon against demon in death matches? Mika didn't think he would—that wasn't the kind of man he was—but she wasn't completely sure. He hated his father so intensely, it colored his view of all demons. What would he do because of that?

She was going to hurt Conor—it was inevitable now—but she had to make sure she didn't annihilate his inner light. The only idea she had on how to do this was to hang around and face the music. He'd be furious at her for stealing his incantation, but at least he'd know she cared about him enough to weather his wrath.

It wasn't much of a plan. She'd have to keep thinking until she came up with a better one. But at least she hadn't found the spell yet. She still had time.

A shimmer of something strummed at her senses, but she ignored it when she heard water in the bathroom turn off. Mika slowly straightened. Conor was going to feel uncomfortable when he saw her, and there was nothing she could do to make it easier for him.

With a soft groan, she stood and stretched. When she felt like she could walk, she headed for the bedroom to gather up some clean clothes. Since she'd hung her clothing by type, then sorted it by color, it was easy to find what she wanted. She picked a pair of jeans that were faded nearly white and frayed a bit at the ankles, and a long-sleeved, fuchsia T-shirt. She heard more water running in the bathroom and sighed. Conor would be a while longer.

Mika dug her comm unit out of her purse and stared at it. She should have monitored her voicemail every day, but she hadn't wanted to hear a message from the Council's minion. She couldn't put this off any longer, though. Reluctantly she checked the display and found two messages. Heart sinking, she hit play.

The first was from her dad. Sitting on the bed, she punched the button to connect to him, and ended up having to leave her own voicemail instead. Just as well. He might hear an edge in her tone and figure something was going on.

Returning to her voicemail box, she went on to the second message. And felt the blood drain from her face. It was from the Council's servant—he wanted to meet with her. Tonight. He gave her the time and place, and Mika closed her eyes. She hit the button to replay the message, wanting to make sure, but he named every code and password that the Council had given her. Because of the intrigue in Orcus, they'd used a complex system, and it was unlikely that someone had broken it.

Damn. She hadn't done a very good job setting up her cover story to get out of the house, and she was going to have to use it. With a little luck, Conor wouldn't look too closely. If he did, she'd have to lie some more.

She tucked her unit back into her purse and took a deep breath. Conor still seemed to be occupied, so she decided to take advantage of the opportunity.

When he was home, he kept his comm unit near his desk, and with a quick glance at the closed bathroom door, she picked it up. Running her finger counterclockwise over the power chip, she drained the charge. She'd never seen him check the level before leaving the house, and she had to hope that held true today too.

Slipping the unit carefully back into place, Mika took another deep breath. There, she'd done it. And she felt guilty as hell. *I'm sorry, Conor,* she thought, but she didn't dare say the words aloud.

What was McCabe up to in the bathroom anyway? As she gently used her mind to probe, her head jerked up. Their watcher was back. He was outside.

Chapter Nine

Mika burst into the bathroom, surprising Conor.

"What the fu—"

"Conor!" She cut him off. "The watcher is outside!"

He tossed his razor on the counter, grabbed a towel and wiped the remaining shaving cream off his face. Although she tried not to let her attention wander, Mika couldn't help but notice that the only thing covering him was the towel around his waist. The man's legs were so muscular that the edges of the terry cloth didn't meet and she had a view of his left thigh. She licked her lips.

He concentrated for a moment. "I can't pick him up. Which direction?"

Mika jerked her gaze from his bare skin and pointed over his left shoulder. McCabe nodded, and she could feel him mentally probe the direction she'd indicated. When he brushed past her, she guessed he'd read the partially blocked energy for himself. It continued to surprise her that an auric assassin wouldn't be more successful at cloaking himself, but she shrugged that off and hurried after Conor.

She stopped short about two steps into the bedroom.

McCabe was naked. Mika could only see his backside, but damn, his body was a work of art. He bent over to yank on a pair of jeans and she heard a roaring in her head.

The need to make some comment—either about his world-class ass or about him going commando—became nearly impossible to resist, but she swallowed the words. As serious as the situation was, she couldn't say either thing—not when she knew what kind of reaction she'd get. She smiled, imagining McCabe acting riled to hide his embarrassment.

While she was ogling him, he stepped into some shoes and grabbed a T-shirt, but it wasn't until he left the bedroom that it dawned on her that he planned to face down the watcher. Mika chased after him. "Conor!"

She caught him at the kitchen door. Putting her palm against the smooth wood, she pushed it shut and stood blocking his exit.

McCabe seemed more puzzled than angry. He asked, "What are you doing?"

"Keeping you safe. You can't go out there now."

"I'll be fine." At the indulgent note in his voice, she tilted her head. Conor? Indulgent?

"Yeah, you will be," she agreed, "because I'm not letting you charge out to confront an assassin who wants you dead."

His hands lightly clasped her shoulders. "Do you have so little confidence in my abilities that you can't trust me to go outside?"

Mika frowned at his misinterpretation. "It has nothing to do with that. I know you can take care of yourself in most circumstances, but you want to face someone—some*thing*—you know nothing about." She reached up and curled her hands around his forearms. "You might underestimate him. You might think you can fight him the usual way, and you can't."

She'd been shopping with her mom in Biirkma when she'd seen one of those assassins make a hit. The results had been horrific and she never wanted to see anything like it again, especially if her mate was the target. An auric blast was much different, much stronger, than the normal offensive magic used by demons. Mika didn't understand how it worked, just that the energy came from two separate sources. An auric assassin could discharge a regular energy blast too, but when they decided to use this, the advantage was all theirs.

Conor nodded but said, "I can take care of myself."

"Yeah? Well, guess what, McCabe, you'd be decomposing right now if it hadn't been for me. And don't you forget it." She glared at him. Sure, he was protective of her; she understood that and knew why, but he was too cavalier about his own safety. It drove her crazy.

She expected him to deny what she'd done, but he surprised her. "Believe me, honey, I appreciate that you wanted to save my ass, and I'm prepared to deal with the assassin. You don't have to worry."

He'd called the attacker an assassin again, which reminded her that Conor hadn't interrogated her. Why not? He wasn't someone who let things go. He should have started to pester her the night of the assault and kept at it until she gave him the answers he needed. But he hadn't. That meant he knew more than he was letting on. She wasn't going to probe yet, though—there was more important ground to cover.

"It's easy to say you're prepared, but how are you going to stop him if he shoots at you today? His magic pierced the protection around your house. He can sit out there and pick you off as soon as you step outside."

"It's not going to happen," Conor growled. "Now stand aside and let me handle this."

His breath tickled and Mika smiled, momentarily overcome by desire. The damn vishtau. "You get me all shivery when you grumble," she teased.

McCabe's curse made her lips twitch. "You're a pain in the ass," he muttered. Then, before she realized what he was up to, Conor released her and walked away. She had an unobstructed view, and Mika was so busy ogling his butt that he was nearly at the main entry before it occurred to her what he intended.

Dire circumstances called for extreme measures. Mika drew on one of her powers, increasing the density of the air molecules across the threshold. She made them so heavy that even Conor wouldn't have the strength to open the door. When he pulled and it didn't move, she had to smother a chuckle. She saw the surprise on his face, and it amused her even more when he twisted the deadbolt a few times before trying to yank it open a second time. His biceps strained as he put everything he had into getting out of the house.

A snicker escaped her, and Conor turned with a glare. "What the hell did you do?" he demanded.

Mika crossed her arms over her chest, leaning back against the kitchen door. "Who, me?"

He stalked toward her, and she felt awareness shoot through her body. Damn, Conor was sexy when he moved— all masculine grace and power. When his hips pinned hers to the wall, another shiver went through her; the rough denim of his jeans against her bare thighs was incredibly arousing. She slid her arms around his neck and leaned forward, pressing her breasts against the solid wall of his chest. Turning her face up to him, she nipped at his chin.

It was McCabe's turn to shudder. His hands tightened at her waist and he made a growling sound.

"Do those glowing eyes mean you're angry or aroused?" she asked.

The fire in his gaze intensified. "Guess," he said. Then he lifted her and put her to one side.

Before he had released her, Mika again blocked the door. She wasn't letting Conor get himself killed, not if she could do anything to prevent it. He used all his strength as he twisted the knob, but the wood didn't budge. Red sparked in his eyes when he turned to her.

"Quit playing games," he demanded.

"This is no game." She reached out and ran her hand fleetingly along the length of his arm. "I won't let you die, and I've never been more serious about anything in my life."

He huffed out a long, slow breath. "You don't get to make my decisions."

"No. Not when . . ." She trailed off. It was probably stupid to remind him, but she was suddenly curious. "If you want to go outside and play so badly, why don't you freeze my powers like you did the night we met?"

With a grimace, he looked away.

"You can't," she realized. "You can prevent me from wielding them, but once they're in use, you can't make them disappear! I'm right, aren't I?" When he made no response, she added, "Do you have to touch me to keep me powerless, or can you do it from a distance?"

McCabe turned to her, his eyes burning. "Stop whatever the hell it is you're doing."

Reaching up, she fingered the ends of her hair and weighed a few factors. Finally, canting her hip slightly, she posed to accentuate her curves. "Sorry, but you're stuck here until I decide otherwise," she said.

His hands clenched and released at his sides as he struggled to rein in his fury. "Do as I say. Move aside."

She rolled her eyes at his order. "Is there anything more predictable than a demon male's response to being thwarted?" It was strictly a rhetorical question, but she knew it would make him angrier. She wanted him pissed off at her and not going outside.

It worked. She could almost see clouds of power amassing around him. A muscle jumped in his jaw. If he'd complained before about his Kiverian side pulling at the leash, it must be about ready to snap the rope by now. He was livid.

"Open the fucking door," he said. Each word was bitten out.

With a smile, she arched her back and said, "I will, after the assassin is gone. But if you want it sooner, why don't you come over here and make me?"

Conor moved so fast that she didn't have time to blink. Suddenly he had her across the room and sitting atop the table. But as he stood between her parted legs, she wrapped them around him and drew him closer. McCabe looked stunned.

"You did this deliberately," he accused.

"Ya think?"

He tried to pull away, but Mika didn't let him. She noticed that he didn't put much effort into a second attempt, and they both knew that if he really wanted to put distance between them he'd easily be able to break her hold. As she watched, some of the anger drained from his gaze.

"You're trouble," he repeated.

"Always." She leaned forward and kissed him. At first, Conor didn't respond, but she didn't stop. Then the tension seeped from his body and he took control.

"Bad for me," he murmured against her mouth.

"Maybe," she agreed between kisses, "but at least you're alive for a bit longer."

McCabe's hands found her hips and he tugged her even more firmly against him. When he had her anchored, one hand moved under her tank top and cupped her left breast. He used his thumb to tease her nipple. With a gasp of surprise, of pleasure, she sank deeper into arousal.

"*Mika.*" His voice was low, husky. Seductive.

"Hmm?" She dropped her head back to give him more room to nuzzle her throat.

"Open the door."

It took a minute, maybe two, for his request to register. As soon as it did, it popped her bubble of excitement. Mika pushed him back—not far, but she wanted to see his face. "Unfair," she complained, but there was no heat in her voice.

He raised an eyebrow. "This again?" McCabe ignored the virtuous look she donned. "You think I don't realize when you use our attraction to divert me? You know exactly what you're doing when you position yourself a certain way." Conor lightly caressed her breast.

When he removed his hand, she smiled, pleased that he knew her so well. "It worked, didn't it? Our watcher left while you were trying to persuade me to unblock the doors."

"What?" McCabe separated from her, faced the direction of the assassin and ran a quick scan. The watcher was gone. "Son of a bitch," he muttered, directing a glare at her.

Mika fluttered her lashes at him. "Can I help it if he didn't hang around?"

Conor shook his head and walked to the sink. With a laugh, Mika hopped off the table and went to him. This was the second time he'd used their attraction to try to manipulate her, and she didn't mind—well, not too much. It was a standard demonic ploy, one she'd used on him, and she thought it was encouraging that his self-command had slipped so far.

When she reached him, she hugged him from behind, snuggling her breasts into his back, and slid her hands from his waist down the front of his jeans. He caught her before she could touch him.

"Don't start," he warned.

"I was only going to make you more comfortable," she said. "That zipper has to be digging into some pretty sensitive flesh."

He cursed then laughed, and Mika smiled. The emotional warmth his nearness caused inside her expanded, filling her body till she felt as if she'd burst. "I love the sound of your laugh," she said, and nipped his shoulder blade through his T-shirt. "I want to hear it more often."

Immediately, Conor went still. He looked pained.

"No." Mika gripped him harder as he tried to pull away.

She sensed his struggle. "I'm not going to push. I just want to say one thing, okay?" Conor didn't reply, but he didn't break away, either. Mika took that as a yes. "You're too serious most of the time. You need to cut that out. I think I can help. Hell, if anyone knows how to have fun, it's me. My family, the others in Orcus, they all . . ." Suddenly uncomfortable, Mika trailed off and broke free.

McCabe caught her before she could escape. "You wouldn't let me get away, why do you think I'll let you leave?" he asked.

She shrugged and tried to evade his eyes. Conor didn't allow that, either. His palm cupped her jaw and tilted her face up until their gazes met. She couldn't read his expression.

"They all what?"

Mika started to give some flip answer, but stopped herself. She'd made a promise that she'd be honest with Conor, and she wouldn't hedge on the truth no matter how uncomfortable it made her, or how vulnerable she felt. Still, she wasn't precisely sure how to respond.

After a few seconds she said, "They don't need me. Don't ask how I know that, either. Maybe it's because my departures have never caused much of a ripple. My returns either. Whenever I crossed the veil . . . Oh, I know my human family missed me when I lived in Orcus, and my demon family missed me when I wasn't with them, but it wasn't like my presence was . . . *necessary*." She shrugged a third time, not certain she'd explained herself.

McCabe gave her an inscrutable look. "And now you think you're necessary to me?"

"I know I am." On that point, Mika was positive. "You might not like it, but it's true."

Just as she needed him. She'd begun to recognize it. Balance. Yin and yang. Light and dark. Male and female.

Something cold settled in the pit of her stomach. Things were so black and white for McCabe that it terrified her. What would he say when he discovered her lies?

With a tremulous hand, she pushed his damp hair off his forehead.

She was in trouble.

Mika felt like a criminal when she left Conor's house. The only thing that kept her from turning around and going back inside was picturing the Council's reaction if she didn't meet with their designee. She'd been able to enjoy a burger, and her freedom from house arrest, but the guilt would come roaring back when she saw McCabe again.

Using a wad of paper towels, Mika wiped up the excess water splashed on the periwinkle counter around the sink. The restroom of the restaurant was empty, but then the diner was sparsely occupied. She was here at an off time, the supper crowd was gone and the evening movie-goers were still watching their shows.

Mika put her purse on the dried area and, after pushing the sleeves of her fuchsia knit T-shirt from her wrists to her elbows, pulled a comb and a barrette from her bag. The shirt was comfortable, and her jeans loose and soft from repeated washing, giving her freedom of movement—something she'd need if things fell apart during the meeting. She didn't trust human minions.

No, contrary to human legends she'd read, they weren't controlled by demons, nor were they possessed. Which meant they could be unpredictable. And they were generally of questionable character. When a human worked for a demon, there was always something in it for them. The Council obviously believed this minion would be trustworthy—as important as this mission was, they wouldn't use someone who hadn't proved himself—but she felt uneasy, anyway.

When she made her rendezvous tonight, she'd be prepared for betrayal. It was the only smart thing to do.

With a grimace, Mika used the comb to gather her hair at the back of her head. When her locks were smooth, she exchanged the comb for the clip and twisted her mane into place. The ends of her hair spiked up and out. It was a fun kind of style, and she stared at it for a moment with a smile.

It made her appear more youthful and innocent—two things that might help with the Council lackey. Of course, looking young might bring about a different kind of trouble with this guy.

Mika shrugged. She could handle a human.

She put her comb away and slung her purse strap over her head. Her money, driver's license and comm unit were tucked into her pockets where they'd be safer, but she carried the small leather bag anyway. It, too, should add to the impression of youth. The shocking pink leather and tiny size were pure teenager.

Or Mahsei demon.

Mika laughed silently. She could easily visualize her mother using something in this style and color, and while her mom looked almost as young as Mika, she was nearly eighty. Of course, for a demon, that wasn't even middle-aged.

With one last primp in front of the mirror, Mika returned to her seat outside. The diner was ringed with booths and she'd grabbed one in the corner. Red vinyl banquettes complemented silver-and-white Formica tables, giving the place a retro feel. She liked it. More tables dotted the open floor, the red-and-chrome chairs brightening the off-white linoleum, and vintage advertising prints decorated the walls.

Mika sighed in contentment. Eating out had been a treat, but one she deserved. After being confined to Mc Cabe's house for days, she'd been going stir-crazy. What with the searching she'd done and the time dealing with Conor and their vishtau, she was ready for a break. Tonight she was going to relax.

"More coffee?"

Mika looked up at the waitress and said, "Yes, please."

The woman's uniform was as retro as the diner. She even wore a plastic pin with her name on it—Rachel. As she filled Mika's mug, Rachel took in Mika's changed appearance and said, "Good thing this isn't a bar. With your new 'do, I'd have to card you."

The waitress grinned and Mika smiled back. "Trust me, if I planned to bar-hop, you wouldn't question my age."

All evening Rachel had chatted with the people at her tables, and Mika found her entertaining. The woman had to be around forty, but she was full of energy and seemed to honestly enjoy people.

"Can I get you something to go with your coffee?" she asked.

Since it was her night to do as she wished—at least until her rendezvous—Mika ordered a slice of French silk pie. She lifted the mug and took a sip as the waitress left. In about half an hour or so, she'd head out. First thing to do would be calling Conor's comm unit to leave her message. With luck, he hadn't noticed his battery was down and she'd get voicemail. If he had realized and switched out power packs, she'd have to do some fast talking.

"I was trying to restrain my curiosity," Rachel said as she returned and slid a pie plate onto the table, "but I have to ask. Why the change in hairstyle?"

"My lover is a little kinky." Mika's lips curved as she imagined Conor's response to that statement. The man was remarkably prudish, considering he was half-Kiverian.

"He likes young girls?"

Mika heard the waitress's disapproval and quickly said, "No, he likes to role-play. A few nights ago, I was a gold medalist in women's wrestling."

Rachel gave a bark of laughter. Leaning forward and lowering her voice, she said, "And now you're doing the 'schoolgirl.' Well, you need the right clothes for this kind of thing. Think of his reaction if you were wearing a uniform. You know, a short plaid skirt, a white blouse and thigh-high stockings. He'll go wild."

The idea delighted Mika. Just the thought of how shocked Conor would be, the look on his face that she imagined, was enough to make glee bubble inside her. "Do you know where I'd find something like that?"

"As a matter of fact, I do." The waitress pulled her order pad out of her apron pocket—another old-fashioned touch—and with a pencil jotted something down. "Check this place out," she said, handing the paper to Mika. "They have all kinds of costumes there, not just schoolgirl uniforms. You could be a maid, cheerleader or a nurse—to name a few."

"Thanks. I'll take a look." Mika decided not to ask how she knew about the store. Some things were better left alone, and she had a feeling this was one of them.

As she slowly ate her dessert, Mika put aside her amusement and considered the upcoming meeting. She needed to be wary, but she couldn't risk offending the minion either. She couldn't do anything that could be construed as distrust of the Council, which would not be well-received if the minion were angered enough to report her. She hated the maneuvering that went hand-in-hand with politics.

With a silent sigh, Mika finished the last of her coffee. Adding a generous tip, she ran her card through the reader and paid for her meal. No more time to delay. The waitress called out, thanking her and inviting her to come again, and Mika must have made the right responses, but her mind was far away. With a wave, she walked to the door and outside.

Full night had fallen while she'd been inside, and as she stepped out into the darkness around the Moondance Diner, she let it enfold her as much as she could, given the artificial city lights and the stupid skywriters projecting ads everywhere. She ignored those as she crossed the restaurant parking lot.

She climbed in her car at the back row of the lot, shutting out the noise by closing the door. There couldn't be any sounds in the background for this call, not with Conor's excellent hearing. This was the part she was dreading, but she had no choice.

Mika put her purse on the passenger seat, pulled her comm unit out of her pocket and punched in McCabe's comm. Exactly as she'd planned, she was connected to his voicemail. Adding just the right amount of frantic worry, she said, "Conor, it's Mika. I had a call from my cousin, and she needs help. She's with some guy who's been drinking, and she doesn't know anyone else at this party. I'm going to pick her up and get her back home." She added the location of the meeting with the minion for authenticity's sake, then disconnected. His unit would record the time, and her alibi would be solid if he started investigating.

Okay, relatively solid. Leaving the house early was one wrench in her story, but unless Conor quizzed his nosy neighbor, Mika figured she was safe.

Her bases covered, she should have felt better than she did, but as she tucked her comm in her pocket, Mika fought nausea. She'd lied again to Conor. "I'm sorry, McCabe," she whispered almost soundlessly. But strapping herself in, she started the car. She couldn't allow guilt to bog her down.

Mika drove the speed limit and parked a few blocks away from the rendezvous point; she'd walk the rest of the distance. Just in case.

She was in a business district, and this late at night, the area was deserted. It was eerie, like walking through a ghost town. Most of the office buildings were low-rise— maybe seven or eight stories—and the mirrored windows covering many added to the spookiness. Mika felt unsettled enough to cloak herself from human eyes.

A slight breeze played with the ends of her hair atop her head, and she tipped back her face to feel it. Wind was her ally, and it soothed her nerves—a bit. After a moment, she continued on. The street lamps glowed gently, but they didn't remove the strangeness.

She spotted a park a couple of blocks down, and realized it was the place mentioned by the minion. The small oasis of green tucked inside the steel-and-glass maze of Crimson City seemed oddly comforting, and Mika nearly laughed at herself. Why was she making such a production out of this?

The streetlight at the entrance was out; she noticed half a block closer and drew to a halt. Something made her shiver. Mika had been telepathically scanning since she'd parked, but now she probed the area carefully, deeply. She wasn't very early; the minion should be close . . . but she sensed nothing. It was as if some void blocked her abilities.

She stayed in the shadows of one of the buildings, unwilling to move forward until she sensed her rendezvous. Something felt wrong. Way wrong. The hair on her nape prickled. Mika probed more, but didn't pick up anyone— or anything. Slowly, almost reluctantly, she turned.

A figure was strolling toward her. He had waist-length blond hair, and on the sides of his face were two thin braids that he used to tie it back in a ponytail. One of the braids had something metallic threaded through it—Mika caught glints of light. The man was criminally gorgeous, with a face that would make any woman stop and look twice—maybe even three or four times.

If she didn't know what he was.

He hadn't cloaked completely. Mika couldn't sense his presence, couldn't hear him, but she saw him clearly. And only the Dark Ones wore their hair like that. Mika backed up a step and he smiled. Though it made him even prettier, the expression sent a shiver down her spine. She edged farther back.

The Dark One stopped maybe twenty feet away and dropped his cloaking. As Mika watched, he started to lift his hand. Her adrenaline surged and she looked around almost wildly. Flight or fight.

She chose flight.

Only, she couldn't move. He was doing something to the physical world around her. She fought, wanting nothing more than to escape before he reached her.

His smile broadened, became more real, but it wasn't a friendly, let's-go-have-a-beer grin. Mika's pulse beat even faster.

"Mahsei," the Dark One said. He inclined his head.

His tones were dulcet, but they sent repulsion through her body and Mika struggled even harder. This situation was *so* not good. Panic threatened to swamp her and she made herself take a deep breath, to think things through. Giving in to overwhelming emotion wouldn't help.

She couldn't move, that was fact, but what about her powers? Mika tested them quickly and found they still worked. Of course, given the type of demon this was, and the kind she was, that didn't offer much hope, but she'd take what she had and fight.

There was no question in her mind that this demon wanted her dead. The same energy that had surrounded the trap she and Conor found that first night now emanated from him. Without doubt, he'd been the one who'd created the snare, which made Mika wonder what else this monster was capable of. Had he broken the Council code and impersonated their minion, setting up a false meeting? Or had he found the minion and forced him to make the call?

Mika shook herself. It didn't matter how he'd drawn her here. What she had to concern herself with was getting away.

"The Council must truly be desperate to send one such as you," the Dark One said. He could have been discussing the weather for the amount of his apparent interest, and there was an edge of disdain in his voice.

"They didn't have many options," Mika admitted. It didn't surprise her that her assignment had drawn the attention of the Dark Ones. She'd never crossed them or done anything to anger them, so what else could it be? "But do you think it's fair to kill me? It's not as if I can refuse any request the leaders put to me."

Her hope to engage him in conversation was in vain. Instead of replying, the Dark One merely shrugged. Then, idly lifting his hand again, he shot an arc of fire at her.

Reflex kicked in and Mika called the wind. With all the strength she possessed, she blew the flame back at him. Mika couldn't singe him or extinguish his fire, but she was able to keep it from touching her.

"Pitiful," the Dark One commented, but he stopped his assault. "You're not going to be much of a challenge."

Mika half-laughed. "Sorry about that. Why don't you free me and see if that makes it more fun?"

For an instant, she thought his lips twitched in reply, but the smile was gone so fast that it must have been her imagination. But the Dark One did loose whatever held her in place. She couldn't run—it was too late for that—but maybe she could put up a halfway decent battle.

Her assailant sent another bolt of fire her way, and wind couldn't deter it. Quickly, Mika threw up the same barrier of dense air molecules she'd used with Conor, but the rope of flame stabbed through as if it weren't there. Mika barely had time to hit the ground. As heat warmed her cheek, she rolled, trying to get farther away.

Suddenly Mika realized her foe was toying with her; fire was probably the least of his powers. She was Mahsei, a demon of the air—not exactly the most powerful of branches. He could destroy her much easier than this.

She tried to think; there had to be some way to counter his attack, some way to go on the offensive, but she was so busy trying to keep him from cooking her that she didn't have a chance. She did notice one thing, though. He was trying to drive her to the entrance of the park. Mika hated the feeling of being herded, but if she stayed put, the Bak-Faru would char her. He discharged another gust of fire.

She started to drop, but at the last instant realized he was aiming low. She leaped instead, levitating herself away from danger.

The flames heated the soles of her tennis shoes, and Mika grimaced as she landed and twisted to avoid another blast. The Dark One laughed. *Good.* As long as he was amused, he'd keep playing with her. Buying time was her best option.

She used a light pole as cover. It wasn't much. Drawing air to her, she turned it into a small whirlwind and whipped it at the dark demon. For a second, it looked good. Then he held out a finger and her attack dissipated to nothing but a gentle breeze. It barely ruffled his hair.

"You can do no better than this, Mahsei?" he asked.

"I'm trying," she muttered, and he laughed again. Maybe she'd do better in a stand-up routine than combat. Or maybe her powers were the comedy. With a scowl, she ran. Glancing over her shoulder, she realized the bastard had actually melted the metal pole she'd hid behind. A ball of terror lodged in her throat. How the hell could she win against a foe like this?

Ducking behind a bench near the park entrance, Mika felt the heat from another blast of fire. While she was huddled there, she examined the dark maw of the entryway. She was close enough now to feel what she'd missed earlier: It was rigged with another trap.

Mika brought up the wind, blowing debris toward the dark demon. He roared with laughter. She didn't blame him; her defense was as pathetic as he'd claimed. Too bad she didn't have command of water—then she'd be able to put out his fire. Of course, if she could counteract his flame, the Dark One would probably bring some stronger magic into play.

Desperately she tried to harness elements of a storm. She had the potential to do this, although she'd never been successful in the past. Things looked good—clouds started to gather, to cover the face of the moon. But the Dark One sent out shot after shot of fire, hardly pausing between bursts.

The bench she hid behind smoldered, and Mika knew time was running out. She tried harder to call the storm, but while more clouds filled the sky, nothing else happened. Daring a quick glance away from her foe, she looked at the snare. What had Conor said happened to those who were caught? Another blast of flame ignited the bench. One more, and her meager cover would be destroyed.

McCabe's words came back to her then, something about demons screaming for a really long time when they were caught in the thing. Mika shuddered again. She was down to two choices, and she wasn't sure which would be worse. Die in the trap or die on the street.

Chapter Ten

Conor opened the door to The Crimson Jim and was immediately assaulted by blaring music and a cloud of smoke. The nightclub was tamer than many, and attracted an upwardly mobile clientele, but after ducking in and out of bars for hours, looking for his contacts, he'd had more than enough of these types of establishments.

Grimacing from the thumping bass, he moved deeper into the club. If he'd been protecting anyone but Mika, Conor would have called it quits an hour ago.

Mika. Every time he thought of her, he felt uneasy. Odds were, he was worrying about nothing. The shield around his home was solid; no one who didn't have permission to enter would get through to hurt her. Conor rolled his shoulders, trying to ease his tension. Maybe after he left here, it wouldn't hurt to give Mika a call and make sure she was okay.

Thinking of her made him frown. How the hell had she kept him prisoner? He'd left as soon as she'd quit doing whatever it was she'd done to the door. She'd probably had a good laugh over the haste he'd shown in escaping, but he was beyond caring about that. Mika could find something amusing in any situation anyhow, and damned if part of him didn't like that.

He shook his head. If he wanted to get out of here before the bar closed, he needed to keep his mind on business. Dodging a sea of bodies on the dance floor, he searched the club.

Mika hadn't asked him what his plan was for finding her stalker. Most people would want a rundown, but in her case, maybe the lack of curiosity wasn't that strange. She rarely behaved predictably, and he liked not having to answer dozens of questions about what he was doing or why he was doing it; though if she did ask, he'd tell her.

His approach was simple. Demons, no matter how hard they tried, seldom blended in for long. It wasn't appearance that gave them away—strong demons were able to shapeshift and indwell, and hell, with contact lenses he could pass for human. But it wasn't as easy to change behavior. Not long term. That was why he combed the paper every day looking for something that set off his internal alarm, and why he talked to people who might hear things that even *The Crimson Post* was unlikely to run.

He thought he'd had it today. The article had been buried in the Metro section on page six, but the small headline had immediately grabbed his attention. *Severed Head Found in East LA*. Granted, humans did stuff like this too, especially if they followed old lore on slaying vampires, but he'd still thought it was worth checking into.

Conor sidestepped a particularly enthusiastic dancing couple and continued scanning the sea of faces. It had been a demon kill, no doubt about that. The person hadn't been beheaded with a knife, axe or chainsaw. Looked like a claw. The LAPD was sure a fang or a dog was their killer, but Conor knew better. It had demon written all over it. He'd spent hours canvassing the area where they'd found the head, but had come up empty.

That was why he was in this club. He'd been trying to track down Marc Hayes since Nat had mentioned his name. The other freelancer was smooth, a good bullshitter, and people liked him. It stood to reason that if Hayes was asking questions, he might have gotten answers. Conor knew that he himself was viewed as antisocial, and not much fun when he did stop to talk.

Maybe Mika was right about him being more alive since she'd come along. It did sort of seem as if his world had burst into full color after a lifetime of monochrome.

He grimaced. She had him thinking too damn much, looking at things he'd never bothered to question. What he needed was to focus on finding Hayes, not to obsess over his woman. His woman? *A* woman. Conor dragged a hand through his hair. *Shit.*

Everything seemed to revolve around Mika now. She'd taken over his house, his job, his body and his mind. And the terrifying part wasn't that she'd done it in a matter of days, but that he *liked* it.

"Can I buy you a drink?" a sultry voice asked.

Conor hadn't realized he'd stopped walking. The woman standing in front of him was a petite redhead with big, dark blue eyes. Her energy said she was human, and her body language said she was interested. Here was a candidate for sex—to blow off the steam Mika had been building in him. He could take this woman back to her place, have some careful sex and walk away without losing any part of himself. That would foil Mika's teasing.

But the woman wasn't tall enough to satisfy; her eyes were too dark and her lips weren't curled in that I-dare-you expression that made him hot. In other words, she wasn't Mika. He desperately tried to summon some interest, but it just wasn't there.

"Sorry," Conor said, and stepped around her.

As soon as he was out of the redhead's view, he scowled. He'd known Mika was trouble the instant he looked into her eyes. Now she had him. Somehow, some way, when he wasn't watching, she'd put him down for the count. Now it was only a question of whether he should take Mika to bed or keep fighting it.

It would be more than sex with her, he realized. She'd take a part of him he'd never get back. Even after she returned to her life, as he was sure she would, she'd hold a piece of his soul. Mika was . . . Mika.

While there were moments of seriousness, moments when she probed his heart and dug around, the rest of the time she was careless. Surely it was her demon half warring with the human. It was a duality in her personality. At the end of this, she'd walk away. How many times had she referred to Orcus as home? Half a dozen? More? And she'd flat out said she preferred living in the demon world.

Then there was her personality. She was lively, light-hearted, and gregarious. He was none of those things. Even if he convinced her to stay for a while, at some point she'd grow bored with him—it was inevitable. If he were lucky, she'd remember him fondly from time to time, but he'd never be able to keep her. She was a lightning bolt, here and gone in the blink of an eye—and capable of leaving behind a great deal of damage.

No, Conor couldn't afford to allow her close. It would already hurt when she left, but joining their bodies would cross some line, erase the small amount of distance he'd been able to maintain. They couldn't have sex. No matter how badly he wanted her.

Stopping again, he released a deep breath and looked around. There was an air of desperation in the club. He understood it now: a fear of spending life alone. Before Mika, he'd preferred being by himself. Now Conor saw his existence would be empty without her.

It was an uncomfortable thought, but hiding wouldn't make the truth go away. He was too pragmatic to pretend nothing had changed. A man couldn't protect himself like an ostrich did—head in the sand and ass in the air.

Picturing Mika laughing over that thought, he made a

low growling sound and forced himself to continue searching the dance club. If he accomplished nothing else, he would keep her safe—and that meant gathering intel. He needed to know everything he could about the bastards who were after her.

Ten minutes later, he spotted the man he was looking for. If Conor had been human, he might have missed him; Hayes had staked a claim on a table in the darkest corner of the bar—not a place where he would be seen or hit on by the ladies. While there were other people nearby, the man seemed completely separate, and his eyes were never still.

Drifting deeper into the shadows, Conor took time to consider the situation. The man had his short brown hair spiked up till he almost looked like a bristling porcupine, and stubble covered his jaw. This wasn't the slick appearance Hayes usually sported. Was he undercover? That didn't make sense—not when it was common knowledge that he was a regular here.

Mika invaded his mind again. Damn it, he needed to focus on Hayes, but his nagging sense of apprehension was back. Conor reached for his comm unit before he knew what he was doing, before he realized the music and background noise would make it difficult to hear. Then he stopped himself, deciding to call Mika as soon as he was done. It was only to put himself at ease, anyway—not because he thought anything was wrong. But the faster he finished here, the faster he could check on her.

He threaded his way through the tables, not making any further effort to conceal himself; surprising someone like Hayes could be a very bad idea.

"McCabe," the man said when Conor got close. "I didn't think this was your kind of place."

"It's not." Conor pulled out a chair and sat, shifting so that his back was against the wall.

"Why don't you join me?" Hayes drawled.

Ignoring the sarcasm, Conor said, "What have you heard lately about demons in Crimson City?"

For about half a second, Hayes appeared startled. Then, without a word, he reached for his beer bottle, took a swig and looked at Conor over the top. Conor met his stare impassively.

"You ever consider trying some small talk, man? You know, a 'hi, how are you' before you start the questioning?"

"It's a waste of time." If Hayes was someone to finesse, Conor would have spread the bullshit, but it would have been without point. It also would have made Hayes suspicious.

The man shook his head and put down his beer bottle. "See? This is why they say you have communication issues. You gotta talk to people, develop a relationship. It's easier to get information when others *like* you."

"I haven't had any problems," Conor disagreed.

"Yeah, right. That's why you're here asking *me* about demons. If you were plugged into headquarters, you would have heard the rumors on your own." With a smirk, Hayes tipped his chair back against the wall and continued. "Of course, maybe you wouldn't know anyway. Not when you're busy playing house with that piece of a—"

"Finish that sentence," Conor warned, his voice quiet but deadly, "and you'll wish you hadn't." No one was going to disparage Mika, not without paying a price.

Hayes seemed delighted. "So that's how it is. Fascinating."

"No, what's fascinating is how the hell you know that I have someone staying with me." Nat being aware of it was one thing; he was downright eerie with his knowledge. But Hayes? Conor didn't like it.

"Is it supposed to be some hush-hush thing?"

The man's obvious amusement reignited Conor's temper. He reached out, grabbed the back of Hayes's chair and brought it down on all four legs. "Not hush-hush, but there's no reason why you should know about it," he growled.

For a moment, it appeared as if Hayes was going to try to stonewall him, and Conor wasn't going to tolerate it. If someone was passing along information about him and Mika, he was damn well going to know who and why. Then he'd hunt that person down and put a stop to it.

Finally Hayes shrugged and said, "It's no big deal. We have a mutual acquaintance who mentioned her."

"Who?" Conor wanted answers. Now.

Maybe the fact that he was running out of patience got through to Hayes, because the man didn't screw around any more. "Calls himself Nat. I don't know his last name, but he's weird."

Great. Nat. Conor didn't know how he'd shut the man up. Hell, he couldn't even find him when he wanted. And odds were good Nat would lie low if he knew Conor were pissed at him. Then a thought occurred to Conor. "Why the hell were the two of you discussing my houseguest?"

"We were talking about you. I commented on how scarce you'd been lately, and Nat told me who you were busy with." Hayes's smirk returned. "And before you ask why you were a topic of conversation, I'll tell you." He reached for his beer, took another pull, then rotated the bottle slowly on the table. "It connects, in a roundabout way, with what you were asking."

"How does my name tie in with monsters?" Conor asked anyway. The last thing he wanted was anyone discussing him. Especially not Nat, who knew he was part demon—it had been made very clear at their last meeting—and about Mika.

"I was asking him about demons, and he mentioned you were asking too," Hayes said.

"What—"

"Shut up and let me tell you," Hayes interrupted.

Conor narrowed his eyes and pinned the man with a

glare. It didn't work, though, and Conor gave up—he wanted this information too much to get caught up in a pissing match. "Go on."

"Did you know there was some top-secret government task force looking into demons?"

Hayes threw that out there casually, but he must have known the impact it would have. It left Conor stunned. Nat had mentioned that humans might be interested in an alliance, but this task force meant actual official involvement. He found it hard to believe that the same people who were trying to rein in vampires and werewolves would want demons on the loose. "No," he said, when it became obvious Hayes was waiting for a response.

"The rumors aren't clear on why or how this group learned to contact the underworld, only that they have. But the most interesting thing about this is that the entire task force has gone missing. No one knows what happened to them."

Conor kept his mouth shut, but his mind was spinning. Were these missing humans tied to the demons Nat talked about? If the info was right, there were at least five in town—each from the darkest branches. And then there was Mika. How did she fit into this? Could she have stumbled onto something important without realizing? Was that why her life was in danger?

He needed to quiz her on a few points, including how often she crossed the veil. The way she worded things, there was no doubt she frequented the Overworld, but did her father summon her every time? And if he'd called her out this time as she claimed, why wasn't he around to protect her?

"You're not going to ask any questions?"

Conor put aside thoughts of Mika. "You told me to shut up, remember?" he retorted.

Hayes muttered, clinked his beer bottle against the ashtray twice and then looked up again. He looked torn, then obviously decided to speak. "Something happened before the task force vanished. I don't know what, but you could smell the fear, see their jumpiness. Then poof, every one of them was gone, including my sister. Foster sister," he corrected immediately.

"You know anyone who was on this team besides your sister?"

"A couple names, not the entire group. But their disappearance was why I was talking to Nat. Officially, there's no word. Personally, I think the task force succeeded and brought demons through. I also think they got more than they bargained for."

"Safe bet," Conor agreed. Damn safe bet. Mika was afraid of these dark demons for a reason, and if someone who was part-demon was terrified, humans would be no match for them.

"It was natural for Nat to mention you were looking into demons, too. . . ." Hayes went on.

Damn Nat. Conor heard the question Hayes wasn't asking, and knew he was going to have to say something. "My houseguest is being hunted by some—she hired me to keep her safe."

"How did she catch their attention?" Hayes asked.

"You don't need to know."

Hayes finally stopped playing with his beer and put his hands flat on the table. "She wasn't a member of the task force, was she? You'd tell me that, right?"

"She's not part of that task force, but that's the last thing I'm saying about her. Client privilege, you know."

Hayes seemed mollified. "Fair enough."

"So. . . . You're looking into the disappearances? Officially?"

Hayes seemed glad to return the favor: "You don't need to know."

Conor scowled. He hated hearing his own words echoed back, but he didn't press. Instead he kept his focus on getting info that would help him keep Mika safe.

"So . . . did you find out anything useful about these demons from Nat?"

"You mean, beyond what types are here and how dangerous they are? Nope. Nat tell *you* anything?"

"Nope," Conor agreed. "But I think he knows more."

"I do too." Hayes grinned, looking more like the man Conor was used to running into at headquarters. "I also know there's no way to get him to share something he's decided not to pass along. I've tried to research him and haven't even been able to prove he exists. If his info weren't always solid . . ."

"I know," Conor agreed. He paused, then decided he better pass the info along: "Nat brought up your name too, that's why I came looking for you. But if I've got the timing right, you talked to him after I did."

With a scowl, Hayes cursed. "I wish I could pick up half the damn intel that man gets, but I don't like this. It sounds as if the son of a bitch is maneuvering us. What do you think he's up to?"

Conor shrugged. "I don't know, but he might bear watching."

"Provided either of us can find him again."

"Yeah," Conor agreed grimly. "If you discover anything else about these demons, I'd appreciate a call."

"Ditto," Hayes replied.

Conor decided to change topics. "So, who are you hoping to spot?" he asked. "That's why you're hiding in the corner, right? Don't know how much good it's going to do you, Hayes. Everyone's aware you hang out here."

That wiped the smile off the man's face. He said, "If I was worried about that, I would have gone to more effort in disguising myself than using hair gel."

"Which means you're hoping someone in particular spots you and comes over. Someone who you'd like to meet in a dark place." Now Conor smirked, enjoying turning the tables. "Who is she?"

"Don't you have somewhere else to be, McCabe?" Hayes responded.

Thoughts of Mika, naked and straddling him, popped into Conor's head. Shit, did he need this? He had to keep his mind off her for a few more minutes. Pulling out a card, he scribbled a series of numbers on it. "Here's my comm code. Use it if you find out something about those demons."

Hayes glanced down and tucked the scrap of paper away before saying, "You didn't put your comm code on your business cards?"

Conor shook his head. "If I put my number on it, people would think I wanted them to call."

Hayes shook his head and reached into his pocket. "You really are antisocial, man." He flipped his own card at Conor. "My code *is* on there. You remember to use it too."

Standing, Conor slipped the card into the back pocket of his jeans and, with a nod, walked away. He was aware that Hayes watched him until the crowd hid him from view, but he didn't worry about it; the man wasn't going to follow.

Outside, it was much quieter. Conor reached for his comm unit, but he felt someone come up behind him. Forgetting the comm, he drew power as he turned and pulled his arm back to hurl it. But before he could fire an energy blast, he recognized Nat.

"Whoa, you've got a hair-trigger tonight," the man said calmly; but Conor noticed he kept his hands in plain sight.

"Why the hell are you sneaking up on me?"

"Can I help it if you're not paying attention?" Nat looked around before closing the distance and saying quietly, "I have something for you. Let's go around the corner."

Conor eyed the dark alley suspiciously. An hour ago, he probably wouldn't have given much thought to following Nat, but after talking to Hayes, Conor was leery. "Hayes had a couple of interesting things to say about you."

"And now you want to know what game I'm playing."

Nat grinned, appearing entertained. "Can't blame you, but you're looking for conspiracies where there are none. I thought the two of you should work together, not duplicate efforts, nothing more sinister than that. I knew it was a longshot, though. Hayes is as much a loner as you are, McCabe."

Shaking his head, Conor silently disagreed, but he wasn't going to argue. "What do you have for me?"

Nat looked around again, and some instinct told Conor the man was nervous, that he wanted off the street and away from the streetlights pronto. "I know what kind of demon you are, and that you can kill me with one good shot," Nat said softly. "I'm not setting you up, honest, but we can't talk here."

When Conor gave a nod, Nat didn't wait. He all but scurried into the dark opening of the alley. Conor didn't hurry. Reaching out, he scanned for a foreign energy sig, but sensed nothing unusual. When he joined Nat, he said, "You didn't seem afraid of the dark demons at our last meeting."

"Let's just say I had a refresher course on what they're capable of and leave it at that." Nat took another hurried survey of the area, then pulled out something from beneath his windbreaker. "Here." He held out the weapon butt first.

Conor took it, examined it. It was slightly bigger than a pistol, bulkier, but definitely not a toy. "What is it?"

"The humans who were experimenting with summonings created it. According to their notes, it's killed every demon they've tested it on. Thought you might want it."

"How'd you get it?" Conor had a lot of other questions, but he started with the most basic.

"Long story, McCabe, long story. This is the prototype and I took all the notes and schematics. I've already destroyed those, so you don't have to worry about the weapon being recreated and used against you or your girlfriend."

"Why give this to me?" Conor asked.

"Instead of keeping it myself or giving it to Hayes?" Nat shook his head. "I'm going underground—you won't see me again until the dark ones are dead. Yeah, I'm frightened, and I'm man enough to admit it. Why you and not Hayes? I think you have a better shot at killing the Bak—" He stopped short. "A better shot at killing them than he does. And if your powers aren't strong enough to take them down, you might need this."

"Why should I believe you?" Conor asked.

"Because I've never lied to you or to your ex-partner." Nat edged toward the mouth of the alley.

"Where'd you run into the dark demons?" Conor pushed.

"That severed head you were investigating tonight? That was supposed to be me. Take them down, McCabe." Nat stepped out of the alley. "Good luck."

Conor didn't waste any time reaching the sidewalk, but Nat was already gone. What the hell was that man?

He heard a giggle and tucked the new weapon beneath his jean jacket just as the nightclub door opened and a couple stepped out. The woman laughed again, and the pair strolled away arm in arm.

Eyeing the door, Conor contemplated going in and telling Hayes what had happened. He had promised to keep the other man informed, but the idea of reentering the club didn't appeal. He'd call Hayes, Conor decided. After he talked to Mika.

Mika. His uneasiness was back and stronger now. Conor reached for his comm unit and flipped it open. He was already dialing his home code before he realized the unit didn't light up. Hitting the reset button didn't bring it back online. He checked the power chip next and discovered it was dead. With a curse, he closed the unit and looked around. Across the street and up about a block was a twenty-four hour drugstore. It would cost him an arm and a leg, but they'd have power units there.

Climbing into his pickup, Conor drove over to the store, parked, ran in, and emerged with the chip he needed. As soon as he was back in his truck, he changed power units and called Mika. There was no answer.

Up till now, he'd been able to keep his anxiety in check by reminding himself of the protection around his house; but Mika wasn't picking up the comm, and worry flooded him. He was frowning at the display, trying to reassure himself that she was only in the shower or something, when he noticed the message indicator was on. Almost reluctantly, Conor hit the button and brought the comm unit back to his ear.

"Conor, it's Mika." His blood ran cold as he heard her voice. Once he had the location, Conor didn't bother listening to the rest of the message. He put his truck in gear and squealed out of his parking spot onto the road.

Damn. No wonder he'd felt uneasy when he'd been in the club. Mika had been off his property and completely unshielded. Maybe he was overreacting and she was on her way back to his house already. Maybe he'd arrive at the place in question and find her healthy, consoling her cousin. *Maybe.* But the address she'd given wasn't a residential area, so unless the kid had been at a rave or some other outlaw party, this was a setup and Mika was in a shitload of trouble. Hell, she might be dead already.

Conor pressed down on the accelerator and blew through two red lights.

He was past it before he saw Mika's sports car parked on the street. Conor slammed on his brakes, put his truck in reverse and pulled over to it. He got out and looked in the passenger window. Nothing was inside except a pink purse. The hood was cold, which meant she'd been parked here for a while.

His adrenaline surged. This wasn't a good sign.

Taking a deep breath, Conor centered himself and

reached out with his senses, looking for her energy signature. He found it almost immediately. She was a few blocks away.

Conor ran, using all his inhuman speed. He wanted nothing more than to hear Mika laugh about the way he'd overreacted, but he didn't think that was going to happen. Not when his instincts were shrieking like this.

When he sensed another presence, Conor cloaked completely and rounded the corner full throttle. He drew to a halt as he saw the figure standing in the center of the street shooting fire from his hands. Mika—where the hell was Mika? He searched for her, finally pinpointing her energy, and focused his gaze in that direction. Her head popped up over the top of a bench, then ducked down again as another stream of fire streaked out at her.

Rushing past a melted streetlight, Conor pushed aside his fear. The bench was in flames, and Mika's assailant was laughing madly. One more shot and she'd be exposed. But he'd be in position before she was defenseless.

Clouds rolled in, as if a storm were trying to form, but Conor ignored them. Instead, he probed the demon and recognized the sig. This was the same bastard who'd created the snare for Mika. Which also meant . . . this had to be one of the Bak-Faru!

Almost as soon as he thought the name, the demon let loose another burst of flame in Mika's direction and turned to look at him. He shouldn't know Conor was there, not when Conor had put enough power into his cloak to hide from any demon, but there was no doubt in Conor's mind that the fire starter knew precisely where he was. Conor recalled how Mika had told him not to say the name of those demons aloud, to not even think it. Maybe he should have listened to her.

When the monster turned back to Mika and raised his hand again, Conor summoned his own power. It jolted him to realize upon which he was drawing. Quickly stopping himself, he summoned fire instead—he didn't need to use *that* when he had other weapons at his disposal which were just as deadly. Weapons that wouldn't cost him his humanity.

Shaken by his lapse, Conor moved, putting himself in front of his woman before he unmasked. He spared a quick glance to assure himself that she was okay, then prepared to attack with both fire and energy spells.

But the dark demon was gone. Or cloaked.

Conor searched hard for even the smallest hint of the bastard's energy. He didn't find anything.

"We need to get out of here," he whispered to Mika. "Stay close." When she nodded, he started another sweep of the area. He had a natural energy shield around him that protected him from magic, and he was sure he could use that to block any shots at her. If he could just figure out which direction they'd come from.

Conor kept scanning and felt her doing the same. "There's another trap nearby," he realized.

"Yes, at the entrance to the park. It's subtler than the one a few nights ago, but I bet it'll get the job done."

This one wasn't baited, Conor realized, but then it didn't need to be; the Dark One had been driving Mika into it. Conor guessed that if she hadn't cooperated and triggered it, the bastard would have killed her where she crouched. A frisson of fear shot through him at the thought, but he pushed it aside. The danger wasn't necessarily over.

"When I give the signal, we're running for that building, the one with the flower shop on the corner. As soon as you reach it, put your back against the wall," he ordered. Mika nodded, and he relaxed an iota. She wasn't going to argue with him. He drew flame and held it in reserve, ready to throw if there was any indication of that demon.

"Try to stay with me, don't get too far ahead or behind. Use me as a shield." Another nod, this one so emphatic that the hair standing up on Mika's head bobbed. "Okay, let's go."

She followed his instructions to the letter. As soon as

Mika's back was against the building, Conor put himself in front of her. He checked the area again. Mika stayed still. She didn't talk or fidget or tease. And that told Conor clearer than words how seriously she took this situation.

The yowl of an alley cat broke the silence, and only then did Conor realize there'd been a dearth of night noises from the time he'd arrived until now. As the tom strolled past, giving him and Mika a lot of space, his tension eased away. Animals were good at sensing demons.

"I think he's gone," he said.

Mika moved out from behind him. For a minute Conor gazed down at her; then he reached out and with his thumb wiped at the smudge of dirt on her cheek. The only thing he could think was how damn close she'd come to dying. If he hadn't felt uneasy enough to check on her . . . The horror he felt was staggering.

Conor dragged Mika against him and held on tightly. He felt her hands rub his back as he lowered his head to hers. The scent of her shampoo—the scent of *Mika*—filled his senses. His mouth found hers. The kiss started out deep and became more urgent. Her taste, the feel of her lips under his, none of it helped his adrenaline subside. Instead, that spiked higher. Damn it to hell, he could have *lost* her tonight.

It was one thing to know she'd walk away at some point—at least she'd be alive, even if she wasn't with him—but tonight Mika could have died. The thought was intolerable. He could survive Mika leaving him, but he would never recover from her death. How could she be so careless about her safety? Didn't she understand how important she was to him? Conor broke the kiss.

"What were you thinking?" he hissed.

He saw about half a dozen different emotions cross her face, but he read one thing plainly: she knew he was beyond furious. There was no indication that she was intimidated by it.

"It might be a better idea to have this fight at home," she said.

And she was right. He took a deep breath, then another. Just because the immediate vicinity was clear, they weren't out of the woods yet. The Dark One could be lying in wait along the route to their vehicles, and no way in hell was Conor risking her again simply because she had him so screwed up that he couldn't see straight.

But she'd referred to his house as her home. Damn, she was going to make him insane yet.

When he had control back, he said, "You're right. And, honey? You can count on us finishing this once we're safe."

"I know." Her smile should have warned him what was coming next. "I just hope we finish more than the argument."

"Mika," he warned.

"What?"

The innocent look that accompanied her question made him growl. "Could you try not to play with my mind until we're back at the house? Please?"

She nodded, her expression overly solemn, and Conor decided that was good enough. He said, "Stick close to me, and if I tell you to do something, obey immediately—got it?"

"Got it."

They traversed the distance to their vehicles without incident, but Conor wasn't ready to breathe easy. He hooked his arm around Mika's waist and pulled her away from her car. "Wait. I want to check things out."

He inspected his truck first. It was clean. He opened the driver's-side door and put her inside to wait, then went over her car. Mika didn't argue, and for the first time, he realized how seriously she was actually taking this. Her earlier humor had probably been more to help relieve her tension. He should have figured it out sooner, but he'd been dealing with his own reaction.

A sense of something off stopped him. Rigged to the engine he found a trap a human would never spot, not created as it was with demon powers. He couldn't even tell what would trigger the energy bomb, not for sure, but there were a couple of possibilities that leapt to mind. It could be geared to Mika's sig, going off when she was within a certain distance for a particular length of time. Or it could be set to explode when the engine hit a designated vibration. Either way, he wouldn't try to disarm it tonight. It was beyond him right now.

Climbing into his truck, he used his hip to bump Mika over to the passenger seat. Without giving her time to say anything, he slammed the door and drove away.

"What about my car?" she asked.

The explosion was strong enough to rock the pickup, so Conor figured that was answer enough. He stepped on the accelerator. The sooner he had Mika back inside his house, the better.

Chapter Eleven

Mika heard the small *snick* as Conor closed the front door, and she moved deeper into the great room. From the corner of her eye she saw him head for the light switch, and in the next instant, the room was illuminated. She took a deep breath and waited. It wouldn't take long for him to start chewing her out, not the way he'd been strangling the steering wheel on the drive home. Anger combined with adrenaline probably continued to churn through his body, and he must be more than ready to release it.

She turned when she felt McCabe behind her, and realized he was furious. Even through his contact lenses, his eyes were glowing redder than she'd ever seen. He vibrated with pent-up energy.

"Why *the hell* did you leave the house?" His voice was almost as quiet and deep as it had been earlier on the street, and that told her clearly how enraged he still was.

Licking her lips, she said, "My cousin—"

"Is an adult?"

"She's only nineteen, and she's as close to me as if she were my sister." Both statements were true. Mika would be as honest with Conor as possible. She curled her fingers into her palms. No matter how much she wished she'd never made any promise to the leaders of Orcus, she had.

"So she—or someone you believed to be her—called and you went haring off without a second thought."

"I *did* think about it." She'd planned carefully how she was going to cover her tracks. That counted. "I even called you," she defended.

McCabe seemed unimpressed. He closed the distance between them and leaned forward. "You left a message," he growled.

"How did you want me to handle it? You were unreachable, and I could never leave Kimi in a dangerous situation."

"What you should have done," he said, "was continue calling until you got hold of me, then *I* could have gone and rescued your cousin."

Mika was unable to speak for a moment. If she'd asked, he'd have driven over to get Kimi? It was that simple, and it stunned her. Demons kept their word to the letter, but they never, ever went one step beyond their oaths. Rescuing Kimi was much more than he'd promised. She felt another shift inside her, and she wasn't sure whether or not it was a good thing. Reaching out, she rested her hand on the center of Conor's chest. The beating of his heart was strong and solid. Just like he was.

"I didn't know when or even if I'd be able to get through to you," she finally said. She licked her lips again, uneasy because she was the reason his comm had been disabled.

Apparently he had no good response, because he switched tactics. "It never occurred to you that the call might be part of a trap?" he asked. "You're being hunted and this wasn't the first attempt made on your life."

"I believed the call was legitimate," she snapped. And so she had. Her rendezvous had given her the passwords the Council had told her. She hadn't doubted for a moment that he was the minion she was supposed to report to.

"Damn it, you could have been killed! Do you understand that?" She felt him inhale deeply, probably trying to regain his self-command. "If I'd been even five minutes later . . ."

Stroking his chest, trying to soothe him, Mika said quietly, "I know, and if you think I'm not scared, you're wrong. The dark demons apparently want me dead, and that's terrifying."

He put his hands on her waist and pulled her against him. "Are you frightened enough to stay in my house from now on? That's the big question."

"Until it's safe, I won't go outside—not unless you tell me otherwise. I promise."

McCabe's eyes closed and he wrapped her in a hug. "That's all I wanted to hear, Mika." The anger was gone. "It about took ten years off my life to see you hiding behind that bench. Don't do that to me again."

"If it took ten years from you, it probably cost me twenty," Mika joked. But it was hard to inject a light note into her voice as she recalled what had happened. She put her other hand on Conor's chest and pushed him back a few inches. "Now, let's talk about the way you placed yourself in danger tonight."

"I wasn't in danger."

"That's a bunch of bullshit. You put yourself between me and a dark demon. You protected me with your body. What the hell were you thinking?"

"I can take care of myself. Don't worry," he snapped.

"Don't worry? Don't worry!" His lack of concern ignited her temper. "You've never faced anyone from this branch before, and you don't know what they're capable of. I do. You can't dismiss them lightly." She gave him a shove. "You know how many times I've told you demons aren't all evil, they're dark? Well, not this group. These are evil. You remember that. They're unbeatable. They're—"

"You don't know what I'm capable of."

The hardness in his voice gave her pause. Just what kinds of powers did he have, anyway? She shook her head. It didn't matter. "I've seen firsthand what these guys have done to demons stronger than Kiverians. Don't shrug it off." She cupped her palm around his jaw. "Do you hear me?"

"You really are worried about me," he said, incredulous.

The absurdity of that infuriated her. Hadn't anyone ever been concerned about him? Someone caring about his well-being shouldn't be so novel an experience. "Yes, I'm worried about you." She stroked his cheek. "You may not put any value on your life, but I do. You're important to me, and I don't want to see you take any unnecessary risks."

So many expressions crossed Conor's face in less than a blink that Mika was unable to name them. "I'm going to protect you. You *hired* me. And I gave you my promise," he added more importantly.

"You could have kept your promise without shielding my body with yours." She knew how their bargain had been phrased, and a demon who'd agreed to the deal Mc-Cabe had said yes to, never would have done such a thing. It humbled her—and horrified her. Conor was honorable and courageous. And what was she? A liar.

"Mika—"

"No," she interrupted, before he could start arguing. "You know I'm right. You could have done a lot of things that weren't as risky and still been true to your promise. I don't want you dying for me. *I don't want that!*"

"Hush, Mika," he said, trying to calm her. "I don't plan to die, but I am planning to keep you safe. Besides, these dark demons are nothing but bullies. Look how fast he ran when someone more equal showed up."

Mika couldn't enjoy Conor's smile. Her blood ran icy cold. "That demon did not leave because you were more of a match for him. He left because you didn't fit into his

GET UP TO 5 FREE BOOKS!

Sign up for one of our book clubs today, and we'll send you
FREE* BOOKS
just for trying it out...with no obligation to buy, ever!

HISTORICAL ROMANCE BOOK CLUB

Travel from the Scottish Highlands to the American West, the decadent ballrooms of Regency England to Viking ships. Your shipments will include authors such as CONNIE MASON, CASSIE EDWARDS, LYNSAY SANDS, LEIGH GREENWOOD, and many, many more.

LOVE SPELL BOOK CLUB

Bring a little magic into your life with the romances of Love Spell—fun contemporaries, paranormals, time-travels, futuristics, and more. Your shipments will include authors such as KATIE MACALISTER, SUSAN GRANT, NINA BANGS, SANDRA HILL, and more.

As a book club member you also receive the following special benefits:

- **30% OFF all orders through our website & telecenter!**
  (Plus, you still get 1 book FREE for every 5 books you buy!)
- **Exclusive access to special discounts!**
- **Convenient home delivery and 10 days to return any books you don't want to keep.**

There is no minimum number of books to buy, and you may cancel membership at any time. See back to sign up!

*Please include $2.00 for shipping and handling.

YES! ☐

Sign me up for the **Historical Romance Book Club** and send my THREE FREE BOOKS! If I choose to stay in the club, I will pay only $13.50* each month, a savings of $6.47!

YES! ☐

Sign me up for the **Love Spell Book Club** and send my TWO FREE BOOKS! If I choose to stay in the club, I will pay only $8.50* each month, a savings of $5.48!

NAME: _____

ADDRESS: _____

_____

TELEPHONE: _____

E-MAIL: _____

☐ **I WANT TO PAY BY CREDIT CARD.**

☐ VISA ☐ MasterCard ☐ DISCOVER

ACCOUNT #: _____

EXPIRATION DATE: _____

SIGNATURE: _____

Send this card along with $2.00 shipping & handling for each club you wish to join, to:

Romance Book Clubs
20 Academy Street
Norwalk, CT 06850-4032

Or fax (must include credit card information!) to: 610.995.9274. You can also sign up online at www.dorchesterpub.com.

*Plus $2.00 for shipping. Offer open to residents of the U.S. and Canada only. Canadian residents please call 1.800.481.9191 for pricing information.
If under 18, a parent or guardian must sign. Terms, prices and conditions subject to change. Subscription subject to acceptance. Dorchester Publishing reserves the right to reject any order or cancel any subscription.

JOIN NOW!

agenda, whatever it was." She brought her other hand up, cradling his face between her palms and tried to convey her urgency. "If he'd wanted, we'd both be dead right now. He could have killed you as easily as swatting a fly."

McCabe looked too damn patronizing. How the hell could she get him to understand the danger when she couldn't tell him about the legend, about the incantation, and how it was believed he was the one who could invoke it? Whether or not that was true she couldn't say, but maybe the dark demons believed it, and maybe that's why the one who'd attacked her had withdrawn: He didn't want to risk Conor.

From time to time in Orcus, there'd been rumbles that the Dark Ones wanted to reclaim Earth. Demons had once ruled this overworld and used humans as their thralls, but something had happened to see her people imprisoned. All demons. With the veil in place, world domination had been nothing except talk—for the most part. But now the Dark Ones believed they'd found someone to lower the barrier.

"You don't believe me," she said quietly. "You think that because I'm weak I'm overestimating their abilities." Mika quirked up the left side of her mouth. "There's nothing I can say to convince you that it's more than my perception, and I'm sorry for that." More sorry than she could say.

Conor tugged her against him, and Mika let her arms slide to the back of his neck. She took comfort in the warmth of his body, in the strength of it. Resting her cheek against his chest, she clung to him.

"I appreciate your concern," he said. "I really do."

"Yeah." She bet he did, since she might be the first person who'd shown any regard for his health.

Conor shifted and stared into her eyes. Then, after a long moment, his lips curved—but it was unlike any smile she'd seen from him in the past. Before she could figure it out, his mouth claimed hers. There was no restraint in the kiss and she returned it the same way, with everything she had. With everything she felt.

His hands went to her hair, freeing it from its clip. She heard the barrette hit the floor and slide, then Conor's fingers were tangled in the strands, holding her still as he devoured her. The taste of him, the feel of his tongue sliding along hers, sent a thrill through Mika's entire body before it settled between her thighs. She clutched his waist more firmly, but couldn't get close enough, not with his hands keeping her away.

Murmuring a protest, Mika tried to convey her displeasure, but he must not have understood. Thwarted on one score, she decided to work on another. She tugged his T-shirt free of his jeans and slid her hands under the cotton knit. Conor's skin was warm, his muscles hard, and she ran her fingers over him, sinking deeper into the simple pleasure of caressing his back.

He broke their kiss, looked down at her and then released his hold on her face. Mika growled, a low animal noise. A part of her registered shock that the sound had emerged, but she couldn't take time to focus on it. Not when every part of her protested Conor's sudden distance.

He shucked his jean jacket and his weapons, then yanked his shirt over his head and tossed it aside. "Wait," he ordered, when she reached for him.

Impatiently, almost quivering with restrained need, Mika waited. And she was rewarded when Conor reached for the hem of her long-sleeved T-shirt. She lifted her arms as he pulled, helping him get it off her. As he stared at her chest, her nipples peaked, pushing against the lace of her bra. Antsy with his continued delay, she shifted from foot to foot. "Damn it, McCabe, hurry up," she complained.

Conor's smile increased her desire. She expected him to strip the bra off her, but he didn't. Instead, he ran his index fingers underneath the edging. It wasn't nearly enough. Before she could protest, McCabe tugged the cups below her breasts, baring her, then he stared some more.

Mika looked down, decided the positioning of the bra did a wonderful job of showcasing her assets and left it where it was. A little bit of clothing sometimes did more to heat a man up than complete nakedness. But her man just stood and ogled her.

Since Conor didn't seem to be able to get in gear, she decided to jumpstart him. Mika slipped the middle finger of her right hand into her mouth to remove it glistening with moisture. She knew how steamed up McCabe became if she touched herself. When her finger was nice and slick, she ran it over a nipple.

His reaction was immediate, and exactly what she'd hoped for. He moved, smashing her back against the wall. Mika hummed with satisfaction and rubbed against his chest. Her nipples stiffened more as they were abraded by his warm skin and chest hair. He went still, as if savoring her touch, before demanding another open-mouthed kiss.

Conor's muscled body wasn't the only thing that was hard, and Mika dug her fingers into his shoulders, trying to drag him closer. He helped. His hands gripped her hips and pulled her into his erection. His groan was muffled by their kiss.

As he kneaded her bottom, Conor trailed his mouth down to her throat. He nuzzled there before nipping at her pulse point. The light sting of his teeth against her neck had Mika arching, pleasure rocketing through her. He used his tongue to soothe the spot, but that wasn't what she wanted. "Bite me more," she told him breathlessly.

McCabe obeyed. Mika dropped her head back, letting him have complete access. Lost in arousal, she hardly noticed him lifting her, not until his mouth found her left breast. Mika held his head, her fingers splayed through his sun-streaked brown hair, and wrapped her legs around his waist. Damn, the man knew how to drive her wild—he used his lips, tongue and teeth until the noises she made were totally animal. Totally demonic.

He took his time before moving to her other breast.

Mika wanted to stroke him, but the position in which he had her only gave her access to his head, shoulders and upper back. She couldn't even rock against him, since she was up too high. If he were human, she would count on him needing to put her down before too much longer, but with his demon strength, Conor could hold her up indefinitely.

"I need to touch you," she gasped.

"Tough." His reply was nearly unintelligible, since he didn't release the nipple he was teasing.

"McCabe!"

Ignoring her, he raised her higher and bit the underside of her breast. Mika felt her eyes go unfocused. She gave up—she was Conor's, and he could do whatever he wanted with her for as long as he wanted to do it.

He made her whimper before he lowered her back to her feet. Mika's knees buckled, and if Conor hadn't been holding her, she would have sunk to the floor. Instead, with a smug smile, he tightened his grip.

"Arrogant," she accused, her voice thick.

His grin widened. She felt his fingers on the clasp of her bra, then felt the tautness beneath her breasts give way. He stripped the garment from her and pitched it to the side. With one arm around her to keep her upright, Conor raised his hand to her face and smoothed her hair back to study her. The stop made her wonder what was going through his head. She knew one thing, though; if he thought he was calling a halt now, the man better think again.

Reaching for the button at his waist, Mika opened his jeans. His hand covered hers as she started to work the zipper. For a moment she believed he was stopping her, and she was ready to bang her head against the wall, but that wasn't his intent. Instead, he lowered the zipper himself, and while she was unable to see his expression, his movements felt careful. That made her recall that he wasn't wearing undershorts. The throbbing between her thighs intensified.

As soon as his hand was clear, Mika reached inside his jeans and ran the backs of her fingers up the side of his shaft. It was a small stroke, his pants were in the way, but it was enough to make Conor jerk.

She had about a second to appreciate the response before he had both her hands pinned against the wall above her head. His mouth ravished hers, demanding compliance and reciprocation. McCabe used his weight to keep her in place while he attacked the fastening of her jeans. He wasn't happy with merely undoing them, however; he pushed them past her hips, and Mika wriggled to help him. Their bodies slid against each other as they both worked to free her of pants.

They managed to get the jeans to her calves before progress came to a screeching halt. He left them there and moved his hand to the flesh exposed by her high-cut panties. There he traced patterns over her flank, stroked the back of her thigh, and when he tucked his fingers under the elastic to grip her butt, she went still.

Desire galvanized her to action. Mika stepped on the back of one sneaker, then the other to get them off. With her shoes out of the way, she lifted a leg, trying to pull out of the faded blue denim. The shift in position pressed McCabe more firmly against her. He broke their kiss with a low groan and her eyes closed as she relished the insistent prodding of his flesh against hers.

She wasn't sure how he did it, but her jeans ended up puddled at her feet. Conor lifted her out of them and strode from the room. Something inside her eased as he put her on the bed and covered her with his body. He wouldn't back out now. Right?

"Get out of those jeans." She nearly growled the words.

"What?"

Instead of answering, she shoved at his waistband, trying to get him naked.

"You're impatient," he told her, but it didn't sound like a complaint.

McCabe got off the bed, but he didn't strip like she'd ordered. "Hang on," he said.

Mika propped herself up on her elbows in time to watch him head out the door. She was going to kill him. No jury in the world would convict her after she told them how many times he'd left her wanting. When she heard him leave the house, she dropped back to the mattress and put her arm over her eyes.

Who said Mahsei weren't scary demons? She'd managed to drive Conor out of his own home.

But not permanently. She sat up when he reentered the room. "You're back."

"Did you think I wouldn't be?" He didn't give her time to answer. "I had to get these out of the truck before things went any farther." Conor tossed a box of condoms on the nightstand.

"Three dozen?" she teased.

"I can always run out and get more." The delivery was deadpan, and it took her a minute to realize he was making a joke. Delighted, she laughed. Until he reached for his pants.

As he pushed his jeans off, Mika caught her breath. The man was magnificent. He fished a condom out of the box. Without taking her eyes from him, she lifted her hips and slid her panties off. She wanted nothing to impede him when he came back to bed.

His eyes ran over her, drinking in every inch. Shifting restlessly, she waited for him. And waited. Mika ran her fingers over her abdomen, then stopped.

"Yeah," Conor said thickly. "Touch yourself for me."

Maybe she'd teased him with that one time too many. "I want *you* touching me," she said.

"I will." He climbed on the bed and sat between her ankles. His hands parted her thighs further, exposing her most intimate flesh. "But I want to watch you touch yourself."

"Will you do it too?" she asked.

He shook his head almost before she'd finished. He looked sheepish. "I'm . . . too close."

For a moment, neither of them spoke, just stared at

each other. Mika knew she could break him, have him on top of her and inside her in seconds. He *was* close, she could see that. But how much hotter could she make him if she did as he wanted? How much better would it be, the longer they felt this uncontrollable desire?

Smiling slightly, she glided her hand down from where it rested on her stomach and opened herself, arching her hips to give Conor a really good view. Since she was so wet already, she didn't bother to moisten her fingers. Slowly she teased herself, and gave some gasps and moans for his enjoyment.

Soon Conor's hands were on the inside of her knees, and Mika lifted her hips as she groaned, both simulating what she wanted to be doing and forcing his palms along her skin. As she rubbed and twisted, she surreptitiously kept her eyes on his face. That would be her best gauge of her performance—and judging from what she saw, she was doing a damn good job.

One of his hands left her. He only stroked himself a few times, but it was enough for her to know that she was affecting him the way she wanted. Mika bit her lip to keep from grinning. While she truly was aroused from their play, she wasn't going to climax—not from caressing herself. But she would give Conor the best show possible.

He surprised her by running a finger through her folds, and this time her groan was real. His calloused touch made all the difference in her pleasure. When he pulled his hand back, she could see her moisture shining on his index finger, and she almost spontaneously combusted when he licked it. Her breathing hitched as she imagined him tasting her for real, but she'd ask him to do that another time.

"McCabe, I'm not going to come without you inside me," she warned, "and if you're waiting for that, we're going to be here a long time."

"Stubborn," he complained.

Mika quit the game. She went to her knees as close to Conor as she could get and said, "I've given myself enough orgasms since we met. It's your turn—and *not* with your fingers. Do you hear me?"

Conor nodded, his eyes burning with red fire, and he reached for her. Before she knew what he was up to, he had her on his lap and straddling him. Mika shimmied forward until her breasts were against his chest. His cock rubbed at her opening and she almost came right then.

She kissed him then, and somehow it wasn't the ravenously hungry kiss she'd meant to give, but a slow, tender caress that held too much emotion. It made her uneasy, but when she lifted her head and saw the look on his face, she couldn't regret it—not when it obviously meant the same to him. Reaching out, she ran her fingers up his jaw.

Conor took hold of her hips, pulling her more snugly against him, and Mika gasped. He bore her down to the bed. Right now, she had a Kiverian male with glowing eyes to pleasure and to take pleasure from; she was going to enjoy every minute. She'd wanted this for so long.

Conor braced his hands on either side of her head and, for a moment that seemed to stretch for eternity, he only stared. It was intimate, unsettling, but somehow exactly right. "Take out your contacts," Mika ordered. She wanted to see his eyes the way they were supposed to be—bright green and shining.

He pulled back and popped his lenses out. There was no trash can nearby, so he put them on the nightstand next to the bed. Mika parted her thighs as he came back, inviting Conor to lie between them. She closed her eyes to savor the feel of him, then met his gaze again. "Thank you," she said, running her finger lightly across his cheekbone.

Without a word, he kissed her. For all the earlier frenzy, Conor was taking his time now. She wrapped her arms around him, pulling him closer, but it didn't speed him up. The kiss remained leisurely, as if they'd already sated themselves.

Mika brought her legs up, tilting her pelvis toward his.

That ended the kiss in a hurry. She nipped his lower lip, and his eyes opened. With a smile that was tremulous, she asked, "How much longer? We both want it. Come on, Conor."

There was a flare of red, and he tried to smile back. It looked more like a grimace, but she knew what he meant. "I want to savor our first time," he said.

Aw, man. "It's already special," she assured him around the lump in her throat. "Because it's you." She hoped he attributed the thickness in her voice to excitement, not sappy emotion. But as she looked at Conor, tremors of need passed through her in waves, and she realized he vibrated the same way. That made his intent to take this slow all the more meaningful.

She reached between their bodies and curled her hand around him, watched the muscle in his cheek begin to jump, and she smiled again. Wriggling to align herself to him, she began to guide Conor inside her. His broad head parted her, pulsed briefly before he started to penetrate and fill her body.

"As hard and fast as you always wanted," she reminded him, withdrawing her hand, not wanting to impede him.

Despite her invitation, Conor didn't move fast or take her hard. Instead, he eased forward one excruciating millimeter at a time. Impatiently, Mika tried to hurry things up, but Conor took hold of her hips, preventing her.

"Damn it, I'm Mahsei, remember?"

"Yeah," he gritted out. "I also remember how tight you were around my fingers. We'll do hard and fast later."

She started to argue, but his expression told her not to waste her breath. With a mental shrug, she decided to enjoy the pace, and she closed her eyes to focus on the experience of Conor entering her.

The steady pressure intensified and Mika braced herself, but before it became painful, he stopped. It cost McCabe; she could see that when she gazed at him again. The man looked as if he were the one feeling the pain: sweat covered him, and his grimace was fierce. Turning her face, she gently bit his throat to show her gratitude.

He seemed to know when she was ready for more, and he resumed moving. Again, he stopped when she started to feel any discomfort. He lowered his head to give her a gentle kiss and said, "We're almost there, honey."

At last he was all the way inside her, and Mika had to concede that McCabe had been right—she couldn't have handled hard and fast, no matter her bluster. Even slow and easy had given her a few moments of unease.

Tentatively, Conor rocked his hips. He watched her closely, but she must have passed the test. He began a gentle thrusting. It wasn't until she moved with him that he smiled and picked up speed.

One of his hands went to her hip, helping her find the rhythm. As she caught on, as they became more attuned to each other, and as she became accustomed to his great size, Mika began to feel really good. Better than good—extraordinary. A soft whimper escaped her, and the way Conor's eyes blazed made her cry out. She became lost in him, and in the intoxicating pleasure his body was giving her. There was nothing for her except Conor.

He shifted her, moving faster. Mika felt something wonderful approaching, a climax better than she'd ever known, and words started tumbling out of her mouth—words spoken in an ancient language. Words she never thought she'd say aloud. They seemed to incite Conor further, and he gave her the hard thrusts she'd begged for earlier. She rolled her hips each time he buried himself inside her, gasping as euphoria built.

Then he leaned forward and bit her. The pleasure-pain drove her over the edge. Arching her hips as much as she could, Mika froze as she found fulfillment, letting the ecstasy wash over her in waves.

Conor held on to her but didn't stop. Her moan became a wail, and still he moved. Her first orgasm had barely subsided before her second hit, and this one was even stronger. She barely heard her voice over the roaring in her ears, didn't know what she was saying. Or what language she was speaking.

Finally, finally, McCabe let go of all control. Almost blind with her own pleasure, Mika saw the red burst in his eyes. Her rapture was so extreme that she needed his body as an anchor.

She heard him choke back some strange words, and then he stiffened, pouring his seed into her. It triggered her third climax and she cried out even more loudly than before.

It wasn't until later, as he lay boneless on top of her, as she stroked his body with gentle hands, that Mika realized something and froze. At the end, she had spoken English. The words echoed in her brain. She'd said, *I love you, Conor.*

Oh, damn. She could only hope that he hadn't heard.

Chapter Twelve

Mika lay atop Conor sometime later, her legs on either side of him. This was one time where even he had to appreciate being half-Kiverian. If they were completely human, she didn't think either one of them would be able to walk. Of course, if they were completely human, he wouldn't have been able to get hard so often. She smiled against his shoulder.

He was still mostly erect, still pressed against her belly, but there was no urgent need to move. Not yet.

Conor had surprised her. She'd expected straight missionary-style sex from him, but he'd been less stodgy than she'd assumed. In fact, she couldn't think of a position they hadn't experimented with—although the female-dominant that she'd wanted to try hadn't lasted long before he'd flipped her on her back.

She had to bite back a laugh. McCabe wouldn't appreciate knowing that his need to be in charge during sex was a demonic trait, pure and simple. Some of the males of lesser branches might be able to handle the female on top, but not Kiverians. Apparently, not even half-human Kiverians.

"What's so funny?" he asked, giving her bottom a squeeze.

"How'd you know I was amused?"

"I can feel the smile, now give."

Mika considered what to say. She wanted to be truthful, but if she told him, it might destroy the mood. Partial honesty, however, could work. "I was thinking about your stamina."

His chest shook slightly, and she propped herself up on her arms. Yep, he was laughing. Mika smiled at his lightheartedness, and swooped down to bite his chin. "Now it's my turn to ask what you find so funny."

"I can't believe you're still thinking about sex." He shook his head, obviously in awe.

Considering the vishtau, she had no trouble believing their attraction, but she wasn't about to get into that. She could imagine his response to the bond far too easily, and it wouldn't be pretty. "Me?" She raised both eyebrows. "And I suppose *you're* not thinking about it?" Shifting slightly, she rubbed against him and felt him react.

There was a flash in his eyes, something that reminded her of his emotional vulnerability, and Mika leaned forward again to kiss him. She went soft and slow. "I'll never tire of you, Conor," she promised. "But it's not only me. It goes both ways."

"Yeah," he agreed, "I guess it does."

Mika settled back against his chest, content with that. The desire went both ways, as did the insecurity. She was the one who'd fallen in love; McCabe had never used the words, never even hinted at them. While she'd managed not to blurt out *I love you* in English again, she had repeated what she'd said in the demon language over and over in the throes of ecstasy. She'd finally realized what she was uttering and been appalled. Despite that, she'd been unable to stop herself from speaking the words the next time. It was a damn good thing Conor didn't understand, because she'd been reciting the ritual to bind herself to her vishtau mate for life.

For life. What the hell was she thinking? At least both of them had to repeat their part of the ritual before it locked into place, and that hadn't occurred. Still, her actions left her unsettled. If the bond had been finalized, she'd never be able to be with another until McCabe died. And it would be the same for him—something he'd despise, when he found out she'd lied to him.

How would it feel to lose a mate forever?

Mika might very well find out. She dug her fingers more firmly into Conor's arms. She cared about him like a soul-mate, and he very well could die. He'd risked his life for her last night, and she knew him well enough to feel sure he'd do it again. And even if he lived through this mess, at some point he'd find out the truth about her, and that would take him from her as permanently as death.

Deciding she didn't want to do any more thinking along those lines, at least not right now, she rocked her body. The feel of Conor's thick flesh against her was reassuring. For now, he was hers.

His hands tightened, forcing her to still, and Mika raised herself up to check things out. Nothing on his face gave any clue as to why he'd stopped her. If anything, his expression was oddly indulgent and he seemed pleased. Giving a mental shrug, she acquiesced. The amount of sun coming in the blinds said it was late afternoon, and she had a question she wanted to ask. "Are you going out today?"

Some of the easiness left him. "Yeah, why wouldn't I?"

Okay. The slight defensiveness suggested that she'd tweaked his ego. Given what she knew about Kiverian males, it probably had to do with her telling him last night that he was no match for the Dark Ones. Mika refrained from rolling her eyes, but it was difficult. Still, he was *her* demon male, and she didn't want Conor to believe she found him inferior.

Leaning down, she nipped his pec before licking and kissing it. "Because," she said, propping herself up on her forearms once more, "we're not done here." Mika rocked within his embrace. "Are we?"

His agreeable expression returned. "Not even close."

"But you are in danger." She couldn't leave it unsaid. "You know that, right?"

"I can take care of myself."

"I know you th—" She cut herself off before he got his defenses back up. "I know you can," she substituted quickly, "but I care about you."

"Trust me." His hands stroked her lightly. "There's nothing to be concerned about. That dark demon didn't seem interested in me. I'll be fine."

The flagrant attempt to pacify her made Mika's temper flare. "Yeah? And what about the auric assassin who shot at you? Will you be okay from him, too?"

Conor's eyes narrowed and his face went hard, and Mika realized she'd revealed too much knowledge regarding who'd shot at him. Before a good dodge sprang to mind, McCabe tossed her on her back and pinned her to the bed. He said, "Start talking. I want to know what you know. *Now.*"

Mika considered her options, and decided to be honest. She'd been drilled her entire life to not share demon lore with any outside of Orcus, but Conor wasn't exactly an outsider.

"Among the darkest branches, a few are born who can wield the power I saved you from the other night. They're always assassins, for that talent can kill any demon."

"Even the Dark Ones?"

She tried to shrug, but because he had her hands pressed to the bed, she couldn't. "I don't know." Before he could push, she explained, "When I said there were few of these demons, I meant it. There are very, very few, and I'm not acquainted with any."

Something flitted through his eyes, but Mika couldn't figure out what. "Why did you refer to them as *auric* assassins?"

"Because that's what I've heard them called."

Conor nodded slowly, and some of his weight eased from her. "What else do you know about them?"

Mika wracked her brain, trying to come up with something he'd be interested in knowing. "Most can only fire one blast before they exhaust their power, but rumor has it that some can fire twice before they have to recharge."

Conor appeared thoughtful. "That explains—"

"Explains what?

That odd expression swept his eyes once more. "That explains why he didn't attack a second time before we made it back inside the house."

Carefully, McCabe shifted away and lay back on the bed, one hand tucked behind his head. Mika rolled onto her side to watch him, but his gaze was focused on the ceiling. If he was thinking twice about being lax with his safety, that was good, but she doubted that was the case.

Pushing the hair from her face, she tried to figure out how to convince McCabe that he couldn't take this lightly. After years of dealing with rogue vampires and werewolves, he was too used to being the biggest badass around. But while he could take down other supernatural beings without difficulty, when it came to the Dark Ones, it wouldn't be easy. And auric assassins were no walk in the park.

Okay, so she didn't know the extent of his powers. Maybe he did have some incredible talents—but they might not be enough. And she was right to worry.

A cold breeze seemed to flow through the room, making Mika shiver, and she moved against Conor's side. He turned his head to look at her, his smile so tender that she felt her heart swell. She was in love with McCabe, whether she liked it or not. And if she wanted more than a few stolen moments, she was going to have to fight like hell once he found out the truth.

"You're chilled," Conor said. He sat up, grabbed the blankets from the foot of the bed and tucked them around her. Once he had her covered, he wrapped his arms around her and rubbed her arms, trying to warm her. "Better?"

"Yeah. Much." She snuggled closer, resting her head on his shoulder. "Thanks."

Instead of answering, he kissed her forehead. It was a simple gesture, but something about it reached her the way nothing else could. It wasn't the same as his endangering his life to defend her, but the way he took care of her, tended to her needs, meant just as much. She traced patterns on his belly, trying to wordlessly convey her appreciation.

Her fingers were beginning to creep lower when he asked, "Did you pick up any rumblings in Orcus about humans attempting to forge an alliance with demons?"

Mika sighed and stopped teasing him. "Why?"

"Two people now have told me they heard rumors."

"That kind of pact would be a Council-level negotiation, and I'm not placed highly enough in society to know about that. It wouldn't surprise me, however."

Conor seemed shocked. "Why the hell do you think humans would want another species loose in Crimson City that's more powerful than they are?"

Mika half-laughed. "You're seeing the situation in black and white. If humans thought they could extract a promise— or control a demon army through some other means—do you think they'd hesitate? Think about it. This city is a powder keg, and as tense as things are, it wouldn't take much to ignite an interspecies war. Humans are at a disadvantage in many ways, but demons are stronger than both werewolves and vampires. Now do you see why some might believe aligning with Orcus is a smart option?"

"It's a stupid option," he muttered. "We both know how demons negotiate and what would happen if they were freed."

Mika shrugged. Some demons would indeed do terrible things. Others would go on living as they always had. The problem was, those who came through the veil would mostly be of the former kind. Humans would think they knew what they were doing, but few actually did. It could quite conceivably be a terrible situation. On the other hand . . .

With a sigh, she tilted her head to look at Conor. "I know you don't want demons freed, but not all of us are dangerous." She wanted to make that clear.

"You think the portal should be opened?" His posture was rigid.

Mika stroked him and thought about it. "I'm not sure," she said at last. "I'd like to see my mom, my gran, my brother and others able to do as they pleased. But the idea of the dark demons running loose among humans scares me."

"They wouldn't be loose for long," he said, his voice hard.

"McCabe, you make me nuts," Mika snapped. She dug two knuckles into his side and twisted. "You can't go hunting the entire branch."

He didn't reply, and she sighed. His need to protect humans from demons was another part of who Conor was, and she'd have to accept it about him. "Why don't we focus now on the dark demon who's after me, and save the rest of them for later?" she suggested.

Some of the rigidity left his muscles. "I'll take care of you, honey," he said. "Don't worry."

"I know you will," Mika agreed, returning to caressing him. She'd have to work on tempering his hatred of demons. "But I wish whoever called these Dark Ones through the portal would send them back already. Although, that wouldn't really solve my problem, would it? I'd still have to deal with them when I return to Orcus."

Mika could practically hear Conor thinking in the silence. Knowing questions were coming, she braced herself.

"Can no one else send a demon back except the one who summoned him?"

"Have you studied anything about summoning spells?" Mika asked. When he nodded, she continued, "Then you know most of them are closed. That means there's a set time the demon can come to this world. Sometimes it's an actual length of time, say a day or a month. But most incantations involve an action." Mika debated for a second, then decided to risk sharing. "For instance, the rauthima summoning ritual allows the male demon to remain only until his orgasm is finished. Since he's brought through the veil in a state of sexual frenzy, his stay in the Overworld is measured in minutes."

Conor's jaw clenched, and she quickly mentioned another example. "Or say humans wanted demons loose until the vampires and werewolves were defeated. That could take years. But if the decision was made, the human who called the demons could revoke the summoning and return them before the action was fulfilled. But only that person could, and no one else. However, if someone knew where the gates to Orcus were located, they could physically push a demon back through. See?"

McCabe nodded. "Yeah, I understand. If you called a demon through, I couldn't return him with a spell—but I could force him back by brute force. Now, what about open summonings?"

Mika shook her head. "There aren't many of those, they're very dangerous. With an open-ended call, no one but the summoner could send the demon back."

"And what if that person died?" Conor pressed.

Mika dug her fingers into him briefly, then said, "Then the demon could remain in the Overworld as long as he wished."

"When your father summoned you, what kind of spell did he use? Is your stay open-ended or closed?"

Mika stiffened before she could prevent it. This was the last thing she wanted to talk about, but she wasn't going to mislead him again. "Summoning spells don't affect me—probably because I'm half human."

Conor was quiet for a couple of minutes and Mika held her breath, hoping he'd drop it. She didn't get her wish. "You told me your father called you forth."

The hardness in his tone made her tense further, but she said easily, "I told you my father has the ability to summon demons."

"And you let me jump to my own conclusions? If someone didn't call you, then how did you get out of Orcus?"

She could feel his stare as he waited for her answer. Taking a deep breath for courage, Mika said, "I don't need anyone to call me. I've always crossed the veil at will."

Conor rolled atop her, his arms supporting his weight. "Can anyone who's half demon and half human go back and forth whenever they want?"

Damn it, she'd known that would be his first question. Mika wanted to tell him that there was no way in hell she was allowing him to go into Orcus to hunt his father, but she knew better. "I don't know," she said, her voice clipped. "Until you, I'd never met anyone else with my mixed heritage."

He nodded, and she didn't like the speculative look on his face. "You've never had a problem in the demon world?" he asked. "I've read that humans can't survive there."

"This is why I led you to believe my father summoned me. You can't go to Orcus." The words escaped before she could stop them. His jaw clenched, and a stubborn expression settled on his face. *Hell.* "You'll stand out," Mika explained. "We read energies, remember? No one pays attention to me because I've lived there my entire life, but do you think a stranger who's half human is going to pass unnoticed and be unremarked upon? You'll never survive."

Conor sat up and started to get out of bed. Mika went to her knees, wrapping her arms around him from behind. She couldn't let him walk away now. She kissed his nape, then the place where his neck met his shoulder. "You don't know that world—I do." She kept her voice soft and non-confrontational. His tension eased and Mika bit his shoulder lightly.

"I've read humans can't survive in the demon world," he repeated.

She bit him harder. "That's right, humans die in Orcus," she agreed.

"But some humans have made it in."

Though it wasn't a question, Mika answered as if it were. "I've never seen any. When I asked why my dad never came to visit, my mom told me he couldn't." She shrugged, her breasts moving against Conor's back. "I checked around after that and was given the same information everywhere I turned. No humans can survive in Orcus."

Conor didn't speak, and after a brief internal debate, Mika opted not to push. Raising herself higher on her knees, she leaned forward and ran her arms over his chest to his belly. Turning her face into him, she kissed and nipped at his jaw.

"Mika." His voice held warning.

"Don't try to tell me you don't like this." She used her teeth on his collarbone. "I know better. I even have visible proof." She looked down at his body.

"You're not going to dissuade me with sex."

"That wasn't my plan, but if you want me to try, I'm willing to give it a go." She was practically falling over his shoulder, trying to reach more of him, but she didn't miss his meaning. McCabe had made up his mind to travel into Orcus. But she still had time to work on him. He wouldn't try anything while he was protecting her.

Showing his incredible strength, Conor reached for her and pulled her around his body. Mika squeaked in surprise but didn't fight. When she safely straddled his lap, she scolded, "Next time warn me before you do that."

"Sorry, honey."

The twinkle in his eye belied his apology, but she didn't call him on it—she adored that gleam. He was far too serious most of the time, far too intense; and this was a happy change. Mika nuzzled his throat, kissing, licking and nipping upward to his ear. If only he didn't feel such hatred for his father. If only he could understand how normal demon physiology had affected what happened the night he was conceived.

Mika froze. Wait a second, that might work. Conor's hands tightened at her waist and she nipped his earlobe. If she could show McCabe that his father wasn't necessarily some cold, pathological rapist, maybe he wouldn't be so fanatic about hunting him. What she had to do was work Conor into a sexual frenzy and then point out a few things. Maybe that would get him to look at his conception from a different angle, get him to see that his father wasn't a monster. McCabe was part Kiverian, and they had the vishtau bond. The edge was off his need because they'd already had sex so many times today . . . but it could still work.

And she knew just how to start—with encouragement—something she doubted he'd heard enough of in his life. Mika ran her tongue around the outside edge of his ear, then murmured softly, "I haven't told you how gorgeous you are." She straightened, smiled at him and wrapped her hands around his left arm. "Look at this—my fingers don't even meet. Do you know how hot that makes me?"

"Cut the bullshit, Mika," he groused.

But she didn't miss the half-dazed look in his eyes, and it made her wonder if he'd ever been told anything positive about himself. That derailed her from her plan for a moment. He needed to hear how special he was, and she put her arms around his neck again. "No bullshit. Every compliment from me will be one hundred percent true. My promise on it. And you know a demon never goes back on her word."

After waiting to see if he had anything to add, she continued: "It's more than your looks, McCabe." She purred his surname like an endearment. "It's you. I love your stalwart honor, your determination, your intensity. I even love the way you grumble when I'm prodding you. I get wet just thinking about you."

She leaned forward and kissed him. As she tried to pull back, his lips clung to hers. There was a hopeful look in his eyes, a hunger, though she had to stare hard to see it. Stroking his nape, Mika weighed her alternatives, but it didn't take long to decide that he was more important than protecting herself. "There's a reason. I love you, Conor."

Her words seemed to hang suspended in time. Mika didn't expect him to return the sentiment, but she had thought to get a response. Still, she couldn't regret saying it—not when McCabe needed to hear this truth something fierce.

Before she could become too uncomfortable, his hands tightened at her waist and he growled low in his throat. "Consider this your warning," he said. Using incredible speed, Conor lifted her off his lap and put her on the bed, flat on her back.

Well, she *had* asked for advance notice when he planned to shift her, but she'd hoped for more than a split second. Mika laughed quietly over his haste before his mouth covered hers.

Humming with pleasure at his eagerness, she raised her knee, resting her thigh against his hip. Conor was in control again, but that was fine. He was already half wild, and she hadn't done much. Yet. Let him hang on to his sanity while he could; by the time she was done with him, his iron command was going to be a thing of the past. The thought made her smile against his lips.

She could feel his sex growing hard, nudging more and

more insistently against the inside of her thigh with every passing moment. Mika wriggled, trying to center him, but Conor didn't cooperate. Raising and lowering her heel, however, made him slide against her leg, and their kiss became less measured. Conor dragged his mouth from hers, licking and nipping his way to her throat. And he turned her own methods against her; he nuzzled her neck, then pinched her pulse point with his teeth. The bite made her gasp and arch her body into his. But as Mika began to throb, she refused to lose sight of her goal.

He didn't make it easy for her. With one last stroke of his tongue, Conor lifted his head. His eyes blazed red fire, just as she was pretty sure hers did too. Knowing she lay with Conor, the Kiverian she loved—her vishtau mate—was enough to make her wild with happiness.

His smile was pure, smug male, and she knew his pleasure was in how aroused he'd made her. Reaching out, he trailed a finger around the areola of her right breast, circling until the nipple drew taut. He moved to the other breast, repeated the motion.

"Stop teasing," she growled.

Mika should have realized Conor would take that as a challenge. He moved, straddling her hips and pinning her to the mattress. Using both hands, he cupped her breasts, pressing them together. As he stared at her chest, he reached full tumescence. Lowering his face, he abraded her sensitive skin with the stubble on his chin. Mika fisted her hands in the blanket beneath her and let him do with her what he wanted.

"Conor," she protested breathlessly as he continued teasing.

Finally—finally!—his tongue flicked one nipple, was there and gone so quickly, it left her gasping. The man was merciless as he played with her, not taking her into his mouth until she writhed beneath him. His erection rubbed against her, and Mika shifted so that she received stimulation every time she undulated. She didn't think Conor had any clue how close she was to coming. Deciding it was in her best interest to keep him ignorant, Mika did her damnedest to limit the noises she made, and to keep her hips from rocking at a frantic pace.

She was right on the cusp when he bit her nipple. With a strangled groan, Mika dug her fingers into his butt and arched into him. Hard. Conor froze for an instant, then worked to plummet her completely over the edge.

A part of Mika realized she was gasping that damn vishtau pledge again, but she didn't care. Her body's only concern was enjoying the ecstasy screaming through it. She finished her portion of the binding ritual at the same time the ripples of pleasure eased.

When she regained her senses, McCabe was leaning over her, his eyes burning into hers. "You weren't supposed to come yet," he said.

Unrepentant, Mika grinned. "Sorry. Why don't you start over and I'll try to hold out."

It took a moment, but Conor smiled. "Have I mentioned that you're trouble?"

It sounded like a compliment, so she ignored the question. She'd failed miserably so far in her attempt to destroy his control, but now that she'd had her fun, she should be able to stay focused. Without warning, Mika shoved Conor on his back.

"Uh-uh," she said, pushing on his shoulder to hold him in place as he tried to rise. "It's my turn."

He made one more effort to get up, but it was halfhearted at best. McCabe wanted to see what she was going to do to him.

Kneeling at his side, Mika took his hand and brought it to her lips. She teased his fingers, running her tongue over each and biting the base of his thumb, before sucking his middle finger into her mouth. Deliberately, she repeated the same technique on his finger that she'd used while going down on him hours earlier. The flare of his eyes told her he remembered, and that he recognized what she was doing.

Conor's body was rigid, his teeth clenched hard enough to make a muscle jump in his cheek. Satisfied, Mika moved to his palm. "I love your hands," she said between bites. "Your wrists too." She gently ran her index finger across his pulse point. "So strong and capable, yet these long fingers make me wonder if you have an artistic side." With a moue to make her meaning clear, she added, "You do have a very talented touch."

She nipped at his wrist and moved to his forearm. "I'm turned on by a man's arms, his shoulders—and, McCabe? You have the sexiest body I've ever seen."

After nuzzling the inside of his elbow, she continued her exploration. Though she was lying close to him, Mika kept her weight on the bed, hoping that position wouldn't trigger Conor's Kiverian need to hold the dominant position.

"I've already told you how I feel about your arms." Mika bit his biceps muscle, then kissed her way to the inside of his upper arm. He shuddered as she licked the skin there.

She made a brief stop at his shoulder, before moving down to his collarbone, then his chest. McCabe had great pecs, and she told him that as she kissed and touched him. She bit the muscle around his nipple and licked that small nub. His entire body went rigid, and she studied him for a moment. He definitely liked this, and she smiled before shifting to his other side. To add to his torment, Mika dragged the tips of her breasts over his stomach.

Conor managed to stay mostly quiet, although she did surprise an occasional grunt from him as she did her best to arouse him. It was a shame he was so contained, but that only inspired her to work harder.

Running her mouth along his sternum, she began chanting the words to the rauthima ritual, her voice softer than a whisper; but instead of making it random, she substituted Conor's name. Mika knew the summoning part of the rite wouldn't affect him, but the phrases that incited sexual frenzy should. She kept herself attuned to him, and saw his hands fist as he struggled to remain still. His body jerked, his breathing became ragged and then he groaned.

Mika moved further down his torso, tracing the ridged muscles over his stomach with her lips. "Damn, McCabe," she said, interrupting the ritual. "I don't know how much weightlifting you do, but it's worth it." She rimmed his bellybutton with her tongue. "You're incredible."

And he was. His abdomen was absolutely perfect. Mika clenched her thighs, trying to control her arousal. She nipped at the flesh below his navel, and looked up at him through her lashes. Conor stared back and, when their eyes met, the world seemed to shift. Or at least her portion of it.

He was her mate. *Hers*.

As she moved her mouth down the line of hair beneath his belly button, Mika reached out and cupped him. He'd recoiled again, and she smiled against his body before resuming the rauthima rite.

His arousal rested against her cheek, but although she gave it a few strokes with her hand, she didn't take him in her mouth. Instead, she sat back on her knees and evaluated him. Still contained. But she hadn't finished the ritual yet. "Make room," she ordered, tapping his inner thigh.

McCabe obeyed with an alacrity that was startling, given his usual disposition. Mika gave a smile she hoped he found sexy, and crawled over to kneel between his legs. Cupping her breasts, she rolled her nipples between her thumbs and forefingers. That earned her a loud, low growl. She spoke the last phrase of the spell she was casting.

It was slightly harder than she expected, but she bent over him without losing her balance. She took his erection between her breasts and used her hands to push herself more tightly around him. Then she started to move. Between the light sheen of sweat on her body and the moisture of his lust, he was able to slide smoothly across her flesh.

Conor wasn't quiet anymore. Between groans, he cursed, and she figured that was his way of trying to maintain control.

Finally, when she felt it was the right moment, she paused. She waited until he looked at her; then, with a naughty smile, Mika bent down and licked the tip that jutted from between her breasts. Then she closed the ritual. She almost felt his self-command snap.

There was nothing contained about Conor as he threw her on her back and covered her with his body. The sounds he made were demonic. And that, more than anything else, told Mika he was completely lost.

Although it was the last thing she wanted, Mika moved her hips, keeping him for a moment from penetrating her. "Conor, remember this."

He looked at her blankly. "What?"

"Remember this moment and how you feel right now, okay?"

McCabe nodded, but he obviously would have agreed to anything to get inside of her. As he slid himself along her sensitive flesh, *she* would have agreed to anything to get him inside her, but she was doing this for him, and she loved him enough to keep sight of her goal. Even as painful as this was.

"Damn it." She pinched his behind, startling him. "Take stock of how you feel right now, of how much you ache for me. I want you to remember this afterward, do you understand?" she demanded.

For a brief moment, there was a lucidity in his gaze that convinced her she'd actually gotten through to him, so this time when he nodded, she went still, allowing Conor to guide himself inside her.

He wasn't slow or careful. This was a Kiverian male who'd been pushed past his limits, and he took her that way, thrusting forward with one, forceful stroke. Pleasure shot through her, making her eyes roll back as she gasped. Knowing that when he came to his senses he'd be anguished at the idea of being too rough, she hurried to correct any misapprehension.

"I'm fine," she assured him. "Hard and fast. The way we both want it."

Without any more delay, Conor slammed into her hard enough to make the headboard bang into the wall. The sound made her smile for an instant, because it was proof of how much he desired her. He bit her, his teeth sinking into her shoulder, and Mika moaned in appreciation.

She dug her nails into his shoulders and, clinging to him, raised her legs, allowing him to drive deeper. That earned her a snarl of approval as he shifted, hooking her knees over his upper arms. It allowed him to penetrate to an even greater depth. But Mika knew there was also consideration in his action: Now she didn't have to work to hold the position.

She lifted her hips as best she could to meet his next thrust. There seemed still to be a tiny sliver of him that was holding back, watching to make sure he didn't hurt her. Deliberately, Mika worked to destroy even that. Since he liked sex-talk, she told him very explicitly what she wanted him to do, how much she liked it. As aroused as she was, the words were coming out one, maybe two at a time, and she was nearly incoherent, but it was enough to sever Conor's last strand of control.

Their mating became animalistic. They bit at each other's shoulders, arms, chests, wherever they could reach. His hands shifted, gripped her sides, and she clawed at her mate as fever raged between them. There was no noise in the room except for grunts and groans and the sounds of their flesh.

Mika reveled in the strength of Conor's body, in the power of his strokes—in the knowledge that she had allowed him a freedom he'd never had with any other female. She'd given him the gift of being able to lose his self-control without worrying.

As he pushed her closer to climax, she couldn't think any more, couldn't do anything but experience their mating. Conor felt so damn good inside her, so *right*.

"Look at me," he ordered, his voice deep and harsh. When she did, he said, "You're mine."

If she'd had the energy, Mika would have cried out with sheer joy. "Yours," she agreed, and he bared his teeth in what could only be a satisfied smile. "And you're mine," she added.

His expression became even more pleased; then he picked up his speed again, forcing her over the edge so unexpectedly that she screamed. McCabe shattered too, and his release intensified hers. The sound that escaped him was inhuman, and she loved it.

She loved *him*.

Mika wasn't sure how long it took before she had enough energy to open her eyes, but Conor continued to lie atop her. He'd released her legs and they sprawled open, boneless. She laughed silently and McCabe muttered a complaint at the motion.

"You know what that grumbly tone does to me," she said, arching her hips. "You're trying to get me hot again, aren't you?"

He lifted his head so she could see his incredulous expression. "Honey, you can't want more."

Raising herself, she gave him a loud, smacking kiss, and with a giggle dropped back to the bed. "Damn, McCabe, that was good. You have to do me like that again. But not right now."

"You sound smug, but you're the one who screamed."

"Now who's smug?" She laughed.

"Hey, I earned the right."

There was such lightheartedness in his banter that Mika laughed again. She liked him this way, wanted to see it more often. "I'll let you earn it again after we heal a little."

"Heal?" He looked down her, and his entire body went rigid. "Damn, Mika—I'm sorry. How bad did I hurt you?"

"You didn't hurt me. The love nips are already closing. Besides, I think you got the worst of it." A drop of blood had trickled from his shoulder to his elbow, and Mika ran her index finger up the path it had taken, removing the track from his skin. "I didn't just bite you, I also scratched up your back and arms pretty good. Do you want me to apologize?"

"No," he said, voice thick. "I enjoyed it. A lot."

"That goes both ways, McCabe. I loved the biting too. Don't forget that I'm as much demon as you are." But now Mika hesitated. Could she chance completing her plan when she'd already worried him about how rough he'd been? In the long run, this would lift some of the burden he carried. Maybe.

"You went all serious on me. What are you thinking?" he asked.

Mika brought her legs in closer, cradling him between her thighs, and said, "Do you remember that moment I told you to keep in your mind? You know, just before you got inside me."

For a moment, he just stared at her, then he said, "Yeah?"

"Could you have stopped?" He looked at her blankly, not understanding. "If I'd said *no*, could you have stopped?"

"You said no?" He appeared stricken. He went so pale, she worried he was going to be sick, and Mika hurried to comfort him, her hands caressing his sides.

"I *didn't* say no. You didn't force me, I swear."

He didn't look as if he believed her.

"I said, *if* I had asked you to stop. I never said stop."

An expression that was almost hopeful skittered across his face. "You're not just saying that, are you?"

"Of course not. I love what we did."

The tension left his body and he collapsed atop her again. That drove home to her just how deeply this affected him. Wrapping her arms around Conor, Mika stroked his back and made soothing noises. She'd never meant to do this to him. She hadn't wanted to cause anguish.

It didn't take long before he pulled away from her, settling to her side. She missed his weight. "What's this about, then?" he asked.

His question sounded angry, but Mika knew it was because she'd scared him. Worried him. Slowly, she sat up and turned to face him. "Do you remember how you were at that point in time? When all you wanted was to have me?"

Conor nodded once, the motion jerky.

"You were frenzied, out of control." Or near enough. That last strand had been negligible, and it had broken.

Another nod. He was closed up again, and Mika rested a hand over her heart. Her chest ached, but she had to do this, had to make him think. If she didn't, he'd never be able to move past his background, never be able to relinquish the hate he harbored. She couldn't let him live the rest of his life like that. Maybe this idea of hers wouldn't work, maybe she was hurting him with no end benefit, but it would take something harsh to make him question his beliefs.

"You don't have to answer aloud. You don't even have to come up with an immediate answer for yourself, but the question is: Could you have stopped if I'd changed my mind at that moment?"

He opened his mouth to reply, and Mika reached out, resting two fingers lightly on his lips. "*No.* Think about it and be honest with yourself. You didn't even hear me at first when I asked you to note how you felt. I had to pinch you to get your attention, and then your mind only cleared for an instant."

Mika paused, hesitated, then plunged ahead. "The rauthima summoning ritual would have left your father just as frenzied as you."

"You recited the ritual. That's what you were murmuring." McCabe jerked away from her touch and got to his feet. She chased after him and grabbed his arm near the doorway.

"Conor—"

"There's no excuse for what that bastard did," he said.

Mika shook her head. "No, there isn't. That's not what I'm saying." Oh, hell, she was making a mess of this. "But maybe you can let go of some of the hate you feel for your father. There are things about being a demon that are unlike being human. We . . . we are what we are. That's not an excuse," she hurried to say before McCabe could turn away, "but sometimes things aren't as black and white as you see them in your mind."

For a moment Conor glared down at her; then his eyes iced over. With cold deliberation, he broke her hold and walked away.

Chapter Thirteen

For three days, Mika had been living in a fool's paradise. She knew it, but was in no hurry to change things; and Conor, it seemed, shared her desire. After he'd walked away from her that afternoon, he'd gone to his weight room and worked out. When he'd emerged, body shaking from fatigue and sweat dripping from him, they'd both begun the pretense.

But acting as if she hadn't used the rauthima ritual, as if she hadn't given him an object lesson, didn't make it go away. It hung between them like a precariously balanced sword, a blade that could fall at any moment. Or maybe it was Mika's guilt giving her that sense. Her lies weighed heavily on her.

She leaned in the doorjamb of the bedroom and watched Conor. He was intent on his computer, no doubt scrolling through the news for some clue to the whereabouts of the demons after her. He was intent on keeping her safe, and as much as she wished otherwise, she really was in danger from the Dark Ones.

His scowl deepened, and he leaned forward slightly. Mika guessed that meant he'd found something of interest, but as she sauntered toward him, it wasn't the screen she focused on. She loved him. Her feelings seemed to grow, to strengthen each day. And it scared her. As intense as her emotions were, Mika knew it would probably frighten her even if she weren't lying to Conor, but the fact that she'd been dishonest, that she continued to hide her mission from him, left her terrified. She couldn't lose McCabe.

When she reached him, Mika slid her arms around his shoulders from behind, relishing the freedom she had in touching him, the easy way he turned to meet her lips.

"Come back to bed," she enticed, although she doubted he'd take her up on the offer. He was already wearing his jean jacket, and that meant he was armed and ready to go.

"Don't tempt me." McCabe powered down the computer.

Mika gently turned his head toward her with her palm and kissed him again. "But we both like it when I do." She smiled and nipped at his lower lip. "Especially when you give in."

Conor stood, breaking her embrace, and taking her hand he pulled her to the front door. "Give me a rain check. There's something I want to look into."

What could she say? He was investigating so that he could protect her. Just because she wanted the world to go away in order to enjoy her vishtau mate didn't mean that either of them could ignore the events swirling around them.

"You know you don't need a rain check," she said. "You can have me anytime, anywhere."

He leaned down to take her mouth, and he was much less controlled, but it only lasted a moment before he drew back. Resting his forehead on hers, he asked, "How the hell do you do this to me?"

"You know you like it." She slid her hands into the back pockets of his jeans and tugged his hips to hers. She started to grind her pelvis into his, but Conor freed himself.

"Hold that thought, honey." Giving her a last peck, he picked her up and moved her to the side.

Let him go, she told herself, and wrapped her arms

around her waist to keep from reaching for him. "Be careful, okay?"

Conor paused. "Stop fussing," he groused, but she picked up a thread of pleasure in his complaint.

"It's my prerogative to fuss." She shifted to see his profile. "I love you."

He made the grumbling noise that turned her on, and started to turn toward her. With a curse, he stopped, shook his head and hightailed it out of the house.

Mika laughed as the door closed behind him. She shouldn't find this amusing, and she sure shouldn't try to prevent him from leaving. There were a ton of books left to get through, and if she didn't find the spell among them, other places to look after that. The humor seeped away and she sighed.

There was wiggle room in her promise to the Council and she was using those shades of gray, exploiting them as much as she could to slow her search. She didn't want to find the incantation, but Mika knew she wouldn't be able to stall for much longer. Either she located the spell or the Council would be in contact to demand answers for her failure.

Reluctantly, she walked toward the bookcase. Before she reached it, a glint caught her eye. Her barrette lay against the wall, probably in the same place where Conor had tossed it the other night. Mika retrieved it and, using her hands to smooth back her hair, she clipped it up to keep it out of her way as she worked.

Instead of tackling her chore, though, she went around the room and pulled the blinds. It was getting dark outside and that's when the watcher came. She'd sensed him the last three nights and didn't like feeling exposed. There was nothing she could do about the lack of window cover in the kitchen, but she simply wouldn't go in there when the lights were on.

Sighing, Mika sank onto the sofa. She'd changed her

mind again; whoever was watching the house and the auric assassin were two different people. An auric assassin was too skilled, too powerful to be unable to cloak himself completely. It couldn't be him outside.

She'd shared her thoughts with McCabe, but he continued to show absolutely no concern for his safety. And the more laid-back he was, the more upset she became. When that happened, he'd try to placate her, and that pissed her off worse. Inevitably their rows led to sex, but that hadn't resolved the issue of how cavalier Conor was about his well-being.

She huffed out a sharp breath and reluctantly pushed to her feet. No matter how much she didn't want to do so, she had to finish this task for the Council. It was more than her promise to them, she reminded herself; she had to do this for her people.

Conor was honorable, but what of the next person capable of wielding the spell? If it wasn't destroyed, could she rely on that individual being of equal caliber? Mika didn't think so —McCabe's integrity was stupendous. And with her family involved, she couldn't risk it: That incantation was much too dangerous to exist.

Dragging the coffee table over to the shelving unit, she stood on it and resumed her search of the books. As the hours passed, she started singing show-tunes to keep herself entertained. Since her grandma Noguchi loved musicals and always had a soundtrack playing in her house, Mika had hundreds of songs memorized.

She'd worked her way through *Into the Woods, Oliver!* and *Annie,* and had just started belting out the title song from *Guys and Dolls,* when she stopped cold, almost dropping the volume she held. She forced herself to carefully slide it back on the shelf. It was no doubt a lost cause, since she'd quit singing mid-verse, but she tried for nonchalance as she stepped from the coffee table to the hardwood floor.

Immediately, Mika scanned for the threat. She didn't see anything, but she felt it. Every instinct she had told her there was danger present despite McCabe's protection, and those same instincts told her it was too late to run.

Too bad she didn't know who or what had entered the house.

She shifted, moving into a better defensive position. Away from the coffee table, she'd have more space to maneuver. Unfortunately she was barefoot, which didn't make her feel real secure, but at least her stretchy leggings and T-shirt gave her freedom to move. Still seeking the threat, Mika mentally scanned again. Something seemed off near the foyer, and she faced that spot.

"You've good detection skills," said a voice as the air shimmered. "Pity they won't save you."

Conor's source had been right—there was more than one Dark One around. The demon who appeared wasn't as pretty as the first, though he was attractive enough if she overlooked the cruel set to his mouth. He was dressed completely in black, something she would have found amusing had things been different, and his pale amethyst eyes were cold, calculating. His dark hair was as long as his compatriot's, and some coppery thread was woven through one of the tiny braids that pulled his dark tresses back into a ponytail.

Something about him made Mika wish she was facing the other guy. Both were evil, but this one seemed more so. He was leaning lazily against the arch between the entryway and the great room, but Mika sensed his alertness.

"How'd you get through the shield?" she asked.

Straightening, he said, "Did you honestly believe that something so feeble would stop me for long? I am Bak-Faru."

He spoke with such arrogance, such superiority, that in other circumstances, Mika might have laughed. Might have, but she doubted it. Only an idiot laughed at a Dark One. Especially when the idiot was facing death.

Mika balanced her weight more evenly and prepared to fight. No doubt she was going to die shortly, but she wouldn't make it easy. Not if she could help it.

"I know little of your kind. I have no way to know what will and won't keep you at bay. Why are your people so secretive anyway?" As she spoke, she kept her voice calm and even—quite a feat, considering that her heart thundered in her chest.

The Dark One looked amused. "Do you think to stall long enough for your protector to return? We've watched, and it's unlikely he'll be back for several hours. And there's little chance I'll lose track of time. Or sight of my goal."

"I know," Mika admitted. "You'll forgive me, I hope, if I ask one question. Why are you trying to stop me from finishing my mission? I am unable to fathom your purpose."

She'd been careful with her words, speaking a bit more formally than usual and making sure she didn't imply the Dark Ones were behaving irrationally, simply suggested that she was too ignorant to understand their choices. Despite her caution, however, the Dark One stared at her. Why had she bothered with politeness? It wasn't as if proper deportment was going to make him change his mind about killing her. Surreptitiously, Mika wiped her damp palms off on her pants and tried to anticipate his attack. Speed might be her one chance at survival.

"We do not want the incantation destroyed. The keeper must use the key and lower the veil."

"You'll be enslaved just like all the other demons if the spell is used. Con—the keeper will be your lord and master."

The Dark One arched an eyebrow and looked as if she were hopelessly slow. "Why would you believe that anyone could subjugate the Bak-Faru? We're far more powerful than that."

"You're trapped in Orcus like the rest of us, aren't you? How'd the almighty Bak-Faru get there if not by the original imprisonment spell?"

His eyes began to glow, and Mika gulped. Too late she

remembered that dying a quick death was preferable to being tortured and murdered. Stories she'd heard, things she'd seen, raced through her mind, and as her knees began to buckle she locked them. No way was fear going to defeat her before the battle even started.

"For a Mahsei, you're very brave. Or very foolish," the Dark One said.

Mika smiled weakly. Foolish was probably closer to the mark. "We Mahsei tend to be impulsive."

"True." The Dark One rubbed his nails against his sleeve, buffing them, and Mika's gut clenched. Time had just run out.

She dived to her left in time to avoid . . . something. It was invisible to her eyes, but she could sense it—and its dangerousness. Whatever it was, it was nothing Mika had witnessed before.

Everything she'd attempted the other night against the blond Dark One had failed, but she had no choice except to try. Maybe luck would be on her side. Instead of increasing the weight of the air molecules around her as a defense, she used her power as a weapon. Calling on everything she had, Mika built the air density around him, hoping to suffocate the dark demon.

Another unnamable attack made her leap into the air. She hit the ground again, rolled to her feet quickly. It was difficult to split her concentration between what she was trying to do with her power and his attacks.

Up till now, her foe hadn't moved, but that changed. He walked toward her and Mika glanced around, trying to choose the best escape route—Conor's house wasn't very big and her options were extremely limited.

The dark demon raised his hand. Its angle made her break left, but it was a feint. She ran directly into a fire-blast from his other hand.

Mika dropped to her knees, singed, agony rolling through her. She'd never felt anything like this before, not even the time she'd accidentally fallen into an electrified fence as a child. Her body spasmed, muscles twitching.

Get up. She had to get up or she was dead. Calling on every ounce of determination she possessed, she staggered to her feet. Her eyes started to roll back in her head and she fought harder.

When her vision cleared, she realized the dark demon wasn't doing anything. He could have finished her off easily, but he hadn't. More cat-and-mouse games, she realized. All she had to do was keep him amused long enough to come up with a brilliant escape. Her lips curved. *Yeah, right!*

She'd stopped her manipulation of the air when she'd been struck, but it hadn't been working anyway. Mika spotted the geode on Conor's desk, and using a combination of telekinesis and wind, she hurled it at the Dark One. It didn't make it even half the distance before he held up a hand. The rock stopped and fell to the floor with a sharp thud. That made the Dark One laugh.

When he sobered, he asked, "Is that the best you can manage?"

"Sorry." Her voice was a croak.

"I'd hoped you'd learned something since your first encounter with a Bak-Faru."

"I'd hoped so, too." Mika took a step back and swayed unsteadily. Man, her head hurt.

Her foe's lopsided smile made him look approachable. Friendly, even—but she knew it was a false impression. Okay, so dark demons were capable of being amused. Of course, they were amused by one liners she tossed out while scrambling to avoid death, but hey, that proved at least that they weren't entirely humorless bastards.

Concentrate, damn it!

Maybe if she combined her powers, she thought, narrowly avoiding another fireblast. Mika swirled the wind in front of her, thickening the mass as she increased its rotation. It made the demon's next shot stray off target, and that gave her hope. She whipped the wind up until it blew strongly enough to pull some of her hair loose from its clip to send it dancing around her face. When the mini-cyclone reached top speed, she directed it toward her assailant. It took work, but she kept the blast on target.

To her utter amazement, she knocked the dark demon back a step. His facial expression remained unchanged, but Mika had a gut feeling he was every bit as surprised as she.

Her moment of satisfaction was short-lived; he sent a barrage her way. Mika tried to form a tornado again, but she couldn't concentrate while trying to get away from the magic he was aiming at her. With him having so much firepower, evading every shot was impossible. Mika was nearly caught by two spells, before the third connected dead-on. Her head reeling, she battled to stay upright. Her brain seemed to be misfiring, but one thought registered: If she went down, there was no way on earth she'd be able to get up again—and she wasn't dying on her knees.

Conor tapped his fingers against the steering wheel as he waited for the traffic light to change. This unusual lack of patience he felt was one more irritant he could lay at Mika's door. He'd never been antsy to get home before she'd arrived, but sometimes the need to be with her nearly staggered him.

Tonight it was something more specific than simply wanting to be with her. From the moment he'd arrived at the location where the bodies were found, he'd had this feeling the whole thing was too pat, too orchestrated. The murders were demon kills, he didn't doubt that; but after a couple of hours of questioning people, the sense that it was a setup had become overwhelming. A setup for what, though?

If someone hoped to take him out and leave his woman vulnerable, they were in for a surprise. He might loathe one of the powers he'd been born with, fear what using it would do to his humanity, to his very soul, but it also came with a damn near unbeatable advantage. Except, no one had taken a shot at him while he'd been asking questions. That made him uneasy, and the sense was again tied to Mika. But this time he knew she was safe: She'd promised him she wouldn't leave the house.

The traffic light turned green and he stepped on the accelerator. Mika was his--she hadn't argued about that. In fact, she'd staked her own claim. Maybe she'd thought he'd be angry, but he'd liked it. Shit, she did have him in the palm of her hand and there was no point in denying it. The only thing to do now was to try to limit the damage Typhoon Mika would leave behind when she blew out of town.

Reluctantly, Conor smiled. He'd miss her like hell when she walked away, but he couldn't regret being with her. For the first time in his life, he felt connected to another person.

But someday she'd leave, head back home to Orcus. Or maybe head out looking for someone capable of saying *I love you*. The idea of another man with her made him scowl fiercely, and he forced himself to stop thinking of it. Instead he focused on all the dead ends he kept hitting in his investigation.

It was unusual: Most demons were smart, he'd learned that years ago, but this group seemed to be unusually cunning. They stayed one step ahead of him, and he felt as if he were chasing shadows.

Conor gripped the steering wheel harder. Mika was in serious danger, and he didn't want to sit around twiddling his thumbs, waiting for trouble. He wanted to be proactive, to take care of the problem before it took care of her. But there was nothing he could do except wait till they tipped their hand.

If it were anyone but Mika, he'd consider a plan of using bait. He could use her to lure the would-be killers into the open at a time and place of his choosing. That kind of advantage could tip the scales in his favor, and he had the weapon Nat had given him. Even though the man had been scared, Conor trusted his info; if Nat said the bulky-looking pistol killed demons, Conor believed it. But because this was Mika, he wouldn't risk that. He would never risk *her*. If anything happened to her because of one of his plans, he'd never forgive himself.

The signal turned yellow. Conor would have floored the gas, but the car in front of him stopped and he muttered a curse. It was late; didn't these people have anything better to do than get in his way? He wanted to get home, to see Mika light up when he opened the door. She'd run her gaze over his body as she walked toward him, checking to make sure he hadn't been hurt; and when she was satisfied he was fine, a look of relief, of joy, would cross her face. Conor closed his eyes, savoring the image. Then Mika would put her arms around him and—

A horn blared behind him, knocking him out of his daydream, and he took his foot off the brake. He had it bad. She'd become too damn important to him and he'd reached the point where he enjoyed hearing her say, *"I love you."* And as much as he liked the words when his cock was deep inside her, he enjoyed hearing them even more outside the bedroom. It gave him a ray of hope that this wasn't only a heat-of-the-moment thing, but real. He knew better, though. He was protecting her, and in a situation like this, it was easy to confuse gratitude with something deeper.

Conor growled, then shook his head. Since meeting Mika, he'd been making sounds that weren't human more and more often. And she liked it. Every time a demon noise escaped, he felt the change in her.

Yes, his sexy little whirlwind frightened him more than any enemy he'd ever faced. She could decimate him—which was scary enough—but the most terrifying thing was what she did to his control. His Kiverian nature was slipping the leash with alarming frequency. Sometimes he didn't realize it had happened until long after the fact. It wasn't conscious on his part. Certainly, he hadn't been attempting the integration that Mika promoted, but it seemed to be occurring anyway. Conor ran a hand over his chin and shook his head. She'd turned his life upside down, and he wanted her to stay, wanted her to keep doing it.

But he knew she wouldn't.

Mika's ties to Orcus, her mistaking some other emotion for love, his somberness—those were just the tip of the iceberg. Conor had seen his Kiverian side scare people: his mother, a woman he'd had a serious relationship with a few years ago, others. He'd never been able to contain his demon nature tightly enough for any extended period of time. Mika was frightened of the Dark Ones. How long till she became scared of him too?

What he'd done to her in bed . . . Conor still felt sick when he recalled Mika's lesson. She'd had him so worked up the other night, he hadn't been able to think about anything except his lust. He sure hadn't heard a word she'd said, not until she'd pinched him, and even then there had only been a moment of focus before he'd sunk back into desire. What if she'd been less forceful about getting him to listen? What if she really had said no?

He used his fingers to wipe away the sweat that beaded on his upper lip. Mika wanted him to wonder about his father's actions on the night Conor was conceived. Her ploy had been a success. He did speculate if the demon had heard anything that had been said, and Conor questioned how assertive his mother had been about breaking through the mindless hunger.

Which made Conor even more determined to remain in command, particularly in bed. Even though they both healed fast, he didn't like that he'd bit her hard enough to draw blood, that he'd left bruises on her soft skin. But despite his regrets, Mika was able to push him out of his head. The wilder he was when they made love, the more she liked it.

Conor started sweating again, but this had nothing to do with fear. Mika wasn't experienced—he'd read that right—but what she lacked in skill, she made up for with enthusiasm and imagination.

Traffic thinned out. He couldn't jump her first thing in the door . . . could he? They hadn't done it standing up yet.

The idea of taking her against the wall, only the bare minimum of clothing shoved out of the way, got him hot. Conor shook his head, trying to clear that mental picture. His body was half-hard just from thinking about it, and he had to get his thoughts on something else or he might not be able to walk by the time he arrived home.

He'd see how Mika reacted when he kissed her. Maybe she'd be fine with a quickie in the entryway. And maybe he should keep his damn mind on his driving before he had an accident.

It seemed to take forever before he parked his pickup on the street in front of his house. He turned off the ignition, but he didn't rush to get out. She'd told him they balanced each other. Conor knew she meant his soberness with her whimsy, but it went deeper. Mika's joy and laughter had pulled him from limbo, and not only had it brought him to life, but it kept him anchored there. He needed her in ways he was only beginning to comprehend.

Stepping out of his truck, he pocketed his keys and slammed the door. Somehow he had to convince Mika to stay with him.

He rounded the hood, already anticipating the feel of her mouth under his. Her pants had an elastic waistband; he could have them down around her knees in no time. Conor's lips turned up ruefully. He had it bad, no doubt about it.

Halfway to the front door, it registered. Conor froze,

scanning with his senses, and immediately realized his protection had been compromised. *Son of a bitch*. He strengthened the energy shield that surrounded his body.

It would have been smarter to enter stealthily; he knew that but didn't give a rat's ass. His woman needed him. Bursting through the front door, Conor took in the scene in a split second. Another one of those damn dark demons was shooting something at Mika from his hands. She looked half-dazed, hair falling into her face, and Conor knew the bastard had her. The great room was in shambles, as if a tornado had gone through it—Mika's way of defending herself, he realized.

The dark demon looked at him, then at Mika. When his hand drew back, Conor struck; with his forearm, he knocked the Dark One's aim off. A fireblast hit the ceiling, leaving a smoldering, charred hole. Conor had to block from his mind what that blast would have done if it had struck Mika.

If he could just hang on to the bastard, he could freeze him—but Conor wasn't given the chance. The demon quickly escaped. Conor pursued, but wasn't able to narrow the distance between them.

"Cowards run," Conor called with a snarl.

The dark demon turned, his eyes glowing, then said calmly enough, "Believe what you will." Finally, firing another blast at Mika, he ducked out the door.

Conor barely had time to intercept. His protective shield held—something he'd wondered about, given what Mika had said about the Dark Ones' power. The magic was the most intense he'd ever felt, but he absorbed and processed it into energy he could use. If only he had a target. His enemy was gone. To verify, he ran a scan, but he hadn't missed anything. He muttered a couple of curses and then turned to check on Mika. She was swaying and he caught her as her knees buckled.

"Honey, are you okay?" he asked.

No response. That wasn't good. He sat down, holding her on his lap. Her whole body shook violently, and when he lifted her eyelid to check her pupils, all he saw was white. He didn't know one damn thing about dealing with this, and he doubted any Emergency Room doctor would know how to treat it either. Conor cursed again and wrapped his arms around her. "Mika, don't die," he begged.

"Not . . . planning . . . on it."

As he cuddled her against his chest, the spasms began to abate. He moved her away and saw she had her eyes open. Conor tried to imagine what the bastard had done to Mika. "How bad is it?" he asked.

She took a deep breath. Her lips curved. "I'm not sure what happened, but . . . I'm okay, McCabe. Relax." And she rubbed the back of his neck, trying to ease his tension.

"You could have died," he growled. She *would* have died if he hadn't come home when he had.

"But I didn't," she argued.

Her eyes were clearing, and her body only quivered with occasional spasms now. That enabled Conor to take his fear down a notch and think. After feeling that demon's power, he knew that Mika was right when she'd said the bastard hadn't run because of him. There was some other reason why the dark demon didn't want to engage, but damned if he knew what.

"Are you okay?" Mika's soft question pulled him from his thoughts.

"Yeah, why wouldn't I be?" he asked.

"You took a hit, too. I was alert enough to see."

"I'm fine. I just hope *that*"—he gestured to the hole in the ceiling—"didn't go all the way up through the roof."

Mika laughed, and Conor relaxed some more. If she could find humor here, then she was okay. With his index finger, he angled her face for his kiss. Keeping the action gentle, he explored her mouth to express the relief he felt.

For a brief moment after he drew back, they only stared at each other. Then Mika said, "I love you, McCabe."

He nodded, unable to speak around the constriction in his throat. Her words filled him with satisfaction. As did the way she said his last name: There was so much affection, so much warmth in her voice that it was an obvious endearment. He for damn sure liked it better than the stupid pet names some women used.

Her avowal made him even more determined that nothing happen to her. Which got him thinking again. How the hell had that bastard dismantled his protection? Only someone who had his permission to enter his property could do that. Conor knew Mika hadn't taken it down and Ben, his former mentor, was in Arizona. He needed to walk the perimeter and see what had happened, see if he could fix things. As long as his security was down, Mika was unsafe here.

A piece of ceiling fell, narrowly missing them and reminding him to check the damage to his house.

"I have to go outside and take a look at what he did to the shield. Will you be all right here by yourself?" he asked.

Her eyes flared. "Of course I will."

"Honey, you couldn't stand up a few minutes ago. I don't want to leave you defenseless."

As if to prove to him how much she'd recovered, Mika got to her feet and moved across the room. "I'm fine," she said.

Conor went to her and pushed her hair back until his fingers hit the barrette. He unsnapped it and, using both hands, gently untangled her locks. "If you need me, yell," he said, and he handed her the clip.

"I will."

After a moment's hesitation, he nodded and headed outside. The night air felt cool, and Conor tipped his face into it, trying to sense any demonic presence. There was nothing.

In the nearly five years he'd lived here, his protection had been impenetrable. It had been tested repeatedly by humans, vampires, werewolves, and yeah, demons. Sometimes he knew when someone tried to cross the energy shield or take it down, sometimes he only suspected. He did know that in the last six months or so, the attempts had become a lot more frequent. But this was the first time anyone had succeeded, and he wanted to know how they'd done it.

Conor checked the two front corners first. Nothing was amiss at either place, but he didn't expect to find anything. With his truck mere feet away, he'd have noticed immediately when he pulled up. Even if he had been in a fog of lust.

He walked along his property line to the back of the house. The third corner checked out okay, too. Which left one last place.

Corner number four was hidden by bushes he'd been meaning to trim for months. As he neared them, Conor noticed they were even more overgrown than he'd realized, and perfect cover for nefarious activity. Damn. He'd have to make this a priority.

Pushing the branches away from his face, he headed behind them to check the last section of his yard. He nearly fell over the body. Crouching down, Conor checked for a pulse. It was there, but weak, and even as he monitored it, the beat grew fainter. There was no blood or other sign of injury, but a Dark One didn't need to leave visible wounds to kill.

As he pulled his hand back, the half-dead man turned his head and Conor grunted in surprise. Ben? His mentor had been the one to let the enemy in? He struggled to fight the overwhelming sense of betrayal. "I don't see any indication of trauma," Conor said, his voice tight. "What did they do to you?"

"Life force spell."

It made an odd kind of sense. The spell they'd used stole

life force energy from a victim and transferred it to the demon. The spell was only capable of extracting a small amount, but at Ben's age, that would be all it would take.

"Do you want me to call an ambulance?" he asked, although there was nothing anyone would be able to do.

"No. It's too late. But I knew if I could hang on, I'd get a chance to talk to you."

"Why?" he demanded furiously. "So you could explain why you turned on me?"

"I was protecting you." Ben's voice was sad. The man tried to sit up, obviously using the last of his energy.

Conor was too angry to rein in. "Bullshit. You destroyed my home's shield and allowed him in! He nearly killed my wo—my client tonight."

"*They*"—Ben emphasized the plural—"are here to protect you from her. The leaders of Orcus want you killed."

Conor would have laughed if he weren't so angry. "If Mika wanted me dead, I'd be dead. She's had plenty of opportunity. Either you're lying, or you were stupid enough to believe their lies. Mika isn't capable of murder."

Ben reached out, clasping his arm with surprising strength. "She's part of a team. She's not an assassin, she's the thief. They briefed her on you and your background, then sent her in. The Council wants a spell you have, and when she gets it, the two assassins sent to kill you will do so. Believe me." His grip tightened for a moment, but the strength didn't last.

"Why should I? Your facts come from Dark Ones. *Demons!* It never occurred to you that they were telling you lies to get at her? You should be smarter than that. They want her dead, and you did everything but roll out the welcome mat."

"Your father . . ." Ben's voice trailed off as Conor stiffened.

"What about that bastard?"

Ben took a deep breath. "He's with the demons trying to

protect you, and he swore to me that he wanted to save your life. I couldn't come to you. I had to work with them. Didn't want you dead. They said . . ." Ben's hand slipped from his arm. "I love you, Conor, like my own son. Couldn't let you die."

The older man's eyes actually filled with tears, and that thwarted Conor's anger. "You've always meant a lot to me too," he said awkwardly. Damn, the man was dying and he still couldn't say those words. He did love Ben, as if the man were a grandfather or an uncle. If it weren't for him, who knew how Conor's life would have turned out? Ben had found him living on the streets of Los Angeles after his mother washed her hands of him, and had taken Conor under his wing, given him a place to stay, and taught him the business of being a slayer.

"Don't worry. I know. . . ." Ben's eyes closed as he winced.

"Thanks," Conor whispered.

"I know too, that you don't want to believe me about *her*. You're thinking they did this to me, so how honest can they be? But your father wasn't part of this. I believed *him*. You won't want to hear it, but he loves you. It was obvious when he talked about you."

Conor could have said a number of different things on the topic, but he didn't. What was the point? Ben would think whatever the hell he wanted, anyhow.

Although Conor knew there wasn't a damn thing any human doctor could do to save him, he asked, "Are you sure you don't want me to call an ambulance?"

Ben shook his head. "Nah. Can't do nothing against this spell. Just promise I didn't die for no reason. Promise me you'll throw her out."

"I promise you won't die in vain, but I won't throw Mika out. I already gave my word to protect her. I'll fulfill the obligation."

"You don't believe me about her?" Ben hissed. "She was

sent for the enslavement spell. I *knew* that thing would be trouble."

"Yeah, I remember. You told me to burn it, that no good could come from finding it. But those dark demons, they're not on my side." He didn't want to believe it. Yet . . . if they were here to protect him, their retreats made more sense. They'd known from the way Conor put himself in front of her that he would die in her defense.

Conor shook his head. He couldn't be buying into this fantasy they'd spun for Ben. "Why send her then, and not a stronger demon? If they want me dead?"

"They knew she'd be able to get closer. She's half human. Like you."

"You know?" That shocked him.

"I always knew. It doesn't change who you are."

A thousand thoughts whirled through Conor's head, but before he could settle on any one, Ben's breathing changed. The wheezy, rattling sound shook Conor and he put his hand on his mentor's shoulder. "Ben, are you all right?" No answer. "Ben?"

The older man's breathing stopped altogether.

Conor waited for it to resume, but it didn't. The urge to throw his head back and howl raged through him, but he fought it. "Rest well," he said. "I guess you know how much what you did meant to me. Thank you."

Slowly, he stood and walked back inside. Mika was alone and vulnerable. He couldn't neglect her any longer.

But how could Ben have conspired with demons? He'd known how they lied.

Mika's a demon. Conor shook off the voice in his head. The Dark Ones were trying to kill her; she wasn't lying about that. She'd be dead already if not for him.

But she'd claimed it was a Kiverian who wanted her dead, and not these two Dark Ones. He knew she read energy too accurately to make that kind of mistake.

Maybe she'd lied to ensure he'd take the job. It was understandable. She'd been scared, needed help and knew nothing would get him on her side faster than being hunted by a Kiverian. Except, she shouldn't have known yet that he hated Kiverians. Or why.

Conor thought back to the night they met, the way she'd immediately known his mother was raped. What he'd said hadn't given it away, Mika shouldn't have jumped to that conclusion so quickly. Unless she had been filled in about him beforehand.

He walked to the front of the house instead of using the back door. Mika couldn't be part of some plot to kill him. If she was, it meant that everything between them was a lie. Everything. And that just wasn't possible.

Chapter Fourteen

Mika paced anxiously, but when two turns around the room left her dizzy to the point of staggering, she sat on the sofa. Where the hell was Conor? It couldn't take so long to just check around—not unless he'd run into trouble. She brought her heels up and wrapped her arms around her knees. If anything happened to him, she'd hunt those bastards down and kill them. Big talk for someone who could have died tonight, and whose head was still swimming from the shots the Dark One fired, but she meant every word.

She wanted to go outside and check on Conor, but she knew better. If he was involved in a fight, her presence would only distract him. She refused to let her worry make her do anything that would endanger him.

No matter how difficult it was to wait.

It was an eternity before she heard the door open. Mika dropped her feet back to the floor and let her eyes eat Conor up. He appeared unharmed, but something had occurred, and from the stone-cold look on his face, it was serious.

"Conor?" she said. She stood, crossing the room to him. "Are you okay? What happened?"

Without answering, he stepped around her and walked deeper into the great room. Pivoting, she went after him, but she'd moved too quickly and her head started to spin again. She braced her feet to keep her balance. The last thing she wanted was Conor to think he had to take care of her. "You're scaring me. Please, are you okay?" she asked.

"Fine."

There was no emotion in his voice, and that frightened Mika more than his expression. When he walked away from her again, she followed and wrapped her arms around his waist from behind. After pressing a kiss between his shoulder blades, she asked, "What happened?"

Another eternity passed; then he turned and pushed her away from him. Okay, some men didn't like to be touched after a battle because they were too keyed up, she understood that, but she didn't think that was Conor's problem. After an even more intense encounter with one of the dark demons, he'd taken her to bed and kept her there until they were both exhausted. Why didn't he want her to hold him now?

For the first time, Mika felt unsure of herself. She linked her fingers together at her waist and squeezed her hands tightly as she debated what to do. Did she continue to push to learn what had gone on outside, though he'd already ignored her question?

As the silence lengthened, she became more uncomfortable. Finally she cursed and said, "McCabe, you tell me what happened out there or I'm going to hurt you myself."

"Hurt me yourself? Has the plan changed, Mika? I thought you were supposed to find the enslavement spell before I was killed."

"There's no plan to kill you! I made them promise—" It wasn't until she saw the flash in his eyes and watched his expression become even more remote that she realized what she'd admitted. She felt the blood drain out of her face. He'd been on a fishing expedition, and she'd taken the bait faster than a shark would chum.

"Conor." She reached for him, but he stepped back, evading her touch. Mika let her hand fall to her side.

"Congratulations, you had me snowed. I trusted you. I believed what you told me. Of course, you went out of your way to make sure it was my cock doing the thinking and not my brain."

McCabe didn't use language like that with her, not out of bed, and it drove home exactly how furious—and how hurt—he was. "It wasn't like that, I swear."

His hands fisted and relaxed at his sides. "You swear? Why doesn't that make me feel any better?"

"I know I hurt you, but I give you my word, I did not use the visht—the attraction between us to complete my mission."

He'd caught her slip; she could see it in the way his gaze sharpened. Mika bit back a groan. Tonight wasn't going well for her. The magical attacks she'd absorbed earlier had left her thoughts sluggish, which was why she was making mistakes. That was small consolation.

Conor closed the distance and, taking hold of her shoulders, glared down at her. "Vishtau. That's what you were going to say, right? *Right?*" he demanded, when she didn't answer.

"You know about the vishtau?" That surprised her.

"Start talking," was all he said.

Mika frowned. Was he testing her? "I don't understand."

"I want you to tell me about the vishtau."

"But—" When the glow in his eyes brightened, she stopped short. Mika tried to organize her thoughts, but she wasn't having much luck. Not only was her mind slow, she was upset. She decided to just be honest. "Sex is pretty casual for most in Orcus. I don't know if it's always been that way, or if it's because the number of males is far greater than the number of females."

When she paused, Conor's hands tightened. Mika continued quickly: "But that changes when a demon meets a vishtau mate. The closest thing to it is the human concept of soul mates, but it goes far beyond that for demons, and most of us hold it in reverence." She shrugged. "Probably because our population is stagnant and we can only conceive with such a mate."

"What?" His tone startled her.

"Well, there have been rumors that the dark demons found another bond that leads to conception, but—"

"I don't give a fuck about the dark demons," he interrupted, pinning her with the hardest look she'd ever gotten from him. "We didn't use birth control that one time."

Although he didn't say it, she knew he referred to the time she'd recited the rauthima ritual. "It was only once."

"That's all it takes." Conor released her and walked away. When he reached the wall, he put his palm against it and leaned forward before cursing a few more times.

Hurt filled every cell in her body before anger replaced it. "You weren't worried before, but now it's a concern? Well, you can put your mind at ease, McCabe. Odds are slim I'm pregnant. The average time before conception is around seven years."

He turned back to her. "*Average*," he said. "That means sometimes it happens faster. Likely, sometimes much faster."

"And it also means that sometimes it takes longer. Like I said, don't worry." Mika flipped her hair over her shoulder. "I can see how much you dislike the idea, and I won't burden you if it turns out we're a more fertile match than most."

Before she could escape, he caught her and jerked her around to face him. "If you're pregnant, you had damn well *better* tell me."

She supposed that meant he didn't plan on waiting around with her to find out. Mika dug her nails into her palms, trying to fight back the pain. She might not like it, but it wasn't something she could hide. Those of demon blood were connected to their children, and he'd be aware of the baby the minute she gave birth. Besides, the chances of her being pregnant were so minuscule that it cost her almost nothing to grant his promise. "You have my word: I'll contact you if it's necessary."

"You better." The growl was so pronounced in his voice that Mika didn't doubt his resolve. For a long moment, he stared at her, maybe judging her sincerity; then he asked, "When did you realize we had this bond? From the start?"

"I suspected before I crossed the veil," she admitted. "And it was confirmed when we met. My response to you was overwhelmingly sexual. That came from the vishtau"—she grabbed his forearm and squeezed—"and not some plan to keep you from thinking about what I was doing." She didn't know why she bothered to explain when he was so unreceptive.

Conor pulled free and walked away. Again, pain swamped her. It hurt something fierce to lose him and she could see him growing more distant already. "I love you," she said quietly.

His reaction was immediate. In a blur of motion, he pinned her to the wall, his hand resting at the base of her throat. He wasn't as threatening as the night they'd met, but close. "I don't want to hear that lie from you again," he snarled.

"It's not a lie." She held his gaze so that he'd know she was speaking the truth, but it wasn't easy with her head swimming.

"It's not real emotion, but some biological connection. It means nothing."

He was so near. An hour ago, she could have leaned in and nuzzled the pulse hammering in his throat. She could have whispered sex words in his ear and enjoyed the results. Now, she didn't dare respond sexually. Though Conor would hate to know this, there wasn't much human about him at the moment; she was facing an infuriated Kiverian male. She trusted that he'd never hurt her physically, but no one with a brain would goad someone in this mood.

"The bond doesn't guarantee strong emotions," she informed him. She kept her tone matter-of-fact. "My parents are fond of each other, but they never fell in love." Mika lost her detachment and reached for him. "What I feel for you is real, Conor—as real as it gets."

If she'd been smart, she wouldn't have said that last part since it caused his temper to spike. All she saw was red in his eyes now, which was strong enough to burn through the green tint in his lenses. "Don't fucking lie to me," he snarled.

Each word was bitten out, and Mika realized he was balanced on a razor's edge. She began to drop her gaze, to act submissive, but stopped as she recalled how much he'd hated it the last time. As furious as he was with her, the last thing she wanted was to enrage him more.

"I swear, no more lies," she said quietly. He looked skeptical. "Demons don't break their promises, you know that."

Some of the fire faded, though his eyes continued to glow. McCabe released her and said, "I want to know everything about why you're here. Start at the beginning."

"Do you mind if we sit down? I *will* tell you all I know," she added hurriedly when his expression hardened once more. "But there's no reason we can't be comfortable, is there?"

After a moment of hesitation, probably trying to decide if she was up to something, Conor stepped away. Mika took a deep breath and tried for nonchalance as she walked to the couch. She couldn't let him know how adrift she felt; in a matter of days, he'd become her cornerstone, and just as she'd begun to rely on that foundation, it had been jerked out from beneath her.

In all fairness, she couldn't blame McCabe. As soon as she'd met him, Mika had known he wouldn't take her subterfuge lightly. She'd even planned to stay around and face the music after fulfilling her mission. Well, the band was playing—too bad it was earlier than she'd expected.

She sat on the end opposite the bookcase and tucked her right ankle under her left knee. Without a word, Conor joined her, sitting as far away as he could get. He gestured. There was no mistaking that the motion meant *start talking*.

"I didn't go looking for this job," Mika said. She was uncertain how much he knew of demon society, but she decided that if he had questions, he wouldn't be shy about asking them. "I'm largely ignored by other demons, and it was a surprise to be approached by an aide to the Council. My first thought was that they wanted me permanently out of Orcus."

Mika smiled at Conor, but he only stared back at her. Sobering, she tugged the hem of her T-shirt and continued. "They had a favor to ask me. That shocked me even more than being summoned to the Council chamber. I'm a weak demon—what could *I* do that they, or some other demon, couldn't do more easily?"

"Get to me." His voice was flat, and Mika bit back a sigh.

"They weren't that blunt. There was some mild ass kissing, but it wasn't overdone. Looking back I can see how they played me, but at the time"—she shrugged—"it seemed legitimate. I felt as if they valued me."

But she'd promised him complete honesty, so she went on. "I was going to turn down the mission, then they handed me your file and told me to look through it. Once I saw your picture and suspected you were my mate, I knew I had to meet you."

"You didn't need the Council's job for that."

"I know. Except, I realized that they wanted you dead. If you had the spell memorized, you could recite it even without a written copy. I bargained with them." She leaned forward, hoping her intensity, her sincerity would pierce his anger. "I told them I'd do it if they vowed not to harm you."

"Sure," he drawled sarcastically.

Mika ignored him. "As I've thought about it, though, I decided they were correct about one thing—that incantation does need to be destroyed. My mother lives in Orcus and so does my gran, my half brother, and other assorted relatives. I won't allow their wills to be enslaved by anyone," she said fiercely. "Not even you. It's not right."

He snorted. "I have no plans to enslave anyone. Do you think I want a bunch of demonic serfs?"

"Well, how was I supposed to know? I hadn't met you yet when I gave the Council my word."

"But you figured it out once you got to know me."

She couldn't decipher the emotion in his voice, so decided to take his words at face value. "I know you hate demons." She quirked up one side of her mouth at the understatement. "But I've also learned that you're honorable. I don't think you'd perform the spell—but it doesn't matter. The Council insisted I make a promise."

McCabe sighed impatiently. "I heard that the first time, and we both know demons never go back on their word. So despite everything that's happened between us, you have no choice."

"Right!" She leaned forward again, optimistic that he finally understood. Maybe he could forgive her.

"Did you promise the Council that you wouldn't reveal your mission to me?"

Hope died. Mika could guess which direction Conor was headed with his questions. "No, but if I told you why I was here and you refused to hand over the spell, it would be the same as not doing my utmost to secure it. And I did vow to give it the best effort I was capable of giving."

"You can assure the Council that you sacrificed everything."

His neutral tone almost disguised the dig, and it took her a few seconds to catch on. "I didn't make love with you for that stupid spell! I went to bed with you because I wanted you, because I lo—" She cut herself off before she finished.

Conor would become livid again if she said that. "It was about us, not my assignment," she finished more quietly.

He shrugged, and Mika rumbled low in her throat. He was determined to deride what they'd shared, and she refused to allow that. Their relationship was special, important. He could deny it aloud all he wanted, try to convince himself that it was part of her ruse, but in his heart, he had to know the truth. Furious, Mika pushed to her feet.

"Sit down," he commanded softly.

Mika sat. She still hoped to overcome his sense of betrayal and the outrage that went with it, and so she wasn't going to make things worse. "What else did you want to know?" she asked.

"How many others are with you?"

"What? No one. Oh, I was supposed to report in to a human minion, and he was to pass along my reports to the Council, but I only heard from him once. Maybe. That might have been a trick to get me—" She cut herself off, but again she wasn't fast enough.

"To get you to that park? Do you even *have* a cousin?"

Offering him a weak smile, Mika said, "Of course I have a cousin. Kimi—Kimiko Noguchi—is real and as close as a sister to me. If she lived in Crimson City and—"

He cut her off. "But she doesn't live here."

"She's in college at Berkeley."

He swore. "What the hell have you told me that is true?"

Mika kept her mouth shut. If she said that she truly loved him, he'd only get pissed off all over again. Besides, she knew a rhetorical question when she heard one.

"Never mind." Conor rubbed the back of his neck. "What about the demons that are here to kill me when you give the nod?"

"Didn't you hear a word I said? I took this job to keep them from killing you. But even if I hadn't, do you think I'd be involved in cold-blooded murder?" She was disgusted. What did he think of her? "I'm not part of some plot to kill you, and I don't know why you keep insisting I am!"

Grabbing her bent leg, he tugged her across the couch until her knee bumped him. "Because I was told there were assassins waiting to take me out as soon as you had the spell."

"Who told you that?" she asked.

"Someone I trust. Someone who's never lied to me."

"Whoever it is, they're wrong. I made the Council *promise* not to hurt you." Mika tried again to recall the exact wording of their vow, but it eluded her. "I was off balance from being called to their chambers, though, from wondering if you were my mate. Maybe I didn't get the oath as solid as I thought."

"You're backpedaling pretty damn fast," he suggested.

She gritted her teeth. "Damn it, McCabe, give me a break. I'm not part of any plot to off you. Didn't I save your life from that auric assassin?"

"That could have been staged to win my confidence. You could simply have been acting like the lying, untrustworthy, demonic—"

Mika growled—a long; low sound. "I'm through being insulted. Yes, I lied to you. Yes, I had ulterior motives for approaching you. But that doesn't give you unlimited free shots at me." She fisted her hand in the neck of his T-shirt and twisted the fabric to yank him closer. "I *love* you, McCabe." She jerked hard on his shirt when he opened his mouth to interrupt her. "I don't care if you don't want to hear. Deal with it. I love you and I'll protect you with my life, so don't you dare insinuate that I'd let anyone hurt you, let alone help them."

With that, she released him and stood up. She needed to get away from him for a while or there was no telling what she'd say or do. She was halfway to the bedroom when he stopped her.

"Come back here."

"No." She didn't quit walking.

"We need to discuss what our story is going to be when I call B-Ops. That can't wait."

"B-Ops? What for?" Curiosity made her turn to study his face. Conor remained expressionless.

"That dark bastard killed a friend of mine and left his body in the backyard. With the signs of a struggle in here, it shouldn't be hard to convince the team that we had a simple break-in, but we need to get our stories straight. I don't want them looking at you too closely. And I don't want them to realize that Ben's death wasn't from natural causes. The Dark Ones are mine, and I don't want B-Ops involved."

Mika didn't offer her condolences about Ben; clearly McCabe didn't want to hear them. But her heart broke for his loss. With a sigh, she headed back to the sofa. This night wasn't over yet.

It was late. Or early, depending on how you looked at it. Conor used his thumbnail to pick at the Evil Twin Brewery label on the bottle he held, and tried to ignore the sound of Mika's breathing. He was at his desk and she was in bed, but he couldn't tune her out. Maybe he wasn't trying hard enough.

She wasn't asleep. He'd only known her for days, and yet he was familiar enough with the rhythm of her breathing to know when she was and wasn't conscious. He would have cursed, but he didn't have the heart for it. Not when he could see the coroner carting Ben away in a body bag. And damn her, Mika had stood right beside him, slipping her hand into his and holding on tight until the vehicle pulled away.

Conor gave up trying to separate the label from the glass and put the empty bottle down on his desk. She'd probably still be hanging on to him if the lead B-Ops investigator hadn't come over. He exhaled long and slow. Mika was one hell of an accomplished liar, and he wasn't talking about how she'd worked him over. The team had taken one glance at her innocent-looking face and fallen all over themselves to make things easier for her after the ordeal of the break-in. Even the females of the group had bought her act hook, line and sinker. Mika was the younger sister each of them wanted to protect. Never mind that she was physically stronger than every single one of them and far more dangerous.

He'd been prepared to use a bit of mind control magic to sway the situation, but it hadn't been necessary—not with Mika spinning out their story so skillfully. She'd added a few tears at appropriate moments, and men had fought to offer her tissues. Even the incident with her car exploding hadn't raised any suspicion—merely speculation that she had a stalker.

Straightening in his seat, Conor ran a hand over the back of his neck and sighed. They'd stuck mostly to the truth: A male had broken into the house and attacked Mika; she'd fought him, and when Conor arrived home, the man had decided the game was up and run. Ben's body had been the hard part, but when Mika said that he'd been coming to town to meet her and give their love his blessing, almost the whole team smiled. Smiled! What the hell?

And when someone collected his thoughts enough to ask what Ben had been doing at their house at that time of night, outside, Mika had simply shrugged and told them he'd been supposed to arrive tomorrow, but must have gotten to town early.

Thinking about it, Conor shook his head. Giving a slight tremble to her lower lip, Mika had claimed she'd been scared, in need of comfort, and Conor had been seeing to her. It wasn't until later when Conor had gone outside that he'd discovered his friend's body. And Mika had managed to make a fat tear roll down her cheek. Shit. The woman was wasted in Orcus; she should be on the big screen.

He heard her shift in bed, and sighed again. Maybe he should be grateful Mika had taken the spotlight. Her act had shielded them both. The idea of lying about what had happened to his friend was more than he could swallow—

and yet he'd had no choice, unless he'd wanted a government inquiry. Then she'd taken over. Conor grimaced. He'd quickly become superfluous, merely the lover who'd arrived in the nick of time.

The worst thing was, in the middle of this performance Marc Hayes had shown up. Someone must have tipped the man off, and it was the last thing they'd needed. He'd watched Mika much too closely—her damn light-colored eyes—and had asked some pointed questions. Conor wished they could have avoided the whole situation, but what was the alternative? Leave Ben in the backyard?

Such falsehoods shouldn't weigh so heavily on him. He knew no one else in Crimson City could handle this situation, that it was up to him to take down the dark demons; but it still felt wrong. Ben had been there for him, and now . . . Conor cut himself off. He couldn't think; not today. The loss was too strong. After he eliminated the dark demons, after he got Mika the hell out of his house, then he'd take the time to mourn.

Sometimes he worried about how easy it was for him to compartmentalize. Ben was probably the one person on earth who'd ever given a shit about him, and Conor had no difficulty locking down his emotions over his friend's death. That seemed wrong. Especially when he was unable to push Mika out of his thoughts.

She shifted her body and he froze, hoping she stayed out of his way. He couldn't look at her yet. Not with her betrayal fresh in his mind. She'd done something crueler than lie. Mika had given him hope, and then snatched it away. When he heard her settle again, he relaxed. But he couldn't help wondering, how close had she been to locating the spell and disappearing?

She'd been through his desk—he'd caught her redhanded—and the moved coffee table gave away the bookcase as the location of her most recent search. Curious, Conor went to the shelves. Moving the table back where it went, he attempted to sense what she'd touched. It was easy to track a person's energy sig, but it was much harder to read traces left on inanimate objects. At least, it was difficult for him.

Closing his eyes to focus, Conor studied the shelves. It took a few minutes, but Mika's presence was stronger at the top. He double-checked and decided that, while the energy was fainter down low, it was also more complete. She'd started there and worked up.

How close *had* she come?

Holding the palm of his hand about half an inch away from the spines of the books, he moved it across the third shelf, then the second. She'd finished with both of those—and recently too, unless he missed his guess. Conor checked the final shelf and found where she'd ended. Seven books. She'd been only seven books away from the one containing the spell.

If she'd started at the top instead of the bottom of the bookcase, she would have put her hands on it right away. If that dark demon hadn't shown up, she might have found it tonight. He rechecked her energy sig and noted that her search had been thorough and careful—not something most people would have expected from Mika, he guessed. But her methodical approach didn't surprise him; he'd seen how precisely she'd organized his papers.

Conor reached for the book, then shot a quick glance at the bedroom doorway. The coast was clear. Returning to the desk, he held the text and stared at it.

The binding was old but not original. Its cover was blank, no title or hint of what was inside, and there weren't many pages. Amazing how much trouble this one slim volume had caused. It had brought Mika into his life long enough for him to trust her, to want more time with her, and then it had taken her away from him. This book was also responsible for Ben's death, and for the dark demons trying to kill Mika.

Leaning forward, he waggled the text in his hands. For

years he'd searched for a way to call his father forward, to exact retribution for his mother's rape. But he'd had a major obstacle—he didn't know who had sired him. And as far as Conor could tell, there were only two ways to draw someone out of Orcus: Either the summoner used the demon's name, or he put out a random request and took whoever showed up.

His mother had chosen option number two, not realizing she'd get a Kiverian.

But this spell . . . Conor ran a hand over the book's cloth cover. He was sure he could use this spell to force his father to face him. Conor simply needed to figure out how to adapt it so that he only brought forth one particular demon and not all of them.

The incantation in its current form would give him power over all demons allegedly, but it would also open the veil between Orcus and the Overworld. That was the last thing he wanted. He was a slayer. He hunted outlaw vampires and werewolves and occasionally demons, whenever they managed to appear. It was his fondest desire to rid Crimson City of demons. Each and every one of them.

Or at least, that *had been* his goal. Conor wasn't as dead set on it as he'd been before Mika. He shook his head. Was he going to think of life this way from now on. Before Mika and After Mika? As if on cue, she shifted in bed again, and he wondered if she were having as much trouble quieting her thoughts as he.

Conor opened the book and stared at the ornate writing. He'd spent years studying, trying to work out the phrasing he would need to call forward one specific but unnamed Kiverian. He'd examined every other summoning spell he'd found, and with the info he'd gathered, it was just a matter of time until he perfected one. Or it would have been. Before Mika.

Nothing was simple any longer.

Congratulations on the vishtau.

He could almost hear Nat's laughter. Conor gripped the edges of the book tightly. He should have checked out what a vishtau was immediately, but he'd been more focused on other things. Like Mika. And the demons running loose in the city. Particularly the Dark Ones.

He didn't remember reading about the vishtau in any of his books, and no one he'd talked with had ever mentioned it until Nat. But there was one person who damn well should have told him what it meant. Her keeping it a secret had been one more manipulation, one more lie.

And she could be pregnant. Shit, he couldn't be a father. What the hell did he know about parenting? It wasn't like he'd had any role models. His mother had considered him her punishment for joining a cult, and his father was a brutal rapist. Conor scrubbed a hand down his face. But if the worst happened, he'd have to deal with it. He wouldn't run from his responsibility.

Standing, he closed the spellbook with a snap and put it back on the shelf. He wanted to go into his weight room and work out some of his emotions, but he couldn't—not with the protection down around his house. While he doubted his foes would return in the few hours left of darkness, he wouldn't chance it. He wouldn't be caught worn out and off guard.

Reluctantly, he went into the bedroom and stripped down to his shorts. He felt Mika awake. She was watching him, but she didn't say anything. Good. Pulling back the covers on his side of the bed, he crawled in and tucked a hand behind his head.

Mika moved, pressing herself against his side. "Conor—"

"Don't touch me," he said. She froze at the coldness of his voice. Tough shit.

Her hand stroked down his chest, and his body responded. That pissed him off. Conor grabbed her hand, stopping it mid-caress, and grunted: "I said, don't touch me."

"But . . ." She trailed off.

"But what?"

"You came to bed."

It was hard holding on to his dispassion when she sounded so bewildered, but he managed. "I'm here to continue protecting you. I need to be close to do so." He turned his head and gave her a hard stare. "I gave my word. But you stay on your side of the bed and keep your hands to yourself, got it?"

"Yeah, I understand." She sounded hurt.

She withdrew slowly, and he fought the need to reach out and drag her to him. He felt cold without her body next to his. And he felt alone.

Pissed off that she still affected him, Conor turned onto his side, putting his back to her. He wasn't going to waste his time obsessing about a liar. There were more important things to consider—like, was his father really in Crimson City?

Ben had once been a good judge of character, but demons lied often and well. The one who had professed to be his father might have said that only to get Ben's cooperation. Those demons must have gone to Phoenix and waited for an opportunity to approach him. To enlist his aid, one had claimed to be Conor's father, and convinced the retired slayer that he had nothing but his son's best interests at heart. Ben was big on family, and Conor had never told him why he felt such antipathy for the man who'd given him half his DNA.

But was it just a lie?

Conor would know the instant he was close enough to read the man's energy signature whether or not they were related. It was unlikely, he knew, but if it really was his father . . .

If it really was his father, then Conor wouldn't have to worry about adjusting the spell or making a mistake and letting all the demons in Orcus run free on Earth. And he could put aside his tentative plan to enter the underworld to search for the man.

It would be easy to hunt the bastard down in Crimson City. Easy to kill him.

Ignoring the disquiet that stirred within him, Conor smiled coldly. Finally, he'd be able to take the son of a bitch down.

Chapter Fifteen

It was amazing, Conor thought as he rounded the hood of his truck, how fast things could change. Less than twenty-four hours ago, he'd been eager to get to Mika, and now he almost dreaded reaching her. He opened the passenger door, and reluctantly took her elbow to help her down. The last thing he wanted to do was touch her, but the pickup rode high, had oversized tires, and lacked a running board. As soon as she was safely on the ground, though, he pulled free. Mika didn't say a word, but her sigh spoke volumes. He ignored it and scanned their surroundings.

It had been a long time since he'd been in this section of LA. The area was rundown, but there were signs of renovation everywhere. Some of the buildings were finished, reclaiming the elegance of their early days, and many others had scaffolding and additional indications of work in progress around them. A year from now, this wouldn't be the same place.

Although it wasn't dark yet, the streetlights were shining, illuminating the sidewalks. Twilight wouldn't last much longer. He guessed they had about an hour till it was night.

"Come on," he ordered without glancing her direction. It still hurt too much to look at Mika, to know she didn't give a damn about him either.

He saw Hayes as soon as they rounded the corner. The man leaned against his beat-up Mustang, arms crossed over his chest. Although he didn't look over, Conor knew he was aware of their arrival.

"What the hell did you bring her for?" Hayes demanded when they reached him.

"Nice to see you again too," Mika said smoothly.

"She has demons after her. I couldn't leave her home alone and unprotected," Conor replied.

Hayes ignored Mika and argued, "You did exactly that a couple of days ago."

"Things changed."

The freelancer muttered another curse. "Some help you're going to be if you're busy babysitting *her*."

Conor heard Mika growl low in her throat, and hooked a hand in the waistband of her jeans in time to keep her from surging forward. She turned her glare on him. "Behave," he warned her coldly. Damn demons and their emotional responses. He turned his icy stare on Hayes next. "Don't use that tone. If you're pissed at me, take it out on me."

"I apologize," Hayes said, addressing Mika. When she nodded, Conor released his grip.

"Are we going to stand here until everyone the neighborhood is aware of us or are you going to fill me in on why you called for backup?"

The other man hesitated, then with a shrug, said, "I've found a couple of demons."

"Where?" If these were the pair after Mika, he could take care of them and get rid of her. There was nothing he wanted more than to have her gone. And maybe the one who'd claimed to be his father was with them. Maybe he would find out the truth or if it had been a lie to fool old Ben.

"See the opening between the two houses to my left? If

you look through, you'll see another building behind them. I think it might have been a small hotel, but it's in rough shape. They're holed up in the lobby—or at least in a large open area located in the front. I want to go in there after them, but I'm afraid they're going to rabbit out the back."

Conor reached out and probed the energy. There were two signatures, like Hayes claimed. One was definitely a demon—not one of the Dark Ones after Mika, but still very dangerous. The other . . . Well, Conor wasn't sure. The energy kept morphing the same way it did with Nat, yet he knew this wasn't his informant.

"It would be better if I went in there after them." How could he allow a human to face a demon darker than his own breed?

This time, it was Hayes who moved. He straightened away from his car and said, "No. I found them, you're backup, nothing more. Got it?"

Since Conor wouldn't want someone else horning in either, he nodded and reluctantly agreed. "Okay, they're yours. Do you have a plan, other than walking inside?"

"Yeah, make them talk, then kill them."

"Oh, that's a great plan," Mika piped up. "Do you know anything about what type of demons you'll be facing?"

"Type? Who the hell cares?" Hayes looked incredulous.

Instead of grabbing Mika by the jeans, Conor hooked an arm around her waist and anchored her at his side. The feel of her warm body distracted him for a moment, and he pushed the awareness away. He understood why she was angry. Humans believed a demon was a demon, and that there was no difference. But Mika would be little threat to anyone unless they cornered her and she was fighting for her life. She'd told him the night they'd met that her branch was mischievous, not dangerous, and from what he'd seen, he concurred with that assessment. At least in that one thing, she hadn't been lying.

"These demons might not know anything about what happened to the team," he cautioned. Conor ignored

Mika's curious stare. "Demons rarely work together, and if this duo wasn't involved, they'll have no idea what you're asking about."

"True, but then these *could* be the demons behind the whole thing. Either way, I'm going to find out. Are you going to help me, McCabe, or do I need to call someone else?"

"I'll help." What else could he do? "What do you want me to do?"

"Cover the back," Hayes said at once. "If they run, try and hold them for me."

"Sure," Mika said. "We'll just—"

"Mika," Conor growled. That would be all he needed: her mouthing off to Hayes and giving something away. The man wasn't stupid, and Mika was impulsive. Who knew what she'd say?

"There's some good cover in the rear," Hayes told him. "I'll circle around to the front and you can get into position. I'll wait ten minutes to enter. Okay?"

Conor nodded. "I'll be ready."

As Hayes walked away, Conor released Mika and checked his watch. He scanned for signatures again, but the pair inside the building hadn't changed position. "What kind of demon is that in there?" he asked Mika abruptly. "It's an energy I haven't read before."

"The stronger of the two is a Grolird. The other is a spinner. Probably one that gave an oath in exchange for protection, since spinners are pretty weak demons."

"Spinner?" It was a reference he hadn't heard before, but he immediately associated it with the creature whose energy kept morphing—spinning—between species.

"It's a slang term. I don't remember what the real name of their branch is because no one uses it."

Spinner. That meant Nat was . . . Son of a bitch. All these years and he'd been getting intel from a demon. No wonder Nat knew what Conor was, knew that Mika was half demon as well.

"Is a spinner stronger or weaker than Mahsei?" Conor asked.

"Stronger." Mika smiled and he had to look away. "They're about mid-range, but still considered weak, especially as far as a Grolird is concerned."

Why the hell did her smile continue to make his heart lurch? He knew she was a liar, knew she'd used him, manipulated him. With perfect clarity, he could recall the times she'd derailed him from questioning her about anything she didn't want to talk about. And despite it all, he wanted her with an intensity that made him ache.

She'd backed off, mostly stopped pushing and provoking him. Probably because it wasn't to her advantage any longer, the cynic in him said. Conor shrugged it off. It didn't matter. What mattered was that he didn't have to deal with her teasing and game-playing.

When he realized Mika was staring at his profile, watching him, assessing, he glanced at his wrist. "We need to get into position," he said. "You get behind me and stay close. And if those two demons do run out the back, you stay hidden, do you understand me?"

"Yes, sir!" She jerked to attention and snapped off a crisp salute.

Conor scowled at her before cloaking his presence from humans. After he felt Mika do the same, he headed for the opening that Hayes had pointed out. As the other man had said, there was plenty of cover, and he kept them behind the overgrown bushes. When they were in position, he dropped the mask and marked the time. Two more minutes.

Those two dragged into fifteen, and Mika started fidgeting. Conor gave her a pointed look, and though she stopped moving, he could feel the impatience bubbling inside her.

At twenty minutes past the mark, she whispered, "What's taking so long?" His glower didn't faze her. "Well?"

"Maybe they're talking to Hayes. Now be quiet."

Just past the thirty-minute mark, Mika stiffened. Conor stared intently at the back of the hotel, but he didn't see anything. He looked over his shoulder and raised his brows.

"Watcher," she said, so quietly he read her lips more than heard the word.

Once he knew what she was reacting to, he found their spy easily. He was stationed to their left, and behind them. Conor analyzed the angles and swallowed a curse. They were directly in the bastard's line of sight. Studying the area, he tried to find a new position, one that gave them cover from two directions, but before he could choose a spot, he detected motion.

The back door flew open and the spinner and the Grolird ran out. One was male, the other female, and there was more than an oath of fealty between them; Conor knew it in the flash of a second.

He moved, and drew the weapon Nat had given him. Hayes would be right behind these two, and no way in hell was he giving himself away as a demon by shooting energy from his hands. "Hold it right there," he ordered, blocking their escape route.

The male demon, the spinner, put himself in front of the female, shielding her as he prepared to fight. She was the stronger of the pair, so what the hell was this about?

"Get out of our way, Kiverian," the male warned.

"Conor, let them go," Mika said from beside him.

"What the hell are you doing? I told you to stay put!"

She ignored him. "They're mated. They'll fight to the death to protect each other, and for what? So Hayes can ask some questions? If he didn't get his answers already—"

The freelancer staggered out the back of the house, pistol drawn. There was blood running down his temple, but he didn't look too battered. Conor had his gaze off the couple for a fraction of an instant, and they took the opening to run.

Swinging around, Conor aimed, but they were already

out of sight. He ran after them, and as he reached the corner he spotted them. Raising the weapon, he took bead on the duo, but he couldn't shoot them in the back. Which Mika should have known, but apparently didn't. She knocked his arm as soon as she reached him. Not only did it throw him off balance, it caused his finger to squeeze the trigger.

Hayes's car blew up in a spectacular fireball.

"Shit," Conor muttered.

Mika misunderstood. "They're vishtau mates, McCabe. I couldn't let you shoot them. They weren't trying to hurt anyone, they just wanted get away."

Hayes drew even with them. "What the fuck happened to my Mustang?"

Mika had the odd urge to laugh. She was sandwiched between Conor and Marc in the pickup, and the men were discussing what had happened. Someone had called the police, and Hayes had called in B-Ops. And when they'd been asked questions, both men had lied.

McCabe had lied! She never would have believed it if she hadn't heard it with her own ears.

She shouldn't find it so amusing. Conor was more furious with her now than he'd been before. She'd hurt him again, and it had been unintentional. Mika did know that he'd never shoot anyone in the back, but she hadn't realized the other couple was fleeing. All she'd seen was Conor and the gun; she'd reacted without assessing the situation. It was her impulsive nature at work.

"Why did you guys say you were after a vampire?" Mika asked when there was a lull in the conversation. "And why did you claim the vampire blew up Marc's car?"

There was dead silence, then Hayes said by way of explanation, "No reason why McCabe's insurance should have to cover the damage."

The men went back to their conversation. Mika sighed. Conor was barely talking to her, and Marc was courteous but uninformative. Apparently, Hayes had held quite a conversation with the demons, but most of what he was telling Conor was no big secret. Mika suspected that the couple had been buying time until they could escape.

Theirs had been an interesting match. The power gap between Mika and Conor was larger, but their mating would be easily accepted in Orcus because the male was the stronger demon. A Grolird female with a spinner as a vishtau mate would face disapproval. Mika would bet that was why they were in the Overworld—and why all they'd wanted was to get away. She doubted the couple would ever cause trouble in Crimson City as long as no one attacked them.

"Hey, McCabe," Marc said, breaking into her thoughts, "why don't we stop and get something to eat? Your treat."

Conor didn't argue. Instead he politely asked, "Mika, are you hungry?"

"Sure," she agreed.

"There's a diner not too far from here," Marc said. "Campy, but they grill a mean burger."

"I know it."

Both men were quiet now, intent on reaching food, and Mika nearly laughed. Amazing how much a half demon and a human could have in common when it came to eating.

Her smile disappeared abruptly as Conor turned the truck into the parking lot of the Moondance Diner. Her heart pounded faster. If McCabe discovered that she'd come here on her way to the park the other night, he'd become even more furious. It wasn't that big a deal, not considering everything, but it would be one more nail in the coffin of their relationship.

Okay, what were the chances that anyone who'd seen her here would be at the diner now? Almost nonexistent. Her biggest problem was the waitress who had served her, but it was likely the woman regularly worked the dinner shift. Since it was the middle of the night, the woman should be home and no threat.

Mika was breathing easier by the time Conor parked the truck. She slid out the driver-side door, her hand lingering in his until he pulled free. Despite that, he kept her close to his side. She realized he was worried, and she wanted to hug him. His care for her had to be more than merely holding to his word; as protective as Conor was, he had to still have tender feelings for her. He *had* to.

As they entered, she scanned the restaurant furtively, then released a silent sigh of relief. She didn't see any familiar faces. McCabe steered her to a horseshoe-shaped corner booth, and she was put in the middle of the two men again. Mika slid closer to Conor, not stopping until her thigh was against his. All three of them had their backs to a wall and a good view of any threat that might come their way. When she smiled at McCabe, he handed her a menu. Mika blew him a kiss and watched the tips of his ears turn red. Damn, the man was adorable when he blushed.

As she studied the choices, a glass of water was set in front of each of them. "Did you want coffee?" a voice asked.

Mika nodded, but she didn't look up. Her stomach had settled somewhere around her shoelaces. The waitress from the other night flipped over Mika's cup, then Marc's and Conor's, before filling each with steaming coffee.

"I know McCabe and Hayes drink theirs black," the woman said, "but did you want cream and sugar?"

Mika had no choice now but to acknowledge the waitress; it would be rude not to. "Yes, please," she said, giving the woman a polite smile. *Please don't remember me.*

Luck wasn't with her. Mika saw the spark of recognition. "*McCabe* is your kinky boyfriend?" the waitress asked. She began to laugh. "I'll never be able to look at him the same way again. A schoolgirl uniform!"

Mika glanced over at Conor. The red of his face could be from embarrassment, but the glow in his eyes meant he was seriously pissed off. Her primary concern had been

Conor discovering she'd been here before. Never, not in a million years, had she dreamed the waitress would mention sexual roleplay.

"What did he wear when you were the woman wrestler?" the waitress continued.

"Wrestler?" Hayes asked in disbelief. He started laughing.

"Mika." Her name on Conor's lips was more a snarl than an actual word.

Mika blanched. The wrestler comment made it glaringly clear that she'd been here *after* meeting him. The waitress was laughing so hard at his reaction that she had to rest her coffee pot on the table. Damn. Mika wished with her whole heart that she'd never made that stupid joke the other night. But who could have guessed that she'd ever see this waitress again, or that McCabe would be a regular here? Or that the waitress would say anything?

Despite the fact that she was already hip deep in trouble, rashness spurred Mika. She battled it, tried to restrain herself, but she'd kept her Mahsei side in check most of the night and it wanted out. She gave Hayes an amused look, turned to Conor and, with a pout, used her best sex-kitten voice to say, "Don't worry, Conor. When we get home, I'll put on my schoolgirl uniform and you can spank me for being naughty."

Chapter Sixteen

Mika wished she'd thought twice before impulsively throwing out that line about spanking two days ago. She'd known what a prude McCabe could be, and yet she'd let her reckless side—her Mahsei side—loose anyway. It hadn't gotten her anywhere, and Conor had been scowling and muttering off and on since. She really had embarrassed him. Probably the only reason he hadn't hauled her out of the Moondance Diner immediately was that it would have led to more laughter. She had a feeling he wouldn't be going back there any time soon, and that he'd be avoiding Marc Hayes for a while. What had possessed her?

With a small grimace, she put aside her regret. It was too late to change things, but she vowed to keep a tighter rein on her impetuosity in the future.

They were out early today. It wasn't noon yet, and the sun was brilliant, making her squint even wearing sunglasses. She glanced over at Conor, but he was intent on the traffic. If another apology would help, she'd offer it without hesitation. But she knew it wouldn't make a whit of difference.

Part of her wished Conor didn't view the world so much

in black and white. That was why he had such difficulty forgiving her—but at the same time, his unbending sense of honor was one of the things she loved about him.

"Where are we headed?" she asked, more to break the silence than because she had any real interest.

"Venice Beach," was his response.

There came no explanation, and Mika needed one. Venice Beach would be loaded with people—especially on a Saturday, and if the Dark Ones chose to attack, the consequences would be disastrous. Mika swallowed her questions. Conor would grow impatient if she asked anything. Partly because he remained angry with her, but lack of sleep also contributed to his irritability. Neither of them was getting enough rest, and that worried her because it affected their powers.

Conor continued to hang close, to sleep beside her. Or, he tried to sleep. The attraction between them hadn't gone away simply because he'd discovered her deceit. Mika was aware of his struggle not to make love to her, but he was strong-willed and hadn't caved, despite her subtle efforts to tempt him.

He'd even resisted her straightforward attempt to lure him into the shower. When she'd suggested that he wouldn't get to her in time if the dark demons came, he'd come and sat in the bathroom, but he'd studiously avoided looking at her when she was naked. Mika knew he caught glimpses of her in his peripheral vision, though, and she'd put on a show behind the glass. It had only worked to leave him aroused. When it was his turn to shower, Mika saw just how much.

Poor Conor. She half-smiled. He hadn't been able to hide his pleasure at her ogling, though he wanted so badly for her to believe he was indifferent. And this enforced proximity would last until he had his protection back in place. Mika's smile widened. Poor, poor Conor.

Her smile faded as she wondered how much freedom

he'd allow her once the field was back in place. He didn't trust her, not one bit. And she supposed he shouldn't.

As much as she wished otherwise, her promise to the Council stood. If the opportunity arose, she'd have to take the incantation to the demon leaders. Conor would loathe her for such a final betrayal. Hell, she'd despise herself, but she'd given her word and couldn't find a way around it.

Shifting in her seat to watch McCabe, Mika pushed her concerns aside. There was plenty of time to worry about this later. Right now, he was only disillusioned with her, angry. He didn't quite hate her. Not yet.

Sunlight made him look younger, she decided, maybe because it highlighted the blond streaks in his hair. She wanted to smooth away the slight furrow between his brows with her fingers, with her lips—and she sighed silently. Conor wouldn't allow her to touch him, and she missed the warmth of his skin.

Her acute sense of smell picked up a faint, spicy scent, and Mika's eyes slid half-shut as she recalled watching him shave. She'd never thought of that activity as sexy, but that had been before she'd seen McCabe doing it. He'd been yummy enough idling with nothing except a towel tied around his waist, but it had been his absolute concentration that caused her to shiver. That same focus she had seen when they made love.

He stopped the truck at a red light, and Conor turned to her. "You're staring," he said.

"Just enjoying the view." When a slight flush touched his cheekbones, Mika smiled and added, "You're adorable when you blush."

"Knock it off," he grumbled. She laughed. Conor appeared relieved when the light turned green again.

She didn't quit devouring him with her eyes until he got into line to park. Mika briefly glanced at the lot, then did a double-take before turning back to McCabe. "You're not seriously going to pay that, are you?"

"What?" He sounded incredulous.

"It's highway robbery. You can't tell me there isn't a cheaper place."

"You're kidding, right?" There was barely a pause. "You're not kidding." Conor looked at her as if she'd just beamed down from the mothership. "I can't believe this. You're *cheap*."

Mika straightened. "I am not cheap, I simply don't think this is a fair price. There are free spots along the street."

"It's the weekend. We'll have to circle forever to get one."

"You don't think it's worth a shot? We can always come back and be gouged later if there's nothing else. . . ."

McCabe muttered again, but instead of turning into the lot when the line of cars moved, he pulled out and off down the street. Maybe he simply didn't want to argue with her, but Mika felt something warm unfurl inside her. She knew Conor thought she was being silly—okay, cheap—about parking, but he'd indulged her anyway.

Twenty minutes later, they were still going up and down the streets and Conor had begun questioning his sanity out loud because he'd listened to her. Everything was filled, as he'd predicted, but she kept her eyes open, sure they'd find something. Soon enough, that happened. "There! See? A van is pulling out."

"Got it." He didn't waste any time zipping into the spot.

Climbing out, Conor pulled on his faded, denim jacket to hide his weapons, then came around to help her down. They were off on the far end of Venice Beach, and while all the parking along the sidestreet was taken, there weren't many people around.

As she and Conor walked side by side, Mika had to wrap her hand around her purse strap to keep from reaching for him. "Are we here for a reason?" she asked, to distract herself.

"Yeah. Someone I talked to on the comm mentioned that Madam Christine was reading tarot here on the weekends."

Since Mika doubted Conor wanted a psychic reading, she asked, "And why are we looking for her?"

"She's the one who originally erected the protection around my house. I want her to redo it."

That didn't surprise Mika. She knew Conor wanted desperately to put distance between them, and the only way he could do that was if he didn't have to hang by her side. As long as the house was insecure, he had to stay close.

They reached the walkway in front of the beach, and he took her hand. Mika was stunned at first, but then she realized he didn't want to become separated from her in the crowds. The beach was packed—some of the people were tourists, some were locals, and every age was represented, from babies in strollers to senior citizens.

The place was a carnival, a riot of noise and color, and Mika found herself entranced. There were shops for T-shirts, tattoos and body piercing. There were street performers singing and dancing, and artists drawing sketches of people. There were clowns turning balloons into animals and painting the faces of children. It was chaos—and it was human life. So different from Orcus. Clasping Conor's hand more tightly, Mika leaned into him and smiled. "This is great!"

Scowling, he said, "Keep watch on your purse."

She went up on her toes and gave him a loud smooch on his cheek. McCabe grumbled some more, but Mika loved his fustiness. And to make him happy, she put her free hand on top of her small, purple bag. The purse didn't quite go with her lilac tennis shoes, but the flats that matched weren't made for walking.

Getting through the crowds of people wasn't easy, and while Mika did her best not to become distracted, she was unsuccessful. Conor didn't know if the woman was giving readings on the walkway or in one of the shops along the beach, so they stopped in nearly every store. Mika wanted to browse through all the interesting things, but satisfied herself with quick looks.

She remained strong until she found the barrettes. They were colorful and whimsical, and she had to have one. McCabe growled impatiently, and she hurriedly looked through the selection before picking a purple one with lime green and orange decorations. While she was at the register paying, she grabbed one of the store's business cards. Her cousin, Kimi, and Kimi's mom would love this place.

As she stepped outside the shop, Mika twisted her hair up and secured it out of the way. It was warm and she didn't want hair on her neck. Besides, she couldn't wait to wear her new purchase.

The instant she finished stuffing the empty bag in her purse, Conor took her hand and tugged her along. "I like your hair down," he complained, and Mika smiled. More and more often, he sounded like a typical Kiverian male.

They hit a few more places, including one that carried the cutest cropped T-shirts. Mika eyed the racks, glanced at Conor and sighed. She'd have to look another time. As he pulled her toward the next shop, she twisted around, trying to memorize the name of the store so she could find it again.

Without warning, he tugged her sharply. Mika fell against his chest and Conor's arms went around her. As soon as she regained her balance, he stepped away. Curious about why he'd pulled her, she turned and saw a young werewolf on rollerblades, juggling bowling pins. He was drifting all over the walkway. Where else but Crimson City would a supernatural creature be performing for spare change from humans?

"Watch where you're going," McCabe warned the kid.

"I think you scared him," she told Conor with a grin when the young werewolf clutched his pins and skated away.

McCabe didn't comment, just said, "Come on."

Hours later, they still hadn't located Madam Christine.

They weren't out of options yet, but it was time to stop for lunch. They'd probably still be searching, but McCabe had been scolded. Mika's lips twitched. While they'd been walking, her stomach had growled loud enough that the elderly couple in front of them had turned to stare. The second time it happened, the woman had told Conor to take better care of her.

They stood side by side. Mika leaned into him as they ate, and watched the men lifting weights in a fenced-off area.

"Why don't we look for a bench?" McCabe asked.

Mika's lips twitched. "I'm fine right here," she said. Conor made a low growl, so low, she barely heard it, even with her demon hearing, and so she added: "Don't worry. Your body is at least as good as any of theirs." She briefly squeezed his biceps through the denim. "Maybe even better."

Deliberately, Mika trailed her eyes from his face, past his chest, to a point below his waist and then back up again. "Definitely better," she purred. *"They* don't make me wet just looking at them."

"You're incorrigible," Conor said. He sounded beleaguered, but she didn't miss the pleased note in his voice.

"Only because I love you, McCabe."

"Bullshit," he said; and it was like flipping a switch, he closed up on her that fast. She hated having to watch her words, hated having to gauge what she said against his possible reactions, but unless he forgave her, there was no choice. The silence was so tense, it was a relief to finish eating and resume the search—some of the fun had gone out of Venice Beach.

Mika could feel Conor become more and more tense as they started running out of places to check. She struggled not to ask, but the question slipped out anyway: "If this psychic put the energy field around your house, don't you have a way to get in touch with her?"

He mumbled something.

"What?"

"I said," he bit out, "I think I might have her business card. Somewhere," was tacked on grudgingly.

"Your filing system."

"If you think I'm so damn bad at organizing things, I'll pull the boxes out of storage and let you at them."

She clenched her teeth to keep from saying anything else. They'd just fight if she did. Conor was frustrated and edgy; she could hear it in his voice. His mess of papers wasn't worth arguing over—even if a trained monkey could do a better job at keeping the paperwork orderly.

The sun was low in the sky when McCabe finally called it a day. The crowds had thinned dramatically, the tourists had gone back to their hotels and the locals to their homes, and it was unlikely that the woman they looked for was still giving readings. If she'd been here at all.

Mika remained quiet as they headed back to the truck. Conor was tense enough that his body nearly vibrated with it. The urge to soothe him, to try and make him feel better, nearly swamped her, but Mika knew he'd pull away. Instead, she thought about what she'd seen today.

Despite her many visits to the city, this was the first time she had come to this beach. She brought her arm up and ran her fingers fleetingly across her barrette. When things were back to normal, she would return. She wanted to spend time exploring the shops for things to buy, not wander around looking for psychics; and she wanted to be able to stop to watch the street performers. One of them had tugged Mika out of the crowd to dance with him. She'd been having fun—until she'd heard McCabe snarl. Her lips curled. Next time she'd come with Kimi, not a jealous vish-tau mate.

Conor wasn't holding her hand any longer, and she missed the warmth of his calloused palm. But things had remained awkward between them since she'd told him how she felt, and they didn't show signs of improving.

Pulling off her sunglasses, she tucked them inside her purse while they walked back to the truck.

As they left the beach farther behind, the area became deserted. Mika felt a prickle of unease go down her spine. If she'd been human, the desolation would make her worry about a mugging, a rogue vampire or werewolf attack, but she was Mahsei—what had her concerned was the dark demons. This was the perfect time and place for them to make their move. She became more alert, let her senses roam.

They'd just turned onto the street where they'd parked when the fireblast streaked by. Mika and Conor tackled each other to the ground behind a parked car. "Not the Dark Ones," she murmured against his ear as they crouched behind the vehicle. Not when that shot had been directed at McCabe.

As he nodded, a second blast separated them. They dove in different directions. They were facing multiple attackers who, while they might want Conor, clearly weren't concerned if she took a hit. She assumed this team included the auric assassin, but he was saving his special energy blast for the perfect opportunity.

Like hell, she decided, and looked around. Her vishtau mate was already firing back, fireblasts of his own directed toward their second attacker.

Their foes had the setting sun at their back, giving them an advantage: Mika was blinded. She might not be powerful enough to make a storm, but she could gather clouds, and she did that now, trying to even the playing field. She wasn't able to block the sunlight completely, but she dimmed it.

Conor spared her a glance. "Nice," he said, sending out another wave of energy.

Mika whirled, avoiding a shot from the first attacker. She wasn't positive exactly where he was, but she called on the wind, rotating it until it became a mini-cyclone, and sent it toward where she thought her assilant was. It might not have stopped the Dark Ones, but these foes weren't quite so deadly, and maybe some blowing debris would slow them down.

After she sent the tornado on its way, she looked around, trying to find shelter, but the position of their attackers left her and Conor with no place to hide. McCabe was busy exchanging fire with the second, but demon number one was abnormally quiet. Where the hell was he? Mika reached out mentally, trying to locate him, but couldn't. Which wasn't good. No way in hell had her trick with the wind been more than a distraction; he wasn't out of the equation yet.

Maybe it was because she had her senses extended, but she suddenly knew precisely where her enemy was positioned. And as her eyes traced the line, she realized Conor was directly in his sights.

It didn't require even a split second of thought: Mika launched herself across the distance separating them and put herself in front of Conor. In the next instant, the energy blast hit her.

Mika staggered, tried to keep her feet. Tried to keep Conor protected. Her body refused to obey. She felt herself start to fall, felt McCabe catch her. Part of her retained enough awareness to realize she'd taken a stronger blast than anything the dark demons had leveled at her. But then, this assassination squad wasn't playing around.

Her lungs burned as she gasped for air. Not a cell in her body didn't feel as if it had been clobbered by a sledgehammer. The intensity was like nothing she'd ever felt. It was almost a gift when her senses began to numb. Almost, but not quite. Her eyesight began to narrow, her view of the world became distant, as if she were staring down a long tunnel, and Mika knew what was happening.

At least she'd saved her vishtau mate. That's what counted.

As her life force drained away, she struggled for a moment more of consciousness. She had one thing left to say. One thing left to do. "I love you, Conor," she rasped.

And then Mika fell.

"No." He whispered the word, but what Conor wanted to do was howl out to the universe. He gathered Mika's body up, held her tightly as he scanned the area. Where the hell were his assailants? They weren't firing. Were they moving into position for another shot? Lulling him into a sense of false security before springing a different type of trap?

He reached for his magic, the power he found too horrible— too demonic —to ever use. If those bastards thought they were going to finish Mika off, they had better think again. His soul was a small price to pay for her life.

He kept scanning, but picked up nothing. Which was odd, since demons rarely cloaked during a battle. But these two obviously were, and had been, only dropping their shields a split second before firing, and raising them immediately after getting their shots off. Why?

The night was quiet. Every instinct Conor had said there was no longer any danger, but he continued to try to locate his attackers. He wasn't ready to trust they were gone—not when this would be a perfect opening. But as time passed and everything remained calm, he decided he had to move.

He lowered Mika to the ground, cradling her head against his chest. She'd deliberately put herself in front of him, deliberately taken the energy blast. "What the hell were you thinking?" he hissed.

There was no answer, and as Conor looked down at Mika's face he realized she wasn't just injured—she was dying.

Too late, he realized she'd meant it when she said she loved him. Probably she was the only person who'd ever cared for him that deeply, and he hadn't believed her, had scoffed and berated her for speaking the words.

And yet she'd said them again and again.

She'd never given up on him.

With a shaking hand, he reached down and smoothed a dark tress off her face. His fingers ran into the goofy little hair clip she'd bought today—it dangled precariously in the ends of her hair—and carefully he unhooked it, slipping it into the pocket of his jacket. His fingers touched his comm unit, which he pulled it out, starting to call for help; then he remembered there was nothing human medicine could do to save her.

"Mika, don't leave me, okay? Please don't leave," he begged.

He jammed the comm back into his pocket and lightly stroked her cheek, ran his thumb across her lips. "Come on, honey, hang in there. Fight. You know you want to tell me I'm an ass. That I should have known you'd never let anyone hurt me."

Half-afraid of what he'd find, he rested two fingers on the pulse in her throat. It was weak, thready. And there wasn't one fucking thing he could do to keep her alive.

"You know," he said quietly, hoping she could hear him wherever she was, "you're everything I've always wanted, all I'd dreamed of finding someday. But I couldn't trust it, I guess. Maybe that's why I was so quick to doubt you, so quick to believe the worst. Maybe I wanted to think you were part of that conspiracy, because then I didn't have to risk anything."

Conor laughed, but his throat was thick and the sound was choked. "All right, you weren't on the up-and-up. I know that. But you made that promise before we met—I should have been able to let go of it." He felt movement. "Mika?"

Spasms wracked her body, and he locked his arms around her, trying to keep her from hurting herself in her thrashing. "Ah, damn. Ah, damn. Honey, please. Don't die. I'll do anything, I swear."

"Anything?"

Conor jerked his head up at the voice. He couldn't see more than a silhouette, but this was a demon, no doubt about it. He wasn't completely cloaked, which was why Conor could see him but couldn't read his energy.

Shit, he hadn't sensed anyone approaching. Who else was out there? Conor scanned, but only sensed some humans. He couldn't trust that, though, not when this son of a bitch had gotten the drop on him. He drew on his power again, ready for anything, and growled, "What do you want?"

The demon held up both hands in a universal sign of peace. "It's not what I want, it's what you want. I can heal her."

Eyes narrowing, Conor tried to pierce the shadows surrounding the demon, but whatever obscured him wasn't natural. If it were, Conor would be able to see his face.

Conor didn't trust anyone who hid so much of himself and demons lied. "You think I'm going to trust you with her?" he snarled.

The demon's reply was matter of fact. "Do you have a choice? Another ten or fifteen minutes and it won't matter. Your mate's dying, I can feel it from here."

Conor's gut told him this demon was concealing something, but he wasn't sure he could care. Mika *was* dying. He knew it; he felt her life energy decreasing every passing second. And Conor would do anything to save her. *Anything.*

"What's the price for healing her?" he asked.

"It is steep. You may not want to pay it."

Maybe a demon wouldn't pay, but Conor considered himself human, and life meant something to him. Especially the life of this woman. Mika was the only person in the world for him—he wasn't letting her go. Not if he could help it.

"Whatever it is, it's yours. If she recovers," he promised.

The demon laughed, and Conor choked back his fury. If Mika died, he would avenge her—and he'd start with this bastard.

"Don't you know anything about negotiating with a demon?" the cloaked figure asked.

Conor glared into the darkness. Every minute Mika grew weaker, and this asshole wanted to play games? "I know that if you don't stop fucking around, I'm going to kill you," he swore.

The demon laughed again. "I'm the only one in Crimson City who can heal her. If I were you, I wouldn't be tossing out threats."

"I'm not making a threat," Conor said. But he made his voice more amenable. He wouldn't cost Mika her chance to be healed. "You said it yourself: time is short. Let's not waste it. You want something, I'm willing to give it to you. It's that simple."

There was a moment of silence, and Conor's heart started to race. Had he pissed the demon off? He hated the damn cloak; it left him blind in a situation where he needed to know what was going on. But before he could call out, Conor heard the demon move closer.

"Very well. I promise to heal your mate, and in exchange you promise . . ." His voice trailed off.

The silence left Conor breathless, but he held Mika and caressed her as a way to remain calm. She was still alive, and if he had to be patient a minute or two longer, he could do it. He *would* do it. His entire world was in his arms, and Conor wasn't letting go.

Half a million years later—or exactly fifteen of Mika's exhalations which Conor was counting—the demon stepped into the light and dropped his shield. "And in exchange, I want your promise not to kill me—or incite anyone else to kill me—by any means whatsoever. Do we have a deal?"

Rage poured through Conor, a rage more intense than anything he'd ever known. No wonder the demon had stayed cloaked, had remained in the shadows. This was the bastard who'd raped his mother.

Chapter Seventeen

"You son of a bitch," Conor growled. Instinctually he gathered power to do battle. "Did you really think I'd agree to that? You deserve to die."

"But does she?" his father indicated Mika.

Conor glanced down, shifting so that he could see her face. It was pale—not merely white, but gray. She wasn't dead, he reassured himself. As if in answer, he felt a soft puff of air against his throat, and something inside him relaxed.

"What's stronger—love or hate? That's the final question," the demon proposed. "Do you love her enough to put aside your hate for me? Because if you can't, she dies and you'll be as responsible for her death as the Setonian that fired the shot."

Mika. She loved him. She loved him enough to put up with his bullshit, to apologize again and again for something she'd promised before they'd even met. She loved him enough to try to breach his fears, and he knew how formidable those were after his past. And she loved him enough to take his place, to step in front of the magic meant for him.

But the bastard was wrong. Conor didn't have to surrender his hate; he only had to give up his need for vengeance. For Mika, he could do that.

Only for Mika.

"I promise not to kill you," he grated out, "or incite anyone else to kill you by any means whatsoever. Word of honor. Now get over here and heal her."

Conor gritted his teeth as the Kiverian sauntered forward. He wasn't moving with as much urgency as the circumstance called for, and Conor had to hang on to his control with both hands. If the bastard let Mika die, all bets were off.

"You need to let go of her," his father said. Conor held on even more firmly. "I can't heal her like this. You have to put her down."

Reluctantly, Conor released Mika and slowly moved back. He stayed close, monitored the son of a bitch carefully. No matter what it took, Conor would watch over his woman.

But the demon never touched her. Instead, he knelt beside Mika, his hands a good three inches above her heart. The only thing that kept Conor from losing his temper was the fact that the energy flowing between the Kiverian's outstretched hands and Mika's body was palpable. Maybe it was imagination, but she seemed to begin breathing a little more smoothly, a little more evenly. Conor wanted to touch her, wanted to push the hair off her forehead, but he didn't dare interfere in any way.

A soft glow developed in the space between his hands and Mika's chest, and the demon began chanting. Conor could only decipher a word here and there, but he recognized an ancient demon language.

Conor didn't dare relax his guard, but as the chanting went on, Mika appeared to become stronger. It seemed as if the bastard really was healing her. When her face regained some color, Conor actually felt the knot in his chest loosen. He fisted his hands at his sides to hide their trembling. It was too early to let relief pour through him, too soon to assume she was going to be fine. When she opened her eyes, *then* he'd believe.

The chanting stopped and Mika's body jerked. Hard.

"You son of a—"

"Her life force is reentering her body. The movement is natural." The demon smiled faintly as Conor eyed him with suspicion. "Think of when you're about to fall asleep and you suddenly jolt awake. Your entire body lurches like this, right?"

Reluctantly, Conor nodded.

"This is similar. It won't be much longer now."

Conor growled, but he settled back and waited. The bastard knew his promise only stood if Mika was healed. As long as he remembered that, Conor could remain calm.

The glow receded as another intonation began. This time Conor was unable to recognize a single word, but he had a sense that this language was older than anything he'd seen. Not that it mattered. He didn't give a damn if the bastard sang "The Star-Spangled Banner," as long as Mika lived.

As the demon drew out a word, his hands shifted to Mika's head. Conor's gaze sharpened, but his father merely circled his palms over her face. Then he went quiet and lowered his arms. Mika didn't move.

"Call her name," his father said, before Conor could accuse him of anything.

He eyed his sire with distrust, then lowered his gaze. "Mika, wake up," he said.

And that easily, her eyes opened. She blinked twice and noticed she was on her back with Conor leaning over her, and her lips curled into a smile. "Now? On the street? Conor, you're such a pervert."

For an instant, he stared at her blankly, then he laughed. "Honey, you wish. You're the pervert who always has sex on the brain." He started to reach out for her, then yanked his hand back. Almost involuntarily, he raised his gaze to his father.

"It's okay," the demon said. "You can touch her."

Conor cupped Mika's cheek in his palm and ran his thumb over her lips. "How do you feel?" he asked.

"Like a twenty-mule team ran over me." The querulousness in her voice made him smile. "I didn't say anything funny," she complained.

"No, I know you didn't, but the fact that you're alive to bitch at all is a miracle."

Well, kind of a miracle. Reluctantly, Conor looked again at his father. He had to force them out, but the words had to be said: "Thank you."

"Merely fulfilling my end of the bargain."

"Maybe, but her life is worth more than yours."

The Kiverian laughed, and for the first time, Mika noticed him. She stared. "You look just like Conor," she said.

Conor felt his relief start to slip away. "What the hell is wrong with her?" he demanded. Mika never moved so slowly.

"Nothing's wrong. She merely needs sleep, and lots of it."

"But—"

"Hey!" she interrupted. "I'm still here, you know." She tried to sit up, but didn't make it. "McCabe, help me."

With one last glower at the Kiverian, Conor slipped his arm behind Mika and gently raised her to rest against his shoulder. She looked around, then leaned more heavily against him. Conor struggled, not wanting to show weakness in front of his sire, but he couldn't hold out. Bending over, he pressed a kiss to Mika's forehead.

Smiling at him, she turned to the Kiverian. "You're Conor's father," she said. It wasn't a question. "I'm Mika Noguchi." When she held out her hand, Conor barely kept from growling in displeasure. This wasn't some damn tea; there was no need for social niceties.

"Sebastian," the Kiverian said, and when his fingers touched Mika's, Conor struggled to keep from knocking his arm away.

"You resemble him, you know—right down to the eye

color. If you got a haircut, the two of you could pass for brothers." Conor felt his body becoming more rigid, and only the fact that Mika had nearly died kept him from snarling at her. Maybe she sensed his temper becoming precarious because she changed the subject.

"You're cloaking us?" she asked.

The demon nodded. "And sending out energy that makes humans find it unappealing to turn down this street."

"I wish I could do that," Mika said wistfully. In the next breath, however, she started giving orders. "Okay, we need to get out of here before someone overcomes the shield he's emitting," she said. Conor nearly smiled. Her mental slowness appeared to be gone.

"How long does she need to stay in bed?" Conor asked, looking at his father.

"Eighteen hours, minimum, but twenty-four would be better." The Kiverian shifted his gaze to Mika. "If you can keep her sleeping that long."

Conor nodded, acknowledging the difficulty. Mika was impatient, impulsive, and she wouldn't be able to tolerate lying in bed—not for long. "You have a way to make sure she sleeps?" he asked.

"McCabe," she warned.

His father got to his feet and put his hands in the front pockets of his trousers. "Do you trust me that much?"

Conor didn't have to think twice. He'd deal with Mika without the bastard's help. "No." But . . . help. That reminded him of something. "You're working with the dark demons, and they want her dead. Why the hell did you heal her?"

"You won't like hearing this, but not because I'm frightened of you."

Conor wanted to stand and face down the bastard, but he fought back his rage. Softly, he said, "You don't know what I'm capable of."

The Kiverian shrugged. "Actually, I do know. I'm a

healer, and you're my son." Conor tensed. He hated hearing he was related to this monster, but the demon continued speaking. "That means there are only two possibilities. After watching you tonight, it's clear you weren't born with the power to treat the injured. That means you must be one of the few who have the opposite talent."

"If you can call it a talent," Conor muttered.

"As for the Dark Ones," the Kiverian went on, "my only promise to them was to do what I could to keep you alive." He paused, glanced at Mika and then continued, his voice low. "Both of them are gunning for her. The dark demons want you to lower the veil between worlds, and they'll do whatever they must to achieve that. Protect your mate closely, because they view her as a threat."

Conor's father glanced around again, but seemed more at ease when he resumed speaking. "There are two auric assassins sent by the Council to eliminate you—both Setonians. I'd thought she was working with them, but learned differently tonight."

Conor read between the lines and made a guess. "The Setonians broke off their attack because the dark demons arrived. That's why they disappeared after Mika was hit."

His father inclined his head. "All demons—even auric assassins—fear the Dark Ones. And with good reason. Whatever stories your woman's told you, believe them. She's not lying. They're the closest thing to true evil I've ever seen."

Then, without waiting for questions, the Kiverian stepped back and faded into his magical fog.

Conor scanned for his father, but picked up nothing. He knew the bastard was still there, though, and he fought to ignore that. Bending down to Mika, he said softly, "Come on, honey, we need to get out of here."

She murmured, and Conor realized she was half asleep. His heart thudded wildly, but some sense told him she was okay, that this was a healing state. He assisted her to her feet and then lifted her into his arms, carrying her to his pickup.

Once there, though, he didn't want to let go of her. Damn, he had it bad. Conor had to force himself to stop holding her, and secure her in her seat. And yet he hesitated, watching the rise and fall of her chest until he was satisfied that her breathing remained even and steady. Then, gently, not wanting to disturb her, he leaned in and brushed his lips across hers before closing the door and going around to the driver side.

Maneuvering the truck home through the streets of Crimson City, Conor drove more carefully than he ever had in his life. But then, he'd never carried a more important passenger. His sole focus was getting Mika home safely.

Mika tried to figure out what was brushing across her forehead. She felt . . . achy, stiff—as if she'd been immobile for days or something. And her head throbbed.

That soft grazing came again, and reluctantly she opened her eyes. McCabe was leaning over her, a concerned expression on his face. "Sorry," he apologized, "I didn't mean to wake you."

It was only after he pulled his arm back that she understood Conor's fingers had been stroking her forehead. She missed their light touch as soon as they were gone. "How long have I been asleep?" she asked. "A hundred years?"

"Nah, only about twenty hours or so."

"Twenty hours? Hell." Mika slipped out of bed and moved.

"Where are you going?"

"Bathroom," she said, and tossed him a get-real look. Did he really think her incapable of going alone?

McCabe was waiting outside the bathroom door when she reemerged. Before she had a chance to protest, he swept her up in his arms and carried her back to bed, carefully tucking her beneath the covers. Once she was settled, he lay at her side, propped himself on one arm and leaned over her.

Mika wanted to sit up, but with Conor hovering, she couldn't, not without bashing her head into his. Of course, there were worse things than being held prisoner by a sexy man wearing nothing except a pair of shorts.

His expression sober, he asked, "What do you remember about yesterday?"

"Everything," she said. When Conor looked skeptical at her assertion, she elaborated. "I took a hit—a serious one, if the way you're hanging over me is any indication—and your father showed up."

"Don't refer to him as my father." Conor's voice was hard.

Mika reached up and lightly circled the muscle jumping in his cheek with a couple of her fingers. "All right," she agreed easily. "Sebastian is the one that healed me, right?"

"Yeah." There was reluctance in Conor's voice. "But don't ascribe any altruistic motives to him. The bastard only did it in exchange for my promise not to kill him."

Damn, Mika thought. She wished she knew what had gone on after she'd passed out. Obviously, she'd missed a few important moments.

Since she didn't feel up to tackling the issue of his heritage, not with her head aching, she simply said, "Thanks."

Some of the fierceness left McCabe's face. "You don't have to thank me. You took that blast because you thought you were protecting me." His expression hardened. "Don't ever do anything like that again—do you understand me?"

"You're welcome," she replied.

Conor sat up and gave her a look she couldn't decipher. "You have no idea how close you came to dying, but I do. I held you in my arms and felt your life seep away."

He didn't say any more, but stared straight ahead. Mika slowly shifted to her knees, the blankets falling away from her as she moved. She smiled faintly at her clothing. McCabe had put her in the purple panties and a matching tank top. She adjusted one of the spaghetti straps and pressed against his back. "I didn't die, so don't think about that."

He didn't reply, and the silence lengthened. Mika leaned forward, ran her hands across his chest, and nipped at his nape before kissing it. She considered it a victory that he didn't tell her to stop or pull away.

"Why did you do it?" Conor finally asked.

Mika froze for a nanosecond, then rested her chin on his shoulder. "That's easy. I love you."

"Let go of me," he said.

Reluctantly, she did. Mika was confused, though. He'd called her *honey* again, he'd been touching her and letting her touch him, why had he suddenly told her to stop? Did he still want her to keep her feelings to herself?

McCabe shifted, arranged a couple of pillows against the headboard of the bed, sat back and patted his leg. "Come here," he said.

If his voice hadn't been soft, if it hadn't held something close to a plea, she would have taken exception. But there *was* that note of entreaty, and so Mika did as he asked. Conor settled her between his thighs, her back to his chest, and wrapped his arms around her. "I told you," he said quietly, near her ear, "not to worry about me, that I wouldn't get hurt. You never should have put yourself in the line of fire."

Mika glared at Conor over her shoulder. "You're not indestructible," she snapped.

"I know that. Damn it, you nearly died—don't you get that? I could have taken that hit without it affecting me."

She broke his hold and turned, going up on her knees and pinning him against the headboard with both hands. "You can't be serious. There is no way that shot wouldn't have hurt you."

He scowled at her, grumbled a bit and then took a deep breath. "One of my powers is protection. I can absorb magical energy and use it."

"But the only demons rumored to be able to do that

are . . . Oh." She gaped. Did he understand what he was saying? Mika stared into his eyes, saw the distaste, the concern, and realized he was aware of exactly what he was capable of. "Well, that explains why you knew more than anyone in the human world should about auric assassins." She began caressing his shoulders rather than pushing at them. "Relax, this stays between us. You're my vishtau mate—your secrets are my secrets."

His hands went to her waist. "I wasn't worried you'd tell."

"What were you—You were concerned about my reaction?"

Conor nodded. "It gives me an unfair advantage. The only people with a defense against it are other aurics. It's a terrible power, demonic in the old human sense of the word. One shot and the victim's dead. I never use it. It's too ugly."

Mika studied him, trying to read between the lines. "You're an honorable man. You're not a murderer." Something occurred to her then. "Do you really think it matters to me what your powers are? Auric assassin or barely able to call up a breeze, I'd love you anyway."

"You told me you'd have nothing to do with a weak demon," he accused.

She had. She remembered. But . . .

"I know I did, but none of them were you," she admitted. He appeared skeptical. She gripped his hand, trying to get through to him. "Even if you were from the weakest branch, even if you weren't my mate—I'd love you still, Conor. Don't you understand? It's you. This goes beyond demon or human, powerful or weak. This was meant to be," she swore. And it surprised her, but she meant it.

McCabe's hands tightened around her waist, drew Mika in until she had to lean against his chest to keep her balance. Since she was right there, she kissed him slowly and thoroughly. She began to ease away, then was overcome by another burst of passion and returned for another, longer kiss. Finally, she broke free and rubbed her nose against his, then sat back far enough to see his eyes. "Well, at least I'll know the next time Setonians attack that I don't need to throw myself in front of you." She laughed.

"Don't joke about that."

"Sorry." She took one of her hands from Conor's face and pushed her hair out of her way. "If I'm recalling correctly, your—um, Sebastian—said there were two auric assassins working for the Council. Before I agreed to do this, I made them promise not to harm you. Obviously I did a poor job of negotiating, but I wasn't involved in any plot to kill you, I swear!"

"I know you weren't." Conor grimaced, visibly steeling himself. "If the idea of everything between us being a lie hadn't hurt so much, I would have seen sooner that you'd never be a part of such a plot."

"What I feel for you isn't a lie!" she snarled. Mika started to pull away, but Conor held fast.

"I know," he said. More softly, he repeated, "I know that now. When you shielded me, I was finally able to look beyond the deceptions. The only times you weren't straight with me was when it affected your job of retrieving the incantation. Am I right?"

Mika nodded, and his fingers spasmed against her back. She said, "Whatever you want to know, just ask. There's nothing I won't answer, and honestly."

He leaned forward and down, and lightly bit her nipple through her tank top. Mika gasped and arched, but he didn't do more. Instead he said, "We don't have to play twenty questions. I know who you are at your heart, and that's what counts. The rest is just details."

She started to smile, but stopped; she continued to feel uncertain. "Are we really okay? You were so angry at me yesterday, and now you're not. I want to make sure that we have everything worked out, that you've forgiven me."

"I'm not mad anymore. Do I like the fact you lied to me? No, but I understand. You made that promise before we ever met, and those of Orcus never break their word."

She nodded regretfully. "If I hadn't promised, I would have come clean pretty quickly. I hated lying to you almost immediately."

"And you're not going to lie any more, right?"

His voice had a slight edge, which made her lips curve, it was so Conor. "With you, I'll be completely honest. I'm not making any promises about anyone else."

He shook his head with a short chuckle, and she reached up to hold him still, then planted a quick kiss on his lips. She enjoyed his laugh. "I *do* love you, Conor," she swore.

"I believe you," he replied.

For a moment, he studied her, something that appeared close to confusion in his eyes; then the expression segued to reluctance. Before she could protest, he moved her so that she no longer touched his body. "We've got two problems we need to solve."

"Only two?" she joked. Her lips quirked up at the corners, and to her delight, his did as well.

"How about, our immediate problems stem from two sources—the dark demons and the Council?"

"Sounds about right. And neither problem will be easy to fix. The dark demons' aims are in opposition to the Council's, so working on one situation will likely exacerbate the other."

McCabe frowned. "Which of the two do you think will be easier to resolve?"

Warmth filled her. He was asking for her opinion, treating her as a partner and not merely someone to protect. She said, "Each has pitfalls, but overall I'd say the Council will be much easier to handle than the Dark Ones."

"Why?"

"Temperament more than anything. The Council isn't a benevolent body by any means, but they're predictable to a degree—they always act in their own best interest. They're also possible to reason with. From what I've heard and seen, not only are the Dark Ones unswerving once they set themselves on course, they're willing to sacrifice anyone or anything to achieve their aims. For them, the end always justifies the means."

"They can't all move in lockstep. There must be dissension," Conor suggested.

Mika shifted to a more comfortable position and leaned against his bent leg. The hard muscles of his thigh pressed her side and distracted her for a moment, but she wouldn't lose her focus, not when McCabe was asking for her thoughts. "Maybe there is dissension," she said after some consideration, "but I've never seen it. Remember, I told you they keep to themselves, and that when they do come out, everyone scatters."

"Yeah, I remember." Conor ran a hand across the back of his neck and scowled. She could see he was weighing their options, and guessed he wasn't too thrilled with them. "Okay, looks like we get the Council off our asses first, then we only will have the dark demons to worry about."

With her right index finger, Mika traced the frown line on the left side of his mouth. *Only* the dark demons? she thought. Those were enough. But she didn't say so. Instead she said, "I know you want me safe, but what you suggested first makes the most sense."

"Yeah. But I don't like it," he growled.

"Of course not," she agreed. As Conor captured her and bit the fleshy part of her palm, it sent a shiver through her. Mika turned her hand, linked her fingers with his and smiled as he kissed her knuckles. But she couldn't fully enjoy the play, not when she was distracted by her thoughts.

The Council's aim was to retrieve and destroy the spell. If McCabe handed it over, they might be amenable to recalling their assassins. It seemed a logical plan, but she hesitated to raise it, afraid it would anger him—afraid that Conor would think she was still scheming to get that stupid thing when nothing was further from the truth. It drove home that, even if he'd forgiven her, the fallout from her previous dishonesty would last for a while.

"Do you have the incantation?" she asked.

"What do you think?" His voice gave nothing away.

Mika hesitated, shrugged. "I think you do, but I could never figure out why you wanted it or what you planned to do with it. I can't imagine *you* would want to lower the veil between worlds."

"I don't, and I don't want all of Orcus enslaved to me either." He paused, and she had a sense that he was deciding whether or not to say more. "The only thing I wanted was to slay the bastard who raped my mother—but I didn't know his name, and randomly calling demons forward until I was lucky enough to get the right one didn't seem quite practical."

"It," she said, choosing her words carefully, "wouldn't have called only your fath—Sebastian—forth. It's not that type of spell."

"Not the way it's written," he agreed.

Mika managed to bite back her gasp. Conor couldn't possibly mean he planned to alter it, could he? Someone like him, who hadn't grown up in Orcus, who hadn't learned even the rudiments of spell creation firsthand, could wreak untold havoc with one wrong word. Again, she had to be cautious with what she said. "You know his name now, you can call him forward using that."

"I know," Conor agreed.

Holding his hand more tightly, Mika took a deep breath and decided to chance diving in. "If all you want is Sebastian, you don't need the incantation any longer, right?"

Conor gave her a hard look. "Stop tiptoeing around and say what you want."

Mika shifted to face him squarely. "If you offered to hand the spell over to the Council, and gave your oath never to cast it, they might agree to call off their killers." Then she remembered another piece of information she'd been told to discover. "By the way, did you make copies or tell anyone else about this spell? They'll want to know that as well."

Mika grew uneasy when he didn't answer. She should have remained quiet, or maybe subtly hinted around until the idea occurred to him and he mentioned it. No doubt he believed this was some new tactic to finish her mission, and an ache began to form in her chest. Maybe they'd never be able to get past her lies, and she couldn't live with him always thinking the worst of her, always examining her words, looking for what she was really saying.

"The only other person who knew is dead," Conor said. The lack of emotion in his voice tipped her off.

"Ben?"

Conor nodded. Mika longed to comfort him over the loss, but she didn't dare to put her arms around him. Not after launching this topic of conversation.

"What are the odds your Council would agree to this bargain?" Conor asked.

"I don't know," Mika replied with a shrug. "If they were on the level about their reasons for destroying the spell, then I'd say the chances are good."

"Would they destroy it? It's a valuable tool." Conor looked down at his hands for a moment, and hers, then met her gaze again.

Mika took a moment to consider. "Yeah," she said at last, "I'm sure they would. They told me you're the only one who can wield it—though they didn't say why."

McCabe pulled his hands free and didn't reply. Mika didn't think that was a good sign, and her regret grew at bringing this up. At least he didn't move her from between his legs. She started to run her hand down his thigh—touching him had become as integral as breathing—but froze when it occurred to her that he might take her caress the wrong way. Reluctantly, she withdrew. How long would she second-guess her actions? And how long would she wonder if Conor was second-guessing her too?

"It doesn't cost you anything to give the spell up—not really," she said quietly. Mika felt uncomfortable, as if she were trying to sell the idea to him. Of course, convincing McCabe wouldn't be a walk in the park, and he hadn't heard the difficult part of the suggestion yet. "You can still summon Sebastian without it, and if you really have no interest in lowering the veil or enslaving the inhabitants of Orcus, why keep it?"

The look she received was stony, but Mika didn't flinch. Not until he accused, "And then you'll fulfill your promise."

"Damn it," she snapped, "do you think I'm advocating this because of the Council? I don't really care about them. I don't love them. My first loyalty is to you, and it always will be. Those guys don't even make my top-ten list."

McCabe scrutinized her long and hard, but Mika met his stare. Even if way deep down she was scared. If he couldn't trust her, they'd never last.

Hell, maybe it *wouldn't* work. Conor was so scarred by his past, he might never be able to open himself up enough to love her. And she couldn't continue to be the only one giving—at some point, she'd have to leave him to save herself.

Mika blinked rapidly a couple of times, and reminded herself not to borrow trouble. This was a problem for the future, not today.

He surprised her by saying, "Let's say I agree to this, how would we approach the Council? Make an appointment?"

She laughed. "They don't take appointments. Anyone who wants to meet with them sits in an antechamber and awaits their pleasure. If they decide to see you, great. If not, it's too bad."

"They want the spell."

"Right—I doubt they'd leave me waiting for long."

His eyes narrowed. "You?"

Mika took a deep breath and prepared to tell him the part of her idea that would make him furious. "Yes. I'd go alone and leave you in Crimson City."

"No."

It was exactly the response she'd expected, and she had her argument prepared. "You can't come to Orcus. They're used to me. No one even blinks at my odd energy sig anymore, but you'd stand out like a neon sign. I told you before, and it's true."

"You can't think I'd agree to this."

Agree to handing her the spell and letting her cross over without him? Of course not; he didn't trust her. But Conor had no reason to fear. She'd bargain hard and carefully with the rulers of Orcus to ensure he remained safe. She wouldn't let him down, wouldn't allow him to remain at risk, wouldn't be rooked a second time. If the Council didn't accede to her demands, if they didn't promise straight out that he'd be safe, she wouldn't give them the incantation—it was that simple.

This wasn't what she addressed first, however. She knew her vishtau mate well enough to understand it wasn't about this one thing. "You can't protect me in the Other World," she said. It earned her a sharp glance. "It's true," she continued, before he could argue. "You don't understand the culture for one thing, and for another, your powers won't be as impressive there. Sure, you'll still have your auric magic, but what good is one blast when we're surrounded by twenty demons?"

"You could do better?" he asked.

Mika smiled, not at all offended. She knew his Kiverian ego was smarting. "Of course not. But as I said, they're used to me—I'd never be caught in a situation like that. Your presence would call attention to us and cause a confrontation."

He grumbled but didn't question her further, and that was a surprise. She'd thought Conor would doubt her, would think she was making it all up to get her hands on his spell. That he didn't, made her feel warm inside—maybe he *could* trust her again. Mika wrapped her arm around his leg and rested her chin on his knee. She was a sorry case, going back and forth between hope and despair like a kid riding a teeter-totter.

"Besides," she went on after a pause, "I'd need you to stand watch on this side. The portal through the veil is in a dangerous part of Crimson City, and I'd hate to return to face immediate attack."

She hoped he didn't question too closely. Yeah, the main portal, the one that was most commonly known, was in a bad part of town, but she was aware of other smaller portals. In fact, she rarely used the main gate because of where it was located. Not only was the area of the city bad, but there were guards stationed on the Orcus side. Mika had never liked the thought of anyone realizing how frequently she crossed.

Conor gave a long, long silence, but Mika didn't say anything, nor did she look away from him. The wait seemed interminable, but she kept herself from fidgeting—barely.

At last, McCabe scowled and said, "Here's how we're going to play it. I have a copy of the book. I'll give pages of it to you, and that's what you pass to your Council. If they agree to leave both of us alone, I'll destroy the original as well as all backup copies."

Mika bent her head and kissed his knee to hide her elation. He was trusting her with something vital to his well-being. When she could talk without him realizing how deeply touched she was, she said, "They'll want to see you destroy the grimoire. If I bring them to the portal, you mustn't cross, even if they demand it. I will clear the view between worlds long enough for them to watch you carry out your end of the bargain."

"But what if me crossing over is one of their demands?"

"I won't agree to it, no matter what." She waved the possibility aside. "Now, we need a code, something I can say that sounds innocuous, but tips you off if there's trouble. How about this? If at any point, I say, 'good news' or maybe just 'news,' then you'll know things have gone to hell—okay?"

"Not okay." Conor moved carefully, shifting her. As Mika went boneless, letting him position her beneath him, he asked, "Do you really think I'm going to send you in there alone if you think we need a code like that?"

She nodded. "Yes—because there's no other choice. I can handle this, I promise, but it doesn't hurt to have contingency plans."

His pale green eyes were intensely bright, and damn, how Mika basked in their glow. She knew the timing was inappropriate, but she couldn't prevent herself from grinning. She loved McCabe so much that it nearly left her reeling. "I won't let you down, Conor. My word on it."

There was a long silence as he considered. "I hope I don't regret this, but we'll do it your way. If things go to hell, though, you get your ass out of there ASAP. I don't want you to get hurt."

"Fair enough. If the situation deteriorates, I'll leave."

He cursed and shook his head. Then Conor lowered his head and kissed her.

She knew where this was leading. Bringing her leg up to cradle him closer, Mika returned the kiss with all the pent-up emotion and desire she held for him. The days where he wouldn't touch her had felt like an eternity, and she urged him on with her mouth, with her body.

Abruptly McCabe pulled away, leaving her on the bed. As he tugged on his jeans Mika sat up and said, "Wha—"

He signaled her to be quiet. Stepping into his shoes, he shrugged into a shirt. Mika went over and held her hands out in a silent question.

Conor leaned forward, put his mouth against her ear, and in a voice softer than a whisper said, "Our watcher's back." Then he was gone.

Mika worried as she pulled on her clothes. Sure, Mc-Cabe had that auric shield thing and so was unlikely to be hurt, but that didn't matter; he was chasing after an unknown. Their spy could be anyone, anything. Of course she was concerned.

But she didn't get lost in the emotion—wouldn't let herself become lost. Her human mind realized this watcher could simply be a decoy to lure Conor away, so others could get to her. She had to be ready, just in case.

She felt more prepared once she was fully dressed, but her anxiety over Conor's absence remained. Her eyes scanned the room, found his weapons, and the knot in her stomach tightened. He's a demon, she reminded herself, he can take care of himself without a gun or knife. No, he wasn't invincible, but he was pretty damn close.

Her gaze kept moving, her mind processing details for any upcoming fight and trying to find advantages. A movement in the doorway caught her eye, and her body tensed to attack. It was a relief to see Conor reappear.

"What happened?" she asked.

He gave a few heated curses. "He had enough of a headstart that he got away. I couldn't chase him as hard or as far as I wanted, though—not with the house unprotected."

Mika nodded, unsurprised. She knew his vigilance was unswerving.

"But I did find out one thing about our watcher," Conor said.

He sounded so self-satisfied that Mika smiled and went to him. Wrapping her arms around his waist, she bit his chin and, when she withdrew, asked, "What did you discover?"

"The bastard's a vampire."

Chapter Eighteen

With Mika slightly in front of him, Conor kept his weapons within easy reach. She hadn't exaggerated how bad this area of L.A. was, and even if they were cloaked, he wasn't going to be caught unprepared. This place made where he'd met her look like Beverly Hills. But was she worried? Hell, no.

Mika was alert, she followed his orders, and she showed no more concern than she had while they'd walked the length of Venice Beach. But he could sense that she was nervous about facing the Council. There were layers and layers here, and just when he thought he knew her, she revealed another.

He didn't like the idea of her going into Orcus alone. Even if he hadn't made a promise to protect her, he wouldn't like it. And while Mika believed her arguments had convinced him to let her go by herself, that wasn't entirely true. The real reason he hadn't fought her on this was guilt.

He didn't trust her completely, and she'd picked up on that.

She'd been willing to die for him, and at a gut level he

still didn't wholly believe in her. Conor understood she'd been trapped by her vow, and he was able to forgive her lies, but he couldn't forget them—and his first instinct was always to take care of things himself. Remorse regarding that had compelled him to agree to her scheme. Almost immediately he'd regretted it, but if he changed his mind, that wounded look would reappear in her eyes. He was in bad shape when his first concern was whether or not he hurt a woman's feelings.

A rat scurried in front of them, and Mika sucked in a nearly inaudible breath as she jumped back. Reflexively, Conor's arm went around her as she collided with him. Shit, the rat was big. Conor scowled, but despite its size, the animal was frightened of them and quickly disappeared.

"I hate those things," Mika whispered.

So did he. Memories of the time he'd lived on the streets after his mother kicked him out swamped Conor before he could put them aside. "Come on, I don't like standing here," he said.

"It's not far now," she assured him.

The only light was from the moon and a few stars visible through the smog of the city, but with the superior night vision Conor's demon genes gave him, that was enough. There were some things he liked about being half Kiverian, and until meeting Mika, he never would have been able to confess that—not even to himself. He'd done some hard thinking while she slept, and sometime during those hours, Conor had admitted something else: If someone invented a magic pill that would make him totally human, he would no longer take it.

That thought shamed him almost as much as his distrust of Mika.

"This is it," she said, and he put aside his thoughts to study their location.

He wasn't surprised to see the CONDEMNED notice; the

building should have been razed years ago. Hell, every structure in the area should have been. This had to be the worst area of the city that he'd ever seen. Or smelled.

"You know it's bad," Mika said, laughter in her voice, "when even the condemned sign is broken."

She turned her head and grinned at Conor over her shoulder, and he felt his heart start to race. Faint traces of moonlight illuminated her face, highlighting the gleam in her eyes and the impishness of her smile. He should tell her to get serious, that this was no time for levity, but he didn't. This was Mika, and he'd missed her like hell. The past few days, she'd been too damn solemn, too circumspect. Maybe she thought he liked her better that way, but it wasn't true. He was grim enough for both of them, and needed her laughter.

In spite of his better judgment, Conor reached out and pulled her to him. He managed to keep the kiss short, cognizant of the danger they were in, but he craved her in a way that went beyond physical.

"Where's the portal?" he asked. Reluctantly, he released her.

"Inside. This way," she said.

She led him around the side of the building and through an opening in the chain-link fence. As they entered, he heard the telltale scuttling of rats. Conor battled his revulsion. Meeting one on the street was bad enough, but dozens—hundreds—inside a confined space made his flesh crawl. Taking a deep breath to calm down was a mistake; the stench nearly overwhelmed him.

"Shit," he muttered, and that was definitely some of what he smelled—along with vomit and the strong scent of werewolf. The last odor made Conor scan more closely, but he didn't pick up any living creature beyond the rats and a cat or two. Good. He didn't want to deal with anyone else.

Mika didn't stop until they stood before a wooden door

with damaged hinges. Light was visible through the cracks. Aside from that, nothing was remarkable, but he could sense otherworldly power. Was the door an illusion, or something else? Whatever he saw, Conor doubted this was the true appearance of the gate.

"I don't like this," he said.

"I know, but I won't let you down, I swear!"

Mika sounded so fierce, Conor couldn't help but smile.

"That isn't what I meant, honey," he said. He decided not to take time to explain. "I just never realized there was a portal here."

"That's the idea." After a pause she added, "Remember, don't cross, okay? I know you'll be tempted, but there are guards on the other side, and we don't know what your powers will be like in Orcus. Finding out during a fight isn't smart."

"I get it," he snapped. He wasn't happy about it. He wanted Mika with him, he wanted her safe. "Be careful."

"I will be—I promise." She went up on her tiptoes, brushed her mouth over his and said quietly, one last time, "I love you, McCabe."

Without waiting for him to speak, she walked up to the door and, after a glance over her shoulder, stepped through without opening it. He stared hard at the wooden portal, but it still looked ordinary. As soon as his amazement passed, Conor took a step to follow her. Her crossing had seemed so . . . final.

"Don't worry," a voice said. "She's survived in Orcus her entire life without you. She'll manage one more day."

Conor turned to confront his father. "Why are you here?" he demanded.

"To watch your back," Sebastian answered smoothly. "Someone had to. You were more focused on your woman than the situation."

Conor opted not to argue. "Planning to cross back over yourself?" he asked hopefully.

"No, and I wouldn't suggest trying to help me

through." The Kiverian smiled and halved the distance between them. "Keep in mind that I'm the only healer on this side of the veil, and if Mika is hurt, you'll need me again."

The truth of his father's words made Conor scowl. Mika's close-call was too fresh in his mind to disregard. And this was almost a joke: The demon he'd hated his entire life, the father he'd thought of as a monster, was a healer, while Conor himself was a bounty hunter, a mercenary, a killer. He had blood on his hands—lots of it—and Mika had recently told him that healers in Orcus didn't fight unless in self-defense or in defense of a loved one. So, which one of them was the monster? The universe had one warped sense of humor.

"Where are your buddies?" he asked his father with heavy sarcasm.

"I've been doing my best to evade them. They're not happy I healed someone they want dead." Conor's father shrugged. "And I wouldn't refer to them as my friends—more like, uneasy allies. They've always known that I worked with them to keep you safe."

Conor went rigid, his hands fisting at his sides. It took a great deal of self-command to keep from launching himself across the room and forgetting the vow he'd made. He couldn't contain his snarl, however, and he was sure his eyes were glowing faintly. Without his contacts in, there was nothing to disguise his anger. "Do you expect me to believe that you give a damn about me?"

"You're my son," came the reply.

As if that were an answer. Conor's growl started low and increased in volume as his rage grew. Conflicting thoughts and emotions hammered at him, and he struggled to hold them in check. Some part of him was stupid enough to want to believe the bastard. Another piece was outraged that the demon who'd raped his mother dared to call him *son*.

And in the midst of this, Conor realized his Kiverian half

was not only free, it had destroyed its cage completely—he could feel his demon blood burning in his veins. That shocked him enough to regain control.

When had this happened?

He reviewed the past few days, but it had occurred so gradually, it was impossible to pinpoint one moment. He wanted to blame the change on Mika, but that was unfair. Yeah, she prodded him frequently, and had encouraged integration of his dual natures, but he was the one who'd undone the leash.

After a brief struggle, Conor stopped arguing with himself; he had more important things to focus on. "If you really want to help, tell me how to get the dark demons to leave Mika alone," he said.

His father stared at him, and Conor stared back. He'd been surrounded mostly by humans his whole life, and the difference in aging was startling. This—like it or not—was the demon who'd fathered him; yet Sebastian appeared no more than a few years older than himself.

Conor now knew why his mother had hated to look at him; his resemblance to this man was strong. They were the same height, and of similar builds, although weight-lifting had made Conor broader, more muscular. Their eye color was identical, and the only difference in their hair was the length. Conor wore his short, while Sebastian's brushed his shoulders. No one looking at them would doubt they were related. He was probably lucky his mother had waited until he turned eighteen to throw him out of the house.

"What has she told you of them?" Sebastian asked.

Conor blinked. It took him a minute to remember what they'd been talking about, and that his father meant Mika and not his mother. "She didn't know a hell of a lot," he said.

"The Dark Ones do keep to themselves." After a brief pause, Sebastian stepped closer, till only a few feet separated them. "They're obsessive, not easily turned from a course once they adopt it. The only way they'll leave Mika alone is if they die. And they're not easy to kill—perhaps not even for an auric assassin."

"Are you saying it's hopeless?" Conor asked.

"No. You have some points in your favor—the biggest being that they want you alive. However, all they need do is render you unconscious, and Mika will stand alone. She's Mahsei. They'll be able to handle her in minutes."

"She survived when they cornered her before," Conor said harshly.

"Because they were toying with her, not because she's a match for them. They enjoy playing games, but twice now they've lost their opportunity to fulfill their assignment. It's a mistake they won't repeat, do you take my meaning?"

Conor nodded grimly. "They'll go straight for the kill. You said I had a *couple* of points in my favor. What's the other one?"

"There are two more, actually. The second is that Mika's your vishtau mate."

Conor turned the statement over in his mind, but it made nothing clear. "So?"

Sebastian rested his hands on his hips and asked, "What do you know of the vishtau?"

"I know that the bond is considered sacred, and that demons can only have children with one of these mates." Conor ran a hand across the back of his neck. Damn, was Mika pregnant? he wondered.

"No, she's not."

Conor's gaze snapped to his father. "How the hell did you know what I was thinking?"

"Relax," the Kiverian said, making no attempt to hide his amusement. "I can't read your mind; there was question in your voice as you spoke. As of yesterday, when I performed the healing, your mate wasn't with child."

Disappointment came out of left field, and Conor was speechless for a moment as he worked through it. What the hell was she doing to him? With the problems he and Mika were facing, he should be thrilled there wasn't a baby to complicate them. He cleared his throat, pushed his emotions aside, and asked, "What do I still need to know about this vishtau thing?"

"Probably a lot." Before Conor could get irritated by the answer, the Kiverian continued, "But the part that will assist you in your battle with the dark demons is the sharing of power. Instead of both of you dipping into your own reserves, you can share one well. Something about that gives extra strength to both demons. Don't ask me why, I don't know, but the sum of the parts is greater than the whole."

More potency in battle sounded good to Conor. "How do we do this?"

"There's a price, I'm afraid."

Conor muttered a curse. No matter how many advantages there were to being half demon, there always seemed to be drawbacks as well. "Nothing's ever easy. Now, how do Mika and I do this?"

Sebastian studied him. "First, you'd have to perform the bonding ritual. Second, both of you would need to show absolute trust in each other. Without it, at best you'll remain two individuals. At worst . . . one of you could destroy the other."

"Explain."

Conor's father grimaced. "At this moment, you're protected from most attacks. If you go through with this, you'll have no defense against Mika. She'll be able to kill you easily, because she'll be behind your auric shield, not outside of it. As I said, it takes trust."

Conor didn't hesitate. "But, after we do it, she'd share the protection of my shield?"

His father nodded. Then he cautioned, "But it may not protect either of you from the Dark Ones."

Although he normally wasn't impatient, Conor found his temper wearing thin. He didn't want partial answers; he wanted everything laid out logically. "Start from the beginning and explain it all," he ordered.

After a brief hesitation, Sebastian acquiesced. He recounted the bonding ritual, reciting both halves. It left Conor stunned for several reasons: first, the finality of the bond. Even if things went to hell between him and Mika—even if she left him—they'd be tied exclusively to each other sexually. No one else would be able to arouse them again, not until the vishtau mate died. It was an odd magical effect, and a daunting prospect. Secondly, he recognized the rite from one of his books. He hadn't been able to decipher its meaning, but somehow he had memorized the passage without trying. The third thing was the most incredible of all—Mika had gasped those words during sex. She'd repeated them each and every time, and although he hadn't understood, they'd incited Conor's passions as if on some level his demon side recognized her call.

Conor barely recovered before his father went on to the second part. That was less concrete, but Conor thought he understood the process. "Most demons don't do this power sharing, do they?" he asked.

Sebastian shook his head. "Most demons don't perform the bonding ritual at all, making it a moot point. But you're correct. Even true vishtau mates rarely have faith in each other to this extent." He paused. "From what I've seen, I doubt you trust Mika completely enough for it to work, either."

Conor scowled. He didn't like the thought of his fath—this Kiverian—watching them that closely. He asked, "What's the third advantage you think we have?"

For a minute, he didn't think Sebastian would go for the change in topic, but with a barely perceptible shrug the demon said, "Well, it's less an advantage than a positive consideration. If you and Mika are successful with your plan for the Council and destroy the incantation to lower the portal, you'll most likely only need worry about the pair of dark demons after you now, and not the entire branch for the rest of your lives."

"Why? You said the Dark Ones are obsessive," Conor argued.

"They are, but this is only one option for lowering the veil between worlds, and from what I overheard, it was always considered a long shot. After all, your position as the person who can remove the barrier is only legend. Many Dark Ones prefer more tangible alternatives. The duo assigned to you will remain fixated on Mika's death and on your invoking the spell, but once it becomes known the grimoire no longer exists, the rest of them should turn their focus to their other plan."

Conor mulled this over. He hoped Sebastian wasn't feeding him a line, because he wanted this over, even if shutting the gate meant Mika left him forever. Above all else—even his selfish desire to keep her with him—he wanted his mate to be safe.

Mika had plenty of time to think. The Council had left her in the antechamber for damn near forever now, and that surprised her considering how eager they'd been to retrieve the spell. Maybe she was worrying about nothing. Maybe. Except, something about the guards on the demon side of the veil had left her uneasy. They'd acted . . . odd, and there had only been three present. Recently, whenever she'd used that portal, there'd always been four. That, on top of this wait, raised her anxiety.

Two other petitioners sat with her, and she unobtrusively studied them. The Nitah woman had given a faint smile when Mika was escorted in the room, but the other, a Elismal male, had ignored her. His snub wasn't unexpected. His branch wasn't as strong as they liked to believe, though occasionally there would be a powerful demon born of the type. Elismals thus had a sense of superiority that was unwarranted, but since she didn't want to start anything, Mika bit back any comment.

With a sigh, she shifted. The small stone room was utilitarian and short on style, but then, why waste resources on making petitioners feel welcome? Even the rug she sat on was thin and worn to the point of offering no ease. Mika's bottom ached from sitting on the stone floor and she shifted again, trying to relieve some of her discomfort.

It was the waiting. Impatience strummed at her, and she struggled to overcome it. She couldn't allow her Mahsei nature to distract her from her goal. It was up to her to ensure Conor's safety, and she wouldn't fail him no matter how long she had to sit.

Mika straightened when the chamberlain appeared, but he didn't come for her. Instead, it was the Elismal that received the invitation, and who shot both her and the other woman a disdainful look before leaving. It made sense that they'd summoned him first. Not only was he here before she'd arrived, but his branch was alleged to have ties to the Dark Ones, and the leaders would be leery of offending him.

It wasn't easy for Mika to curb her antsiness, though—not when she knew McCabe would be worrying. And the longer this took, the greater the likelihood he'd use the gate. He'd absolutely refused to promise that he wouldn't come after her.

The Nitah went back to her book, leaving Mika to occupy herself with her own thoughts. There was nothing she could do about Conor except fret over what action he might take, and that increased her fear for him. She needed to rid herself of it immediately. If she faced the Council in this state of mind, they'd sense it and use it against her. She had to be cool and confident when she walked into their chamber.

To keep her thoughts from straying to her vishtau mate, Mika considered what he'd discovered about their watcher. It made sense that it was a vampire, perhaps, but his shadowing of them made her wonder if he was working alone or was part of the interspecies conflict in Crimson City.

She'd like to believe she was jumping to conclusions, but if Conor had heard rumors of humans looking to ally with demons, it was likely that vampires and werewolves had picked up the same information. What better way to make sure a coalition never came about than to reach accord with Orcus first? Maybe the watcher had waited near the portal for someone to be called across. It wouldn't be easy to trail most demons, but he'd been lucky and she'd come through. Mika swallowed her humorless laugh. She'd been having so much fun playing secret agent at the time, it was unlikely she would have noticed if she'd been followed by an entire army.

But why had he wanted to follow her? She had a guess. Demons were scarce in the human world. Maybe he'd wanted to learn more about them before using the gate. Vampires could do what werewolves and humans could not—cross the veil and survive.

There was no telling with whom Orcus would choose to align, but one thing was clear: Both the Council and the Dark Ones wanted the barrier between the worlds gone. And Mika doubted either human or vampire was ready for the consequences. Both groups thought they'd be able to control her people, but they would quickly learn otherwise.

Mika fidgeted again before she caught herself. *I'm cool and collected. Not impulsive.* She needed to use her humanness, and to retain complete control during the meeting. The irony of her weakness being an asset wasn't lost on her, but she had to focus on one thing right now—remaining in command. Breathing slowly and deeply, she reined in her emotions. She lost the rhythm when the Elismal stormed through the room, but resumed her calming breaths as soon as he was gone. By the time the chamberlain returned and summoned her, she'd reached a state of composure.

Inside, at the far end of the room, the four councilors were seated on large pillows positioned atop a dais. It gave them the height advantage whether the supplicant remained standing or was allowed to sit on one of the intricately-patterned rugs provided. Hanging behind the leaders was an elaborate tapestry with a human king bowing before a demon council—his lords and masters.

This was only Mika's second visit to the Council Chamber and it was as impressive this time as it had been the first. High, vaulted ceilings provided a sense of majesty, which was accentuated by the many richly woven tapestries adorning the stone walls. Mika's gaze absorbed every detail of the lavishly appointed room, lingered on each work of art.

Guards armed with swords were stationed on either side of the platform and at each entrance. Most of the weapons had jewels embedded in the hafts, but Mika knew they weren't ceremonial. Each guard was a well-skilled soldier, and sworn to obey the Council until death. Curious, she checked their energy sigs. A number of them were Grolird, one was Setonian and several more were Kiverian. The only branch who wouldn't think twice before starting trouble in here were the dark demons.

Mika continued forward until she stood before the Council, and folding one hand demurely over a fist, she bowed low. She didn't rise until she was bade do so.

"You have the incantation?" en-Tanith, the Council leader, asked.

"Yes and no."

One of the councilors shifted angrily at her reply; another scowled menacingly, and nin-Siath, the lone female councilor, glared at her. There was a soft glow in the demoness's pale yellow eyes which told Mika how poorly her answer had been received.

"That is not an acceptable response," en-Tanith said. "Either you have it or you do not. Which be it?"

"I have a copy. The original remains with Conor Mc-Cabe. He wishes to make a bargain, and has agreed that I may act as his emissary before the esteemed Council."

The level of anger in the chamber rose at her words. In her peripheral vision, Mika saw the guards shift, blocking the exits should she be foolish enough to try an escape. This response was not unexpected, although she'd hoped they would give her a chance to speak. Her gaze swept the room, instinctively looking for alternatives should she need to run. There were deeply-set windows about twenty feet above the floor, and though they were narrow, she felt sure she could get through one—if she could only reach it before the guards caught her.

"You told him of your mission?" The question was hissed.

"I did not—my word on it, en-Tanith. There were Dark Ones in Crimson City working to ensure I did not acquire the spell. They enlisted the aid of a human, a friend of Mc-Cabe's. This man passed along the information regarding my assignment."

The four councilors exchanged glances, and Mika took another deep breath. She forced her fingers to loosen their grip on her fist; she couldn't show any trace of nerves.

"Explain further," nin-Siath ordered.

"One of the Dark Ones confronted me, and because I am so beneath him in power, deigned to answer my questions. He claimed his people are too strong to be enslaved to anyone's will, and that their goal is to have the incantation invoked and the veil lowered, so that they may rule the Overworld as all demons once did."

The councilors leaned toward one another to quietly discuss her information. When there was a lull, Mika added, "I told him that, since the Dark Ones are imprisoned in Orcus just as every other demon is, that perhaps they weren't quite as potent as they like to believe."

That brought immediate silence, and all four stared at her as if she'd lost her mind. Mika ignored the disbelief. She'd told the leaders this for a reason. They might think she was insane, but demons respected courage. What she'd done had taken guts.

"He was there to kill me. I didn't think I could make the situation worse by mentioning this—until I recalled their penchant for torture."

"And yet you stand before us." En-Tanith sounded surprised.

"McCabe arrived and shielded me." Not that they cared about her well-being, but they required an explanation. "The Dark Ones want him alive to recite the spell, although I don't know why it is believed only he can invoke it and not any other half-demon."

The councilor on the far left—the one who had scowled so furiously at her—spoke up. "The legend is quite specific: only a half-demon who is also an auric will have the strength to implement the incantation."

The statement brought rebuke from the other councilors. and an argument ensued. While they chastised him for being too free with facts, Mika ran through the legend as she knew it. In the version she'd heard, there was no mention of an auric—but she wasn't surprised that the leaders had info that the rest of the population did not. There were many demons, particularly those on the lower end of the power spectrum, who felt that they were told no more than what the Council wanted them to know. It had always been this way.

When the disagreement seemed to be abating, Mika put her thoughts aside and waited. Though she was curious how they'd discovered Conor's abilities, she didn't dare ask. It would be the same as admitting what he could do, and she wouldn't verify anything for them. Their spat ended, and they turned their attention to her.

"What type of bargain does he seek?" en-Tanith asked.

She had to be careful here. "In very general terms, Conor McCabe would be willing to trade the spell—and to take an oath never to recite it—in exchange for his safety."

There was a brief silence. "We must confer. Withdraw to the far side of the chamber."

Bowing her head to show her respect, Mika backed away from the dais until she reached the farthest wall. She knew they weren't deciding whether or not to take the deal—they were deciding whether or not to bargain on a *possible* deal. Even if they consented to a discussion, they might opt to decline any pact she'd offer.

They also would try to take advantage of her. But what the strong rarely understood was that the weak could be better at negotiating. They had more need to be. Mika only hoped she was sharp enough to close every loophole this time.

As her wait lengthened, she grew concerned about Conor. What was he up to? Was he becoming impatient enough to cross the veil? There was no hurrying the Council, and if they agreed to haggle over terms, the discussion would be protracted. She couldn't rush this and miss an opening to help her vishtau mate.

At last they signaled her to return to the platform. "You stated that you have a gesture of his good faith. We would see this now," nin-Siath directed.

"It's in my trousers." Mika didn't move until she received a nod allowing her to proceed. From the rear pocket of her jeans, she withdrew some folded paper: a reproduction of a few half-pages of the grimoire. She held them up. "May I come forward and hand these sheets to you?" she asked.

En-Tanith's nod held such pomposity, Mika fought the urge to smile as she passed the paper to him. He glanced down, then handed the sheets to the councilor on his right. It would have been easier to make an electronic copy and let them read from her comm device, but human technology didn't fare well in Orcus. If turned on, her energy pack would explode in less than a minute—hardly the right tone for negotiating a truce.

It seemed an eternity before nin-Siath asked, "He is willing to give us this incantation?"

"He is willing to destroy it and all copies." Conor had refused to bargain unless he was the one to incinerate it.

"We do not trust this."

She'd known they wouldn't, but Mika also knew this was a sign that negotiations had begun. "I have the ability to make a tiny portion of the veil transparent for a brief time. McCabe will not cross the portal, but the esteemed Council will be able to watch him obliterate the book."

They weren't pleased by that either, but moved on to another point. She wondered if it was a very minor item and they'd squabble later, or if it was a possible deal breaker, something to be held till the end and only raised again if agreement was reached on other issues.

Fifteen minutes into discussions, en-Ulsef, the councilor holding the papers, roared a protest that the entire incantation wasn't provided. The sudden silence in the room was overwhelming, then accusations began to fly. Nevermind that they knew this was only a gesture of good faith, not a duplicate of the spell, they were looking for an advantage and wanted her on the defensive. Mika didn't become flustered, instead she found herself growing impatient with the theatrics. The high emotion wasn't entirely faked—passion ran high in demons—but it was wearing thin.

When it became obvious that Mika wasn't going to respond as many normal Mahseis would, the Council calmed down and tried a different approach. That didn't work either. And that's when the serious bargaining began.

It quickly became clear why nin-Siath did the majority of

the talking; she was the most skilled negotiator of the four, and Mika not only had to stay alert, she needed to think several steps ahead of the councilor. Forty-five minutes later, Mika had sweat running down her back, but they'd reached a compromise on every point—even on who would destroy the spell. They'd finally conceded that Conor could do the honors, but had insisted that the remains of the book be given to them. She hadn't been able to find any reason not to agree to that, even if it was a rather unusual request.

They still weren't finished.

The scribe who sat to the side of the dais read back what was agreed, and Mika and the leaders debated word choice for each and every provision, each and every sentence. It was exhausting, but it was important that there be no wiggle room for them to use and have Conor later killed.

Leaning over the scribe's shoulder, Mika read through the document carefully, examining it for misspellings, strange-looking letters—anything that could nullify a term. The words had an odd slant because the scribe was left-handed, but everything was as it should be. The Council hadn't attempted to cheat, and that indicated respect for her, as well as respect for her skills as a negotiator.

"All is well?" the councilwoman asked.

Inclining her head, Mika said, "All is well, nin-Siath." She closed her hand over her fist and bowed again. Such formality was necessary with the leaders.

"Then we shall seal the bargain." En-Tanith held his hand out toward the scribe. When he had the contract, he laid it flat on the table in front of him, spoke quietly and pressed his finger to the paper. A fine mist rose from where he touched, and he waited for it to clear before passing the paper to the next councilor.

As chief negotiator, nin-Siath was the final councilor to place her mark. The agreement was then returned to the scribe, and Mika was bidden to press her own finger upon the page.

As the mist around her hand dissipated, the Council leader intoned, "It is done."

Mika felt some of the tension leave her body. It had been necessary to make the bargain in this manner, to ensure every point was transcribed accurately, and that each councilor had put their seal on the pact. It was the only way to ensure whoever succeeded these councilors would be bound by the same contract.

By the time the document was properly filed, impatience ate at Mika. When they started to discuss in which manner they would travel to the portal, she grew frustrated enough to scream, but forced herself to maintain control, to wait for the members to decide who would be part of the group and which position they would assume in the array. It seemed like a bunch of bullshit to her, but she wanted them happy.

At long last, they set off. The procession of the Council and their entourage through the narrow streets of Biirkma brought more than a few curious stares. Mika tried to ignore them, but she felt sure when she returned to Orcus, she'd be facing questions about this parade.

There were only two sentinels at the portal when they arrived, but the leaders didn't seem to think it odd, and Mika shrugged off her own uneasiness. Things must have changed during her visit to Crimson City. At an order from the Council leader, the two men stood down and moved to the side of the small room. She could only hope that Conor had waited, and that the missing guard wasn't dragging her mate's lifeless body off somewhere.

"Proceed," en Tanith dictated, and pointed toward the gate.

Mika slowly approached the portal. When she reached it she turned back to the Council and said, "I need to straddle the veil to make a small part of it transparent. I am not leaving." She wanted that clear. "You'll be able to talk directly to McCabe through this window that I create."

She received permission to continue, and Mika stepped

into the door. Holding out her hands so that her palms were flat, she concentrated all her being on making the gateway's molecules transparent. Slowly, the veil began to clear.

Chapter Nineteen

Conor was ready to climb the walls. Or to charge through the veil. If Sebastian hadn't been there, he probably would have done it already, but the Kiverian had pointed out something Mika hadn't. She'd stressed that Conor would be in danger if he went through; Sebastian had mentioned that Conor's presence could put *Mika* at risk. Conor hadn't thought of that, but the bastard was likely right. Damn woman.

Yet, Conor couldn't grouse too much. Not with that weird warm feeling that developed whenever he thought about what she'd done. No one had ever cared for him so deeply. No one.

Worry made him pace back and forth in front of the door. "She's been gone too long," he said.

"No," Sebastian replied calmly. "Depending on the Council's whim, they could make her wait two minutes or an entire day."

"They want the incantation," Conor argued.

"That doesn't mean they'll see her immediately."

Conor stopped and turned to Sebastian. "Power games," he muttered. "I hate them."

"The Council doesn't." The Kiverian leaned his shoulders against the wall and crossed his arms over his chest. "Have some faith in Mika. She's weak, but she wouldn't have suggested this unless she learned to deal with situations like this long ago."

Mika wasn't weak, not in the ways that counted, but Conor didn't say that. Demons from Orcus obviously viewed strength in terms of their powers, but that was inaccurate. She might not be able to send a bolt of auric energy at an attacker, but she could stay calm and come up with a plan. That put her miles ahead of those demons who merely reacted. Emotional responses were fatal in battle, and so he'd take Mika at his back over any all-powerful dark demon any day.

"How long do you intend to hang around?" Conor asked, changing the subject. Mika was no one else's business.

"Until your mate returns."

That wasn't what Conor had been asking. He'd meant, how long was Sebastian staying in Crimson City; but he didn't rephrase the question. "In case she's injured?"

"No, I'm staying to keep *you* safe. You're too emotional, and rushing to Mika's rescue will cause nothing but trouble."

This demon thought he was too emotional? Ignoring that, Conor squared off with the Kiverian. "Keep me safe? What the hell do you care?"

The man's eyes narrowed. "You're my son," he repeated.

Every muscle in Conor's body went rigid, his hands fisting and releasing at his sides. "Don't call me that," he growled.

"Not using the word"—Sebastian straightened—"doesn't change who you are, and it doesn't change how I feel about you."

"Feel about me? You don't know me! Hell, you didn't even know I existed until a few days ago."

"You're wrong."

His quiet words stopped Conor cold, then rage roared through him. He took a step forward before he regained command. "When?"

"When did I know? I felt you take your first breath." Before Conor could think of a response, his sire continued. "Demons are connected to their children."

"Forever?" The idea was horrifying.

Sebastian shook his head. "Only until puberty." He paused, started to speak, then stopped. Then, shrugging a shoulder, he said, "At times I felt your need of someone. I would have been there if I could have, but the veil kept me in Orcus. This is the first I've been free since you were born."

It was a lot of information to process, and it took a second for the implications to dawn on Conor. The bastard meant he hadn't been out of the underworld since the night Conor was conceived. The fury returned, and this time, nothing was going to stop him from—

The portal wavered. Okay, one thing could stop him— Mika's return. Except, only part of her appeared. He saw her right arm, her leg, part of her torso and could just discern the side of her face, but she didn't finish crossing. "Mika? What's wrong?" he asked. She didn't answer and he closed the distance fast. "Mika?"

Was she stuck? Conor started to reach for her arm, planning to pull her the rest of the way through.

"Don't touch her!" his father cried.

"Why the hell not?" Conor glared at him.

"Because you could kill her. At the very least, you'll hurt her badly. She's not in either world right now, and the veil does unusual things to the physical body."

Conor jerked his hand back. He didn't know why, but he believed the Kiverian. There was nothing he could do except wait, and he hated that. Damn it, he'd already been cooling his heels forever. Anxiously, he watched, leaning forward and silently urging her the rest of the way through. But instead of Mika emerging from the ether, a rectangle began to appear in the wall. It gradually became more distinct.

Four faces suddenly peered through at him, three male and one female. "He can hear us now?" the woman said.

Mika's answer reassured him. She was deliberately standing there; she wasn't caught in the veil.

"Conor McCabe, this Mahsei claims she's your emissary. Is this true?" the female demon asked.

"Yes," he replied.

"And you give your promise to abide by each term of the agreement that she has negotiated?"

He began to say yes—it was on the tip of his tongue—but before Conor gave in to the urge, he started to think. Never sign a contract without reading it, right? Maybe he had better find out what Mika had committed him to. The demon repeated her question, and Conor said, "Before I give my word, I need to hear what the terms are."

That hadn't been the right thing to say. The four demons turned to Mika and chewed her out. Loudly. "You're a fool," Sebastian hissed from his side.

When the Council returned their attention to him and had their scribe read the provisions of the agreement, Conor knew the Kiverian was right—he'd been a fool. Mika had orchestrated an airtight deal, and when the recitation was complete, Conor didn't hesitate to give his word to uphold it.

"Now, we will watch you destroy the grimoire, then you may pass the remains of the book to the Mahsei."

Conor didn't care for the demoness's tone, or the way she referred to Mika as an object and not a person, but he obeyed. He looked around for something to hold what would be left of the book, but he didn't see anything appropriate.

"Here," Sebastian whispered, and tossed Conor the discarded lid to a paint can. It wasn't as large as he would have liked, but there weren't any other options at hand.

The Council stood, their faces nearly pressed against the rectangle to watch. Conor glanced at Mika, wanting to share his humor, but he wasn't sure if she could see him or not. Deciding to put on a show for the leaders of Orcus, he held up his hand and telekinetically called the book to him. He raised his other hand and brought forward the copies. Making sure the demon leaders could see, he placed both loose pages and grimoire atop the the paint can lid and gathered energy. Then, directing it through his hands, he incinerated them. When he finished, there was nothing left but ashes.

He picked up the lid carefully, but he'd concentrated his power so well that it was cool. Mika had an arm extended, and when the lid hit her hand, her fingers closed around it. She took it through the veil, and he saw the councilors relieve her of it.

The councilors looked at him, and the woman said, "Your word that there are no more copies. We must have that."

"Every copy that I know of has been destroyed, you have my promise," Conor vowed.

"That will do." The woman gave a regal nod before the rectangle closed.

As impatient as Conor was, It seemed an eternity before Mika finished crossing and stepped into the dank, smelly room with him. His hands took her shoulders.

"Are you okay?" he asked.

"Fine."

Unconvinced by that short answer, he examined her from head to toe, looking for some sign that she was hurt. When he didn't find one, he pulled her against his body and wrapped his arms around her. The next time she went to Orcus, he was damn well going with her. He couldn't handle such stress again.

"I'll be taking my leave," Sebastian said.

Conor ignored him, but Mika didn't. Much to his displeasure, she stepped away and gave his father a polite good-bye. A protracted, polite farewell. Finally, Sebastian left and they were alone again.

"You never told me about the bonding ceremony between vishtau mates," he accused.

With a shrug, she tucked her fingers into the front pockets of her jeans. "Why bother? It's not that important."

For some reason, her offhand answer pissed him off. "Maybe not," he said with a growl, "but Sebastian mentioned a second ritual, one where we can share powers."

Her face tightened, and a soft glow grew in her eyes. "Did Sebastian also mention that it only works if both mates believe in each other to the depths of their beings? That it's dangerous because if one mate turns against the other, they can utterly destroy them?" She gave her head a shake, tossing her hair over her shoulder. "Maybe you realize now that I won't physically harm you, but you don't trust me. We both know that."

"I trust you."

"Bullshit, McCabe!" Her eyes glowed red. "You didn't even have enough faith in me to agree to the pact I negotiated with the Council until you heard every damn detail."

Shit, she was hurt by that; he could sense it beneath the anger. There was nothing he could say that she'd believe, so he didn't bother to try. "We're doing both rituals," he demanded. Only that would prove his trust.

"No." She pivoted, but he caught her arm before she made it more than a few yards. "Let go," she snapped.

"Listen to me. If we do this, you'll share the shield I have, and you'll be safe when I fight the dark demons."

She stared at him, then Mika coolly pulled her elbow free of his grip. "First, it doesn't matter what your powers are. I won't be able to use them if you don't trust me. You don't. End of story. And second, did Sebastian mention what the bond entails? Like the fact that once it's done, you'll never be able to have sex with anyone else? I'll be it for you until one of us dies."

Conor curled his hands into fists to keep from taking hold of her again. "Yeah, he mentioned that."

"And you still want to go through with it?" Mika

sounded incredulous. Conor wasn't sure what that meant. When he nodded, she snorted. "It would be for nothing."

"I'm tired of hearing that." He did reach for her then, clasped her hips and pulled her close. "It's good between us," he said quietly. "I can be happy with only you for the rest of my life." He tried a smile, but it wasn't returned.

"You're such a sweet-talker. Just what every woman wants to hear before binding herself to a mate for life—I might be stuck with you, but at least the sex is good."

"You're the one who's been obsessed with sex this whole time. And that isn't what I said." He was pissed off again. "Besides, if you didn't want the bond, why did you keep saying your part every damn time we were in bed?"

"It wasn't every time."

"Like hell. Whenever you were close to coming, those words started pouring out of your mouth. If that's what works, I can always tug your jeans down and take you against the wall." He didn't miss her blush, and that blunted some of his anger. "Sorry," he apologized gruffly. "I didn't mean to be crude."

"I don't mind that," Mika said. At last, her arms went around his waist. "It's just . . . things are shaky between us. I don't know if I can bond with you and still know to walk away if it becomes too destructive. Do you understand?"

"I'd never hurt you, don't you know that?"

"You'd never hurt me physically. But emotionally? Not intentionally, no, but I love you and you don't feel the same way about me. Eventually, that's going to hurt." Before he could respond, Mika put two fingers over his lips. "It's not your fault. If I'd been truthful, maybe we could have built something between us. But I lied and you can't get past that."

Conor searched for a way to sway her, but Mika could be damn stubborn when she wanted. "You haven't given me much of a chance to recover, and I *have* gotten over some of it already. With more time, it could be a non-issue," he promised.

"Finding out you can't let it go after we've done the ritual isn't smart. Imagine it—tied for life to someone you hate."

Cupping her face with one palm, Conor leaned nearer. "I could never hate you. Even when I was pissed as hell, I didn't hate you. You're worrying over nothing."

If anything, her stubborn expression became more pronounced. "Why don't we head back to the house?" she suggested, ignoring what he'd said. "We can argue there."

"We're not leaving here until we finish both rites."

"Then we'll be breathing this rank air for a long time."

He nearly smiled. Although she drove him insane with her mulishness, he liked the fact that she went toe-to-toe with him. But how the hell would he convince Mika to agree to his plan? It was obvious she'd dug in her heels.

Manipulate her. Conor started to dismiss the idea—after all, it came from his demon side—except . . . Except she'd manipulated him. He might have been lost in a fog of lust, but he hadn't been blind to her tactics. Mika had used his attraction to her and her body to get past him more than once. It wouldn't be difficult to turn the tables; he knew her weaknesses. He could have her repeating her half of the ritual in minutes. But was that fair?

Gazing down into those sexy champagne-colored eyes, Conor decided fair didn't matter. The only important thing was keeping Mika alive. If that meant pushing a few of her buttons, he'd do it and deal with the consequences later.

"The extra power boost would help when I face the dark demons, but I bet I can take them down without it," Conor said. He kept his tone casual and, running a thumb across her cheekbone, lowered his hand back to her hip. "You're exaggerating how strong they are, anyway. I absorbed magic from one of them already, and it wasn't that big a deal."

There was a moment of confusion in Mika's eyes before they started to glow again. "I did not exaggerate! They're dangerous and the blast you took wasn't full strength."

Conor tightened his fingers on her hips, then relaxed them. With a stiff smile, he said, "It doesn't matter. If you won't bond with me, I'll have to battle them with what I have. And as much as you might wish otherwise, the showdown is coming. They want you dead and I won't let that happen." He read the look on her face: She'd taken the bait. All he had to do now was reel her in. "Know this, I'll fight for you until I take my last breath."

"I told you, I don't want you dying for me!" She tried to pull away from him, but Conor held on.

"You don't get to tell me what to do. If the Dark Ones want you, they'll have to go through me. It's that simple."

Mika attempted to free herself one more time before sagging against his chest. "Damn you," she said quietly.

Gathering her close, Conor bent until his mouth was next to her ear. "Bond with me, Mika. Give me a better chance against them. That extra power might make the difference."

"It's pointless." But she didn't sound adamant any longer. He knew he had her.

"When I square off with them," he said, "I want every advantage, but if you won't share the rites with me, I'm still going to meet them." He debated adding more, but decided if he were too blatant, she'd catch on. Instead, he said, "We have to try."

He thought she was going to argue further—he saw her reluctance—but with a sigh, she capitulated. "Okay."

Something inside his chest eased at that one, unenthusiastic word. Conor knew he should feel guilty for playing on her need to keep him safe, but he didn't. What he felt could be summed up in a single word: satisfaction.

"The female starts the rite," he reminded her. No way in hell was he giving her a chance to think this through.

Mika rested her forehead against his shoulder, but Conor moved her far enough away to see her face. When she tried to drop her gaze, he caught her chin in his hand. He wanted her to look at him, to *see him,* when she spoke.

After a brief hesitation, she began. He'd heard the words before, while he was buried deep inside her, but they were more meaningful now. For the rest of his life, there would be no one else, and as Conor looked down at her, he couldn't imagine ever wanting another woman. Mika was his in ways that went far beyond physical.

Her lips trembled as she finished speaking, and Conor brushed his mouth across hers before beginning his part of the rite. He didn't understand most of what he said in this demon language, but he could feel power building. And as he reached the end, Mika repeated the closing words with him.

It was as if his entire life had lacked clarity, and at last, he'd adjusted the focus. Then came a flash. A thousand different images of Mika kaleidoscoped through his mind before they stopped short and he saw *this* Mika again. The shift was so sudden, Conor felt off balance, but as his gaze locked with hers, the world righted itself. She was his anchor, his sanctuary.

As soon as he stood steadier, Conor said, "Sebastian helped me memorize the words to the second rite. Do you know them, or do you need me to tell you?"

"I know them. Every demon in Orcus does, although it's rarely used." She turned her head and kissed his palm, looking up at him again. "You get to start this one—for all the good it'll do."

"Honey, try to remember our roles. You're the optimist and I'm the pessimist," he joked.

The corners of her lips tilted, the first smile he'd seen from her in what seemed like days. "I love you, McCabe," she said.

"I know," he replied. And he was only beginning to grasp how much. To say that they were tied was an understatement—*merged* was closer to the mark. Conor finally understood Mika's reservations about joining, what with things unsettled between them, but she'd done it anyway to keep him safe. This seemed more significant than the way she'd shielded him with her body, although he was unsure why.

The ritual was quick. A few sentences for him, a few for her, and then they closed it. "Nothing feels different," he said.

"That's because you don't trust me," Mika replied, freeing herself from his hold.

He wanted to draw her back—Conor felt cold without the heat of her body against his. But he resisted. "Do *you* trust *me?* You're sure I'm going to hurt you emotionally. If not now, then in the future. Sounds like you don't believe in me, either."

Mika opened her mouth, shut it, paused, then said, "There's something wrong with your argument, but damned if I can figure out what it is." She smiled but looked strained. "Can we get out of here now? I'm sure the rats are plotting against us, and I don't want to be here when they decide to attack."

"Yeah." Conor closed the distance between them and took Mika's hand. "Let's go home."

Bonded. She'd bonded with McCabe. The thought kept echoing through her head as they made their way out of the dilapidated structure.

As a girl, Mika had spent hours daydreaming about meeting her vishtau mate. And although she'd known that demons rarely performed the bonding ritual, she'd fantasized about that too. But in her many scenarios, her mate had always demanded the permanency, because he loved her too much to do without her.

With maturity, Mika had started thinking more sensibly. It was unlikely she'd ever use the words she'd memorized. Most mates lived together, had children yet never bonded; and chances were that her life would follow that pattern as well. She'd reconciled herself to what would most likely come to pass—at least, that's what she'd believed. But when McCabe had ordered that she bond with him—not out of love, but to keep her safe—the caricature of her dream had left her feeling hollow inside.

Holding Conor's hand more tightly now, she sidestepped the carcass of a rat. She couldn't wait to exit and get away from the sights and smells here. This was something else she'd never imagined as a girl—performing her bonding rite in a derelict building. Mika shook her head. Time to give it up and deal with reality.

She loved Conor. Maybe they could make it work between them. Maybe he'd learn to believe in her. And maybe in a while, her heart would stop aching and she'd get over the fact that he'd bonded with her only to protect her and increase his powers.

McCabe let go of her hand when they were outside. "When we get home," he said, "we'll practice sharing power. I want you to be able to use my shielding capability."

Mika opted not to repeat the trust thing. He knew, so why belabor the point? "I'm willing to try," she said.

His lips quirked, and she felt her pulse kick up. His smiles were still rare, but were they becoming more frequent? She hoped so.

"Not just try," he said, "succeed. Hell, honey, we're both obstinate enough that we should be able to do anything we set our minds to."

"If it were that easy, every demon would be capable," she complained. She made a face at him. "You, me—stubbornness is a demonic trait."

Conor stopped, gave her a quick kiss, and then urged her along once more. What the hell was going on with him tonight? Mika had expected him to complain about being lumped in with demons, but he hadn't so much as grimaced. Granted, he'd come some distance in accepting his Kiverian nature, but she'd at least expected a sneer.

They approached the fence encircling the property, and

Mika scanned the area, trying to pick up any threats. Nothing. No one was close enough to trigger any alarm bells in her mind, and she bent over to get through the chain-link.

"Wait." Conor stopped her from squeezing through the hole and studied the area. "Go ahead, but stay aware."

Nodding to show she heard, Mika shimmied through the opening. As soon as she got clear, she moved forward and stood guard. Because of his size, Conor would be vulnerable when he went through, and she wouldn't leave him unprotected.

"Mika," he said when he stood beside her. "Stay close to me and stay alert." His soft voice indicated he was worried about eavesdroppers, and she ran another scan.

Still nothing.

"You picking up a presence?" she asked.

"No." He ran a hand over his nape and looked around, then Conor's gaze met hers. "I just have a feeling something is off."

She nodded. McCabe had been in dangerous situations for a long time, and his sixth sense would be very developed—not that she would discount any of his feelings, anyway. How many blocks away had they parked? Mika sighed silently. Once again, she hadn't been paying attention. At least this time she'd been focused on how to approach the Council and not busy playing some game in her head.

The neighborhoods they walked through seemed more sinister than they had earlier—there were shadows everywhere and a million places for someone or something to hide. Conor didn't rush, but he did keep moving at a good clip. There was a watchfulness about him, a sense of readiness that both relieved Mika and raised her level of anxiety. She had to be prepared too; she would never stand by and let him do all the fighting.

Every sound made her heart race. Every scurry of a rat made her think someone had caused it to run. Every whir of machinery made her nerves pull tauter.

With her superior vision, Mika didn't need the street-lights to see, but the fact that they weren't working added to the eeriness of the night. The area was deserted, and even a gang of werewolves would be a welcome sight right about now.

They rounded a corner, and Mika hesitated. There was a . . . stillness that was unnatural. "Conor," she whispered.

"I feel it. We'll go around. Come on." His arm went to her waist to turn her. Not that she needed it; Mika was more than happy to go in another direction. She felt McCabe tighten his hold a nanosecond before she completed her pivot, and saw what had made him tense.

Without a word being exchanged, she and Conor turned again, but the way they'd been walking was blocked. The dark demons were making their move.

Chapter Twenty

They were trapped.

With buildings on either side of them, there were only two directions to move, and the Dark Ones had both covered. Mika glanced over her shoulder—the first Bak-Faru had crossed a lot of ground. One shot: that's all it would take to finish her off.

Up ahead on her left, there was an alley—a possible escape route if they could reach it quickly enough. But just as humans couldn't outrun a bullet, demons couldn't outrun an energy blast.

Maybe, though, McCabe could get away. The dark demons wouldn't know he'd destroyed the grimoire. Without that info, they'd want him alive.

One glance at Conor's face, though, told Mika not to bother suggesting he leave. He'd never do it.

"I don't know what your powers are," Conor said quietly to her, "but direct the strongest of them at the demon in front of us when I squeeze your waist. Got it?"

"Yeah." If she combined a couple of her magics, like she had the second time she'd faced a Dark One, maybe she could affect him in some small way again. Mika gathered energy and held it, awaiting McCabe's signal.

For an instant, she almost felt him. It was as if Conor were reaching out for her, and instinctively she tried to close the distance, but a wall stopped her. The distraction almost made her miss his cue, but when his hand tightened, Mika released her whirlwind of thick air. At the same time, Conor discharged a blast of energy. Their two magics intertwined and raced toward the Dark One. She'd never heard of demons trying something like this before, but it was an incredible idea: their powers melded into one, a glowing cyclone that held her mesmerized.

The blond-haired Bak-Faru made no effort to move. In fact, he opened his arms, arrogantly daring the power to come to him. It did. The energy slammed into his body and tossed him several feet through the air before he landed on his backside. Mika smiled with satisfaction at the sight.

"Honey, there's two of them," Conor reminded her.

She stiffened and glanced behind her. While she'd been admiring their handiwork, the other Dark One had started strolling toward them. Why wasn't he attacking? The small distance wouldn't affect his powers.

Keeping himself between her and the black-haired demon, McCabe urged Mika toward the alley. She understood his goal now. Conor didn't want a confrontation; he wanted to get away and fight the Dark Ones some other time. Like, maybe when they'd worked out how to share powers?

Another peek showed the dark demon was unalarmed by their movement, and by his compatriot's struggle to regain his feet. The Dark Ones were here together, but acted always as individuals. Mika tried to decide if that gave her and Conor an advantage, but doubted the lack of teamwork would change the outcome of this clash. Those two *were* from the strongest demon branch.

The blond demon stood at last, but he didn't appear entirely steady. She and Conor ran faster, but the alley remained more than fifteen yards away. The Bak-Faru with the dark hair continued his unrushed pace. At ten yards from the alley, Mika knew why.

"It's a trap, Conor."

Cursing, she watched him size up the situation with this new piece of info. To escape, they'd need to make it past one of the dark demons. If they couldn't, there was nothing to do but stand and fight. And die.

Conor used all his speed, pushing Mika back against one of the dilapidated structures with his body in front of hers. Mika could only peer over his shoulder, but she didn't argue, not with the intensity radiating from him. Their position allowed a solid view of both dark demons. The blond one had recovered and strutted toward them the same as his compatriot; only, he looked pissed.

"This is pointless," Conor called out. "I won't allow you to harm her."

There came no response; they simply continued walking.

"I destroyed the incantation—"

"Conor!" Mika protested. At the same time, the blond Bak-Faru threw back his head and roared in fury.

Conor ignored him and added; "And I don't have a copy. It's gone."

The Dark Ones came to a stop and shared a glance. The rage on their faces was terrifying.

"He's lying," Mika said desperately. "While he did destroy the original spell, he does have a copy. He can still lower the veil."

"What are you doing?" Conor demanded in a whisper.

Mika ignored him. The Dark Ones would be able to hear anything she said, and she couldn't tip her hand—not when they were furious and the odds were already against her. "You know," she said, addressing them, "that only a half-demon who is also an auric assassin can do this, and Conor may be the only one born of that description since our imprisonment in Orcus. Another like him may not come for millennia. Do you want to lose this chance?"

"Mika, be quiet."

She shrugged him off. "They know what you are, as does the Council. It's part of the legend, although most demons are unaware of all the details." It was silly given the circumstances, but she wanted Conor to understand that she wasn't betraying him. "I didn't know myself until I was told today."

The two dark demons met and started conferring; they were so enraged that their gestures were almost caricaturish. They would have been humorous if the situation weren't so precarious. *Please let them believe me,* Mika thought.

"What were you thinking?" she asked Conor, her voice barely a breath of sound.

"No incantation means no need to consider you an obstacle."

Mika gritted her teeth and took a deep breath. "You thought they would just walk away if you didn't have the spell?"

McCabe nodded. Hadn't he listened to her when she'd told him the Dark Ones were obsessive and irrational? They weren't going to shrug this off and leave. Ever.

"You were wrong. If you don't have the incantation, then your life becomes as worthless to them as mine. Luckily, you held on to a copy." She tacked that on for the Bak-Farus' benefit.

Although Conor never looked at her, Mika knew he finally understood what she was getting at. The dark demons were vindictive, and someone would pay if the spell was gone. Who better than the Council's agent, and the half-demon idiotic enough to destroy the grimoire?

McCabe put his hand behind him, pressed it against her hip, and gave her a nudge to the left. If he thought they were going to get out of here because the Dark Ones were talking, he was mistaken. A burst of flame hit the wall close enough to singe the hair on her arm.

Before Mika could stop him, Conor pulled a gun. She

knew he didn't want to stand and wait for the Dark Ones to kill them, but taking the offensive wouldn't help their situation. He returned fire and some kind of orange beam shot out of the weapon, but the blond demon was a split second faster than the blast headed his way; while he was winged, the Bak-Faru avoided serious injury.

Before Conor could shoot again, the dark-haired demon directed heat at his gun; Mika could see the glow. McCabe fought to hang on, but when the weapon became unbearably hot, he had to drop it. The demon didn't let up until the weapon became an unidentifiable lump of molten metal. Satisfied that the threat was taken care of, the Dark One held out a hand and emitted an invisible energy wave. Mika barely had time to sense its movement before it crashed into her.

Since Conor shielded her, he took the brunt of the attack, which drove him into her, hard. The wall stopped her, and she stopped McCabe. As soon as he recovered, he straightened, and she gasped for air.

"Are you okay?" he asked.

Mika nodded, since she couldn't yet speak. She'd had the wind knocked out of her, but was otherwise fine —for now. If a dark demon could hurl them so forcefully with no problem, how the hell were she and Conor going to get out of this mess? McCabe went back to protecting her, and she felt a shift in energy. He was adding power to his shield, she realized.

Pushing her hair out of her face, Mika decided they needed a plan. Her magic wasn't much, but if Conor could continue to mix his power with hers the way he had earlier, maybe they could do some damage. And then there was his auric talent.

Of course, that would be a last-ditch, desperation move. If Conor fired, he would lose his shielding and be vulnerable. Assassins using the auric blast tended to attack and then get the hell out of Dodge. Only, McCabe wouldn't run—not unless they were both able to get away.

Mika froze. The dark demons appeared to still be talking, but something told her they'd reached a decision. Mika jumped onto Conor, pushing him to the ground.

The shot burst overhead and left a three-foot hole in the brick building directly behind them. McCabe rolled, shoving her beneath him. She twisted, trying to see the Dark Ones. "Damn it, let me help you!" she cried.

"Stay still."

Since he had a much better view of the situation than she, Mika obeyed instantly. Conor curved his body around hers, tucked his head in, and she braced herself. The dark demons released a barrage of energy; she could see the glow in her peripheral vision and sense it surround them. Some of the assault went astray, but the rest was absorbed by her vishtau mate.

McCabe didn't flinch.

"Conor?" Mika whispered.

"I'm okay, just don't move. I told you, I can absorb their energy." He gave her a small smile. "And they're going to be mighty unhappy when I fire this back at them."

Mika grinned with sheer relief. He was all right. She repeated that over and over as the assault continued.

Their faces were only inches apart, and the more Conor was hit, the brighter his eyes glowed. This wasn't caused by anger or arousal, but some third source—one she knew nothing about. Was it something unique to auric assassins?

The bombardment stopped suddenly, and McCabe lifted his head. "Oh, shit," he said.

"What? What's happening?"

"We've got more company."

At his grim tone she twisted, trying to see what was going on, but he pressed her down, keeping her covered. She complained, "If you're not going to let me look, at least fill me in."

"The Council's assassins have shown up."

"Oh, no. There won't have been enough time for word to reach them that their assignment's been scrubbed," she answered his unasked question. "I'd guess the Council is making arrangements to contact them even now."

Conor nodded. "I think our four friends are arguing over who gets to kill us." He sounded torn between amusement and horror.

Mika sighed. "That won't last long."

"I know. Okay, we're going to stand up—that will give us more options. I need you to move with me, keeping yourself behind my body. Got it?"

Mika nodded. Conor shifted slowly to his feet, and she maneuvered with him as he'd ordered. At last she was able to see their enemies again—just in time for a Dark One to attack one of the assassins. She would have watched further—anyone fighting a Bak-Faru was a spectacle not to be missed—but McCabe growled, "We can't go left or right. How about up? How high can you jump?"

Unsure what he wanted of her, Mika looked at the adjacent building. With her talent for levitation and a boost from the wind and air . . . yeah, she could get to the top. "I think I can make it to the roof—although it'll be close," she warned.

"That's five stories," he said. He sounded shocked.

"Um, that wasn't what you were asking?"

"The fire escape—Never mind," he decided. He glanced over his shoulder at the squabbling demons. They were standing in the street, exchanging fire. "You'll be vulnerable in the air, but I think it's worth the risk. Get up to the roof and go down the other side of the building. Then run like hell."

"What about you?" she demanded.

"Listen to me." He glanced again at the skirmish, then bent down to glare into her face. "If you're gone, I won't have to worry about protecting you or getting both of us out of here. If you leave, you're not deserting me, you're helping me."

As much as her heart rebelled at the thought, she knew

what he said was true. He was at a disadvantage with her present. "If you get hurt, I'll make you pay for this—understand me?" she swore.

Conor smiled, his lips quirking up in that sexy way he had. "I won't get hurt. Now get out of here before they get tired of fighting each other and decide to take care of us."

She nodded and gave McCabe a quick kiss, then trailed her fingers along the side of his neck as she pulled back. "Be careful!" she ordered.

Crouching, Mika used a combination of her leg muscles and her ability to levitate to launch herself skyward. She thinned the air around her to reduce drag, and added a boost of wind. As she passed the fourth floor she began to lose momentum, and she willed herself to make it that last story.

Mika started to reach forward to grab the roof, but stopped at the last second. As she fell back to earth, Conor glared at her. "Why the hell are you here?"

Despite the danger in their situation, she smiled at his grumbling. "About a third of that roof is gone, and the surrounding walls look like they could collapse at any minute. I didn't think it would take my weight, and I couldn't reach the part of the roof that appeared solid."

"Shit." Conor looked over at the demons, and Mika followed his gaze. It resembled a shootout from some old Hollywood Western, only instead of guns, the combatants were using fireblasts and energy waves. It was amazing. She'd never seen anyone stand against the Dark Ones before, but the auric assassins not only were fighting, they were holding their own.

"Let's try the power-sharing thing again," Conor said. He must have read her skepticism, because he added, "Work with me here, honey."

"You can't force yourself to trust me," she warned. He gave no response. Time was running out, so she gave up the debate—it was better to simply go along. "Okay, ready when you are."

She felt Conor reaching for her and Mika tried to visualize herself opening to him with every breath she took, with every beat of her heart. There was that sense of almost, but the barrier remained between them. It was thin—their own personal veil—but it held McCabe back as surely as if it were a fortress. She wiped away the perspiration that was dripping down his forehead toward his left eye.

"It's okay," she told him. "I still love you."

Something in his gaze shifted, became more intense—if that were possible. Conor cursed, and Mika rested her hand on his chest, rubbing gentle circles over his heart. She wasn't giving up; she'd fight until she took her last breath. Yet Mika knew the outcome didn't look good. McCabe might be a powerful Kiverian, but because he insisted on protecting her, he was in as much trouble as she, and there was no changing his mind.

Stepping closer, Mika wrapped her arms around his waist and looked up at him. "I love you, Conor, and I don't regret a thing. It was all worth it to have this time with you. I wish it could have been longer, but even a lifetime wouldn't have been enough." Going up on her toes, she nipped his chin and kissed him. Then she prepared to do what she must.

Mika was saying good-bye. She believed she was going to die, and she was saying good-bye. Conor tightened his hold on her. Didn't she realize he'd never let that happen?

But the logical side of his brain kicked in. There might be nothing he could do to prevent it. If they couldn't escape, it would be only a matter of time before they were killed.

He let Mika break the kiss, but kept his arms around her. Where were the recriminations? Why wasn't she berating him for his lack of faith? She'd done everything possible to atone for the lies she'd told. Not only had she gone into Orcus and bargained with the Council on his behalf, she'd nearly died protecting him. She would have died, if Sebastian hadn't shown up.

It's okay. I still love you. She'd said that after it was obvious he was the one preventing the merge.

She still didn't blame him for not believing in her.

The irony wasn't lost on him. All he wanted to do was keep her safe, and yet he was the reason she was going to die.

Conor gazed into her eyes. There was nothing there but unshakable love and trust. An ocean of trust. How could she look at him like that when her death would be his fault? How could she continue to love him?

"Come on," Conor said. He took her hand. While their four foes were busy fighting each other, he and Mika would try to slip away. She didn't hesitate, didn't argue, simply moved with him.

It had been a bad idea. They made it half a block before a blast of energy hit Conor. One glance back showed the demons had banded together. And, shit, Mika was unprotected. Conor looked for a defensible position, somewhere that gave her maximum protection, but . . .

A second blast nearly caught her.

That settled it. As much as he hated fighting in a corner, that was the only place she'd be safe: behind him and protected on her sides. He hauled Mika to the nearest tenement, put her where a tall staircase met the building, and stood in front of her to face the threat.

Conor had collected quite a store of power from the earlier attacks, and he called on that now. Compressing it into a tight ball, he hurled it at the nearest Bak-Faru. The blast packed a hell of a wallop, but the results weren't what he'd hoped for—the bastard staggered but didn't go down. There'd been a bigger effect when he'd infused Mika's cyclone with his own energy.

"Can you send out that tornado again?" he asked.

"Yeah, just say when."

He waited until a volley of energy passed, then gave her the signal. The attack didn't have the same outcome. His foes must have learned to compensate.

Conor absorbed more blasts of magic, and stored them—for all the good it would do. He felt Mika at his back. Why couldn't he wholly trust her? What else did she need to do to prove herself? No sooner did he ask than he knew the answer. It wasn't her; it was him. He couldn't trust *anyone* completely.

As he struggled to beat back the demon fire hurtling at him, Conor thought about that. It didn't take a college degree to figure out why. He'd always known how flawed he was, and to keep others from finding out, he kept them away. It was self-protection.

But he'd never been able to hold Mika back; she'd ignored his *Keep Out* signs and barreled ahead. Maybe that was why he'd gotten so angry when she'd lied to him. He'd latched onto it as an excuse to push her away before she discovered that he wasn't worth loving and abandoned him.

A fireblast roared over his head and hit the building. He heard Mika hiss with pain as debris—chunks of brick and mortar—rained down on her. "Mika?" he called out.

"I'm okay," she replied. "It stung a little, that's all."

Pissed that she'd had even a moment of pain, Conor hurled several bolts of energy at his enemies. They leapt to the side and walls exploded behind them.

He was an ass. Mika wasn't going to leave him. Shit, she'd stood fast when anyone with sense would have walked away long ago. She'd refused to take his attacks personally, had laughed at them—and had made him laugh. Conor felt her breath near his ear, and knew she was peering over his shoulder. He reached behind his back, touched her. The demons were again moving forward.

His hand tightened on her flank. "Get down!" he ordered, a split second before a tidal wave of energy rolled toward them. The demons hadn't combined their powers, but they were attacking side by side. As the power crest hit the stairs and building, the wave narrowed, became more concentrated. Became more powerful.

His shield wavered under the onslaught . . . but held.

Yet, in that split second, he knew absolute terror for Mika. The thought of her dying was unbearable. And that's when the pieces fell into place. He suddenly understood.

He loved her.

That was why he'd insisted she bond with him. Not because of the power-sharing, but because he'd wanted her tied to him in every way possible. If they were bonded, she might walk out and leave him, but she could never allow any other male to touch her while he was alive. It had been selfish as hell—and he'd do it again and again, because she was his. She always had been. And he was hers—heart, mind, body and soul.

The Bak-Faru and the auric assassins broke into another argument. Each blamed the other pair for the failure of their attack—or at least to take out Conor's shield.

An assassin fired at the dark-haired Bak-Faru, and another mini-battle ensued. This time, Conor and Mika didn't have the option of attempting to slip away; they were trapped against the building and their foes were too close.

Despite the situation, Conor had the weird urge to grin. Mika was his woman. His mate. His world. Finally, he had someone who loved and accepted him. Someone who wasn't afraid of his nature or his temper. Someone who wasn't cowed by his distance. Hell, Mika was someone who refused to *allow* distance between them.

Now that he'd figured out how much he loved her, he was damned if either one of them was going to die. Not tonight, not until they were old and had shared a lifetime.

He reached for Mika. Kissing her, he tried to mesh their souls. That damn obstruction remained. And yet . . . he suddenly saw that it was insubstantial, and he ripped through it easily. Conor felt her surprise; then Mika welcomed him. And as her love surrounded him, he knew he'd found completion.

Chapter Twenty-one

Mika wanted to wrap her arms around Conor and hold him forever. She felt his crushing loneliness—and she felt his quiet relief as it ended. Something had happened to make him trust her, to make him open up, but she was damned if she knew what.

They'd have to talk. Later. Right now, they had four enemies who were still dangerous, even if high emotion had them acting stupidly. She needed to figure out how to share McCabe's shield, and to tap into some of his other magic, then they could go on the offensive and stop cowering in this damn corner.

At first, it was . . . awkward. There was some stumbling around before it clicked and she had his protection around her. The rest of his powers—well, she'd figure those out later. "Let's go kick some butt." Mika smiled. "Then we can go home and have hot, adrenaline-charged demon sex."

He shook his head, seeming amused despite himself. "Are you sure you can hold the shield?" he asked.

If he wasn't so sweet, she would have rolled her eyes—he still had to learn to trust her competence. But she appreciated his concern. "I've got it, I promise. If you're ready, let's go before they remember they're here to fight us, not each other."

Conor grabbed her arm before she could race past. "That shield doesn't make you invincible," he reminded her.

"I know. I'm the one who keeps telling *you* that."

He growled, a low, demonic sound. Poor McCabe. She frustrated him endlessly, and no doubt, would continue to do so for the rest of their lives.

Shaking his head, he said, "Don't send any energy toward the assassins—they'll collect it and use it later. And don't—"

An arc of fire from one of the Setonians stopped him short. "Any more instructions?" she asked sweetly.

"To hell with it. If you run into trouble, yell." And with that, McCabe shouted some kind of battle cry and rushed forward, leaving Mika flat-footed. Cursing, she chased after him.

The blond Bak-Faru threw a ball of energy at her. It hit dead-on, stopping her for a second. Mika didn't know which of them was more surprised that it didn't cause any damage, her or the Dark One, but she recovered first. After directing a whirlwind toward her assailant and his buddy, she glanced over at Conor. He'd taken on the Setonians, leaving the Bak-Faru to her.

A side of her mouth quirked up. She knew why McCabe had zeroed in on the auric assassins. If she couldn't use her powers against them, then that fight came down to sheer brute force, and as with humans, demon males were stronger than the females. The Bak-Faru were more appropriate for her to handle.

And he obviously believed she could do it.

"Haven't you learned any new tricks?" the golden-haired demon asked. She still couldn't get over how gorgeous he was. Evil shouldn't be so pretty.

"I'm Mahsei. I have to work with what I've got," she replied. At least, she had to work with her own powers until she figured out how to use some of Conor's.

The other dark demon, the one with dark hair, growled

low in his throat and muttered a complaint about too much talking. He shot a fireball at her.

Mika started to duck, then remembered she was protected. It was an odd experience, one that held her enthralled. The energy hit her and evaporated, while she stood in a tranquil bubble. The intensity of the assault and her own shield astounded her.

Conor had spoken of absorbing the power, of being able to use it later, so if she could collect this, she could do amazing things. Mika tried gathering it—and it worked! A short laugh of exuberance escaped her before she could stop it, and that pissed off the blond demon. He cast more magic at her, which she also added to her energy stores.

How cool was this? And she doubted McCabe even gave a second thought to the talent.

It was almost a disappointment when the Bak-Faru quit blasting her. She had a great deal of their power, and once she figured out how to gain access, she was going to use it. Mika grinned. Damn, this was almost fun—or it would be if the stakes weren't so high.

Quickly, she glanced over at McCabe—he was holding his own, even two-on-one—then movement jerked her attention back to her own foes. The pretty blond was rushing her.

Mika shifted her feet so that her weight was evenly balanced, and braced herself. She didn't have the smooth moves of a martial artist, but her dad had taught her some down-and-dirty street fighting. Just in case. She doubted the dark demon had an equal amount of skill. For one thing, he'd attacked openly, giving her time to prepare, and for another, the way he charged made her think of a frat boy spotting a keg. He likely was used to killings that were much easier than this.

When he reached her, she easily deflected him with a forearm and, hooking her foot behind his ankle, pushed hard, tumbling him to the ground. Mika jumped back, evading the fist he aimed at her knee.

As he started to climb to his feet, she took a couple of running steps forward and, with the full momentum of her body, kicked him in the groin. The noise he made was like nothing she'd heard before from either human or demon. The blond Bak-Faru collapsed back on the street and curled into the fetal position.

But, demons recovered more quickly than humans, and Mika couldn't risk him rejoining the brawl. She hesitated, cringing at the thought, but it was life or death, and she couldn't play nice. Down-and-dirty, she reminded herself. And with her eyes open only enough to aim, she let loose with a roundhouse kick to Blondie's temple. His head whipped to the side and he went limp. It was hard to hide her reaction, but she couldn't display weakness, and that was how remorse would be viewed.

Mika turned her attention to the other dark demon. She'd expected him to jump in and double-team her as she'd fought his partner, but he hadn't. He stood nearby and appeared amused, as if he were watching a show. There might be some tension between the two Bak-Faru, and maybe she could exploit that.

Before she could figure out how, though, he moved.

Not normally, however—he teleported. It was a talent she had never seen before, and he went from twenty feet away to directly in front of her. His blow to the side of her head was hard enough to make her vision go black.

Instinctually she ducked and wove, backing out of range until she could see again and fight. As she retreated, Mika's heel hit the curb and she stumbled. That clumsiness saved her life. The Bak-Faru's second blow would have broken her neck—if he'd landed it cleanly. Instead, her sudden stagger threw off his aim, and while her shoulder hurt like hell, she was alive to complain. This Dark One was adept at hand-to-hand.

Her vision was back but blurry, and she blinked a few times to clear it. Mika half-expected to see Conor bearing down with murder in his eyes, protecting her, but it was just her and the dark-haired Bak-Faru. A glance to her left showed McCabe had his own trouble.

The Dark One took her by surprise. Instead of another physical move, an incredibly intense arc of fire erupted around her. Instinctively she flinched, but her shield held.

He moved close enough for her to kick. She knew he'd be expecting her to aim for his crotch, so she delivered a thigh kick instead, her shin striking four inches above his knee. Her dad would be proud—it was the ideal place to land the blow.

But Mika didn't stop. While her opponent was recovering, she moved closer and brought her arms up. With one hand protecting her face, she delivered an elbow to his temple. It snapped his head back, and she caught him in the other temple with her opposite elbow.

Certain he was reeling, Mika made the move for his groin, but he turned in time to evade. The force of her kick sent her staggering, trying to regain her balance, and the Dark One came for her throat. Bringing her forearm up, she knocked his hand away and took a swing. She grazed him, but didn't manage the blow she wanted.

"Aren't you going to taunt me?" she jibed. Maybe she could rile him, cause him to lose his temper and make a mistake. "Or are you too busy concentrating on being beaten by a weaker demon?"

The Dark One sneered. "You can do no better than that, Mahsei? Your verbal jabs are as feeble as your magic."

They circled each other, each looking for an opening. "I guess I haven't watched enough WWE," she joked. That earned her a blank look. "Professional wrestling," she explained. He didn't understand and she shrugged. "Guess you don't get out of Orcus much." Then she laughed, mocking him. There was a flash in his eyes as the comment struck home. She continued, "Luckily, I can come and go as I please. I don't have to wait for a human to call me forth, don't have to make pacts with them or owe them any favors. Not like you."

The Bak-Faru's eyes were glowing now and Mika knew she was on the right track. "I could push you back through the gate and you'd be trapped in the Other World again. For all your great powers, you're as helpless as the weakest of demons when it comes to the veil." She laughed derisively. "What's your debt to the human that summoned you?"

She kicked out, aiming for his thigh, but he jumped back in time and it was nothing but a glancing blow.

"We killed them," he growled, his voice ferocious. "And ate their hearts."

It was supposed to scare her; instead, Mika laughed. "Poor Bak-Faru. Who's going to call you out next time now that your stooges are dead?"

Red burned in his eyes, and Mika blocked his next assault with her forearm, preventing the dark demon from striking her with the heel of his hand. They returned to circling each other.

He snarled, "It's unnecessary. The veil is coming down—if not by your Kiverian half-breed, then because of our alternate plan. There will be no need to summon me or any other of the Bak-Faru—Earth belongs to us, and we will rule it again as we did before our imprisonment."

Mika rolled her eyes. "That's quite a speech, but I don't see any walls down yet. Demons have tried since the beginning to free themselves, and haven't succeeded. Your second plan is surely nothing more than another Bak-Faru joke."

Mika whirled away from his lunge. The Dark One was seriously pissed, and out for her blood. Her idea of enraging him had seemed smarter before she'd succeeded.

Suddenly, he disappeared.

Mika froze . . . and figured out what he was up to a few seconds too late. He'd transported himself directly behind her. His hands went around her throat, and his fingers tightened. She brought her own hand up, trying to wedge her fingers between her neck and his grip, but his hold was too secure. Swinging her elbow back didn't work, either. He was too far away from her and, because of his strength, the Dark One didn't need to use his body as leverage to strangle her.

With no good physical response, she had to call on her magic. Now seemed like a good time to work out how to use the energy she'd collected. As her vision began to dim, she decided to go with instinct. She had nothing to lose.

Mika thickened the air molecules around the dark demon, pressing them in on him. Gathering the power she'd amassed, she used that to intensify her own talent. She visualized the heavy oxygen atoms wedging in his lungs, crushing the delicate cells. She pictured the air outside his body pushing with the weight of the entire planet against his chest. Holding those images firmly in her mind, she directed her power to carry them out.

The dark demon released her, and Mika fell to her hands and knees, gasping for breath. Her throat burned as if she'd swallowed a blazing sword, but she didn't let up on the Dark One. Not until she heard yelling. One of the voices belonged to Conor.

McCabe. She had to check on McCabe.

Mika tried to raise her head, but it was heavier than her neck could lift. Gray mist obscured her vision, and she forced herself to breathe slowly and deeply.

Gradually, her eyesight began to clear and she gained enough strength to search for Conor. He appeared bloodied, but he was on his feet and he was still holding his own. Good. She needed a few more minutes before she could stand. She coughed violently and her stomach heaved. Mika swallowed hard, not wanting to vomit all over herself. Okay, maybe it would take more than a few minutes.

She hoped the dark demon was dead, since he hadn't attacked again, but she knew she had to find out. Bracing herself, she turned until she saw him. Yep, he was dead. His chest was caved in.

Mika's stomach heaved again. Looking away, she did some more deep breathing—and some more hacking. She'd never killed anyone before, had never even tried, and she wanted to cry. Intellectually, she accepted that he would have strangled her without a second thought, that it was either kill or be killed, but emotionally . . . Well, it was going to take some time to come to terms with this.

Thinking of what she'd done reminded her to check on the dark one that she'd kicked. She lurched over to him, and looked down. He was still out, and given the speed with which demons healed, that surprised her a bit. She couldn't have . . .

Mika stared at his chest, but she didn't see it move. She tried to crouch beside him, but was unsteady enough that she ended up on her hands and knees. Tentatively, she reached for his throat, searching for his pulse. She couldn't find one.

Before she could double-check, she heard a triumphant shout and looked up. The Setonians had knocked Mc-Cabe down.

Her heart in her throat, Mika lurched to her feet. This wasn't good. He was vulnerable, prone. Anger bolstered her strength, and she ran toward her mate, intent on helping him. No powers, not against these guys, but they weren't paying any attention to her. Mika adjusted her angle and lined up to strike one of the assassins.

When she reached him, she let fly with a roundhouse kick. She caught the Setonian under his ribs, and his response was immediate—he flew off Conor and didn't get up. She gave a cry of victory. No one hurt her vishtau mate without paying a price—not while she was able to defend him!

Mika turned her attention to the second auric assassin, but he'd thrown himself at McCabe. The two were rolling around on the ground, each trying to keep on top.

She was caught up in watching the fight, willing McCabe to take out the demon, when she sensed motion. The first Setonian was headed back for her.

Despite the damage from the kick she'd delivered, the assassin still had the advantage. He outweighed her by a good seventy pounds, and he was close to Conor in height, which made him about half a foot taller. And he had training. The Setonian was a hired killer—he'd know many different fighting methods and be adept at them.

He sent a burst of flame at her. It didn't last long. His facial expression didn't change—not really—but something told her he'd figured out that she was sharing McCabe's powers.

The Setonian moved in. He didn't grab her—that would allow her some leverage. Instead, he took a swing. Mika ducked, but it was a close call.

His eyes were flat, sober, and held no glow. He was deadly serious, and she doubted he would allow himself to be taunted into precipitous action or distraction. Mika tried to take the offensive, but he countered her every strike. She almost ended up on the ground, and knew she couldn't risk that. She dodged and weaved to avoid his blows. If he connected, if he knocked her down, she was finished. He wouldn't hesitate to go for the kill.

But she couldn't continue to dance around. Conor was locked in his own fight, and she couldn't count on his help anytime soon. She had to save herself. The question was how. If she tried to wield her powers against the assassin, he could amass the energy and use it against her.

Mika took a punch to her side, not quite able to get out of the way in time, and wheezed as the air was driven from her lungs. Air. That was her area of mastery. She couldn't direct her powers at him, but what if she worked on the oxygen outside his shield? He had to breathe.

Estimating how far his protective bubble went, Mika started altering the molecules around it. Delving into the pool of power she shared with McCabe, she stripped the air until it held so little oxygen, no living thing could survive. Around those atoms, she created a dense wall to keep the thin air encapsulating the Setonian.

At first, her foe didn't understand what was happening. She saw his confusion, but he continued trying to reach her. Only, the more effort he put out, the faster he used up his oxygen.

"Mahsei. Air and wind," he realized.

The words were soft, forced out between gasps, but she heard them. And now that he knew she was responsible, Mika prepared herself, ready for whatever he tried.

His choice was unexpected. Since Conor had been so unconcerned about the auric blast, she'd assumed his shield held against it—yet that was the weapon he chose to level at her. He fell to his knees, but she sensed him continuing to call on his power. Mika glanced over at McCabe, but he and the other demon were busy. Cautiously, she backed away.

Just as he began to keel over, the assassin summoned enough magic. The blast lit up the protection surrounding Mika more brightly than the Vegas Strip, but her shield didn't waver.

By the time the brightness dimmed, the assassin was dead. It wasn't any easier for Mika to bear than her first killing—she quickly glanced at the Bak Faru—or the second, but she didn't have time to think about it. Squaring her shoulders, Mika ran toward Conor. She winced when she drew near enough to see his face. He'd taken a pounding, but so had the Setonian he fought.

It took a few deep breaths to calm her temper enough to think How could she help? She couldn't jump into the middle of the fight, that would be stupid, but with the two males so close together, she'd have to be very precise to use asphyxia. Conor swayed and that hardened Mika's resolve. She'd be careful, and if it appeared as if she were affecting McCabe, she'd stop.

She started to thin the air molecules—attempted to anyway. Something blocked her; Mika could feel a barrier. Calling on more power, she tried again, and again, but the same thing happened each time.

Conor staggered back a step, and with a smirk, the Setonian met her gaze. It was only for an instant, but it told her what had happened. When she and McCabe had been attacked, and his shield had wavered, Mika had felt Conor adjust it. He'd compensated for the actions of their enemies. This assassin must have done the same thing and neutralized her weapon.

For a few minutes, she stood and watched, desperately trying to come up with some new idea. A breeze gusted strongly enough to blow her hair into her face, and impatiently, she shoved it out of the way. *Wait a second.* Maybe that was it.

Of course, she'd need to get Conor clear, but this might work now that she could call on his power. Drawing deep within herself, Mika began to gather a storm. Clouds rolled in, obscuring the moon, and the wind blew forcefully. When a low rumble of thunder echoed through the night, she smiled. Thunder followed lightning, and that's what she wanted.

Now that she'd created the storm, she needed control of it. That wasn't quite so easy. She'd never reached this point before, and it was mostly guesswork. Trying to force the storm didn't work; neither did using the wind to shape it. With a frown, Mika thought some more.

If you can't beat them, join them.

As soon as the saying leaped into her head, she knew it was the answer. Mika merged her consciousness with the storm, became part of it. Its primitive fury was exhilarating, but she couldn't allow herself to get lost in the feelings. Conor needed her.

She waited for an opening, but her vishtau mate never broke far enough away for her to risk a lightning bolt. It became difficult for her to stay blended as she kept hearing the grunts and the sounds of fists meeting flesh. Finally, enough was enough.

"McCabe, get the hell away from him. Now!" she cried.

Oops. Maybe she shouldn't have done that. It distracted Conor and he was struck hard. He went flying several feet in the other direction.

On the plus side, the assassin headed for Mika. When he was far enough away from her mate, she called a spear of lightning down, striking the Setonian directly in the center of his chest. The noise he made was indescribable. It sent a shudder through her, and Mika knew she'd be hearing it in her nightmares. The Setonian's body convulsed on the ground, flopping around in a sickening display. She turned her head away and closed her eyes.

A few moments later, Mika disengaged from the tempest and carefully dispersed it. She took a step toward McCabe, but she had vertigo so bad that she had to shut her eyes once more to block out the spinning world, and to get a handle on her nausea.

She felt movement, and she figured it was Conor coming to check on her. The arm that went around her throat told a different story. Before she could react, a second arm went over her body, pinning her arms to her torso.

"You're going to die for what you did to me," a voice hissed.

She opened her eyes, but everything continued spinning crazily and Mika couldn't keep them open. It didn't matter, she knew it was the blond demon. How had she missed his pulse? "Did you take a look at your friend?" she rasped, and as she asked the question, called on her powers. Only, nothing was there.

What the hell? She tried again, but no dice. The shield was present but felt shaky, as if it wouldn't take much to destroy. She delved deeper, looking for the pool of extra power she'd been using, but couldn't access that either.

The Bak-Faru murmured near her ear how he planned to torture her before her death, showing the ugliness of his nature. Pretty or not, the Dark Ones were aptly named.

McCabe, she thought, I could use some help now.

But she couldn't see him. She didn't know how badly he was hurt. Mika tried to work herself free, but her dizziness hampered any defensive move she attempted.

"Let go of her," Conor's voice called out.

Mika smiled faintly. Her mate's words were music to her ears. She opened her eyes long enough to see that Conor was in bad shape, swaying unsteadily, with blood running down his face. It sobered her, and she tried to tap into her powers again.

"She's going to die, and there's nothing you can do to protect her, Kiverian. Look at yourself. You're marginally capable of standing, but beyond that?" Mika felt the Dark One shrug, but his hold didn't loosen.

While she couldn't swear to it, she thought she sensed McCabe trying to access their well of power, too. She was fairly sure he'd come up empty.

Conor made a noise that was pure demon—there was nothing remotely human about it—and she nearly smiled again. He was accepting all his Kiverian nature. He and her captor made more threats back and forth, and while the Bak-Faru was distracted, Mika fought to get free.

She was no more successful this time than earlier. The Dark One tightened his hold on her neck, slowly cutting off her air. Who would have guessed this frat boy of a monster, the least practiced in fighting of her four enemies, would be the one to bring about her death?

Mika forced her eyes open. She wanted to see McCabe before she died, and puking on herself was the least of her worries.

As their gazes locked, she read determination from Conor—resolve. The demon squeezed harder and Mika choked, trying to take in more oxygen. She became light-headed and slumped back against the Dark One.

Then she felt it: McCabe was calling on his auric energy. But Conor never used that power. He'd told her he never would—that it was too ugly, too evil. That it would cost him his humanity.

"Hold still." She wasn't sure if he whispered the words or merely thought them, but she heard and obeyed.

Mika closed her eyes, and in her mind's eye she pictured the energy blast that sailed from Conor's hand to the head of the Bak-Faru holding her. The dark demon fell backward, and she was dragged along, landing on top of him. As soon as his hold slackened, she rolled, twisted and crawled to put distance between them.

She felt hands take her arms and she writhed frantically, ignoring her stomach's protests. "It's okay, honey, he's dead."

At Conor's voice, she froze and opened her eyes, then clamped them shut again. "Everything's whirling so violently," she gasped.

"Then come here and let me hang on to you until it stops." He pulled her onto his lap, and wrapped his arms around her.

Snuggling into his chest, Mika tucked her face against his throat. His blood felt sticky against her cheek, but she didn't move. "How badly are you hurt?" she asked.

"I'll be fine tomorrow. How about you? How bad off are you?" His hug firmed, then loosened.

"My throat's been better, and this vertigo is making me sick, but I'll be fine tomorrow too. That storm did something to me," she confessed. "I don't know what, but it screwed me up."

She wanted to ask questions, but Mika didn't have the energy for a serious conversation—and she doubted McCabe did either. There would be plenty of time to discuss everything later; their enemies were finally dead.

It took about ten, maybe fifteen minutes for the nausea to recede, and carefully, Mika opened her eyes. The street stayed steady, and she smiled against Conor's skin.

"Better?" he asked.

Mika nodded. Looking him over, she asked, "Can you walk? We should get out of here before someone finds us."

"Yeah, I can walk, but you're going to have to get up by yourself. I won't be able to help you."

Mika nodded, and stood. There were definitely more graceful ways of doing so, but she didn't care; she and Conor were both alive, that's what counted. Besides, Mc-Cabe didn't look too slick either as he got to his feet. When he swayed, she hurried and wrapped her arm around his waist.

"Are you sure you're okay? We could try to call a healer." She meant Sebastian, but she wasn't telling him that.

"I'm fine," he grumbled. "Get my comm out of my pocket, though, would you, honey?"

"Who are you going to call?" she asked, handing over the unit.

"Hayes. I lied to cover his ass, so he can lie to cover ours."

The subsequent comm conversation was terse, with Conor giving just enough info for Marc to know what the situation was and what they needed him to do; then McCabe ended the call and handed Mika the unit. She tucked it in her pocket as he said, "Let's get out of here. Hayes is only a few minutes away and he can handle this without us."

They walked along the sidewalk, McCabe leaning into her side for support. Mika said, "I never thought I'd say this, but I'm going to have to ask for a rain check on the wild sex. I just want to sleep."

"Maybe tomorrow," Conor said, and Mika caught his smile.

That sounded promising, didn't it? Tomorrow? It meant he was keeping her around, right? She thought about that for a few blocks before she said, "You should make me your partner. After all, I did take down three demons to your one." She winked at him and held her breath.

He laughed. "You don't have to brag, honey. I know you did a good job. I also know that you've never killed before and that you're dealing with a lot of emotion because of it."

Mika swallowed hard as those feelings rushed back. "I don't want to talk about it."

"You're going to, though. But later. Not now."

She wanted to argue with him, but didn't. He was right;

she was going to need to discuss it with someone who understood what she'd done, and what she was going through emotionally. Conor had killed vampires, werewolves, demons—he'd get it.

"You used your power," she said, changing subjects. "The one you said you'd never use." Well, that came out smooth as hell, Mika thought with a frown. She risked a glance at her mate, but he didn't seem angered by her comment.

"Yeah, I know." She thought he was going to leave it at that, but without prodding, he added, "I'd use it again to rescue you, too. I had nothing else left. There was little choice."

"I know," she agreed.

Conor's truck came into view, and Mika breathed a sigh of relief. They were both quiet until they reached it.

"Your dizziness is gone? Completely?" Conor asked.

"Yeah, why?"

"You get to drive." He pulled the keys out of his front pocket. "My eyes are swelling shut."

Mika helped Conor into the pickup, then went around to the driver side and climbed up and in. Turning to Conor, she said, "Thanks. For saving me. I know what it cost you to use that power."

"I'm half Kiverian, and I'm an auric. You were right: Denying it doesn't change what I am. Or who I am. 'The bamboo that bends is stronger than the oak that resists.' I get that now—*really* get it. I could have stayed stubborn and refused to use that power, and you would have died." His hands fisted tightly enough to turn his bruised knuckles white. "And that would have broken me." His gaze, even with his face so swollen, was intense.

"I love you, Mika," he said.

"What?" She couldn't have heard right.

"I love you." His voice was gentler this time. "You're the best thing that's ever happened to me, and more than I deserve—I know that." Mika tried to interrupt, but Conor reached out and squeezed her hand. "Let me finish. We both know you put up with more shit from me than anyone should have to, but give me a chance to make it up to you. Give me a chance to change. Just don't leave yet, okay?"

Mika leaned forward and brushed her lips over his. "McCabe, I love you too. I've been telling you that for days, and I'm not going anywhere." She smiled. "You'll have to throw me bodily out of your house—and even then, I'll come back and fight."

"*Our* house. And you're definitely better than I deserve," he laughed.

"Wrong," she disagreed. "I'm exactly what you deserve. And before you put me up on some pedestal, I'm a long way from perfect."

"Wrong," he said, echoing her, "you're perfect *for me*."

She had to kiss him for that—gently, since his poor mouth was as messed up as his face. His fingers splayed through her hair, lightly caressing her head. Mika stayed frozen after the kiss ended, needing to be near him. They both could have died tonight.

"Honey," he said softly, "this is the wrong place and time—there's nothing romantic about it—but . . . will you marry me?"

Mika straightened away from him, studying his face. "Marry? McCabe, we've done the bonding ritual. That's much more permanent than any human ceremony." She even felt a bit of disdain for the mortal rite.

But Conor was adamant. "I pushed the bonding thing on you, and there's nothing we can do about that. But this time I'm asking. Will you marry me?"

She suddenly heard what he wasn't saying: He needed her to choose him freely, without any outside force—not even his own—swaying the decision. She'd argue another time—it wasn't entirely accurate that he'd pushed her to bond with him, since the only reason she'd hesitated was her belief that he didn't love her. But that would be best saved for later, too.

"I will marry you—anywhere, anytime, in any ceremony you wish. I love you," she said for the millionth time. It never felt like enough.

The corners of his lips turned up, and he and she shared another long kiss. Conor finally broke away and said, "I'm too old, too big and too sore to make out in the truck. Let's go home, honey."

Reluctantly pulling away, Mika buckled up and started the pickup. Home? That sounded exactly right.

Epilogue

Mika McCabe stepped out of the shower and reached for a towel. The wedding and the reception had gone off far more smoothly than she could have hoped. Sure, some of her human family thought getting married on the beach underneath a full moon was strange, and that a luau dinner was even odder. And yeah, Conor had growled a little when he'd spotted his father, but overall she couldn't have asked for a better day.

There had been only one notable absence. Conor's mother.

Just thinking about it made Mika scowl. Tracking the woman down hadn't been easy, but she had done so. She'd tried talking to her on the comm first, but as soon as Conor's name came up, his mother had disconnected. So, on a day when Mika knew her mate would be busy, she'd trekked all the way out to Timbuktu to invite the woman to the wedding in person. Mika had even promised to forgo inviting her demon family if the woman agreed to attend; she knew how much her presence could mean to Conor.

The trip had been wasted. As soon as she'd introduced herself as McCabe's fiancée, Mika had gotten the door closed in her face. Her second visit had garnered the same response, and she'd finally conceded defeat. If his mother wanted to cling to her bitterness, there was nothing Mika could do to change that. But she felt bad for her vishtau mate.

The comm rang and she heard Conor answer it. Deciding not to eavesdrop, Mika tuned out the conversation, but she had to shake her head. McCabe had been making an effort to become less isolated, but he should have left the unit turned off tonight. Of course, the chances of another call coming through were next to nil, so she guessed there wouldn't be any more interruptions.

As she finished drying off, Mika secured the towel around her and reached for some scented lotion. She rubbed it between her hands to warm it, then began smoothing it onto her skin.

Her lips tilted as she thought about how secretive their wedding had just been. With tensions continuing to escalate in Crimson City, they'd decided the presence of her mom, gran and brother, Nic, needed to be kept quiet. Okay, *Conor* had thought it was a good idea to be cautious, and she'd agreed because he'd been so tense. It had all worked out although it was the first time her human and demon families had met, and there were some iffy moments.

Mika sobered. When she'd gone to retrieve her belongings and to tell her mom about Conor, things had felt . . . odd in Orcus. She'd talked her dad into summoning her three relatives for more than just the wedding. It was still a closed ritual, of course; but instead of going immediately back to the Other World, her family would be spending some time on her dad's estate up near San Francisco.

Mika didn't know who would have the more difficult adjustment to make—the humans in the Bay Area or her demon family. But at least her dad and mom—okay, at least her dad—would keep a lid on everyone.

Mika's grin returned as she thought about how her parents had been acting tonight. They believed they'd been discreet during the wedding luau, but she had a pretty good idea that she and McCabe wouldn't be the only two having some hot sex tonight. She didn't pretend to understand her parents' relationship, but for years she'd suspected they had clandestine trysts. Mika shrugged. It wasn't her business.

Putting the cap back on the lotion, she wondered where Conor's father was living. Nearby, she guessed, since he had repeatedly shown up trying to bridge the chasm with his son, but he kept a very low profile. Mika was glad someone besides Marc had been at the ceremony for her mate, and maybe Sebastian's persistence would eventually soften McCabe.

She turned when she heard a knock. "Yeah?"

"That was Hayes on the comm," Conor said through the wooden door. "He had news about our watcher."

Mika stiffened. They'd sensed his presence tonight, and that had been the one dark spot in the evening. "What did he say?"

"He went through the veil into Orcus." When she remained quiet, processing that information, Conor said, "Mika?"

"I heard. It makes sense," she answered slowly. "I thought he might be studying us to learn about demons."

"Maybe," Conor agreed. "But at least we don't need to worry about him anymore. There'll be plenty of other demons to keep him occupied—probably for the foreseeable future."

McCabe had that right. Mika laughed softly as he walked away from the door. Imagining what the vampire would be facing in the Other World, Mika almost felt sorry for him. Almost.

She tugged her towel free and tossed it in the hamper. The red silk chemise she shimmied into had thin, spaghetti straps and ended high on her thighs. There were tiny V-string panties that went with it, but Mika didn't bother with those. McCabe would have them off her in about two seconds anyway. With a smile, she reached for the clip she'd used to keep her hair up and dry while she'd been in the shower, and let her tresses tumble free.

Time to go have some wild demon sex. The mere thought of her husband aroused her, and by the time she reached the bedroom, she was already primed. She stopped short in the doorway and watched Conor tie a second black bandanna to the headboard.

"What are you doing?" she asked.

He glanced over his shoulder, then did a double-take. His reaction was everything she'd hoped for, and her smile returned.

"You like?" she asked, making a slow pirouette.

His growl, and the red glow in his eyes, were all the answer she needed. Conor had given up fighting his Kiverian nature. He continued to wear his tinted contacts outside the house, but when they were alone, he didn't bother. Mika loved that—and not because she needed him to be demon, but because she wanted him to accept himself. Like she now accepted her human side. On that front, he'd been making exceptional progress.

"You were going to tell me what the bandannas were for," she prompted when Conor did nothing but stare.

"They're there so you can tie me up."

Mika laughed. "Bondage, McCabe? I can't believe I married a pervert." She shook her head, but she was delighted.

His growl denoted frustration rather than arousal. "You wanted to be on top, right? I figured . . . well, if I was restrained, I'd be less likely to . . . Well, we'd be able to do it in that position."

She grinned. "You're incredibly sweet." And he was. They'd tried more than once to mate with her in the dominant position, but they'd never made it long before Conor flipped her on her back and took charge. Of course, *that* was damn good too.

"Do you want to thank me now for finding Madam

Christine's business card in that mess of papers I filed for you?" Mika teased. "Or do you want to wait until after I make you scream?" She knew he'd never allow himself to be vulnerable without the protective field back around the house.

"Honey, you're the one who screams," he reminded her.

Mika hid her laughter with effort. "Are you bragging, McCabe?" When he merely shrugged, she shook her head and pointed something out. "You know, though, that you'll be able to break free no matter how tightly I tie the knots . . ."

He nodded. "I know. The restraints will be more a reminder than a true imprisonment. At least, until we get something that can hold me. . . ." He grinned.

Mika felt a burst of pure pleasure. "If I'd realized what you had planned, I would have bought a dominatrix costume instead of the nightgown," she joked.

That earned her another grumble. "If you don't want to try this, just say so. I can do without the cracks," he complained.

"But I *do* want to try it." Mika closed the distance between them and wrapped her arms around his waist. All Conor wore was a pair of unfastened jeans, and she took a moment to stroke the bare skin of his back before biting his shoulder. Looking back up, she said, "Think of the teasing as a bonus you only get with me."

His hands slid down her hips and under her chemise until he was cupping her bare bottom, and his lips quirked. "I think of the teasing as something I *endure* to have you," he replied.

Mika laughed. Conor still didn't banter with her enough, but it wasn't as rare as it had been. She liked to believe that was her influence. Sobering, she said, "Thanks. I know giving up control isn't easy for you."

"Well . . . I trust you," McCabe said. He leaned forward and kissed her slowly and thoroughly. "I love you, honey."

"I love you too."

And that was enough seriousness. "Now, are you going to strip out of those jeans or do you want me to yank them off?"

"You're the boss," he laughed.

Carefully, Mika pushed the denim down his legs until Conor could step out of them. "Sit on the bed," she ordered. He obeyed with a smile that made her squirm. "Grab the headboard." When he complied, she straddled him, making sure she rubbed against him every time she shifted.

Once she had Conor's hands secure, she sat back and shrugged until the thin straps of her chemise fell down her arms. A few wiggles bared her breasts. Then, keeping her eyes locked on his, Mika provoked McCabe unmercifully with her hands, mouth, teeth and body. Despite what he said, she knew she might never get him in this position again, and she was taking advantage of it while she could.

He gripped the rails of the headboard tightly enough to whiten his knuckles, but he didn't break free. He made it clear, though, when he'd reached his limit.

"Honey," he said, his voice thick and grumbly, "we're going to tie you up next time, and I won't forget any of this."

His eyes promised retribution, and Mika smiled as she reached for him, guided him inside her body. She'd love every second of his payback, not only for the physical pleasure, but because it meant that Conor had learned to play.

CRIMSON CITY

Don't miss any of this fabulous series!

CRIMSON CITY
Liz Maverick

A TASTE OF CRIMSON
Marjorie M. Liu

THROUGH A CRIMSON VEIL
Patti O'Shea

A DARKER CRIMSON
Carolyn Jewel
November 2005

SEDUCED BY CRIMSON
Jade Lee
March 2006

CRIMSON ROGUE
Liz Maverick
April 2006

Patti O'Shea
THE POWER OF TWO

The U. C. E.: In the 21st and 22nd centuries, the United States changed and grew. Now the "United Colonies of Earth" dominate the globe. But a mysterious voice is broadcasting treason, inciting revolution and referring to an enigmatic figure named Banzai Maguire.

To find Banzai, the U.C.E. assigns Cai, whose neural implants allow her to sit back in a control chair and feed information to her partner, the dark-souled Jacob Tucker. He's as rigid as he is deadly…or handsome. But this time, Cai needs Jake to trust her completely. Whether he likes it or not, she can't sit back while he fights the bad guys. Wherever this mission takes her, Cai is gonna be the one kicking a little tail.

Tiger Eye

Marjorie M. Liu

He looks completely out of place in Dela Reese's Beijing hotel room—like the tragic hero of some epic tale, exotic and poignant. He is like nothing from her world, neither his variegated hair nor his feline yellow eyes. Yet Dela has danced through the echo of his soul, and she knows this warrior would obey.

Hari has been used and abused for millennia; he is jaded, dull, tired. But upon his release from the riddle box, Hari sees his new mistress is different. In Dela's eyes he sees a hidden power. This woman is the key. If only he dares protect, where before he has savaged; love, where before he's known hate. For Dela, he will dare all.

Susan Grant
The Scarlet Empress

Shot down over Korea, modern-day U.S.A.F. fighter pilot Cameron "Scarlet" Tucker is put in bio-stasis. She wakes 170 years later to find her best friend survived, too—the "legendary" Banzai Maguire is being held for treason in the country that was once her beloved United States.

Cam has her own problems. She's in the masterful hands of Kyber, the emperor prince whom Banzai just escaped. And he won't get fooled again. With a mysterious Shadow Voice urging world revolution, and her friend in chains, Cam wants the sexy dictator on her side—and maybe even closer. But her role in the thrilling mission to save her country must come first. It's time to give a royal butt-kicking, and Cam knows just where to start.

Dorchester Publishing Co., Inc.
P.O. Box 6640
Wayne, PA 19087-8640

52597-6
$6.99 US/$0.99 CAN